An account of the zombie apocalypse that swept across America

Nicholas Ryan

LG, A – PBS&ST

This book is dedicated to my two sons.

Acknowledgements:

A great many people offered their technical skill, their expertise and their experience to make this book as accurate as possible. To everyone who helped – you have my most sincere thanks. A full list of everyone who contributed appears at the end of the book.

PROLOGUE:
The Fist of Allah...

LUT DESERT, SOUTH-EAST IRAN.

There were three men remaining and the instructor assembled them in a semi-circle near the tents.

The midday sun blazed, and the air was still. The heat beat down like a heavy weight and the silent immensity of the desert enfolded them. The men sat in stony silence while the sweat prickled from their pores, and the scalding air seemed to sear their lungs.

The camp was crude – just a dozen canvas tents daubed the color of ochre around the remains of a small fire pit, and a single wooden hut no larger than a prison cell, with a hessian sack hanging across the opening. The instructor stood before the men and withered them with his stare for long silent seconds.

"What you are about to embark upon is a holy jihad that will change the world forever and unite all Islamic nations against the infidel," the instructor said. He paced before the men, his boots dusty, his fatigues crusted with three weeks of grime and sweat. He stopped mid-stride and glared at each of the assembled men, measuring them with the force of his gaze. His beret was pulled down low but it did not diminish the intensity of his eyes. They blazed with the fanaticism of a true believer, and he saw the same passion reflected in the gazes of those men gathered around him. He hooked one hand inside the webbing of his belt and rested the other on the release catch of his pistol holster.

They were all hard men, made harder by the intensive desert training. They were unshaven and unwashed, rugged and lean.

They were the lions of Islam.

"Tomorrow we will leave this place and return to Tehran. In seven days from now you will each embark on your journeys. God willing, in a month the world will be changed forever," the instructor promised. "The cause you fight for is great – there can be none greater. Each of you will die a glorious martyr and be welcomed into Paradise."

The three men closed their eyes and bowed their heads as if in solemn silent prayer, or reflection. The instructor stood amongst them and began to recite short passages from the Koran, and his voice rang out across the barren empty desert as if his prayers might reach the very ear of Allah.

*

Before sunset, two Mercedes 911 trucks appeared from out of the undulating desert, driving at low speed. Their trays were covered with heavy canvas tarpaulins and the trucks jostled and swayed on worn springs as they came out of the dunes and onto the hard pan of sandy earth. The vehicles were painted in desert camouflage and their big round headlights were blacked out to narrow slits. The trucks pulled up at the edge of the camp and lurched to a halt.

The driver got out of the lead truck. He was covered in dust and sand that crusted in his hair and clung to the sweat on his brow. He was a small man with dark nervous eyes. He saw the instructor striding towards him and he snapped to quivering attention and saluted.

The soldier had a wad of papers clutched in his hand. The instructor ignored the man, his eyes narrowed as he carefully inspected the trucks. He grunted, and then turned back to the driver.

"How many prisoners?"

"Twelve. Sir."

The instructor grunted again. "Soldiers?"

"Eight," the driver answered, and there was a fearful tremor in his voice. The instructor was a big powerful man. The sleeves of his tunic were rolled up exposing huge muscled forearms. He stared down at the driver and his gaze was withering. "They are in the second truck with the cages."

The instructor nodded.

"And our guest?"

"He follows," the driver offered.

The instructor frowned. "You had orders to bring him with you." His voice began to rise and there was a menacing edge to his words. The driver seemed to shrink before him.

"He would not come in the truck," the driver was suddenly defensive. "He refused. He insisted on being brought in a car."

The instructor reeled away, muttering darkly. He scanned the edge of the dunes searching for a telltale feather of dust but saw nothing. His lips compressed into a thin bloodless line and he snarled back at the driver.

"Get everything set up. Now!"

The driver spun away, relieved, and ran to the cabin of the second truck. A moment later eight soldiers appeared from under the canvas flap of the vehicle. They were dressed in rumpled desert camouflage BDU's and carrying G3 battle rifles with collapsible stocks. The soldiers looked tired and ragged under their helmets. They bustled to the rear of the first truck and formed up in a semi-circle.

"Out!" one of the soldiers shouted. He climbed up through the heavy canvas tarpaulin and barked a string of guttural insults.

The prisoners came out into the soft dusk light, their hands and feet manacled like death-row convicts. There were a dozen men, each of them thin and gaunt, their steps shuffling and uncertain. The soldier prodded them with the barrel of his rifle and kicked at their legs until the prisoners were herded into a tight knot of cowering misery between the two vehicles.

The driver ran back to the instructor and saluted.

"Get the cages. I want them set up over there," the instructor said. He pointed to a place on the edge of the camp that was in the lee of a sand dune.

The driver turned away yelling instructions and six of the soldiers began unloading heavy iron pieces.

Each length was like a section of iron bar fencing, four foot high and four foot wide with hooks and brackets at either end. The soldiers assembled the cages in a line, with two prisoners inside each box. There were no doors, and no locks. The prisoners squatted on the ground while the cage was built around them and fastened together with long iron spikes. They sat, docile, the fight and will to live long ago beaten from their bodies.

They were captured Iraqi soldiers. They were naked, shriveled and skeletal. Their starved bodies were crawling with vermin that clustered around the pubic hair of their genitals and on the open wounds across their backs and legs. Some of the men were covered in dried faeces that had crusted to their legs. One of the prisoners began to groan softly. He clawed at the blindfold with his cuffed hands, but a soldier slammed the butt of his rifle into the man's ribs. The prisoner howled in pain, exposing a ruined mouth full of broken shattered teeth and bleeding gums. He cringed away to the far side of the cage and his whole body was racked with the slurred sounds of his sobbing.

It took fifteen minutes for the cages to be assembled. When it was done, the three martyrs were summoned from their tents. The sun was setting behind the undulating line of distant sand dunes and a chill wind came hunting across the desert so that little dust devils kicked up around their feet, drifting across the sand like smoke. The men were carrying AK47's. One of them scraped away the black ash of the fire pit and set about lighting a new fire.

Night comes quickly in the Iranian desert. Within minutes the sunset was in the dying stages of its spectacular light show and the temperature plunged. The men fed more wood into the fire and a shower of sparks rose up into the starlit sky.

The eight guards had gone back to their trucks. They huddled round the vehicles smoking. They were tired. The journey from Shahdad had been long.

The instructor gathered the martyrs around the fire and his face was made demonic by the flickering golden light. He glanced pointedly over his shoulder at the soldiers and then back to the men around him.

"None of them must live," he said simply.

The martyrs opened fire. The range was just twenty yards and the eight soldiers were caught in a withering hail of lead.

One of the guards threw down his gun and tried to run. Two of the martyrs caught him in a crossfire of bullets that stitched a ragged line from his torso to the top of his head. The impact jerked him backwards like a puppet on a string, his arms flailing as he was slammed against the side of the truck and collapsed dead to the sand, leaving red streaks of his blood spattered across the canvas tarpaulin.

The two drivers were asleep in the cabin of the first truck. Rough hands dragged them to the ground. They stared up ashen-faced. One of the martyrs put his boot on the first driver's chest to pin him to the sand, then pressed the hot barrel of his AK47 against the man's forehead and executed him. The second driver's bladder emptied itself, and a dark stain spread across the crotch of his fatigues as he cried out in wide-eyed terror. The martyr who had dragged him from the truck forced the barrel of his gun down the man's throat and when the driver's cries had subsided to muffled whimpers, the martyr fired.

It was over in a matter of seconds.

The instructor walked amongst the dead, his face hard as granite. Blood had soaked into the sand so that it crunched beneath his boots.

"Bury them," he said. "Behind the line of cages."

They gathered the rifles up and tossed them into the back of the first truck, then laid the bodies out at the foot of the dune and dragged the loose sand down over the dead. The twelve caged Iraqi prisoners watched on with empty hollow eyes.

As the last soldier's body disappeared beneath the sliding desert sand, headlights suddenly flashed in the distance. The instructor's eyes narrowed. The lights were close together and low to the ground. A car. Not a truck. He watched the twin beams flicker and jounce as the vehicle came towards them at high speed, groping for the hard earth of the ancient camel route between the shifting crests of the dunes.

The Land-Rover's engine howled as it crested the shoulder of sand. Pale dust boiled out from under its wheels. It braked to a screeching halt beside the trucks and there was a raucous, drunken burst of laughter from the back seat, followed by a high-pitched feminine giggle.

Then the driver of the Land-Rover cut the engine, and for long seconds the silence of the desert returned so that the only sound was the ticking ping of the vehicle's exhaust as it cooled.

The instructor stepped briskly towards the Land-Rover. It was an old vehicle, the desert-camouflage paintwork scratched and gouged back to the bare metal.

The driver saw the broad-shouldered figure approach, and even in the soft flickering light of the campfire he was soldier enough to sense the big man's authority - and his simmering temper. The driver threw up a rigid salute.

"You're late." The instructor said.

The driver bobbed his head apologetically but said nothing. Instead his eyes flicked to his two passengers, as if that gesture was explanation enough.

There was a man and a woman in the back seat of the vehicle. The man was slouched in one corner and the woman in the other. The woman had the hem of her dress rucked up around her milky white thighs and her legs were spread wide. The man's eyes were glittering with hungry pleasure, and when he glanced up at the instructor there was a dark scowl of annoyance on his face.

"You are interrupting," the man said in heavily accented English.

He was hugely obese, maybe sixty years old, wearing a rumpled linen suit stained with sweat beneath the armpits. His hair was grey and his face angry red, burned by the harsh unrelenting sun. He had a grimy handkerchief in his big pudgy hand and he mopped at the sweat on his brow as he glared up at the instructor with black eyes that were almost lost within the folds of paunchy skin.

The instructor's eyes flashed with annoyance and his expression darkened. He bit his lip and flicked a glance at the girl. She was thin – maybe nineteen – certainly not older. She had dirty blonde hair that cascaded down to her shoulders and a pale face, artfully concealed beneath heavy makeup so that her skin on her cheeks seemed to glow. Her eyes were huge and dark, framed by long artificial lashes. She had one hand down inside the elastic of her panties, and in the other hand was a half-filled glass. She met the instructor's gaze and in her eyes was a brazen challenge.

The instructor's expression turned to disgust. He turned back to the man. "You can play with your filthy whore when the test is complete," he said.

The man raised a mocking eyebrow. "My whore?" he laughed, but the sound was bitter and resentful. "She's not my whore. She's a Polish *prostitutka* your government provided for my comfort and pleasure. A fucking Polak! They couldn't even find me a good Russian girl, so they bought me this diseased little wretch." He wrinkled his nose, and then sighed heavily, as though he had made the same protest countless times.

The Russian's eyes lingered between the girl's spread legs for a moment longer, and then he heaved himself from the Land-Rover and glanced around the camp, taking in everything in an instant. The girl slid across the seat and stood beside him. She saw the three dark dangerous men clustered around the campfire, and then the prisoners squatting in their cages, and she smoothed her dress back down her thighs with her fingers and tottered on high heels in the soft sand, swaying slightly. She reached out for the man's shoulder to steady herself, but he brushed her away.

"Why do you people insist on everything being done in the fucking desert?" the Russian complained. "You would rather live with the camels?"

The instructor's expression stayed blank, but there was rage simmering behind his eyes. The Russian pig was an offence to Islam, and the instructor's mind played across the pleasure of killing the man: sliding a knife up under his ribs and watching the life drain out of him. It was enough for him to keep his voice controlled.

"We like secrecy," the instructor said flatly. "You should know that by now."

"Da," the Russian nodded sagely. "After seventeen months in this stinking hell-hole I should know."

The instructor smiled, but there was ice in his eyes. "You could always leave, comrade. You could always return home to your mother Russia." He knew that wasn't true. The man would never see his homeland again. In fact he would not see the next sunrise.

The big man looked pained and sad. He knew the Iranian was taunting him.

"To face life in prison? My government does not look highly upon its scientists who sell their skills, even to the camel-loving desert nomads in your government, my friend. I would be killed if I return."

"I am not your friend," the instructor said with an icy smile. "And I would kill you right now if I were able to. If you were a Muslim, you would have been dead long ago for your blasphemies. It is only while you remain useful that you live, Russian. Remember that. Once the entire world has learned to embrace Allah and the faith, men like you will be ground into dust."

The two men glared at each other, the Iranian instructor's face intense with his hatred, and the Russian scientist's face bemused. The scientist nodded in concession, but then waved a fat finger under the other man's nose. "But you can't kill me," he said. "Your government still needs me. That's why they bring me vodka and whores and turn a blind eye as I commit every offense against your blessed Allah. *Because they need me.*" His expression suddenly turned malevolent. He shoved his finger hard into the instructor's chest. "And as for Allah? You camel humping apes have been promising Allah's wrath against the world for hundreds of years. And what? What have you achieved? Nothing," the Russian spat contemptuously. "You live in the dirt like animals, and you smell like unwashed pigs. You are uncivilized, and that will never change," he said with the defiance of a man who had long ago realized he was doomed to certain death. "You beat your women, you think fucking is a sin and even drinking is evil." He shook his head "You are a backward race of thieves, nothing more. Now, get my fucking bag from the Land-Rover and show me my quarters. I will be ready to commence in an hour."

The instructor jerked his head at the driver, and the man snatched up a leather briefcase off the passenger seat. The Russian shoved his way past the instructor and the girl followed.

"Soon," the instructor's rage seethed like lava, although his face remained expressionless. This man was not the only Russian scientist in Iran. The Supreme Leader employed many of the Godless pigs as whores to service the Islamic struggle. Some were employed in the nation's nuclear program. Others were hired for gold to train and advise the military – but the instructor had never met any of them. He had only met two other Russians, and they were buried in the shifting sand on the edges of the camp.

The instructor turned back to the martyrs around the fire and sent them to their tents. Then he walked a slow circuit of the campsite, wandering past the row of cages and then around the trucks and Land-Rover. He walked stiffly, with his fists clasped tightly behind his back and his head lowered in thought.

He was choosing a good place where he would bury the Russian.

"Allah be praised."

*

It was completely dark when the Russian tugged aside the hessian cloth across the cabin door, and stepped out

14

into the glow of the firelight. The night was cold – the temperature had plummeted as the last of the day's heat was sucked from the desert sand. The Russian fastened the button of his trousers and re-buckled his belt, then looked round for the imposing shape of the instructor.

He was sitting around the fire, squatting over the flames, amidst the dark, expressionless faces of the martyrs. "We will begin," he said. "I want to be away from here before sunrise. I have meetings in Tehran with your leaders."

The instructor looked up into the face of the Russian and he nodded, his expression blank. He knew the Russian did not have meetings. He knew because his orders were to kill him as soon as the demonstration was complete. He got to his feet and the men around him stood dutifully.

He waved to the three martyrs. "Arrange the trucks and the Land-Rover," he said brusquely. "I want their headlights on the row of cages."

It took a few minutes – long enough for the Russian to fetch his briefcase from the hut. He set it down on the hood of the Land-Rover. Inside was a bottle of vodka, a small leather pouch the size of a woman's purse, and a row of slim vials, each two inches long. The vials were packed within thick black foam that had been cut to hold the vessels. Each vial was sealed, and beside each one was an aluminum tube with a screw cap.

"These are for your men," the Russian said, pulling one of the vials carefully from the clutch of its foam padding. "The vial goes inside the aluminum tube for transport," he demonstrated, slipping a vial inside the cylinder and screwing the cap back on carefully. "It should be kept this way until the time to open it and inject the virus. Understand?"

The instructor nodded. He took the cylinder carefully between his fingers, unscrewed the lid and slid the vial into the palm of his hand. It was half an inch round. The liquid

15

inside was clear as water. The top of the tube had been sealed.

"The contents must be injected immediately," the Russian said.

Again the instructor nodded. The previous Russian scientist who had come to the camp a week earlier had gone carefully over the transport and storage procedures, but this was the first time he or his men had seen the actual virus. The instructor passed the cylinder and vial on to the martyr beside him, and then began to issue the other vials until there were three glass tubes remaining.

The Russian took the leather pouch from the briefcase and unzipped it. It opened to reveal several syringes, an assortment of needles, and a stethoscope.

He rigged a syringe and filled it with the contents of one of the vials.

"Enough for ten men," he said. "Come. I will show you."

The Russian strode across to the nearest cage. The two prisoners cowered away, but the cage was small. They pressed themselves against the bars. The Russian reached into the cage and snatched at one of the Iraqi's thin frail wrists and clamped his fingers tight. The man made a pathetic whimpering sound. The Russian jabbed the needle into the man's arm and injected a small amount of the virus.

Nothing happened.

He trapped the second prisoner's foot and one of the martyrs reached between the bars to hold the leg steady. The Russian shot the second prisoner full of virus and then leaped back quickly, as though the prisoners might explode.

Nothing happened.

"The virus works quickly," the Russian said. He went to the fire and threw the syringe into the flames. Then he went back to the hood of the Land-Rover and prepared the next round of injections.

Suddenly the first prisoner went rigid, as though charged with a surge of electricity. There was no room within the cage and the sound of his leg breaking was like the crack of a bat hitting a ball. The man's eyes rolled in their sockets and his back arched, bending to an impossible angle. A scream of agony split through the still night and was abruptly cut short.

The man was dead.

The second prisoner wailed in terror – and then his body went into spasms. He writhed and thrashed. He raked his fingers at his face, clawing at his eyes, and then a bright gush of blood burst from his mouth and he slumped dead against the cold bars of the cage.

"Reanimation takes place anywhere between a minute and forty-five minutes after death," the Russian said casually, as the instructor stared fixedly at the bodies of the two Iraqis, twisted in the agony of cruel murder. "It depends on the victim, and their physical condition. In the case of these poor pathetic wretches, the next stage will happen soon," he said.

"Explain," the instructor demanded, even though he knew the workings of the virus.

The Russian didn't answer immediately. Instead he went to the second cage and injected one of the prisoners.

"It is a pathogenic virus," the Russian said, "that induces rapid death in the victim, and then reanimation sometime shortly afterwards."

"How?"

The Russian frowned. "Do you really want to know?"

"Of course," the instructor said.

The Russian sighed irritably. He had a headache from the vodka. He rubbed his forehead. "Death comes quickly once the victim has been infected. Usually within thirty seconds. Once death has occurred, the virus re-wires the victim's nervous system," he said vaguely, "although not entirely. The machinery of the pathogen spreads through the blood system. It takes a minute for blood to circulate through the body of an average person, and once the pathogen begins to break down, it starts inducing an immune response. The pathogen produces a highly volatile state. In essence, the reanimated ghoul uses the body's capabilities much like a parasite. What the pathogen creates within that body is a creature that cannot feel pain, cannot reason, and is governed only by one biological instinct – the urge to reproduce through biting and infecting. That instinct will drive it until the time it decomposes."

"They become living dead?"

The Russian nodded. "They do not feed. They do not drink, nor do they sleep. They kill until they collapse."

The Russian went quickly along the line and injected one prisoner in each cage. When he was finished he was sweating, despite the near freezing temperature. He leaned heavily against the side of the Land-Rover. His hands were shaking. He needed a drink. He checked his wristwatch. It had been nearly twenty minutes since the first two prisoners had died.

"What is it called, this thing of terror?" the instructor asked. "Does it have a name?"

The Russian smiled bleakly. "When I was back in Soviet Union I worked in chemical weapons labs," he said proudly and his chest puffed out. "We were perfecting many things, but not all were success," he said. "Some things became not what we expected. Some things became worse," he winked conspiratorially as though he were sharing a State secret. "This was called F1-st," the Russian explained. It had no other name."

The Iranian instructor's English was passable but it was not a language he was comfortable with. The Russian picked up a branch of wood from the fire and scratched the letters large in the sand at the man's feet.

The instructor sounded them out silently, and then more clearly.

"Fist," he said, and there was a sudden sense of righteousness and awe in his voice. "The Fist of Allah."

*

Even for hardened men who were accustomed to death in all its forms, the killing of the uninfected Iraqi prisoners was difficult to watch. The men who had died under the needle suddenly rose, like wild animals, snarling and hissing. Their eyes blazed with manic hatred as they tore at their fellow captives. The scent of blood seemed to enrage the infected, and their voices rose to high wailing shrieks as the virus drove them berserk. In just a few frenzied minutes it was all over. The dead lay mutilated in the cages and the infected prowled and snarled and hissed at the assembled martyrs, shaking the bars with strength that was borne from blind madness.

The Iranian instructor stepped forward warily and paced along the line of cages. Blood seeped into the sand and the undead thrust their clawed hands through the bars of the cage and lashed out at him like wild animals. At the end of the line, he spun on his heel and called out to the Russian.

"And so the ones they have attacked – they too will reanimate within forty-five minutes, yes?"

"Da," the Russian nodded.

"How do you kill them?"

The Russian smiled wryly. He cocked his thumb and finger into the shape of a gun and put it to his temple. "You shoot them in the head. Destroy the diseased brain. It's the only way," he said.

The instructor frowned thoughtfully as he came back to the Land-Rover.

"You do not have an antidote, Russian?"

"No. Not yet. I am still working on this matter."

The instructor shook his head. "Not any more."

He pulled his pistol from its holder and thrust it between the big scientist's eyes.

There was a split-second of dangerous silence, and then the Russian laughed. It was a bear-like growl; a wheezing breathless sound that shook his big fleshy frame. "You can't shoot me," he chuckled. "I just told you, I have not yet created an antidote. Without it, even you camel-loving apes would be infected once the virus is released. It will sweep around the world, cross all borders, and leave your filthy piece of desert barren of all life. Not even your fucking Allah could save you then."

The instructor raised his eyebrow.

"That is the very last time you blaspheme," he said coldly. Your insults to Allah signed your death warrant long ago."

The Russian's face became outraged. He spat in the instructor's face. "Do it then!" The Russian held his hands wide, inviting his own execution. "But if you kill me it will be the end of your Muslim dream. I have told you – there is no antidote."

The Russian was wrong.

The instructor pulled the trigger and the bullet tore through the back of the Russian's head in a pink cloud of blood and gore. He fell backwards into the sand, eyes still wide with a frozen expression of disbelief and shock as the sound of the shot echoed into the dark night.

The girl was asleep on a narrow cot when two of the martyrs burst into the hut. They dragged her naked into the glowing firelight and forced her onto her knees. The instructor executed her with a single bullet to the back of her head and she fell forward into the sand.

"Take a long look," he raised his voice and clenched his fist. "Look at the cages and know this is what you will become – glorious killing machines to champion the Muslim cause against the infidels. Warrior lions who will take Allah's Fist to America, and destroy it with a single mighty blow."

The martyrs began to chant, raising their weapons and thrusting them above their head. The instructor listened to the sound of their voices swelling with the force of their fanaticism, and he knew they were ready.

"Allah be praised."

At midnight the instructor began executing the infected. The cages were dismantled and each bloody body dragged onto the fire. Then the hut and tents were burned.

At dawn the next morning - just as first light was breaking across the rim of endless desert horizon - the Lions of Islam boarded the trucks and Land-Rover, and set out on a journey that would change the world forever.

TEHRAN.

The meeting took place in a secret underground command center that sprawled deep beneath the Abbas Abad district in the north of the capital. The area was the location for the offices of the state security forces and the Organization of Islamic Culture and Communications, and so he was surprised when the driver by-passed each building complex and drove on past several foreign embassies.

The vehicle turned, and then turned again, finally braking to a halt in front of a non-descript brick building on

Mirzayeh Shirazi Avenue. It was dark. The instructor stepped out of the car. The night sky was brilliant with the light of a million stars, and in the cool still silence of the city he could hear the distant sounds of evening prayers, carried on the breeze from the Mosalla Prayer Grounds.

Three men were waiting for him on the footpath. They were dressed casually, but the instructor sensed the awareness of them. It was in the way they held themselves, and in the steel of their eyes. They were military, and he stood passively and allowed them to search him before being escorted through the heavy wooden door.

The building was a two-story empty shell. Inside was a foyer where four uniformed members of the Revolutionary Guard stood on alert. Each of the soldiers wore a black beard and was dressed in combat uniform. Behind the soldiers was a small, slim man, who stood beside a set of double doors.

The man was wearing a dark, western styled suit over a crisp white shirt and black tie. His facial features were classically Persian. The nose beneath the dark eyes was hooked, and the jet-black hair was closely cut atop a high-set forehead. He watched the instructor being searched by two of the Revolutionary Guard, and then nodded. A faint flicker of a smile touched his lips.

"Welcome captain," the man said. His voice was almost effeminately soft, and cultured. "The mullahs have just arrived from prayers. They are waiting for you."

The double doors were opened from within by two more guards, and the man led the instructor to an elevator. They rode down in silence, and when the doors whispered open again, the instructor was forty feet below the embassy district of Tehran and standing in a wide well lit passageway.

"This way," the man said softly. He led the instructor into a vast network of tunnels, their footsteps echoing in the eerie silence of the cavernous complex, and finally came to a halt outside a wide wooden door attended by two more guards. The man nodded and the soldiers stepped aside. He pushed the doors open and led the instructor inside a conference room. There was a polished timber table in the middle of the floor with a dozen chairs nestled around it. The lighting in the room was softer than the flaring fluorescent light in the passageways, and the air carried the faint scent of tobacco smoke.

Standing, waiting for him at the head of the table was a black-robed Ayatollah.

He was a thin, elderly man, his expression made thoughtful and studious by the over-sized glasses that rested on the beak of his nose. He was dressed in a Palestinian *kaffiyeh* and a black turban. His long untrimmed beard was streaked with silver strands. In attendance at either side of the Ayatollah stood four heavily bearded *hojjat-el-Islam*. They were younger men, perhaps each in their sixties, the instructor guessed. They were dressed in black robes and wore white turbans.

"*Salam aleikom*, captain," the Ayatollah said. He was softly spoken, yet his voice carried unmistakable authority. "You have performed your tasks most admirably."

The instructor said nothing. He bowed his head and the Ayatollah summoned him closer with a wave of his hand. The instructor marched to the head of the table and stood stiffly.

"How many martyrs remain to carry the war to the Great Satan and its allies?" the old man's voice took on a sudden edge.

"Three," the instructor said. "One was killed during our time in the desert training and preparing."

"And where are these jihadists?"

"Do Ab, your Holiness."

The Ayatollah frowned. "The training camp?"

23

"Yes, your Holiness. It has been abandoned for some months. The martyrs wait there in secrecy for your order."

The Do Ab Training Camp was a remote installation in the north of the country. Little more than a cluster of crude huts, the camp had been left abandoned since the beginning of the year.

The Ayatollah nodded thoughtfully. He turned and glanced at the clerics who stood around him.

"Have you preserved all secrecy?" one of the *hojjats* asked suddenly. He was the tallest of the four men, his eyes hooded beneath dark bushy eyebrows. He had a long drawn face, and his skin was grey as ash.

The instructor nodded. "There are no witnesses."

The Ayatollah studied the instructor carefully, his expression suddenly darker, and made grave.

"Are they ready to take the holy war to the infidels?"

"Most ready, your Holiness," the instructor said. "As are we all."

The Ayatollah smiled and nodded benignly. The answer was as he had expected. "Good, my son," he said and suddenly reached out and placed his hand gently on the instructor's arm. "Because it has been decided that you will join your men as the last martyr, captain. In one week from now, you will go to America and lead the war against the Great Satan yourself."

*

When the instructor had been escorted from the underground complex, the small man in the western business suit returned to the conference room. The Ayatollah was waiting for him, alone.

"It is time to begin the immunization," the Ayatollah said. "All soldiers and important religious and political members will be the first to be immunized against the virus.

24

Once this has been done, the Army will go into the cities and towns and will immunize all men aged between thirteen and fifty. After that you may immunize the women – but only those of a suitable and useful age. The rest will need to trust their fate to Allah."

The young man nodded gravely. He bit his lip, as if to stifle the futile protest that leaped to his throat. The Ayatollah saw his expression and nodded benevolently. "Speak your mind, Ahmed."

Still the young man hesitated. He had raised the matter before. He clasped his hands together as if in prayer. "Your Holiness, might we consider an alternative plan for the martyrs?" he offered cautiously. "Sending them all to just one destination within America...? Might we not be better served if they were separated? This would cause the virus to spread more rapidly, yes?"

The Ayatollah smiled beneath the dense bristles of his heavy beard. "It is necessary," he said patiently. "The touch of a finger does little to cause pain, and yet those fingers together and bunched, Ahmed... become the fist of Allah."

MIAMI, FLORIDA.

The man came in through the door of the convenience store wearing a brown jacket that was worn at the cuffs and frayed around the collar. He had a crop of black hair and dark sunken eyes. He went to the refrigerators along the side wall and reached for a bottle of water. When he came back to the front of the store he set the bottle down and lifted his eyes to the cashier behind the counter.

"You are Mohsen Gheydari," the man said.

The attendant flinched. He had never seen the man before. He bobbed his head and smiled with polite caution.

"And you have a family," the stranger said ominously in stilted, faltering English.

Mohsen froze. He felt an ice-cold chill of dread run down the length of his spine. He stared at the stranger. The man's eyes burned with an intensity like fanaticism. Mohsen had lived in America for fifteen years. He was an American citizen with a wife at home and two sons who played soccer and attended school.

"Yes…" he said softly.

The strange man smiled – a flash of brilliant white teeth, made all the brighter by the dark olive of his skin.

"I am here to remind you that you are still a son of Iran."

Mohsen felt his hands begin to tremble, and the blood seemed to drain away from his face. The stranger reached into his coat pocket and laid a photograph down on the counter.

Mohsen Gheydari felt his knees buckle beneath him.

The photograph was an image of an elderly lady and two younger women, perhaps aged in their thirties. All three of the women were on their knees. Standing on either side of them were black uniformed men, their faces concealed by balaclavas so that only their eyes and mouths could be seen. The men were holding automatic weapons to the heads of the cowering women. In the photo, Mohsen could see the old lady's face was slick with tears of terror.

"Your mother is not well," the stranger said. "Nor are your two sisters, Mohsen," the man's voice lowered and filled with menace. "They wish you would return to Tehran to care for them, but you have made your life here, in the West. This is very bad, but still you can save them from a terrible, terrible death."

Mohsen stared up into the hard eyes of the stranger. He could feel himself on the verge of weeping. He licked his lips nervously and then impulsively reached out for the man's hand.

"Please!" he pleaded. His face was wrenched into a rictus of distress. "Do not harm them!"

The stranger pulled his hand free of Mohsen's grip. "They will be safe, provided you fulfill the task you have been set. Your homeland needs you."

Mohsen Gheydari nodded his head, a gesture of submission and defeat.

*

"You will hire a fast boat and you will take it offshore tomorrow night. Do you understand this?" the stranger asked.

Mohsen jerked his head. The stranger laid a map out on the counter of the convenience store. The doors were locked, the store closed for the night.

"You will take the boat to this point," the man stabbed at the blue coastal waters with the tip of his finger. There you will wait. Just before dawn the following morning a freighter will meet with you. It will come from the south. Do you understand this?"

Again, Mohsen nodded his head. The stranger looked satisfied. He folded the map and handed it to Mohsen. He left the photo on the counter.

"Four men will disembark from the freighter. They are our Iranian brothers. You will bring them back here to Miami."

Mohsen frowned. "Is that all?" he asked incredulously. Somehow he had expected that much more would be demanded of him.

"That is all," the man said. He smiled then — a warm charming smile that sparkled in his eyes. "Do this, Mohsen, and your mother and sisters will be safe. On this, you have my word."

Mohsen stared at the man for a moment, then the blaze of the stranger's eyes compelled him to look away. "Very well," he said. "Where shall I take these men?"

"Bring them into the city to the place where you hire the boat from… but do not speak to them, Mohsen. Do not utter a word or even look at them unless they first speak to you. It is best if you do not see their faces, or befriend them. They are soldiers of Allah."

*

The four men came down the side of the freighter's rusted hull, swinging from a rope ladder as the ship rolled gently in the offshore swell. Mohsen conned the speedboat closer. The water foamed white as the big outboard engines growled. One by one the men leaped aboard the boat. The last man had a canvas bag slung over his shoulders. When all the men were safely aboard, Mohsen opened the throttles and the speedboat lifted up onto its plane and dashed away into the dawn.

"Slow down," the Instructor from the desert camp growled. "Bring no attention to us."

Mohsen obeyed. He stood at the wheel of the boat, his legs braced against the rolling ocean swells and nudged the lever to ease power to the engines. The sleek hull dropped back down into the rolling crests and the Instructor grunted.

Mohsen was trembling. He kept his eyes fixed straight ahead. He recalled the stranger's warning in the convenience store the night before, and the photo of his mother and sisters was in his shirt pocket as a reminder. He would do nothing to jeopardize their lives.

The sun came up, spilling orange and golden light across the ocean. Gulls wheeled overhead, and the gentle breeze carried the smell of salt and a fine mist of spray. The hours went by with slow certainty until a haze of brown smog stretched like a scar across the far horizon. Mohsen pointed. "Miami," he said.

He heard the sound of footsteps close behind him. He could sense the presence of one of the men standing nearby. "What time is it?" a voice growled. It was the same man who had snapped at him to slow the boat as the freighter had sailed away to the north.

Mohsen held up his arm, turned his wrist. "It is ten-thirty," he said. The man checked his own wristwatch and grunted. The other three martyrs synchronized their watches to Miami time.

"How long until we reach the city?"

"Perhaps another hour, but I can go much faster if it is imperative."

"No," the man said. "There is time. Draw no attention to us."

The four men were dressed in dirty, faded denim jeans and khaki colored shirts that were grimy from their passage aboard the ship. The instructor opened the bag and handed fresh clothes to the other men. Quickly they changed into clean, casual clothes.

The staggered skyline of Miami seemed to rise from out of the ocean, made glittering and mirror-like by the brightness of the sun. The four martyrs stared in awe. "Behold the Great Satan," the Instructor said, his voice hushed yet quavering with the fervor of a zealot. "Here is the beast we have come to slay."

*

When the details of the city were clear, and they could see the arch of a bridge that seemed to span two peninsulas of land, the Instructor made his way forward and stood at the bow of the boat. He narrowed his eyes, studying the coastline with the gaze of a predator. He could see the mouth of the harbor, sparkling blue beneath the bridge, and beyond it the clutter of gleaming buildings that seemed to cling to the narrow strips of sand.

"Is that where we go to?" he pointed at the channel.

"Yes," Mohsen said. "I have chartered the boat from a company inside the harbor."

The Instructor nodded. He stepped back a pace, then whipped his muscled forearm around Mohsen Gheydari's throat. The man cried out in a shriek of white fear. The Instructor pulled the man off balance so that his back was arched and his chest swelled tight against his shirt. Then, from within the pocket of his jeans, the Instructor produced a knife. He plunged the blade into Mohsen's heart, burying the weapon to the hilt. He held the man upright until his shirt was soaked with blood, and then he heaved the body over the side of the boat.

*

The four men abandoned the speedboat at the edge of a marina and disappeared into the crowds of weekend tourists who had come to the waterfront to shop and eat. They walked in a tight knot, their faces rigid, their bodies tight with tension. The noise of the city was an assault on their ears. The crowds were thick throngs pushing and rushing for no apparent reason. The streets were filled with cars and trucks. The Instructor stepped to the side of a busy road and threw out his hand urgently.

A taxi pulled across a lane of traffic and jerked to a halt.

The Instructor leaned through the open passenger-side window of the vehicle. The driver was a plump man with no hair on his head, and fat meaty arms. He was grossly overweight. The interior of the vehicle smelled of greasy food and stale sweat. The Instructor smiled.

"Excuse me," he said in broken awkward English. "We would like to go here." In his hand was a piece of paper that had been cut from a magazine. The paper was crumpled. The Instructor smoothed it out and smiled warmly again.

The taxi driver frowned. He reached across the passenger seat and took the clipping. He looked at the four men speculatively. "That won't be cheap," he said.

The Instructor dug a fist into his pocket and offered a wad of American money. He had a thousand dollars in new fifty-dollar bills. The taxi driver peeled off four of the notes and tucked them into his shirt pocket.

The four men climbed into the taxi and the car sped away from the curb.

"Sun Life Stadium it is," the driver said.

It was 1pm, Sunday afternoon.

*

The men had seen sports stadiums in Iran, but nothing to match the sheer grandeur of the structure that seemed to fill the windshield of the taxi as the vehicle entered the vast parking lot. The four men peered out through the windows in hushed wonder. There were thousands of cars – more cars than any of them had seen in their lives.

The taxi lurched to a halt and the driver jabbed a pudgy finger through his window. "That's the entrance," he said. "Just follow the crowds."

The men got out of the taxi and the vehicle sped away in a belch of grey exhaust, riding low on its springs and swaying like a boat as it disappeared from sight. The Instructor glanced at the three other men gathered close to him. "Remember why we are here," he sounded the warning. "We are martyrs for the great cause. Do not fail your families or your country."

*

There were thousands of people, the Instructor saw, dressed in green and orange. Many of the people were sitting in their seats waving giant orange fingers that seemed to be made of foam. The noise of the crowd made his head pound so that he longed for the vast emptiness and solitude of the desert. He found a seat beside several young women. They were sleek and glossy with the exuberance and confidence of youth. Their bodies were tanned brown and they wore shamefully skimpy clothes. They screamed at something that suddenly happened on the sports field but the Instructor did not bother to look. Instead he watched the young women from the corner of his eye. They leaped from their seats and hugged each other. They were laughing. One of the women peeled off the bright colored t-shirt she was wearing so that everyone around her could see her bra. The Instructor turned away. He felt a flush of dark color burn his cheeks. He heard the women giggle gleefully and wondered if they were taunting him.

"Godless whores," he hissed under his breath. He felt his temper begin to flare, but he suppressed it. He clenched his fists tightly and searched the sea of faces for the other three martyrs. He could not see them, but he knew they would be ready. The Instructor glanced down at his watch...

*

At third down and eleven on the forty yard line, everyone in Sun Life Stadium seemed to sense the Miami Dolphins were about to call a passing play. An anxious hush descended upon the vast crowd.

The quarterback took the snap and rolled out to his left. Downfield the wide receiver suddenly jinked off his right foot and burst away from his cover, running fast towards the Packers end zone. The quarterback threw the pass and the ball sailed on a perfect arc through the air.

Seventy-six thousand fans rose to their feet, following the trajectory of the spiraling ball and holding their breath.

The hands of the Instructor's wristwatch ticked over to one fifty-nine pm.

He rose calmly from his seat and reached into the pocket of his jeans. In his hand was a small leather case. He unzipped the opening. Inside was a small syringe and the vial of virus the Russian scientist had given him at the desert training camp.

The Instructor filled the syringe and glanced at the clock. He began to count down the seconds. His hands began to shake.

"Allah be praised."

The Instructor felt the prick of the needle pierce his skin, and his vision began to blur. He heard the crowd cry out in a sudden roar of wild excitement followed by a thunder of applause that seemed to roll around the stadium like a great wave of sound.

It was two o'clock.

*

Sun Life Stadium was the perfect killing ground − a vast press of bodies confined by seats and choke points at the entrance gates.

That was the Instructor's last thought as he fell back in his seat, suddenly dead.

No one noticed.

Two minutes later he got to his feet.

It was the instant that America was changed forever.

The zombie lunged for a young blonde woman close beside it. The girl was in her twenties. She was swinging her t-shirt above her head and bouncing up and down in the narrow space between the seats. She was wearing a black bra. Her skin was honey brown, gilded by the Miami sun. The zombie grabbed her by the arm and the girl screamed. The zombie reefed the woman off balance, and as she turned her face and saw the hideous thing that held her, it lunged and tore at her nose and eyes. Flesh ripped, blood gushed. The girl thrashed and kicked. Blood sprayed high into the air and spattered like rain across the shoulders of the people nearby. The girl screamed again. The zombie had spat out her nose and had its hands tangled in the hair at the back of the girl's head, holding her still while it bit at her eyes and the soft flesh of her cheek. The girl fell to the ground, her body awash with blood.

The zombie roared. It was a high-pitched snarling sound. Blood spilled down its chin. It turned its head, saw another woman. This one was older. She was standing beside two young children. The zombie hurled itself at the woman and she went crashing backwards to the hard concrete. The zombie tore at her chest with its clawed fingers. The woman's heels tapped spasmodically on the ground as the ghoul dug into her flesh and tried to tear out her heart.

People started to scream. A man stepped forward and grabbed the ghoul by the shoulders. The zombie turned and snarled at the man. He tried to back away but it was too late. The zombie dropped down onto its haunches and then lunged to attack. The guy went over backwards, tripping over a chair and crashing into other spectators. He was crying out in fear. Around him other people began to move away in panic. The zombie retched up fresh blood. Its eyes were red and crazed. It sank its teeth into the man's arm and tore away shreds of flesh until the bone was exposed.

The screams became louder. A ripple of frantic movement seemed to spread out through the vast crowd, as if rocks had been thrown into a calm lake. The ripples reached out and eventually collided, just as the panicked people did in the stadium. Suddenly the sound of cheers became the high keening wail of terror. People were crushed as they clawed and fought their way towards the exits. Children were left behind or lost by their parents. The weak and elderly were trampled. White panic spread within the stadium until the sound of their collective voices was a wail of mortal fear and horror.

The zombies raged through the dense press of bodies, and it was a slaughter.

A white-shirted security guard came running into the stands with his weapon drawn. The crowd swirled past him, running in sheer panic. They were screaming. The guard saw a young blonde woman stagger towards him. She was wearing just a black bra and tiny white shorts. She was drenched in blood and half her face had been ravaged. Soft flaps of flesh hung from her cheek.

"Jesus!" the guard gasped. He took a step towards the woman. She tilted her head to the side at an impossible angle and her tongue slithered from the ruined lips. She licked at the air as if tasting it. The guard froze, and then took an uncertain step backwards. A big heavy-set man wearing a Miami Dolphins jersey went lumbering past, knocking himself and the guard off balance. The gun went off and the sound was deafening. Then the zombie woman flung herself at the two men, slashing with her clawed fingers and tearing at flesh. The guard screeched. He fired blindly, hitting the zombie in the chest. The bullet tore through her body, punching a neat hole just above her breast. Brown slime oozed from the wound. The zombie threw back her head and her blood-soaked hair flailed. She howled and then went berserk.

Around Sun Life Stadium the wails of fear rose to a crescendo. The crowd at the turnstiles was frantic. They were pressed so tightly together that children caught between the bodies suffocated, and a man died of a heart attack. There was no room for him to even fall. He died standing up. Glass windows shattered. The concrete ground became slippery with blood. The undead stalked towards the exits and ripped a swathe of blood and horror through all those who were unable to escape.

In the vast parking lot a heavily pregnant woman wearing an over-sized Green Bay Packers jersey ran screaming, clutching at her stomach. Her face was painted in gaudy colors but not even that could mask the terror on her face. She wailed and sobbed as she ran. She reached a concrete barrier and stole a terrified look over her shoulder. One of the undead was running after her. It had been a man. Now it was a terrifying apparition of horror. One of its arms was missing, but it ran as though compelled by mindless fury. It hunted the woman. She cried out and pushed herself away from the barrier, trying to escape in the maze of parked cars. An SUV reversed in a juddering screech of smoking rubber. The vehicle knocked the pregnant woman to the ground and the zombie pounced on her. It tore her neck open and then perched astride her chest, feasting on her soft flesh. The woman shrieked until she died.

A man came running from one of the nearby cars. He had a gun in his hand. He stopped ten paces short of the zombie and spread his legs, throwing up the weapon and clasping it between both hands. He fired once into the air, and the zombie turned its head towards the gunman.

"Back away!" the man shouted. His face was twisted in shock and fear. His hands were trembling. The dead woman was lying in a pool of her own blood. The zombie had severed her head with its teeth. It looked up into the man's eyes and then vomited blood down its chin. The man backed away. He aimed the gun and fired, accidentally shooting another woman who was fleeing the terror. The victim went crashing to the ground in a sprawl of arms and legs. The zombie rose slowly from its haunches. It was awash with the pregnant woman's blood. It stalked towards the gunman and he turned and ran.

The zombies slashed and tore into the press of bodies, infecting some with the virulent spread from their own bloody wounds, and turning other victims with the savage bite of their teeth. To be touched by them was to die and rise again. To be bitten by them was to die and rise even faster. The zombie plague erupted across the city of Miami like a series of staggered detonations, as some people were reanimated within just minutes, and others who had merely been scratched became the undead with agonizing slowness.

TV news reports from the stadium were broadcast live across the city. What had begun as a routine weekend sports broadcast became a shocking real-life horror story. People spilled from the nearby buildings and ran panicked into the streets. Cars jammed the roads. Families overloaded the cellular phone networks and landlines to call friends and relatives. People frantically packed memories of their lives and weapons and blankets into their vehicles, and choked the highways. There were thousands of traffic accidents. Cars collided and caught on fire. The sky began to fill with smoke. Buildings burned down and power poles went crashing to the ground, cutting electricity to large sections of the city.

It was Sunday.

Bloody Sunday.

The day America died.

TEHRAN.

The young man came into the conference room of the underground bunker and bowed deeply and respectfully. The Ayatollah greeted the man with a kindly inner peace touching at his lips.

"It is done," the young man said as he straightened. He handed the Ayatollah a piece of paper. "It is the beginning of the end for the Great Satan."

The Ayatollah cast his eyes to the heavens...

And he smiled.

Thirteen months later…

PART 1: 'OPERATION CONTAINMENT' The Interviews…

NATIONAL SECURITY COUNCIL MEETING ROOM, THE WHITE HOUSE:

Richard Danvers, the architect of the Emergency Homeland Defense Plan, was a tall man with a lean and wiry frame that bristled with a kind of restless energy. I guessed him to be in his sixties. He had a long, drawn face that was darkly tanned and a close-cropped head of grey hair. His eyes were sharp and penetrating, set amongst a fine web of wrinkles. He sat back in a chair near the end of the long wooden table and regarded me carefully.

"Take a seat," the man gruffed. I had the feeling he was resentful. He watched me like a hawk, his eyes drawn to the folders and notebooks I had in my hands.

"No recording devices," Danvers warned. "I'm giving you this interview because our Commander In Chief has ordered me to, but you're not leaving here with anything on tape."

I frowned, sat down across the table and fixed him with a stare. "That's not how I understood this interview would be conducted," I said.

Danvers's expression never changed. His features seemed carved out of stone. He leaned forward slowly and propped his elbows on the polished wooden tabletop. "I don't give a shit," he said mildly. "That's how it's going to happen. I talk, you write, Mr. Culver. No recording."

"Sure," I said. I flipped to a new page in my notebook and snatched a pen from my pocket. Danvers sat back in his chair and swiveled, casting his eyes around the room.

The subterranean meeting room below the White House looked oddly colonial. The low ceiling was elaborately molded, the dark wood wall panels divided by arrays of multimedia screens and maps of the world. The lighting was subdued. It was quite a small room, dominated by the big table we sat on opposite sides of. There was a pitcher of ice water on the table, and a couple of tall glasses.

Danvers waited until he was quite sure I was settled and then steepled his fingers together like a high-powered corporate executive. He narrowed his eyes.

"Tell me what you want to know," he said warily.

I sighed. I actually didn't know where to start. I shrugged. "Why are we meeting here, at the White House?" I asked.

Danvers smiled, but it was a bleak, grim expression devoid of any humor. "It's where I was first handed the job of coordinating America's response to the outbreak of the zombie virus," he said. He sat back and the leather chair squeaked as he shifted his weight. "The President sat in that seat right there," he pointed to the chair at the head of the table, "and called me over."

"Over?"

Danvers nodded. "I was in the room. It was a crisis meeting of the National Security Council. There were only seven people in attendance, plus me. The Vice President had invited me. I wasn't sitting at the table. I was standing against the wall, feeling completely out of place."

"Who was at that meeting?"

Danvers shrugged. "The usual," he said. "The President, the Vice President, the Secretaries of State, Defense and

Energy, and General Wallace, Chairman of the Joint Chiefs of Staff… and the Director of National Intelligence."

I made a face. "That's a high-powered meeting. Did you know why you were invited to attend?"

Danvers nodded. "I had a good idea," he said. "The Vice President had filled me in beforehand. I just wasn't prepared for the kind of authority I was about to be handed."

I nodded. "So that was the meeting where the President nominated you as 'the Architect', right?"

The man across from me looked almost embarrassed. He nodded his head slowly. "It fell to me to devise the Emergency Homeland Defense Plan."

I hesitated for a moment and then took a chance. Danvers was a formidable presence, almost intimidating in the way he seemed to fill the room with his energy. "That must have pissed a lot of those people off," I said.

Danvers blinked, and then slowly smiled. "Yeah," he said. "It did. General Wallace was furious. Almost everyone in that room saw the zombie outbreak as purely a military issue – a war that had to be fought on American soil. Naturally they thought the best qualified people to co-ordinate our defenses was one of their own."

"But the President didn't agree."

"Not entirely."

"Meaning…?"

Danvers closed his eyes for a moment like maybe he was assembling his thoughts, and the room became absolutely silent. I could hear myself breathing and the gentle hum of the air-conditioning. Finally he fixed me with narrowed eyes.

"Let's get one thing straight before we go on," he said. "The reason we are alive today – the reason America still exists – is because we had a President at the start of the zombie outbreak who was a man who believed in his convictions. Our President was the kind of man the late great Ronald Reagan would admire. He believed in the might of America, and understood our rightful place in the world. He knew we had to be decisive, regardless of the protesting left wing sympathizers who called the outbreak a humanitarian disaster. It was – but it was also a fight for survival. The President understood that."

"How did that understanding affect America's response when the first cases of the outbreak were reported in Miami?"

Richard Danvers got out of his chair and went to a large map of the United States spread across the far wall. It was a hugely detailed map, almost ten feet wide and about six feet high, set within an ornate dark wooden frame and hung on the wall like it was a seventeenth century masterpiece. He beckoned me over with an abrupt wave of his hand.

"By the time that NSC meeting was convened – just ten days after the first cases of the outbreak were reported, we had already lost the southern sector of Florida," the man explained, sweeping his hand across the map and covering an area northward from Miami to Cape Coral. "The local police forces had been overwhelmed. The National Guard got swept away. Panic was quickly becoming a pandemic. The President acted swiftly."

"By appointing you."

Danvers shook his head. He turned to face me and we were eyeball to eyeball. He was taller than I had first thought. His eyes were like daggers. "The President's plan was in three stages," Danvers explained, and then began counting off his fingers. "Containment, Conquest and Compression. He tasked me with the role of coordinating the Containment phase. The rest of the plan was passed on to more suitable leaders."

I shrugged. "Why you?" It was a simple question that had puzzled so many commentators around the country.

The answer seemed veiled in as much mystery as the man himself.

"The President knew of me," Danvers said evasively. "I was an engineer, not a soldier. My expertise was in global disaster relief. The President saw the outbreak of the infection as a disaster, not a war. That's why he chose me for the job. It was felt that the country needed someone who could step back from the natural impulse to respond with immediate military action, and instead, build a defense."

"Which is why you were called the 'architect'."

He nodded. "That name came along because of the defensive line I designed."

I frowned. "Then why are you so secretive? You're a national hero, and yet there is just one photograph of you circulating in the media – an image that's about ten years out of date. Why aren't you standing next to the President with a chest full of medals and giving press conferences?"

"Because I'm not a fucking politician!" Danvers suddenly sparked, and I got my first glimpse of the man's famous temper. "I don't kiss babies, and I'm not trying to get elected. I'm not a film star, and I don't need celebrity. I'm a patriot, Mr. Culver, not a glory seeker."

There was a pause. I saw something move behind the man's eyes – the shadow of some emotion that passed in an instant. When he spoke again, his voice was once again calm, restrained.

"I saw what the Army didn't see," he said softly. "I saw a swarming enemy that was unlike anything America had ever fought against before. In the history of our military conflicts, we had never faced an enemy like the undead horde. Normal tactics, even our technology, were absolutely useless. It called for a different kind of thinking. The President appreciated that."

We stared silently at the map for long moments. My eyes were drawn to the dark line that stretched from the Carolina coast all the way across to the Mississippi River: The Danvers Defense Line.

Richard Danvers must have sensed the direction of my gaze. He studied my face for long moments, as if he was trying to read my thoughts.

He sighed. "Once the President appointed me, I went to work immediately," he said. "I drew up a plan that would contain the infected." He swept his hand across the map. "Ever heard of the 'Maginot Line'?"

I had. I was a student of twentieth century history. But I shook my head.

Danvers's expression turned blank. His eyes became distant like he was recalling information. His voice became flat, almost conversational without the underlying barb of aggravation.

"The Maginot Line was a line of concrete fortifications, obstacles, and weapons installations that France constructed along its borders with Germany way back during the 1930's," Danvers intoned. "The line was a defensive response based on the French experiences in World War I and was constructed during the years leading up to the Second World War.

"The whole idea behind the French plan was to create a fortification that would provide time for their Army to mobilize in the event of attack."

Danvers paused for a moment. "Follow so far?"

I nodded.

"You see the French looked back at World War I and saw the success of static, defensive combat and figured the same kind of tactics would likely be employed if war ever broke out in Europe again. Military experts extolled the Maginot Line as a work of genius. It was – it just wasn't the right tactic for the times. The line was an engineering feat of brilliance, but it came too late. The world, weaponry and tactics had move on.

"While the fortification system did prevent a direct attack, it was strategically ineffective. Ultimately, the Germans simply went around the line, outflanked the entire defensive installation, and swept through France regardless."

"So you used the inspiration of the Maginot Line as a template for the Danvers Defense Line?"

The man nodded. "It was perhaps the most difficult, most painful decision I will ever make," he said. "I had to accept surrendering the lives of Americans in five states, in order to keep the rest of the nation safe. It weighed on my conscience – it still does – but there was simply no other way, no other alternative. We had to build a line that could be defended, and that meant we needed time."

"Thirty four days, right?"

Danvers nodded his head. "You've done your research."

I said nothing. Danvers filled the silence.

"In thirty four days we constructed a line that stretched from Wilmington, in North Carolina, through Raleigh and Durham, across to Knoxville, Tennessee and into Nashville. The western leg of the border ended in Memphis, and used the Mississippi River as a natural barrier all the way down to New Orleans." He stared at me for long silent moments, trying to see if I understood the significance of the achievement. I did, but it was hard to get a sense of proportion.

"Over eight hundred miles of trenches and fortifications," he explained. "One of the most incredible engineering feats this country has ever witnessed, given the urgency."

I stared back at the dark line on the map, seeing the bulge of it through half of North Carolina and the undulations that linked the major cities across Tennessee.

"Trenches, right?"

"No," Danvers shook his head. "To call the defensive line merely a trench is to minimize the significance of what we created. It was more than a long line dug into the ground."

I had seen photographs of sections of the Danvers Defensive Line. The trenches that had been dug were wide tracts, with coils of barbed wire that were reminiscent of historic images I had seen in books about the Great War a century earlier.

"What we did was mobilize America's construction industry and the Army's engineering corps into one vast orchestrated machine that dug trenches twenty feet wide and eight feet deep. We then built firing platforms for the troops to operate from, and laid thirty feet of barbed wire ahead of each trench."

I looked puzzled. "Barbed wire? Surely that wouldn't have been a deterrent to the infected?"

"It wasn't," Danvers admitted. "It was a hindrance. It slowed them down so that as they pressed against the defensive line, they were snared. That gave our troops time to take head shots." He grinned, but it was unconvincing. His mouth twisted out of shape leaving his eyes haunted.

"And the forts you built? How crucial were they?"

Danvers looked pleased. I sensed the installations that had been sprinkled along the defensive line were something he was proud of.

"The forts," he sighed, like he was recalling a particularly fond memory. "Each one was a mile square built of high chain link fence, topped with barbed wire," he explained. "And each fort had several observation towers for snipers. There was one gate in, and one gate out." He went to the table and snatched at one of my pads of paper. He had a pen in his pocket. He leaned over the table like a general explaining tactics to a subordinate.

"We built each fort on a major intersection," he said and drew a large cross to indicate the overlapping roads. "The fort was built on the road running south, straddling the blacktop, with the actual intersection beyond the rear wall of the fort." He drew a box over one of the arms of road, and then drew gates at either end. "You see the fort was a mile square – and the gate we built made use of the road that already existed. That meant refugees could come in through the gate and be safe. It also meant our patrols could operate in zombie infected areas. The rear gate allowed us to mobilize troops along the defensive line by using the road that ran east to west along the intersection. It meant, in the event of a zombie attack somewhere along the trench line, that we could send troops from the nearest fort to reinforce the line without having to send them across difficult terrain. The intersecting roads gave us smooth lines of supply and reinforcement."

I nodded. I appreciated the genius behind the simple plan. "And the forts were twenty miles apart, right?"

"Approximately," Danvers said. "It depended on the intersections we had at our disposal. We built each fort a few miles south of the major cities along the line."

I stood back, glanced once more at the big map, and then down at the hastily scrawled drawing Danvers had made. "It seems that the Containment strategy you devised is a cross between World War I trench warfare, and the kind of forts we built back in the wild west when the cavalry were fighting Indians."

Danvers grunted. "That's a fair appraisal," he admitted. "When I developed the plan for the line I had to consider the type of enemy we were going to be confronting. As I said before, America has never fought an enemy so primitive that it rendered our superior technology ineffective – until the zombie outbreak," he spoke with the force of complete conviction. "I knew modern warfare, built

47

around technology, was not the answer. I found the solution, ultimately, in our history."

"You make it sound simple."

The man shook his head. "It wasn't simple," he said. "It was hard work and it involved great sacrifice. 'Operation Containment' wasn't just about building this defensive line, it was about the missions our brave soldiers undertook in the course of the operation. The line gave us a base – a place to defend, but once we had that containment line built, we still ran operations in zombie infected areas as part of the initial response. America has a lot of heroes they don't know about. That's why I agreed to this interview. I want you to tell the people of this country about the heroic dedication of the men and women who pledged to defend them."

I nodded. I already had several more interviews lined up with combatants who had been actively involved in 'Operation Containment'.

I sat back down at the table and gathered my thoughts for a moment. I had a dozen pages of scribbled notes. I flicked back through the pages quickly. I realized my writing was so scrawled, I would be lucky to read the mess later.

"What was the biggest challenge to 'Operation Containment'?" I asked after a long moment. "I mean apart from the logistics of building the line. Was it in the operations that were conducted in zombie territory, or dealing with politicians…?"

Danvers stared hard at me. Slowly he sat forward and thrust his face close to mine so that I could not mistake the gravity in his expression.

"The numbers," he said, like it was some secret that until this moment had never been revealed. "The sheer numbers of the enemy," he shook his head and seemed to become lost in his own brooding thoughts for several minutes. Finally he sat upright, and pressed his palms flat against the tabletop. "By abandoning Florida, and conceding that we couldn't defend Mississippi, Alabama, Georgia or South Carolina, we created an enemy army of about twenty eight million," he said the words slowly, making sure I understood the significance. "Twenty eight million mindless ghouls that couldn't be stopped, couldn't be reasoned with, couldn't be dissuaded, but could only be killed by a bullet to the brain. Think about that," Danvers said, and then lapsed into pensive silence while I tried to grasp the enormity.

I shook my head slowly. It was an impossible number to conceive. More than ten percent of the nation's population had been infected. I knew too that southern parts of North Carolina and Tennessee had also been forsaken.

"Look at it from a military point of view," he went on with a kind of macabre relish to emphasize his point, "and you'll understand better what we were dealing with."

He got up again and went to one of the blank multimedia screens on the opposite wall. He pressed some buttons and the screen filled with red towers, like some kind of a graph. Danvers stood before the screen like a college professor about to give a lecture.

"The People's Republic of China has the biggest Army in the world. Know how big?"

I shook my head.

"About two and a quarter million," Danvers said. I blinked. He went on remorselessly. "The US Army is the second biggest in the world – about 1.5 million, followed by India and North Korea, both with over a million men." He was pointing at each red column on the big monitor as he rattled off the numbers. "Russia has about a million, then comes Turkey, South Korea, Pakistan, Iran and Egypt, all with somewhere around half a million men. Know what that means?"

I shook my head slowly.

"It means that by surrendering those five states to the zombie infection in order to buy enough time to prepare a solid defensive line, we were confronted by an undead army that was *three times the size of the world's ten largest military forces, combined.*"

Danvers paused to lean across the table and pour himself a glass of water. He didn't offer me one.

"At the time of your appointment, the government had no idea that the zombie virus was in fact an act of terrorism perpetrated on the United States by Iran, right?"

"That's right," Danvers said solemnly. "We thought we were dealing with something extraordinary – something we had never seen the likes of before, but we thought it was like an Ebola strain, or some other virulent mutation of virus. We had no idea until several months into the war that this was all some gruesome terrorism plot."

I was tempted to probe further, but I didn't. Instead I kept the questions focused on 'Operation Containment'.

"You said you ran operations during those early stages containing the virus," I began. "How many, and what was the nature of them?"

"I didn't run the operations personally," he explained. "They were military, and – in some cases – civilian exploits. But to go into detail it would be better if you interviewed the combatants yourself."

I nodded. "Can you at least single out some of the main events that you felt were significant during the months that 'Operation Containment' was in effect?"

Danvers nodded carefully, "Sure," he said, like he was keen to merely get rid of me. I had the feeling that his patience was wearing thin. "Mission Warwax, Mission Hawk's Wing, and Mission Exorus. When you speak to the men involved, you'll understand the heroism of our troops on the ground, and the terrible sacrifices they made during those first few months when we held the undead back, and gave our military time to assemble and prepare."

Richard Danvers stood up, extended his hand across the table. Whether I liked it or not, the interview was over. I nodded my head, muttered something about being grateful for his time and cooperation, then turned for the door where a uniformed soldier had suddenly appeared. I was half way out the door when Danvers called out to me suddenly, "Oh, and see if you can find anyone willing to talk about the 'Silverbacks' and their exploits... if any of those men survived."

"The Silverbacks?"

"A group of retired soldiers," Danvers said sketchily. "They were from Georgia. They were kind of like a resistance group. We owe them a lot."

THE PENTAGON, ARLINGTON VIRGINIA:

With a different school guidance counselor, Raymond 'Tug' Horsham might have ended up as a butcher, or maybe a school bus driver. He had a wide friendly face, a ready smile, and the kind of sparkling eyes that store owners look for when they employ their Santa Claus each Christmas. In short, he looked nothing like my impression of the hardheaded General who had been appointed by the President to oversee 'Operation Containment', and the man who coordinated the initial military defensive response of the nation.

The original SAFCUR (Supreme Armed Forces Commander Undead Response) was waiting for me when I entered his Pentagon office. He looked me over carefully, and then gestured for me to take a seat on the opposite side of a large desk. An aide was running down a list of his other

51

appointments for the day. Horsham dismissed the young man with a nod and a friendly smile, and held the expression right up until the door finally closed and we were alone.

Not a second longer.

"What do you want?" Horsham's voice crackled like electricity.

I was shocked. The transformation from the genial public persona to the private warrior was startling. He fixed me with baleful eyes.

He was a big man – broad and solid in the shoulders with a bull neck and thinning grey hair.

He put his hands on the desk and laced his fingers together.

"Sir, my name is Culver..."

"I know," Horsham said. "I didn't ask who you were, son. I asked what you want."

As a journalist, I've conducted interviews with all types of people. Some try to win you over with charm. Others become adversarial in the hope that you'll be intimidated and shy away from asking the hard questions. But I didn't sense that with Horsham. I simply got the impression that he was a no-nonsense man with limited time. I hoped I was right.

"I want to know the truth about 'Operation Containment' and your role in the defense of the nation during the zombie war," I said, and sat up straight, meeting his steely gaze and refusing to blink.

"The truth?" Horsham's voice was a deep rumbling bass, the kind of voice that reminded me of thunder rolling across the sky. I was hoping he'd give me the clichéd *"you can't handle the truth!"* and go all Jack Nicholson on me. He didn't.

"The truth is that a lot of fine young men and women died in defense of their homeland."

I nodded, and flipped my notebook open to a blank page.

Horsham's phone rang suddenly. I caught the man's eyes and silently offered to step out of the office, but Horsham motioned for me to stay put. He snatched at the receiver and swung round in his chair so his broad back was to me. I heard his voice, low and muttering, but paid no attention.

Instead, I gazed around the Pentagon office.

There was a map of Old America on the wall behind him, next to an old American flag, still with the original fifty white stars in the top left corner. His desk was huge – like some kind of a barricade maybe, and there was a credenza against one wall. There was nothing on the man's desk apart from the phone and a 49ers football helmet. Not even a framed photo of children or a wife. He had both.

His uniform coat was on a hanger, pressed and immaculate, displaying a chest of military decorations and ribbons.

The office had a sense of being temporary – as if Raymond Horsham was subconsciously preparing for a recall back to real soldiering. There was nothing here that the General couldn't pack into a duffle bag and be on the next plane back to the front line.

It was an unexpected insight into the man.

Horsham swung round in his chair and dropped the phone back into its cradle. He took a deep breath, and then narrowed his eyes like he was making a judgment call.

"Fire away," he said at last. "Ask whatever you want and I'll give you the honest truth."

I relaxed just a little. Horsham did the same. He leaned back in his chair.

I had to ask about the flag and the map. I sensed that the relevance of those pieces would reveal a glimpse into the man's personality and temperament. "The flag," I gestured. "Is there any significance?"

"Absolutely," Horsham said. His shoulders went back an inch. "It's still my flag, and it always will be – and America is still my country… and it always will be."

I frowned. I could understand the passion, but I struggled with the practicality – especially from a man with a reputation for being pragmatic.

"The zombie infection broke out thirteen months ago," I said gently. "Operation 'Containment' lasted several months, and then we transitioned into 'Conquest' and 'Compress'. We've exacted retribution against the Iranians. The horde has now been driven back behind the Florida border. Isn't that enough? Isn't the war over – or as over as it's ever going to be?"

"No." Horsham said, and his voice seemed to boom around the room. "The Middle East might have changed as a result of our wrath, but America has not, and will not. The war isn't over. It's won, but it's not over – and it won't be over until the last zombie is eliminated and driven from the face of the earth, and Florida is reclaimed as American soil."

"So you don't support the new America? The re-drawn maps and the new flag?"

"No," he said again. "Too many proud men and women have spilled their blood in mud around the world for over a century fighting for that flag you see behind me, and defending *all* of the land on that map on my wall. We owe it to them to fight the fight until the world is right." It sounded like a powerful slogan, and I wondered if he had ever used that speech to rally the troops he had led into battle against the zombies.

But I didn't ask…

"You were appointed SAFCUR, and as such, you were the man responsible for fortifying and defending the Danvers Defense Line. Correct?"

He nodded. "Correct."

"I'm interested to know how you went about that, especially in those early weeks when the zombie hordes were rampaging through the southern states," I said. "Was there a sense of panic, or confusion? How did you pull the necessary armed forces together to man such a long line of fortifications?"

Horsham turned his head a little and I got the sense that he was glancing at the map of Old America. He sighed.

"The military response was incredibly professional and organized," General Horsham said. "The biggest issue we had was dealing with the spread of civilian panic. Roads were choked with traffic all the way through Virginia, Kentucky, Missouri... so logistically there were difficulties getting our forces on the ground," he admitted. "Initially we were able to man the trenches with National Guard troops, and almost the entire 82nd Airborne Division."

"Almost?"

Horsham smiled thinly. I think he sensed right then that I had no idea exactly what an entire airborne division constituted.

"It was only the third or fourth time since the Second World War that nearly the entire 82nd Airborne was in the air with the majority of its equipment," he explained. "A force so vast that it had to be airlifted into combat by around one hundred and fifty Air Force C-130 Hercules and C-17 Globemaster III's."

He fell silent for a moment, and I began to appreciate the enormous logistics of the operation.

"The 82nd Airborne Division has been called America's fire brigade – they're the guys we call on in an emergency. They're based out of Fort Bragg... and that made them perfect. Bragg was on the southern side of the containment line, and when the Danvers Defense Line was initially approved, the Secretary of Defense argued long and hard to make Bragg part of the defense. It did no good. So the 82nd was re-deployed further north, and into Tennessee. But as you can see, having these guys so close to the conflict made their deployment a no-brainer."

I nodded. I had read accounts of heavy equipment being left behind as the Division was re-deployed. Horsham saw it differently.

"We didn't abandon any equipment," he said pointedly. "We simply left the Air Defense Artillery and the 319th Airborne Field artillery behind. The plan was to pick up that equipment once the operation moved into the 'Conquest' phase."

I scribbled quickly. General Horsham was opening up, and I sensed my best tactic was to stay quiet and let the man talk. I nodded encouragingly, and my pen raced across the page.

"We flew everything out of Pope Air Force Base, dispersing the 504th Parachute Infantry Regiment and the 505th along the Tennessee perimeter line, and the 325th into North Carolina. The 307th Engineer Battalion was sent to Memphis – the western tip of the line – to begin bridge demolition work. Their efforts were supported by the Air Force."

"Were the engineers the only troops sent to Memphis?" I asked.

He shook his head. "We used the old Millington Naval Air Station as a staging ground when the Defensive Line began to take shape and we were funneling more troops into the trenches," Horsham explained. "Twenty odd years ago Millington was a major military installation but it was downsized. When we moved in it was housing a smaller Personnel Center for the Navy, but it still retained most of its original facilities, and the old runway was still there. The runway had been transferred to civilian use. We took it back."

"Did you feel prepared for the approaching conflict?"

The General paused and rubbed his chin. "We had a lot of men, but it wasn't nearly enough," he confessed. "And abandoning equipment, and aircraft goes against the grain," he grumbled. "But we needed to deploy with great speed. Leaving Bragg and Pope in the dead zone was militarily stupid, in my opinion. If the Danvers Defense Line had been given into the hands of someone with a true appreciation of the military considerations, my guess is that it would have been drawn up differently."

I sensed some friction, and like any good journalist, I tried to pick the scab off the General's wound. "So you weren't a fan of Richard Danvers? That must have caused difficulties, considering you were appointed SAFCUR."

Horsham's expression became frosty. His posture stiffened. He stared at me for long silent seconds and I could sense him bristling with a barely concealed flash of temper.

"Danvers did the job the President appointed him to do," Horsham said carefully, like he was reciting these lines from some kind of a prepared, censored media statement. "As SAFCUR, I operated with the restrictions I was handed. They weren't of my making – they were mine to make what I could with."

I smiled wryly. "Spoken like a politician," I said.

The General didn't share my smile. He tensed. "No," he said, and thrust one of his fingers at me. "Spoken like a career soldier who is accustomed to dealing with the idiotic decisions of politicians and bureaucrats."

More silence. The interview had taken a confrontational turn and I tried to steer it back on course, back to aspects that were more comfortable for the General in the hope that he would once again be forthcoming.

"Sir, you've had an extremely distinguished career. You've seen action and led men in every major theater of operations for many years. How was the zombie war different to other military conflicts, in terms of attitude?"

"Attitude?"

"Yes. In terms of morale?"

Horsham hesitated and his broad face creased into a series of frowns. He stared towards the ceiling for a moment.

"I guess the closest I can figure would be to compare it to 'Desert Shield' and the defense of Saudi Arabia back in '90-'91," he said after a long moment. "From a purely operational point of view, both conflicts were the same – that period where we hastily assembled the men and equipment necessary to construct a cohesive defensive line. In every other aspect," Horsham assured me with a steely gaze, "the zombie war was unlike anything I have ever encountered before."

It was the kind of comment that deserved a significant moment of silence, so I kept my mouth shut and made notes. I flipped over to a new page.

"You were SAFCUR I," I began, suddenly finding myself looking for a delicate way to pose the question I wanted to ask. "And yet, despite the success of 'Operation Containment' under your leadership, later in the war, another General was appointed to lead 'Operation Conquest', the second phase. Can you tell me why? Did you fall out of favor with Washington?"

General Horsham cut across the question brusquely, waving his big hand in the air like he was swatting away my words.

"Horseshit," he said, his voice like gravel. I sensed it was a question he had been asked privately more than once, and that it was an issue that irritated him.

"Son, the military isn't full of the same ego-driven characters that populate Capital Hill," he said. His voice leveled out, losing some of its sting. He glanced around him and his eyes fastened on the 49ers helmet. I saw a glint come back into the big man's eyes. The General smiled thinly.

"I was picked to run 'Operation Containment' because I

have a reputation for playing good defense," he said, slipping into a football analogy. "My job was to hold the line, and I did that. "But a good team is also made up of a strong offense, and special teams. When we transitioned into 'Operation Conquest' and 'Operation Compress', the President called on men who had reputations for their offense. Make sense?"

It did. I nodded.

"And when we finally discovered the whole zombie war was initiated by an Iranian terrorist plot, well... the President decided it was time for the special teams to take the field. One man can't run every play – each task required the leadership of the best man for each individual job."

"Have you ever actually met 'the architect', Richard Danvers?"

"No," the man's voice snapped like a whip.

I changed tack again. Interviewing the man was like walking through a thorn bush.

"Was there ever a time during those first few weeks when you were pulling together America's military resources behind the Danvers Defense Line that you were worried?"

General Raymond Horsham stared at me, and for long seconds he said nothing. The room was deathly silent, and I began to wonder if it was a question he was simply unwilling to answer. Then, slowly, the set features of his face seemed to crumble just a little and I got a brief, haunting glimpse of the man behind the soldier.

"Every night," he said, his voice lowered to little more than a whisper, but somehow was made more powerful. "Every single night I worried that the infected would spread north and press against the line before we were prepared."

"Because...?"

"Because we weren't ready," he confessed. "We would

have been overrun. The scenario haunted me right up until the first major conflict when the undead horde crashed against the line south of Asheville, North Carolina. It was the first time the defense had been tested."

"The Battle of Four Seasons, right?"

Horsham smiled, a drawing back of the lips that was without warmth or humor. "Hendersonville," he said. "They called it the city of four seasons. That's where the name came from," he shrugged.

"That engagement was the first organized conflict of the zombie war. It must have given you some confidence."

The General shook his head. "I always had confidence in the men under my command," he said. "American soldiers are the best trained in the world, and remember, we were fighting on home soil. They were committed and dedicated... and brave. What troubled me was that I was leading them into war when we were under prepared. I didn't know how broad the front would be. I didn't know whether we could hurl the undead back. I didn't know if the tactics would work because we'd never fought such a primitive and unique enemy before."

I seized on the General's last comment because it was one aspect that had troubled the military in the frantic weeks leading up to those opening battles. I cocked my head to the side and looked quizzically at Horsham.

"You know, that confuses a lot of people," I said.

"What?"

"That comment you just made about the enemy being so primitive," I went on. "General Horsham, the common misconception from commentators when the war first began was that the American Army had an enormous technological advantage."

Horsham shook his head emphatically. "We did have a huge technological advantage," he said. "But it was fundamentally useless." He leaned way back in his chair and then reached into a drawer or a shelf beneath his desk. He tossed a stack of folders onto the polished timber tabletop. They skidded across the surface.

"We have the most advanced weaponry in the world," the General grumbled. "We have the kind of technology that out thinks, and can out smart every other major military force on the planet. But it's useless when your enemy has no technology at all. You're not countering their capabilities."

I shook my head. I didn't understand. I went to flip open the cover of the top folder, but the General slapped it closed with a thump of his fist like it was full of state secrets. The sound of his hand was like a hammer. I flinched.

"Those reports are not for you to read," he barked. "They were merely to indicate the huge amounts of intelligence we were able to generate in the first weeks of the conflict — satellite images and the like. All of it useless."

I was still shaking my head. "I don't follow."

The General sighed. "Smart bombs, missiles... even artillery was no direct match for the undead, because the only way to kill them was to destroy the brain," he grunted. "Sure, you might get a few kills from missiles or shrapnel, but you're laying the entire southern part of America to ruin for no real advantage — turning it into the kind of wastelands we saw in World War I between the trenches." General Horsham made a tight fist with his hand and his words suddenly shook with passion. "This was a dirty war — a close range conflict that we hadn't fought for a hundred years. There was no remote control killing, no combat fought beyond the horizons... it all came down to our men on the ground with rifles and automatic weapons face-to-face with a relentless, mindless enemy."

I had filled the rest of my notebook, but I sensed there was more here to be discovered if I could only ask the right questions.

"You mentioned tactics just a few minutes ago," I said thoughtfully. "Do you mean the tactics you employed leading up to the Battle of Four Seasons?"

The General nodded. "Hendersonville was the location of one of our forts, straddling the I26 south," he explained. "But further south of that fortification, I also had armored convoys – light mobile units of Humvee's that were scouting the terrain, and Black Hawks flying constant reconnaissance patrols. They were our whiskers."

"Whispers?"

"No," he shook his head. "Whiskers – like a cat. We used them to 'feel' for the enemy. At the time we were frantically pulling troops into the defensive line, but I wanted eyes in the dead ground, sensitive to the spread of the infected, and also capable of rescuing any refugees that were fleeing the carnage. The Humvee patrols had strict orders not to engage – they were merely scouts, tasked with rescue. When the zombies began coming into contact with these units, we knew we had run out of time."

I was puzzled. "Couldn't you get that intelligence information from satellites?"

The general tried to smile, and then decided it just wasn't worth the effort. "Sure," he conceded, "but apart from the real-time delays between when the information is gathered, and when it was passed through to SAFCUR Command, have you ever seen a satellite rescue a refugee?"

I got the point.

The general shook his head. "Satellite imagery was helpful, but not telling," he said. "Sure, we've got a sky full of birds and I could have tasked every one of their cameras to scour Alabama and Georgia as the plague swept north. But satellites are just photos. They can tell you the 'what' but they can't tell you the 'why'. They can't tell you about the on-ground factors. Even the live-feed drones that relayed images back were barely useful because there was nothing vital they could tell us. HUMINT was more precious to me."

"HUMINT?" The military has a profound fascination for acronyms.

"Human intelligence," the General explained. He looked at me as if it was a term I should have known. "Eyes, ears... men on the ground. It was risky work for those men in the Humvees, but it was essential. And the Black Hawks crews took great risks too, probing deep towards Columbia, Atlanta and Birmingham in the search for survivors."

General Horsham looked pointedly down at his wristwatch and then at the closed door of his office, as though he was expecting to be interrupted at any moment. I sensed my time with the man was running short. I started to close my notebook, and then tossed out my last question like it was a hail Mary pass that I hoped he would catch and run with."

"Why didn't we base our response to the zombie outbreak on CONOP 8888?" I asked.

Silence.

Not the amiable silence you experience when two old friends have run out of things to talk about and are happy just to sit and reminisce – this was one of those ominous silences that precedes a thunder storm. The atmosphere in the office suddenly became charged.

"That plan was a load of shit," Horsham exploded. "A useless piece of marketing trash that made no strategic or tactical sense. Christ, it was supposed to have been a Pentagon document, but I tell you, no one I came across even knew it existed until the media got hold of it."

On April 30th 2011, the US Strategic Command drew up a document that outlined the way the American military should deal with an undead apocalypse, entitled CONOP 8888. The plan was also known as 'Counter-Zombie Dominance'. The document came to light in 2014 and was featured on hundreds of online blogs, with commentators going to great lengths to point out the glaring inadequacies of the policies outlined.

"It was a joke," Horsham's tone was almost offended. "Some hair-brained idiot's idea of a way to fictionalize preparedness for a raft of real world threats. We looked at that plan for five seconds and threw it in the trash."

"Like that promotion the CDC came out with at the same time?" I asked. "That Preparedness 101 for Zombies?"

"No," Horsham shook his head. "Not like that at all." The big man was bristling with frustration and temper. He got up from his chair and leaned across his desk, planting his big hands on the tabletop and thrusting out his jaw. "The CDC plan was actually useful. It alerted people to natural disaster preparedness by using a fictional zombie apocalypse as a way to attract interest from the public. It served a very valuable purpose. CONOP 8888 was the opposite. It was a destructive divisive load of rubbish that should never have been written, and never seen the light of day."

BARKSDALE AIR FORCE BASE, LOUISIANA: 608th AIR OPERATIONS CENTER

Lieutenant Colonel Greg Pike wanted to make one thing clear.

"The Air Force didn't bomb every bridge along the Mississippi River," he explained to me patiently as we stood outside the Air Operations Center at Barksdale. "The Air Tasking Order we worked off specified seventy-two bridge structures. They're the ones we bombed."

"How many B-52 aircraft were involved in the mission?"

I asked. I had my notebook ready, pen poised.

"Nine," Pike said easily. "The 8th Air Force was tasked with the mission and the job fell to the 2nd Bomber Wing here at Barksdale, and elements of the 5th Bomber Wing, stationed at Minot Air Force Base, North Dakota. They were responsible for the most northern bridges across the river."

"Only nine B-52's? That doesn't seem like a lot of aircraft for such an extensive operation?"

Pike gave me the kind of special look I imagined he reserved for journalists and politicians. "The ordnance we dropped were JDAM Mk 84 bombs," he explained brusquely. "They're two-thousand pound bombs. We allocated two weapons for each bridge and each of the aircraft carried sixteen bombs. Do the math."

I did, and then asked another question quickly.

"Can you tell me how long the actual procedure took, from start to finish?"

The Lieutenant Colonel smiled amiably enough. He grabbed at his nose and tugged at it, then stared up into the sky for a moment as if he could hear an aircraft overhead. "We flew the missions over two consecutive days, right at the very outset of the infection," the man said. "This would have been around the same time the President approved the plan for the Danvers line. We had the job of securing the west flank of the perimeter. Most of the work was done on the first day of the operation. On the following day a three-ship cell went back over the targets to re-strike any bridge still standing."

There were over two hundred and twenty bridges along the Mississippi River. Seventy-two accounted for roughly a third of those. I stared at the Air Force Lieutenant Colonel and made a face to express my confusion.

"What happened to the rest of the bridges?" I asked.

Pike was a tall man, and when he smiled, it reached all

the way to his eyes and left little dimples in his cheeks. He was immaculately dressed in uniform, his regulation-length hair neatly parted on the side and just beginning to turn from black to grey. His eyes were bright, and he had that peculiar far-away gaze I had seen in other pilots – the look of a man who was accustomed to staring at far away distances. He had a high forehead and perfect white teeth.

He smiled again, as if to show them off to me.

"The smaller bridges were left in the hands of the Army Corps of Engineers," Pike explained. "They were demolished at the same time, and the ferries that operate on the Mississippi as far north as Memphis were all moved to the west bank and placed under the control of elements of the Arkansas and Louisiana National Guard."

"Do you know why?" I asked.

"Why do you think?" The Lieutenant Colonel fixed me with a stare. He folded his arms across his chest.

"To prevent opportunists from operating the ferries during the outbreak?"

Pike smiled, and nodded his head. "Exactly," he said. He glanced pointedly at his wristwatch. "Are we done here?"

"Not quite," I said quickly. Pike sighed and shuffled his feet. "Look, I was told this would be quick," he said, and there was a grumble of aggravation in his voice. He didn't want to do this interview.

"Can you tell me what it was like to fly those missions?" I asked. I wanted to know how they were different from other similar tasks the B-52's might have been called upon to perform in overseas theaters of war.

The Lieutenant Colonel suddenly became more serious, as though this question was at least deserving of his attention.

"It was surreal," he said, like he was confiding something personal. "It was the most poignant mission I have ever

66

been a part of."

"Poignant?" I frowned. It was such a powerful word, and so unexpected. "In what way?"

Pike unfolded his arms and wrung his hands. "It was on home soil," he said. "That was the first thing. In my life I never thought I would see the day when war came to America… when we were fighting to defend our own nation, rather than protect another." He shook his head. "It really hit home – flying over those bridges and knowing we were destroying history and infrastructure because war had come to the USA. It still gets me…" his voice trailed away and for a moment he was silent and lost in a rising tide of his own emotions.

"And in other ways also?" I prodded gently.

He nodded. "The B-52 is the mother of all killing machines," he said with a pilot's passion. "For over fifty years those BUFF's have been the backbone of America's strategic bombing capabilities. Hell, during Desert Storm a flight of B-52's flew from here to Iraq, bombed targets, and then flew home again," Pike said proudly. "We were in the air for thirty-five hours and flew fourteen thousand miles non-stop. Now, suddenly, we were flying short hop operations and hitting targets just over the horizon."

I began to understand the impact the bridge-bombing missions along the Mississippi had had on this man. For the first time, perhaps, warfare was incredibly personal.

"You called the planes BUFF's a moment ago. What does that mean?"

"Big Ugly Fat Fucker," Pike seemed to take some delight in sharing the term of affection. "Or if you prefer the sanitized version, Big Ugly Fat Fellow." He smiled then, but I wasn't sure if it was because he was pleased, or because the joke was on me.

"Did it feel like other bombing missions at all?"

"No," Pike admitted. "Not to me, anyhow. It was devoid

of every stimuli."

What the?

I looked at the pilot, puzzled. "Um... what?" I tried to be delicate.

"Flying those missions was almost like operating a simulator," he explained. "There were no nerves, and there was no sense of flying into danger like every other combat mission. No one was firing at us. No one was trying to defend the bridge. No enemy fighters were hunting us. There was nothing. It was so antiseptic, and yet at the same time incredibly harrowing, because of the significance of what we were doing."

I had imagined high altitude bombing would create a sense of distance and remoteness for these pilots – something I thought I would be less likely to find in the soldiers who fought so close to the enemy. I was wrong. Distance did not diminish the wrench of a man's patriotism, nor the anguish of the duty they were called on to perform.

It was a somber, sobering moment for me.

"Dropping bombs on a target from high altitude must be fraught with its own perils," I said slowly. "Things like accuracy, for instance..."

The Lieutenant Colonel shook his head. "It's not like what you imagine," he said. A little bit of color came back into his face, as though he had brought his emotions back under control. "In World War II, high altitude bombers were happy if they landed ordnance within three thousand feet of their target. Today, we're accurate to forty feet because of the GPS power of the JDAM attachments."

I was impressed. He saw it on my face. But I was also a little confused.

"Forgive my continuing ignorance," I began, and Pike went out of his way to stifle a meaningful laugh, "but what exactly are these JDAM devices? You mentioned them earlier in the interview as well."

"JDAM stands for Joint Direct Attack Munition," the Lieutenant Colonel said, then waited impatiently until I wrote everything down. "It's a guidance kit that we use to convert 'dumb' bombs into all-weather 'smart' munitions. Once a bomb is equipped with a JDAM kit, it is guided to the target through a guidance system that works in conjunction with a GPS receiver."

"And that's what makes it accurate?"

"Yeah," Pike said dryly. "What we aimed at, we hit. All the bridges tasked to us were destroyed." Pike's expression remained bleak, but despite the emotional strain of the bombing mission, a tiny trace of pride crept into his voice for a mission successfully accomplished.

"I just hope I never have to fly another mission like it," he said softly.

NAVAL STATION NORFOLK:
NORFOLK, VIRGINIA

The Petty Officer shook my hand and smiled because he was supposed to, not because he was pleased to see me. "You're John Culver?" He glanced down at the credentials clutched in my fist that I had carried through the security checks.

"Yes," I said.

The man nodded. "I'm here to escort you to the Vice Admiral's office. He's been waiting for you."

I shrugged an apology. Gaining access to the world's largest naval base wasn't just a stroll through the gates. "Sorry," I said. "I wasn't expecting such a lengthy processing procedure."

The Petty Officer looked at me like maybe I should have. He turned on his heel and I scurried to follow.

I got lost in the maze of buildings. The vastness of the naval base was overwhelming.

"Naval Station Norfolk supports seventy-five ships and over a hundred aircraft," the Petty Officer sketched an outline of the base as we walked. "It is made up of fourteen piers and eleven hangars. As well as being the largest naval base in the world it also has the highest concentration of US Navy forces."

I didn't write any of this down. I was struggling to keep pace with the sailor.

"It's the home port for five aircraft carriers, just as many cruisers, seven submarines and more than twenty guided missile destroyers. And that's just the main combat vessels."

"It's impressive," I admitted. "Were all these warships employed during the blockade of Florida?"

The Petty Officer stopped suddenly and turned to face me. He was scowling, as though I had asked a sensitive question. We were standing outside a building that looked much like an office block. "The Vice Admiral's office is on the fourth floor," the man said instead. "Someone will meet you inside the front doors. They will escort you the rest of the way."

I frowned. "He's not on a ship?"

"No. He's in his office."

I was somehow disappointed. I had expected to find the man standing on the bridge of a huge aircraft carrier with binoculars slung around his neck.

I went through the glass-fronted doors.

Another Petty Officer looked up from behind his desk in the foyer. He set down his pen and came striding across the polished floor. "Culver?"

"Yes."

"You're late."

"I know."

"The Vice Admiral has been waiting for you."

"I know."

The man's expression became almost sympathetic. He took my credentials and looked them over carefully, then handed them back to me with a sigh. "Brace yourself," he muttered ominously.

We rode the elevator in silence.

On the fourth floor the Petty Officer knocked on a door at the end of the corridor.

"Come!"

The man pushed open the door for me and backed away.

I stood on the threshold of an office that was smaller than I had expected. The walls were lined with framed photographs and bookcases. There was a map of old America on one wall and a battered leather chair in a corner. There were shelves of naval memorabilia and a window that offered a view of murky grey warships far in the distance. A desk that looked like an antique dominated the floor space. It had ornate legs and a wide polished timber surface. It was covered with papers and the edges were scattered with small silver frames and a miniature model of an aircraft carrier.

It was gloomy in the room. The drapes had been partly drawn across the window. The air smelled of expensive cigar smoke.

The man behind the desk stood up.

Vice Admiral Walter Greenville threw down the papers in his hands and glared at me. He was of average height, maybe in his late fifties or early sixties. Beneath the uniform he looked like he still worked out. He had grey hair, parted neatly on one side and a ruddy complexion. His eyes were deeply set behind silver-rimmed spectacles and overhung by a heavy brow. He looked me over carefully and seemed unimpressed. "You're late."

"Sorry... sir," I said. "I got held up at the main gates."

The Vice Admiral grunted. We didn't shake hands. He dropped back down into his seat and gestured for me to sit down. There was a straight-backed chair across the desk. I sat down and waited.

The Vice Admiral went back to reading his reports.

I sat in awkward silence for exactly six minutes – the precise amount of time I was late in arriving for the interview. Finally the Vice Admiral picked up a pen from his desk and signed the papers in his hand with a flourish. He snatched off his glasses and stared across the desk at me.

"I agreed to give you thirty minutes for this interview," Walter Greenville said. He had a deep rumbling voice – the voice of a man who was accustomed to authority. "You wasted six of those minutes by arriving late, and making me wait. I have taken another six of those minutes making *you* wait." He leaned forward and reached for one of the silver frames at the edge of his desk. He turned it around and I saw it was a small clock. "You have eighteen minutes left."

I nodded, and reached for my notebook. I had planned to ask this man about his background. He had graduated from the US Naval Academy and had enjoyed a distinguished career. Now I only had time left for questions about the zombie apocalypse.

"You were overall commander of the naval blockade along the Florida, Georgia and South Carolina coast when the zombie infection first began to spread," I began. "Could you tell me how you went about organizing an operation of that size?"

Greenville swayed back in his chair. He rested one hand on his hip and rubbed at his chin with the other hand.

"It wasn't anywhere as difficult as people might have assumed," The Vice Admiral explained. "The blockade operated under the name 'Operation Vulcan'. It was our mission to create an iron-tight blockade of the waterways along the east coast and the Gulf to prohibit the possibility of infected victims making it offshore in pleasure craft or light aircraft."

"And you say that was easy?"

"No," the Vice Admiral corrected me. "I said it wasn't anywhere as difficult as some observers might have imagined."

"Why?"

Greenville shifted his weight in his chair. The soft leather squeaked. He had a file on his desk. He held it up for me to see and then set it down again.

"In 2008 we conducted a similar operation. It was called 'Operation Brimstone'. It was a Joint Task Force Exercise, known as JTFEX 08-4. It commenced in July of that year of the Eastern US Atlantic coast from Virginia to Florida."

"You practiced a blockade against the possibility of a zombie infection as far back as 2008?" I was shocked, and a rush of outraged and alarmed questions bubbled to my lips. I found it incredible that the government had been aware of the possibility of a zombie-like infection for so many years and kept it quiet from the nation.

"No!" The Vice Admiral slammed his hand down on the table like he was crushing something. "'Operation Brimstone' was a multinational US naval exercise that included British, French, Brazilian and Italian naval forces as part of a proposed plan by the Bush administration to conduct a blockade against... ironically... Iran."

"Iran?"

The Vice Admiral nodded. "At the time there was a plan to blockade that country, and we conducted the 'Operation Brimstone' exercise to drill and train for operations in shallow coastal waters such as the Persian Gulf and the Straight of Hormuz."

I sat back. I felt disoriented. The Vice Admiral was staring at me, his features fixed into a stone-like expression.

"So… the training exercise is relevant because you actually drilled for a similar event in the same waters?"

"That's correct," Greenville said. "In 2008 we drilled with the *USS Theodore Roosevelt* and its Carrier Strike Group Two. The same aircraft carrier operated as part of the blockade against the zombie infection. We also had a second Carrier Strike Group built around the *USS Harry S. Truman*, which operated in the Gulf of Mexico. Both aircraft carriers were supported by Aegis class cruisers, as well as destroyers and several frigates."

"What did each component contribute to the blockade?" I asked curiously. "I mean I can understand the aircraft carriers, I guess. You needed the aircraft. But what about the cruisers and the smaller craft? How did the whole operation work?"

The Vice Admiral planted his hands on the desk and pushed his chair back. He got to his feet and stepped towards the map of old America he had on his wall. It was a large map broken into two parts – one showing the eastern coastline in particular detail. He swept his hand over Florida.

"Imagine three rings," the Vice Admiral said," and drew a circle with the tip of his finger like the outer atmosphere of a planet. "That's where the carriers were stationed. Here, and here," he pointed at a spot in the Atlantic and then at another place in the Gulf, up near the Panhandle. "Inside that circle was another, closer to the coastline. That's where the Aegis class cruisers were stationed. Those warships have radar systems that can track hundreds of air and surface targets simultaneously. We used them as our eyes and ears, supplemented by AWAC aircraft that were launched from the aircraft carriers. Every air and surface movement along the coastline was monitored and investigated."

"By the fighter planes aboard the carriers?"

The Vice Admiral nodded. "Sometimes," he said. "And sometimes they were picked up by the vessels we had operating inside the inner ring – the one closest to the shore. That's where the frigates and destroyers were on active patrol."

I stood back from the map thoughtfully. It seemed as though the blockade had been comprehensive. But had it been effective?

I turned to the Vice Admiral. "Were there many incidents?" I asked tactfully.

Greenville made a kind of pouting expression with his lips, like something was suddenly distasteful.

"The first few weeks of the outbreak were a real test for us, both in terms of light aircraft traffic and sea traffic," Greenville explained. "It was decided to destroy the A1A causeway to isolate the mainland from Key West, and then we routed all aircraft to the Naval Air Station on the island. The carriers were flying air combat patrols around the clock, and every aircraft was treated as hostile. It was chaos – the Naval Air Station at Key West was never set up for that kind of heavy traffic – but every aircraft had to land there for clearance. Any plane that refused was shot down."

There was a moment of heavy silence. "Was there?"

"Was there what?" the Vice Admiral wanted me to spell the question out. I did – delicately.

"Was there any light commercial aircraft that were shot from the sky by your fighters because they refused to land at Key West for clearance?"

"Two," Greenville said. "Both aircraft were intercepted by fighters launched from the flight deck of *USS Theodore Roosevelt* and terminated."

Another long heavy silence.

"And were there any incidents on the water? I know Florida has a huge recreational boating fleet. There must have been hundreds of thousands of people trying to escape the apocalypse in speed boats."

The Vice Admiral nodded. "We had several incidents in the Gulf, but most of the issues were along the east coast. And not only from within Florida. One pleasure craft off the coast of Georgia had to be sunk when it refused to yield to a destroyer that had been dispatched to intercept it."

"How did you manage all of that ocean traffic?" I shook my head incredulously. I could visualize thousands of small boats in the waters off Florida, racing out to sea, packed with frantic survivors trying to flee the terror.

"Each and every boat was intercepted and boarded," the Vice Admiral assured me. "No boat was permitted to pass through the inner-most circle of our blockade without being cleared by our inspection teams."

"And you were able to enforce that?"

He nodded. "As I said, the first few weeks were intense. After that the air and sea traffic along the east coast and into the Gulf all but ceased." He shrugged his shoulders. "By then, no one was left alive."

I frowned, looked at the map again, and then down at my notebook. I had pages of scribbled notes that would have to be deciphered after the interview ended. "Just going back a step," I puzzled. "What happened to the boats that refused to yield to the blockading frigates and destroyers? You said you shot two planes down. There must have been at least as many incidents with boats – probably a lot more."

Greenville nodded. "A *lot* more," he agreed, and there was emphasis in his words. "And it was an altogether more dangerous situation for us. When a plane would not detour to Key West, we were able to prosecute an attack from a safe distance with the fighters. But when a boat refused to give way to the frigates, we had the choice of either firing at the vessel or somehow forcing it to stop."

"So you opened fire?"

Greenville shook his head. "We didn't want to do that. We knew a lot of those boats would be filled with good people in terrible fear for their lives."

"So you risked the boarding parties lives? Surely there must have been some concern that at least some of the fleeing boats carried people who might be infected."

"We used patrol boat drones," The Vice Admiral said.

I flinched. "Pardon?"

Greenville smiled bleakly. "Patrol boat drones," he said again. "At the outbreak of the zombie infection it was still considered experimental technology – that's why you haven't heard of them in operation before. But the Navy had developed a system where small boats – almost any small boat – could be operated like a drone aircraft. They were guided by a remote-control system."

The Vice Admiral went back to his desk. I went back to my chair. Greenville reached out for the scale model of the aircraft carrier and plucked it up into his hand.

"Imagine this model is a patrol boat," The Vice Admiral said, turning the little ship over in his hands," and imagine this clock is an aircraft carrier, or even a cruiser."

I nodded. The Vice Admiral set the framed clock in the middle of the desk and put the tiny model beside it. "The unmanned boat drone is designed to leave the vessel it is protecting and attack an enemy threat. The idea is to have a swarm of these unmanned drones close to the key vessel. When a threat appears several of the drones will swarm towards the enemy, encircling it and keeping it well away from the cruiser or carrier they are protecting."

"How does it work?"

"The technology is called CARACaS. The Office of Naval Research has been working on the idea for a couple of years. Some time ago they started live tests on the James River in Virginia. Those tests demonstrated how the drones could protect a major vessel travelling through a narrow water straight. We used the drones to isolate and encircle pleasure craft that would not yield to our blockade."

"And it worked?"

The Vice Admiral nodded his head. "Very effectively," he said. "Rogue boats were encircled and detained by drones. Any vessel that tried to break through the blockade or deliberately disobeyed our orders was kept at bay. We didn't board them for forty-eight hours to ensure that everyone aboard was free of infection."

I was writing this all down as quickly as I could. My hand raced across the page while the Vice Admiral sat back in his chair. I could feel his eyes upon me. When I looked up at last, he had shifted his gaze back to the map on the wall.

"Can you tell me what the CARACaS acronym stands for? I think it would be important to mention in my article."

"Control Architecture for Robotic Agent Command and Sensing," Greenville said, annunciating every word clearly for my benefit. "Using those unmanned platforms off Florida gave us the ability to diffuse the danger of infected people escaping offshore without risk to US Navy personnel."

I sat back and flicked through the notes I had scrawled. "How long did the blockade last?" I asked.

"It's still operating as we speak," Greenville said, which surprised me.

"Really? Why?"

"Because we're thorough," the man leaned forward and propped his elbows on the desk. His expression became defiant. "Because we never rest. Because it pays us to be eternally vigilant." He sat back at last, and some of the tension seeped from his posture. "We still have a force in the Atlantic and the Gulf. Not the same kind of Naval force that upheld the blockade, but elements of it… and we will continue to do so."

"Until…?"

"Until such time as the zombie infected are eliminated and Florida is returned to the United States of America. Because until that happens the war is not won, and we cannot rest."

FEMA REGION IV TEMPORARY HEADQUARTERS, NASHVILLE, TENNESSEE:
DISASTER EMERGENCY COMMUNICATIONS DIVISION

"FEMA was part of the initial Danvers plan," Tom Deighton explained to me as we walked around the organized chaos of a parking lot in downtown Nashville. "Our management actually consulted with Richard Danvers directly, and I am proud to say that the FEMA Region IV Disaster Emergency Communications Division was one of the very first units on the ground."

"Here?"

Deighton nodded. "Right here, in this parking lot," he said.

Tom Deighton was the Region IV Regional Emergency Communications Coordinator at FEMA. He had held the demanding job for almost nine years. When the Danvers Defense Line was drawn up, FEMA representatives played a hand in the process, and the team from Region IV was relocated to Nashville before the first trenches were dug.

"Traditionally Region IV served the south eastern states of Alabama, Florida, Georgia, Kentucky, Mississippi, North Carolina, South Carolina and Tennessee," Deighton explained. He was a big man, broad across the shoulders, and carried weight in his gut that might have been muscle when he was younger. He had a rounded face and was just a few grey wisps of hair away from being bald. "Naturally, our knowledge of the areas affected by the zombie infection made us one of the lead groups as the outbreak began to spread."

"What exactly was your role?" I asked.

The parking lot was filled with military vehicles and a collection of other trucks from different agencies. Although the defensive line had now been relocated well south, Nashville was still being used as the command center for the military, and the civilian organizations that had been drawn under the armed forces umbrella.

"We were very careful at the outset not to overplay our hand," Deighton confessed. "We had been made well aware of the hierarchy, and we established ourselves as a valuable asset to SAFCUR and his support staff."

"So this could never be called a FEMA operation?"

"Oh, hell no!" Deighton suddenly became animated. "For God's sake, don't write that in your article. FEMA was one of several support agencies to the military – that's all."

In previous years, and during previous natural disasters, FEMA's reputation had taken a battering through some damning media coverage. The organization was still licking its wounds after the chaotic response to Hurricane Katrina – and that had been around a decade ago.

"Fair enough," I said. "I understand." To placate him I even flipped open my notebook and made a note of the fact. He still wasn't satisfied. He looked over my shoulder and read what I had written. "Underline *'support only'*," he said.

I did. "Happy?"

Deighton nodded, and then visibly relaxed. He struck me as being a tense man – someone who walked a permanent tightrope of frayed nerves. Maybe it was the stress of the job.

I looked around the parking lot. We were in the shade of the AT & T building, a multi-story office building in downtown Nashville. I had heard locals affectionately refer to the building as 'The Batman Building' and I could see the clear resemblance of its skyline to the cowl worn by the fictional crime fighter. The complex had been commandeered by the military for its headquarters.

There were three white FEMA trucks parked nearby. I started walking towards one of the vehicles and Deighton shuffled behind me trying to catch up. "What's this?" I asked, pointing. The truck looked like a long armored car. It was all square box-like shapes and there were communication dishes and antenna, like bristles, sprouting from the top of the vehicle. There were doors built into the sides of the truck body with steps down to the ground. The doors were closed.

"That's one of our three MERS vehicles here in Nashville," Deighton explained. "Mobile Emergency Response Support. They have been the key to our division's involvement in the outbreak."

I walked round the truck slowly. "What does it do?"

"It's a communications center," Tom Deighton gave me the simple answer. He was sweating. Even in the shade the day was warm and sunny. He mopped his brow with a handkerchief and blinked at me myopically for a moment. "When the zombie infection began to spread, our key function was to provide an early center for communications," Deighton went on. "There was so much panicked traffic – we had everything from cell phone calls to ham radio operators. We were able to help compile the incoming communications and present it to SAFCUR and his staff. Some of the information was intelligence-based," Deighton lowered his voice like we were in the pages of a pulp fiction spy thriller. "People holed up in their basements reporting the spread of the infection. Others were panicked. They were trapped and surrounded. They were calling for rescue. We took everything that came in, and gave the military the opportunity to monitor the infection's spread from real-life reports, as well as orchestrate their responses for those civilians who were desperate to be rescued."

I arranged my features into a look that would convey I was impressed. "Didn't the military have their own system?" I asked.

"Sure," Deighton said, "but you can never have too much information. SAFCUR and his key personnel regarded the data and temporary communications infrastructure we provided as being essential to their eventual success."

"And you're still here on site?"

"Our role hasn't diminished," Deighton looked almost offended. "In fact it's about to be dramatically increased."

I raised an eyebrow in surprise. "Really? Surely most of the communication from the infected zone went quiet months ago. There's practically no one alive in Florida to speak to – is there?"

Deighton's smile was grim. Not a smile at all, really.

"Sure," he nodded his head. "Incoming civilian communication dried up after the first few weeks. Since then the contacts have mainly been from survivalist types on their ham radios. They're hunkered down and refuse to come out. They simply won't leave."

"So…?"

"So we're preparing to move into the dead zones," Deighton went back to his espionage voice. "It's been over a year since the outbreak, and several months since the success of 'Operation Conquest'. Now the Army is saying that 'Operation Compress' has reached the stage where the Florida border is considered stable. FEMA will be one of the lead units moving into the dead zone to begin the clean up. And it's happening soon." This last little gem of information was delivered along with a suitably breathless gasp.

"Really?"

I find that the easiest way to make some people talk. As a journalist, you try all kinds of things to get people to loosen up. Sometimes it works. Sometimes it doesn't. Simply questioning the person's last comment was a standard kind of technique that encouraged the subject to expand – because when they expanded on their statement, they invariably gave you more detail, and that made for a more comprehensive story.

"Really?" I said again.

Deighton nodded his head. "The entire FEMA organization is moving its Federal Headquarters to Nashville," he said. "It won't just be our few MERS trucks from the Disaster Emergency Communications Division… it will be the whole show. And we'll be on the ground for as long as it takes to get America dusted off and back on her feet again."

I smiled. I felt like Deighton was waiting for some kind of congratulatory slap on the back. I grinned at him instead. "Well, that's good news," I said without conviction. "I'm sure everyone across the rest of the country will be relieved to know the clean up operation is going to be left in FEMA's capable hands."

We shook hands. Deighton frowned at me like he wasn't sure if my words were a sincere compliment or dripping with sarcasm.

I left the man wondering…

LANGLEY AIR FORCE BASE, VIRGINIA:
55th FIGHTER SQUADRON

The 55th didn't belong here.

The squadron of F-16 Fighting Falcons had called Shaw Air Force Base in South Carolina home until the zombie apocalypse had forced the sleek jets north during the first desperate days of the outbreak. Now the 'Fighting Fifty-Fifth' ran its operations out of Langley... and would probably continue to do so, even though Shaw AFB had now become part of the re-claimed dead zone – that grey area between the original defensive line and the current post-apocalyptic perimeter built around much of Florida.

I stood irritably in the shade and checked my watch. It was getting late. I took another long look into the afternoon sky and saw a dark spec, high amongst the clouds. As I watched the shape descended and quickly took on the detail of four F-16's, roaring overhead before coming in to land.

I paced across the concrete with frustration, as the roar of the approaching fighters became an assault on my ears.

The F-16s rolled to a gradual halt beyond the shelter building where I stood. Ground crew rushed forward to the sleek warplanes, and crew chiefs propped ladders next to each fighter's bubble canopy. One of the pilots climbed down, tugging at the straps of the full-faced helmet as he came directly towards me.

I nudged one of the nearby ground crew. "That's Captain Harper, right?"

The man squinted, staring from the shade, out into the bright glare of midday sunlight where the F-16 seemed to crouch like a bird of prey on the verge of flight.

"Yeah," the man said. "Call sign 'Moses'."

I stood and waited. The pilot came closer, bulky with flight suit. The helmet came away at last, revealing a tress of red hair that cascaded down to the woman's shoulders. She pulled it back into a neat bun, and then smiled slightly. She tucked her flight helmet under one arm and held out her hand.

"Are you John Culver?"

I nodded. "Are you Captain Tony Harper, call sign 'Moses'?" I knew my tone sounded incredulous, because I was. I was expecting a man – not this rather attractive young woman with piercing green eyes that glinted with mischief.

"That's Toni, with an 'i' she said. Her head came to the level of my shoulder.

"And your call sign is 'Moses'?"

Toni Harper nodded. "I'm a natural redhead," she said.

I nodded. "I noticed."

She smiled wryly. "Well the guys took their understanding of that fact to a lower logical level… and I got Moses as a call sign. Something about a 'burning bush…' she arched an eyebrow playfully.

I got it.

Captain Harper led me deeper into the building and then up a set of stairs to a room overlooking the wide expanse of the base. The walls were carpeted for soundproofing, and the afternoon sun was just beginning to angle in through the tinted windows.

She fetched a can of soda from a refrigerator and unzipped the front of her flight suit. She was wearing a yellow t-shirt.

"Want a drink?"

"No, thanks." I said.

Toni Harper dropped into a comfortable chair. She popped the soda and sipped. "Sorry for keeping you waiting. What would you like to know?"

I dropped into a seat beside her. I was still coming to terms with the fact that this experienced fighter pilot was a woman. Of course, I had known there were women pilots in our Air Force, but I hadn't expected to meet one who had been assigned combat duty during the zombie apocalypse.

85

Harper stared at me speculatively, and then narrowed her eyes as though she could read my mind. "Get over it," she said flatly. "I'm a woman. I drive fighter planes."

I nodded, somehow feeling guilty, or sexist, or narrow minded.

... or maybe all three.

"Your squadron was one of the first units activated for a particular role very shortly after the outbreak of the infection," I said. "Did the relocation from Shaw to Langley cause disruptions during those early missions?"

Captain Harper took another sip of her soda, and glanced, distracted, out through the big windows as another F-16 suddenly clawed its way into the air ahead of a blooming heat haze and a mighty roar that seemed to shake the sky. When the fighter was out of sight, she turned her attention back to me.

"We're a combat ready unit," Captain Harper explained. "We're trained to deal with disruption, and even dislocation. We were in the air and on the job an hour after the mission tasking came through."

I reached into my bag for my notebook. "And the mission itself – the 55th were essentially flying combat patrols over the Danvers Defense Line, even before the barrier was completed. Is that right?"

Toni Harper nodded. She set the soda down on a side table.

"We started patrolling the skies above the defensive line just as the first heavy engineering equipment began tearing up the earth," she explained. "We were tasked with F-15's from the 336th to run the line from the east coast across to Memphis. For simplicity, we flew along the 36th parallel north on an east to west route, and then back again."

I nodded. I knew the 336th fighter squadron was based out of Seymour Johnson AFB, near Goldsboro, North Carolina. Unlike the jets of Toni Harper's squadron, the

Eagle squadron's home base was behind the Danvers Defense Line.

"What exactly was the mission," I asked. "As I understood it, you were basically enforcing a no-fly zone. Is that correct?"

Harper shook her head. "No. It's not correct." She smiled thinly and then scraped her fingers through her hair. "We were tasked with the responsibility of stopping all commercial aircraft and helicopters from flying *into* the quarantined area," she said. "And for the terms of our mission, that area was basically anywhere below the 36th parallel from the east coast across to the Mississippi River."

I nodded, because I understood what she was saying. But I didn't understand why.

"Why?"

Harper's smile became strained. "When the apocalypse first broke out in Florida, everyone who had a light commercial plane, or could charter a helicopter flew as far the hell north as they could," she said and there was a hint of aggravation in her tone, like maybe I was wasting her time. "But the government didn't want opportunists swooping into Florida and preying on those left behind. We didn't want the skies being criss-crossed with gung-ho air jockeys trying to make a fortune by renting out their planes and helicopters like mercenaries. It was too dangerous."

"In terms of air safety?"

She nodded. "And in relation to the spread of the infection," she added. "Those first few weeks were chaotic. There were so many rumors and so few hard facts, no one was even sure about the delay between when a victim was bitten, and when the virus re-animated the corpse."

I was puzzled. "But surely any means of escape from the infection…"

Captain Harper shook her head and her hair swished across her shoulders like the flick of a jungle cat's tail just before it attacks. "No," she said adamantly. "The pilots of those helicopters and light aircraft were a risk to themselves, and to everyone they flew – and a risk to the massive military contingency that was trying to establish a defensive perimeter. We needed the skies clear, and that's what the 55th fighter squadron was tasked to do. And we did it."

"At the cost of civilian lives?" I questioned pointedly.

Harper arched her eyebrow and her gaze became black. She stood up and bunched her fists, her posture defiant and bristling. She glared at me like she was trying to locate my jugular vein. "Listen," she thrust a finger at my face. "The Air Force had plans to rescue as many refugees as we could, flying them out of designated evacuation locations in transports. But we couldn't. In the end, the plague spread too quickly, and the danger became too great. Washington tore up the planned operation. But if we had been ordered in, we would have gladly gone."

Captain Harper turned on her heel and stalked across to the window. She stared silently out across the air base, and I could see the tension in her shoulders as she fought to compose herself.

"I didn't mean to imply…"

"Forget it," she turned her head and snapped with frost on her lips. "Just finish asking your questions. I have more important places to be and more important things to do."

I shrugged. "How did you go about intercepting the helicopters and light planes? Were there a lot of them?"

"AWACs," Toni Harper said crisply. "It's an airborne early warning and control system. We had AWAC aircraft high above us. They would pinpoint the threats and we would be tasked with investigating."

"Were there a lot of incidents?"

"Yes," Captain Harper said. The woman certainly knew how to hold a grudge. Her tone remained curt, almost seething. "In the first few weeks we were flying non-stop patrols and being tasked to targets almost constantly. Once the light plane pilots and helicopter jockeys understood we were serious, the number of attempted incursions declined dramatically."

I took a deep breath. "There was one reported incident…" I started to say. "A media report that a Bell JetRanger helicopter was shot down by an Air Force fighter over Tennessee for violating the no-fly zone. Did you hear anything about that?"

Harper shook her head. "It was a lie," she said with finality. "That helicopter crashed. It wasn't shot down."

I raised a questioning eyebrow. "How can you be sure of that?" I asked.

"Because I was on patrol the day that incident happened," she said in a flat monotone. "I know the pilot who was involved, and I'm telling you it was a crash. The Air Force has the footage, filmed from the nose of the F-16 that was flying on a course to intercept. There's no scandal – just confirmation of exactly the dangerous practices we were trying to prevent occurring."

I let the matter go. Toni Harper might have been a lady, but I sensed that to pursue the shooting down of the helicopter would be like prodding a snake with a stick. I tried to smooth the waters.

"I'm sorry about what I said earlier," I made a placating gesture with my open hands. "I guess I was just surprised that you could be so callous about civilians being left stranded in the middle of the apocalypse, and that you could actually advocate leaving them there… in the hope that a military evacuation might have been orchestrated instead." I shook my head.

Toni Harper's eyes blazed with hostility, but also something else – something so fleeting and elusive that I didn't recognize it – until it was too late.

"I'm not callous," she said. The anger that was in her

voice lost its way and somehow became sadness. "My mother and father, my kid sister, and my grandmother all lived in Orlando."

She stalked for the door. I thought the interview was over. Just before she left the room, she turned back. There was a glistening tear on her cheek.

"I'm a professional," Toni Harper's voice trembled. "It tore my heart out knowing my family had a chance to be saved, but couldn't be."

FORT RILEY, KANSAS:

America has always cherished its heroes, turning them into larger-than-life public personalities – even celebrities. And yet the first real hero to be recognized during the zombie war was perhaps one of the most humble and unassuming men I had ever met.

He was waiting for me patiently in a hangar at Fort Riley, a slight tall man, leaning casually against the canopy of his UH-60 Black Hawk helicopter. Chief Warrant Officer Sam Grear, Bravo Company, 2nd Battalion of the 501st Combat Aviation Brigade shook my hand and smiled with the kind of expression that suggested he was acutely embarrassed by the attention.

He was wearing a 'pickle suit', a green one-piece aviation uniform that had been replaced by the Army a few years earlier. Grear had bright blue eyes, and a peculiar far-away gaze. I guessed him to be in his early thirties.

We walked out into the bright sunshine, while all around us mechanics bustled like bees around the huge hulking shapes of 2nd Battalion's helicopters.

"You're uncomfortable about this, right?" I asked.

Grear gave me a sideways glance, and nodded his head.

"I know you want to interview me about the rescue ops we flew during 'Operation Containment'," he said. He was softly spoken man. "I just don't understand why. A lot of crews have done what me and my crew did." He shrugged his shoulders. "They deserve attention too."

I nodded. "But I can't interview them all, Sam," I said. "And the Army thinks your exploits deserve to be known and appreciated by everyone. They've nominated you and your story as being indicative of the heroism our pilots have shown. In a way, you're a spokesperson for all the other guys. Think of it that way."

He put his hands behind his back, clasped them together and kept walking. He was frowning thoughtfully. After a hundred yards of stony silence he stopped suddenly and lifted his face to mine.

"Okay," he said. "What do you want to know?"

I had some prepared questions, based on the newspaper accounts of Grear's actions I had read. I flipped open my notebook.

"According to what I have read – and what the Army has so far released – you were flying your Black Hawk helicopter on a reconnaissance and rescue patrol when you spotted several survivors, fleeing from a large swarm of zombies. Is that right?"

Grear made a face. "No," he said, and shook his head. He took a deep breath. "My copilot, Chief Warrant Officer Mike Tolliver was the one who first sighted the refugees."

I nodded. "Okay... so tell me what really happened. Let's set the record straight."

High overhead helicopters circled in the sky like lethal birds of prey so that the air was alive with the distant pulse of beating rotors.

"2nd Battalion is GSAB – general support. That means we fulfill a range of different functions," Grear explained. "So when the plan came for a series of sweeps into the dead zones of Georgia, as part of Mission Hawk's Wing, our unit was one of the first ones mobilized." The pilot paused for a moment to see if I understood him. I did. He went on.

"We were flying missions throughout the day, concentrating our efforts around Athens and Atlanta – they were our areas of operation. We went in with four Delta snipers aboard –"

I cut him off. "Your crew? How many men?"

"There was me and Mike Tolliver upfront, and we had two crew chiefs, Staff Sergeant Kim Wilson and Staff Sergeant Paul Rolandson in the back of the bird. They were on the miniguns."

I nodded. "Right," I scribbled down the men's names. "And you had four Delta snipers aboard as well."

"Correct," Grear nodded. "The cargo door was open on both sides of the bird and the Delta boys were in the opening as we swept over the dreads."

"Dreads?"

"Undeads," Grear shrugged. "That's what we call 'em."

I made a note of that. Grear watched me writing everything down, like it was important to him that the record be accurate. I looked up at him, encouraging him to continue.

"It was just after oh-eight hundred, the second week after the Danvers Defense Line had been finalized," he began. "The defensive line was beginning to fill out with troops from around the country. We still weren't ready for a major attack, but we were getting there quickly. The orders came down for us to start flying ops looking for refugees that had somehow escaped the apocalypse further south."

I studied the young man's face. "How did you feel about that?"

He shrugged his shoulders. "I joined to serve," he said simply. "I was glad to do my part. My whole crew was. Mike had family in Florida. Most of the men I know were affected in some way or another."

I nodded, and then remembered something. "You weren't always a helicopter pilot though, were you?"

Grear looked a little surprised. "How did you know that?"

It was my turn to shrug. "Research," I said vaguely.

He regarded me carefully for a moment, and then we started walking again. Grear began to talk.

"I was a Marine before I became a pilot," Grear revealed. "When I was nineteen I went to train in the Marines. I went through Officer Candidates School at Quantico. Every candidate starts out as a sergeant, and I enjoyed the training, but three years later I was injured... and out of the military for two years."

I frowned. "You didn't go off and find a new career?"

Grear shook his head. "I wanted to serve," he said again, and I could hear the commitment and passion in his voice. "So I eventually joined the Army to be a pilot, signing on as a specialist at basic training and a sergeant at Warrant Officer Candidate School. After graduation I went to flight training school."

I was impressed. The man had been dedicated. "Any regrets?" I asked.

Grear shook his head and smiled humbly. "No," he said. "I love flying."

We walked for a little ways in silence. One of the circling Black Hawks came in to land, and for several minutes the roaring sound of the chopper made conversation impossible. As the big helicopter's turbines and rotors slowly wound down, I flicked back to my list of prepared questions.

"Tell me about that operation in more detail," I encouraged. "What happened when Chief Warrant Officer Tolliver saw the refugees?"

Grear nodded his head. "There were six of them," he began, "running along the road. We were operating a few miles north of Atlanta. There were burned out and abandoned cars choking the highway. We were flying low, maybe a hundred feet of altitude, certainly no more than that. Mike saw movement and when I looked down through the helicopter's chin bubble I saw a couple of kids and four adults. The adults were running, dragging the children by the hand, almost pulling them off their feet. I could see the panic in everyone's faces, even from a hundred feet. One of the men in the group stopped suddenly."

"He just stopped and did what?"

"Nothing," Grear said. "The guy just stopped running and stood in the middle of the blacktop for a few seconds. Then he collapsed."

"And that's when you decided to land in a nearby parking lot, right?"

"No," Grear shook his head. "There was a parking lot but we couldn't land there – or anywhere nearby," he said. "There were simply too many power poles, lines... strike zones that we traditionally stay clear of."

"So what did you do?"

"There was a field about a click away," Grear said. "We started to circle around towards it, but then one of the crew chiefs saw a swarm of dreads, about five hundred yards behind our refugees. They were coming on fast – too fast."

"You hadn't seen the ghouls before that moment?"

"No," Grear said. "We thought the refugees had seen our ship and were simply running towards us. We didn't realize they were being chased."

"So what happened next?"

Grear's eyes became kind of vacant, and his voice changed completely, it was bleak and flat, lacking any timber or resonance, as though he was deliberately trying to sanitize his account of all emotion and simply recall the facts.

"I threw the bird into a tight turn and told the crew

chiefs we were weapons free, and then swung the Black Hawk broadside to the road. The guns were 7.62mm miniguns. They fire up to four thousand rounds per minute."

"And so your men opened fire."

"No," Grear said. "They waited until I had put the helicopter between the zombies and the refugees. I dropped to just twenty or thirty feet. We were hovering right across the road. Staff Sergeant Kim Wilson opened fire, and so did the Delta Snipers."

"You took a great risk," I said. "I imagine there was no margin for error."

"There wasn't," Grear admitted. "And breaking discipline – dropping that low in an area filled with potential strike zones –was something that frightens the hell out of the best pilots. But at the time I didn't see any alternative."

I wrote all this down as quickly as I could. The sun was starting to sink towards the horizon and two more of the helicopters that had been circling high overhead dropped down out of the sky to land. Grear suddenly turned on his heel, and we started back towards the big hangar.

"What happened when your crew chief opened fire?" I asked.

"All hell broke loose," Sam Grear said, and for the first time I saw a wry smile on the serious young man's lips. "The minigun tore into the dreads and flung them back like they had hit a wall. It ripped them into pieces and left them spread and spattered across the highway."

"But they weren't dead, of course."

"No," Grear said. "Some of them went down and stayed down. Some of them were so badly torn apart that they no longer posed an immediate threat. But it wasn't the end of it."

"What happened…?" I prompted.

"I swooped along the road and set the helicopter down in the middle of the freeway. It was tight. An eighteen-wheeler had overturned and spilled its cargo of boxes across the pavement. I sat the helicopter down in front of the truck, about two hundred yards ahead of the refugees."

I had to ask the question. "Were you calm?"

Grear shook his head. "No," he said. "I was scared. So was Mike, but we were well trained, and in moments like that you fall back on your training. It's what gets you through. I wasn't really frightened until later on when I thought about the risks I had taken... but by then we were back at base being debriefed."

"What happened once you set the Black Hawk on the ground?"

Grear frowned, like suddenly he had to think hard. "Everything happened very quickly," he confessed. "Like it was a blur. The Delta boys took up firing positions on either side of the road and crew chief Staff Sergeant Rolandson jumped down onto the blacktop and started running towards the refugees."

I shook my head. I could imagine the bravery of this man and the rest of his crew. I doubted whether I would have been so courageous in similar circumstances.

"What happened?"

Grear narrowed his eyes and frowned. He wasn't looking at me – he was staring off into empty space. "The noise was chaotic," the young pilot said quietly. He shook his head as if the horror of that clamor was still reverberating in his ears. "The helicopter, the screaming of the refugees, the sniper fire coming from either side of the bird – everything was a roar of confusion. I could see the dreads through the side window of the chopper. They were gathering themselves around a couple of burned out cars just down the road. The distance was hazed with swirling smoke. The dreads started forward – started to run at us, and I could see the terror on the faces of the children. The sound of the dreads got louder – I could see their bodies were twisted with the madness of their infection. Then, one of the kids fell over. She lay there in a crumpled heap and then got up again, limping and crying. There was blood spilling down her leg. One of the women tried to scoop the child up in her arms but she must have been too heavy to carry. Mike was thumping at his harness, just about to get out of the chopper and run forward to help. I stopped him. Through the coms I told crew chief Wilson to ready the minigun."

"But you were on the ground, right, and the refugees were running towards the helicopter?"

Grear nodded. "I was prepared to take off, hover just above the road to give the miniguns a clear field of fire over the heads of the civilians if it came to that. We knew we had other birds in the area, and that if we could hold the swarm of dreads at bay long enough, another ship might be able to drop down and pick the refugees up."

I could see the scene playing out in all of its gruesome horror in my imagination. I could visualize the sheer terrified desperation of the fleeing civilians, and the dreadful fear that must have gripped them as the snarling zombie horde began to spring forward to hunt them down. "But it didn't come to that?"

"No, thankfully," Grear said with a sigh. "The little girl got up and took a few staggering steps. Then one of the Delta guys ran forward under the cover of the other snipers. He snatched the child up one handed like she was a sack of rags," Grear shook his head. "He was still firing from the hip, running back towards the helicopter with the kid tucked under one arm like it was nothing."

"You got them all?" I asked.

Grear nodded. "Three women, a man and two young girls. We got them all to safety before the dreads were able to regroup and reach the helicopter. Crew chief Rolandson carried the civilian who had collapsed over two hundred yards on his shoulder. That was heroic."

We walked the rest of the way back to the hangar in silence. There seemed to be nothing left to say. Sam Grear's modest, humble recollection of his bravery and that of the men with him on that fateful flight had said it all.

I shook the man's hand and looked him in the eye. "Thank you," I said, like the words had more meaning than merely my thanks for his time. He looked at me, and then smiled slowly.

"Are you going to interview any of the civilians − the people my crew risked their lives to save?"

I shook my head. "No," I said. "I'm just trying to record America's military response in these interviews."

There was a brief moment of silence while Grear considered me. Finally he leaned closer, his voice still soft and serene. "Make an exception," he said. "Talk to one of those people we saved. Because if you don't at least mention the human aspect of this whole damned horrible war... then what were we fighting for?"

He leaned back, his gaze steady and implacable. "I joined the Army to defend America. Those people are what we're all fighting for. Let them have a say."

I thought about that. Grear had a point. But there was a problem.

"I... I wouldn't even know where to find them?" I gestured.

Grear smiled again, so that for a moment, he almost looked at ease. "They're less than an hour's drive away," he said. "They're in a temporary refugee camp outside of a little town called Blue Rapids."

'CAMP K14', OUTSIDE OF BLUE RAPIDS, KANSAS: 39°40'55"N 96°39'33"W

'K14' was not the kind of refugee camp I was expecting. There were no high wire fences and no armed guards. The camp was made up of maybe a hundred large canvas tents, set out in the kind of precise lines that only the military could have managed.

'K14' was spread out across open grassy fields just beyond the limits of a picturesque little town named Blue Rapids in the north eastern corner of Kansas. It reminded me of a massive summer camp. Here were the temporarily homeless and the dislocated – the people who had been fortunate enough to flee from the zombie horde, or, like Gloria Kingsman, been fortunate enough to have been rescued by helicopter pilots like Sam Grear.

There was a family, communal atmosphere. Groups of young children ran through the tented areas, crying out and laughing, while mothers pegged ragged clothes from the guy ropes. There were a couple of trucks parked by the side of a nearby road, and soldiers in green fatigues were unloading food and water supplies onto hand carts. In the middle of each tented line, huge bonfires burned in drums as the afternoon light gradually turned to the radiant colors of sunset. Here and there, I could see the muted glow of lamps burning behind thin canvas walls.

Gloria Kingsman was a woman in her thirties who looked a decade older. She had been living in the camp with her two daughters for over a year since that fateful day on the highway north of Atlanta. The time had not been kind to her. She looked thin, and there were dark shadows of fatigue smudged below her eyes. Her face was pinched with stress. She sat on the edge of the canvas chair with her legs crossed and her hands fidgeting in her lap. She stared at me, and I had the impression there was something hollow about her – as though all the energy and vitality had somehow been drained away.

"You want to talk about the men who rescued us, right?" she made it sound like a question, but it wasn't. The camp personnel had already told her about my planned visit the evening before.

I nodded anyhow. "That's right," I tried a friendly smile. "I just wanted a few minutes of your time to check some details."

"You've spoken to the pilot, Sam?"

"Yes. He suggested I talk to you."

"Why?"

I shrugged. "He thought you might provide some interesting insight," I offered vaguely. Gloria Kingsman nodded her head like the explanation made enough sense for her to be satisfied. She sighed and pushed at her hair in a heartbreaking moment of feminine vanity. "Where do you want to start?"

I took a breath. "I'd like to know about the events leading up to your rescue," I said. Gentle voice, another friendly smile. Mrs. Kingsman looked like she was on the ragged edge of a nervous breakdown. "If you feel up to talking about it again."

She lit a cigarette and inhaled deeply. She was swinging one leg like it was the swishing tail of a cat. She looked over her shoulder. There was the distant sound of a child crying somewhere in the camp. She listened for just a moment – realized it was not one of her own – and then seemed to shut the sound from her mind.

"Larry – that was my husband – and me were from Grantville, Georgia," she explained in a soft accented voice. "When the infection broke out down south, we decided to pack up and head as far north as we could. We had two little ones. We packed the car and headed for Atlanta."

"Did you know about the Army's defensive line they

were constructing?"

She shook her head. "No," she said. "We had heard things on the radio, but there was so much confusion, we just didn't know what to believe. We only knew we had to get the little ones as far away from trouble as we could."

"So you went to Atlanta."

"We tried," Mrs. Kingsman said. She dropped the butt of her cigarette in the grass and crushed it under the heel of her shoe. "We didn't get more than a few miles. The roads were impossible – abandoned cars and trucks, people panicking, fights on the streets. There were gunshots. Cars were on fire and there was looting. It was anarchy. It took us almost a week to get to Atlanta, sleeping in abandoned cars or under trees while Larry kept watch with his rifle during the nights."

"It must have been a frightening ordeal."

"It was," Mrs. Kingsman lit another cigarette and inhaled anxiously. "The screams in the night were terrifying – blood-curdling cries that went on and on."

"From the undead? Were they pursuing you?"

"No," she shook her head. "It was from all the looting and killing. People were insane with panic and desperation. Larry saw one man shot by a young woman who stole his bicycle." She shook her head like it was still something she couldn't come to terms with. "For a bicycle!"

Even a year after the event, those days filled with terror had left deep emotional scars.

Maybe ones that would never heal.

"You mentioned Larry, your husband," I began delicately, already sensing there was no good news to come. "Was he the man that Sam Grear and his crew rescued that day outside of Atlanta?"

"Yes," Mrs. Kingsman said. Her voice had dropped to a hushed whisper. "He had collapsed on the road. He had been carrying our youngest for the last ten miles on his back.

When we saw the helicopter come out of the sky, we all started to run. But Larry... well it was his heart. It just gave out, I guess."

"He died?"

"No," the woman said. "Not right then." Tears began to well up in her eyes and her shoulders began to slowly shake. She turned her head away and I heard her sob. When she turned back to me, her cheeks were wet, her eyes huge wells of agony and sorrow. "They got him to a USAMRIID hospital in Knoxville. They thought maybe he had been infected. He died there."

"I'm sorry," I said. The words sounded trite.

Through her tears, Gloria Kingsman smiled suddenly. "It was like Larry knew we were safe," she sniffed. "He knew we had made it to safety. That seemed to be all he was hanging on for."

I looked away, gave Mrs. Kingsman time to compose herself. A young girl's face appeared from behind the nearest tent. The kid saw me and ducked back out of sight.

"Your daughters are safe though, right?" I asked.

"Yes," Mrs. Kingsman said. "Thanks to Sam and the other men on board his helicopter that day. They risked their lives to rescue us. It was something I'll never forget, and never be able to repay them for."

I jotted a few quick notes and then looked around the camp one last time. I got to my feet slowly and held out my hand. Mrs. Kingsman forced a quivering smile. "When do you return home to Grantville?" I asked.

The woman's smile flickered for another moment, and then slid off the edges of her mouth. She shrugged her shoulders. "No time soon," she admitted.

I frowned. "But... the undead are back behind the Florida border defensive line now. Surely you..."

Mrs. Kingsman shook her head. "The government says it will be at least another year before we're repatriated," she

102

said. "The area is still official dead zone, and the damage... well apparently it's just like New Orleans after Hurricane Katrina."

She fell silent for a long moment, and it was like she was seeing the ruins of her future stretched out ahead of her like an endless road of broken ground. She lifted her face slowly, and her eyes flicked to something beyond my shoulder. She smiled wanly, then lifted a languid arm that was deathly pale. "Hi Ty," she said.

I turned. There was a man in his thirties standing between the rows of tents with a young girl on his hip, maybe six or seven years old. Beside the man was an attractive young woman with a bob of sandy hair and a quirky smile that seemed to make her eyes sparkle behind the lenses of her glasses.

Gloria Kingsman waved the couple over. The man held out his hand.

He was tall and solidly built. He had clear, defined features and a beard that was just beginning to turn white along his lower lip. He smiled, and the expression hung from the corner of his mouth as he set the girl down on the ground beside him.

"Ty Harrison," he said as we shook hands. "And this is my girlfriend, Sarah."

I nodded.

"This is John Culver, Ty," Gloria Kingsman introduced us. "He's a journalist. He's been interviewing me about the apocalypse." She bit her lip, then leaned closer to me. She lowered her voice to a whisper, but it wasn't necessary. The man and woman could hear every word she breathed. Perhaps she was just being polite. Perhaps it was just genteel manners. "Ty and Sarah were in Bradenton when the infection broke out. They barely escaped."

I looked up at the man. He was silhouetted against the sinking sun. "Is that right?"

The man nodded. He glanced sideways at the woman beside him, and there was some silent exchange of messages, or perhaps memories.

"Care to tell me about it?" I offered. I reached for my notebook. The man sighed, and then let go of a shuddering breath as if the tension he had been holding onto had suddenly leaked from him. He dropped down into the long grass like he needed to.

For a long moment the man said nothing. He just stared down at the ground, his gaze distant, his facial expression rigid. When he finally began to retell his story, his voice seemed to come from far away.

"I owned a comic book store," Ty Harrison said. "We had just opened that week."

I raised an eyebrow. "A comic book store? What was it called?"

He smiled wryly. "Tytan Comics," he said. "The store was on US41 in Bradenton."

I frowned at that. I wasn't instantly familiar with the town. He must have caught the curious wrinkle in my expression. "Bradenton is an hour south of Tampa Bay," the man explained. "We had just renovated the store and opened for business."

I made a note, then looked back at the man. The young woman with him was standing close by his side. The little girl clung to the woman's hand.

Ty Harrison lifted his eyes to mine. "At first I... I thought it was all an elaborate hoax," he confessed. "The store had just opened for business, and I thought Sarah had organized some kind of extravagant promotion to let the locals know, and maybe attract a little bit of publicity." He shook his head. "I saw these people running down the street. They were covered in blood. Some of the wounds... they were ghastly."

"And you thought it was a stunt?"

He nodded again. "I studied special effects make-up," Ty explained. "I thought it was all a Hollywood-type event."

He sighed, then glanced away and stared into the empty distance.

"When did you realize it was the real thing?"

"When the first body came crashing through the glass windows at the front of the store," he said.

"What?"

He nodded. "A young woman came running down the sidewalk. She was dressed in blood-soaked tatters. Shreds of cloth were just hanging from her. She stood outside the window and stared in through the glass. She was swaying from side to side. She slapped her palm against the window and it left a smear of blood."

"So you did what? Started to run?"

"No," Ty Harrison said. "I actually went towards the door to open it for the zombie."

"You're kidding, right?"

He shook his head. "I was calling out to Sarah. She and my daughter were at the store that day to help with the grand opening. They were out back, unpacking the car. I was calling out to her about how cool the whole thing was, and asking her how much of the advertising budget she had blown."

I made a face. I could imagine the scene. The man was walking towards his death. "What happened?"

"Sarah saved my life," he said. "She came into the store and saw the zombie hammering its fist against the glass. Sarah screamed. I mean really screamed. The kind of terrified cry you hear in all those horror films. It turned my blood to ice. I froze. Then a car went crashing through a shop front across the street from the comic book shop. It just crashed through the building and caught on fire. The zombie turned at the sound, then turned back and snarled at me."

"And then you started to run, right?"

"No," Ty Harrison said. "I had a baseball bat in a glass cabinet. It was a display piece that we wanted to use in the store. But as I went towards it, the fucking zombie woman just hurled herself through the goddamned window! That's when I started to run."

"And not a second too soon," the woman standing beside him muttered. I glanced up at her. She had a serene, graceful aura; she radiated a sense of calm that I had rarely encountered before. She was smiling fondly down at the young girl. "Ty only just escaped," she said.

The man sighed again. "We got into the store room and slammed the door shut. I could hear the zombie pounding its fists on the door. I could hear it snarling. There were sirens wailing in the background and other screams started to fill the air. It was like a scene from a riot. Chaos."

"But you escaped?"

Ty Harrison took a deep breath. "My car was parked out the back of the store. We were still unpacking boxes of comics. We managed to get into the car and drove about three blocks before the road was filled with crashed cars. Some of them were on fire. There were dead bodies lying on the road and undead zombies crouched over them, tearing at their flesh. There were thick spreading stains of blood on the blacktop, and corpses still trapped in a couple of the vehicles. The street was filled with running, screaming people. I don't know how many were human and how many were…. were zombies. It was just one horrifying nightmare."

"How did you escape?" I asked. Despite myself, I found I was leaning towards the man, drawn in by the tale of horror.

"A guy in a school bus!" Ty Harrison said, and his voice rose an octave at the incredulity of it. "There was a guy driving a school bus. He came crashing around a corner on two wheels, driving like a lunatic. He looked like Rambo. He had a gun thrust out through the side window and he was driving with one hand. The bus clipped the front of our car, and then stopped. I could see the guy shouting at us. I looked at Sarah, and made a snap decision. We leaped from the car and jumped aboard the bus."

"Were there other survivors?"

"About ten," Ty Harrison said. "They were mostly women and children, shaking and crying. We climbed aboard, and the bus went right through the tangled wreckage of cars and exploded out through the other side."

"To freedom."

"To freedom," Ty Harrison agreed. "Eventually."

I sensed there was much more to the story of this family's escape. But it was quickly getting dark. "How long are you here in Kansas?" I asked. "Have the authorities told you anything?"

"We're some of the lucky ones," he admitted. "I have family in North Carolina, behind the old Danvers Defense Line. "My father is retired military. We're being moved next week."

I shook hands with the man, and the young woman. They were indeed lucky. Many survivors like Gloria Kingsman were facing long uncertain futures in the refugee camps. At least for this couple, and one young child, there would be a new home.

ABOARD '*USS MONSOON*' (PC-4): NAVAL AMPHIBIOUS BASE, LITTLE CREEK VIRGINIA

Covered in glory but shrouded in mystery, the elite US Navy SEALs are one of the most elusive and covert military organizations in the world. The men who make up the teams are private, quiet men – but also some of the most lethal combatants ever to go to war.

That covert mentality pervades all levels of the teams, and as I boarded Patrol Boat, Coastal, *'USS Monsoon'*, at the Naval Amphibious Base at Little Creek, I was again reminded of the strict rules for interviews by a uniformed naval officer who greeted me on deck.

"Culver?"

I nodded.

"He's waiting for you below," the officer said with a jerk of his head, then raised a warning finger at me. "No pictures and no names – no kidding. Understand?"

I understood.

The Naval Amphibious Base, Little Creek, is the largest installation of its kind anywhere in the world. It's the major operating station for the amphibious forces of the nation's Atlantic Fleet. Little Creek is an inlet on the southern shore of Chesapeake Bay. The base is sited at the extreme northwest corner of Virginia Beach.

I followed the man down narrow steps and through a tight maze of steel corridors to a small cabin below decks.

A man was waiting for me – just a man wearing a pair of denim jeans and a black shirt. He looked ordinary in almost every way: average height, average build, average looks.

Predatory eyes.

We shook hands. The officer who escorted me disappeared.

"Call me Mike," the man I came to meet said in a low rumbling voice.

"Is that your name?"

"No," the SEAL smiled easily. "But that's what you can call me in your article."

I nodded. "Do you want a surname?"

He shrugged. "Sure," he said. "How about Wainwright?"

"Is that your real surname?"

"No."

I made a face, and shrugged. As far as interviews go, this one hadn't started well.

There was a narrow bunk in one corner of the cabin, and bolted to the adjoining wall was a small desk beside a straight-backed chair. Mike Wainwright dropped comfortably down onto the bunk, and I scraped the chair back and sat down.

We stared at each other across the small space for several seconds. Wainwright looked to be in his late twenties. He had short dark hair and a shadow of stubble on his jaw. His gaze was disconcerting. It felt like he was sizing me up – deciding how he would kill me if he had to. I wondered if that was the kind of thought that randomly went through such a man's mind when he walked down the street, or ate dinner at a local restaurant. Was that the way an elite soldier's mind worked... or was there a difference in the mentality of the man who went home at night and the one who went to war?

I wasn't about to ask.

"What can you tell me about the operation that became known as Mission Warwax?" I asked, flipping open my notebook. "It's one of the most secretive exploits of the zombie war... in fact nobody even knew the SEALs were in action during the apocalypse until just recently."

Mike Wainwright shrugged his shoulders in a casual gesture, but when he spoke, there was an edge of intensity and purpose in his voice.

"Operational security is something that extends well beyond when the operation is completed," the SEAL member said. He fell silent for a moment as though measuring his next words carefully. "At least it does when special units are involved."

"Why?"

Wainwright sighed, clasped his hands together and looked me in the eye. "A few years ago SEAL Team 6 went hunting bin Laden, and shortly afterwards our Vice President at the time made a public statement attributing the success of the operation directly to the SEALs. It was an unprecedented gaffe. It put a target on every one of the guys backs – something we didn't appreciate," Wainwright said gravely. "It's not the sort of mistake that should ever have been made, especially by such a high-profile politician who should have known better... and it's not one the Naval Special Warfare community want made ever again. Now we're even more circumspect about what we say, and when we say it. That's why you haven't heard of Warwax before now."

I looked at the man, my expression incredulous. "Surely an attack against a zombie horde is very different in terms of your operational security than a raid against a terrorist organization like al-Qaeda?"

"Sure," the SEAL said. His smile twisted slowly and blood darkened his cheeks. "But practice doesn't make perfect. *Perfect practice makes perfect.* And operational security is about perfect practice. The zombie war has been won – the horde has been pushed back within the borders of Florida... but there are other threats around the world looming."

Wainwright paused again and his lips compressed into a thin line of frustration. He sprang to his feet and paced across to the cabin door then spun on his heel and came back to the bunk again. He looked like a caged lion prowling.

"On any given day, US Navy SEALs are deployed in over thirty countries around the world," Wainwright explained carefully to be sure I understood. "Today I'm talking to you from Virginia Beach. Tomorrow I could be posted to operations in Africa, Asia, Europe or the Middle East. What makes the SEAL teams so effective is our covert nature. It's the dark cape we drape over ourselves that allows us to operate so effectively."

Good line!

I wrote down everything the man said.

"Fair enough," I conceded. "I take your point, and I assume your identity is one of the things that needs to be protected. What about details of the mission, though? Can you tell me when Warwax took place, and what the nature of the operation was?"

Mike Wainwright sat back on the bunk and seemed to relax a little. "On one condition," he said with care. "Anything you write about this mission must be cleared with SOCOM public affairs before publication."

I agreed. "Done," I said. We shook hands. I wanted the story. I had heard whispers about the fabled Warwax mission, and I sensed this would be the only opportunity for any of those events to be revealed.

Wainwright took a deep breath, and started talking.

"Mission Warwax was executed by SEAL team members just twelve days after the initial outbreak of the zombie virus. It was a rescue operation, conducted around Boynton Beach, Florida to secure several trapped civilians. The mission was a success, although we sustained some casualties while carrying out the mission."

I wrote Wainwright's description down, but it was cold and clinical – almost remote. I wasn't about to settle for the bare bones of his explanation because I sensed there was much more to be revealed.

"You say the mission took place less than two weeks after the initial outbreak. That was when Florida was burning and the zombie hordes were rampaging across the

111

state. It must have been a chaotic environment to infiltrate."

"It was," Wainwright agreed. "We're talking about a time before the Danvers Defensive line had even begun to take shape, when the US was first coming to terms with the horror of the infection," Wainwright went on. "The situation in Florida was a nightmare." He shrugged. "But we were on a tight schedule. The civilians we rescued were in real jeopardy."

"How many?"

"How many what?"

"Civilians?"

Wainwright paused for just a second. "Eleven," he said slowly, "and one VIP."

My ears pricked up. Wainwright saw the change in my expression. He held up a hand like he was stopping traffic. I opened my mouth to fire off the question and closed it again.

"No," he said. "I can't tell you details," intercepting the question before I could ask it. "All I can say is that the VIP was a powerful politician you would know. You might even vote for him one day."

I sighed. The journalistic instinct in me wanted to probe for details, but I sensed I would be up against a brick wall. I let it go – for the moment.

"How did the operation come about?" I asked instead. "Was it just a matter of a radio message and then the SEALs went into action?"

Wainwright laughed. "Before SEALs teams go anywhere, the mission must be authorized and planned," he explained patiently. "The first we knew of it was when the unit commander issued a Warning Order."

"Meaning?"

"Meaning we were isolated and briefed. We went through the Patrol Leader's Order, and then had twelve hours to prepare – to sort out kit and weapons."

I frowned. "The Patrol Leader's Order – what exactly is that?"

"It's a formal briefing," Wainwright offered. "We go over the mission in five logical steps that cover the situation, the mission, the details of the execution, how the mission will be supported and the command structure. We also had satellite imagery of the target location, and cell phone recordings from the trapped civilians."

I made notes then shook my head slowly. I felt I was losing the essence of the operation in military techno-speak. "So what exactly was the mission? In simple terms, what did the SEALs do on Boynton Beach?"

Wainwright looked at me thoughtfully. "You will clear everything before publication, right?" He asked again.

I nodded. "Scout's honor."

He sighed. "We took a full platoon of sixteen SEALs to Florida, aboard this patrol boat you're on right now. We took up station off the coast and the platoon split up into two teams of eight men to board rubber Zodiacs at oh-two hundred hours.

"We paddled in towards the shore. Intelligence told us that the twelve civilians were holed up on one of the top floors of an apartment complex.

"A few hundred yards off the beach, beyond the surf zone, our two scout swimmers slipped over the gunwales of the Zodiacs and swam to the shore to secure the landing. We waited. It took several minutes before we got the signal. Then we paddled through the surf and the team inserted on Boynton Beach. We dragged the boats up above the high-tide mark, and the lieutenant leading the patrol moved us off immediately towards the building."

"How far away from the location were you when you landed?"

Wainwright shrugged his shoulders. "We had a hundred yards of sand and then grass," he said. "There were buildings built right on the edge of the beach. The target location was behind the front row of buildings." He made an open-handed gesture. "So maybe it was five hundred yards."

"And you had to pass beyond the first buildings?"

"That's right," he said. "There were steps from the beach to the apartments. They had all been built on the edge of the sand, supported by a network of steel piers and pylons, like the ground had been reclaimed and then reinforced to take the weight of the structures and stop them sliding. The point man for the patrol went forward, and he was on edge, let me tell you!"

The comment surprised me. Wainwright's account had been so dry up until this moment the sudden revelation caught me off guard. "How did you know that?" I asked.

"Because I was the point man for the patrol," he said, his features suddenly softening a little. "I was the one out front."

I suddenly became more interested. "That must have been intense."

Wainwright nodded. "Pucker time," he said softly. "It was a direct action op, and I knew I was responsible for the safety of the patrol and the civilians," he explained. "I went forward carefully, and the night was alight with fire and filled with terrified screaming."

"What did you see?"

"I went up the steps and took position by the wall of the closest building," Wainwright said quietly. "The whole waterfront seemed to be ablaze. There were thick clouds of smoke hanging low in the air, and flames licking from the smashed windows of every apartment I looked at. I could hear the sounds of screaming, growling, snarling.... it was like a war-zone. In the distance there were security alarms going off and the far away sounds of cars and trucks. Closer, I could hear running feet – hundreds and hundreds of people running."

"Zombies?"

Wainwright shook his head like he didn't know. "Probably," he guessed. I saw one young woman hurl herself out of a five story unit. She just crashed through the glass and her body folded over the balcony. She screamed all the way down and hit the concrete pavement about forty feet away from where I was concealed. Something moved in the shadows. It ran over to her – a big hulking shape – and it dragged her away."

"What did you do?"

Wainwright shook his head. "I followed through with the mission," he said it like it hurt, but that discipline and focus had masked his instinct for compassion. "I was carrying a military version of a twelve-gauge shotgun, loaded with rounds of double-ought buckshot. I waved the patrol forward, and as they moved, I went at a run to the far edge of the building."

"The back corner?"

"Yeah," he said. "The apartment complex the woman had fallen from faced the beach at an angle, with a concrete driveway out front. The bottom of the building was all parking garages for the residents. From where I was standing I could cover those garage doors and also see beyond the front rank of beachside apartments."

"Could you see your objective building – the one containing the civilians and the VIP?"

Wainwright nodded. "There was a narrow road between the units. It ran parallel to the beach, lined with low shrubs and ferns. I went to the edge of the road and the patrol came up behind me. The lieutenant formed us up in two squads."

I took a breath and tried to visualize the scene Mike Wainwright was describing to me. "How far from the road to the target building?"

"Only fifty yards," he guessed. "Once we crossed the road, there was lawn and concrete driveways that encircled the actual building."

"And how high was the building?"

"Eight stories," Wainwright said. "The civilians were on the sixth floor."

"Was it on fire?"

He nodded. "The top floor was on fire. Flames were pouring out through several windows. It looked like it had been burning for some time. And there were other fires closer to the ground floor. The whole façade of the complex was blackened. It looked like it had been hit by bombs."

I wrote everything down. Now that we had reached the details of the mission, Wainwright had become more candid. The stern reserve had slipped away. I wondered how much of his story I would actually be able to publish…

"What was the plan, now that you had reached the road?"

"Two teams," Wainwright explained. "One would secure the perimeter and the other would enter the building and reach the trapped civilians."

"What team were you a part of?"

"I went into the building."

I paused and took another look at the man I was sitting across from. Physically he was in no way extraordinary. What made him an exceptional warrior was his mental discipline, his innate bravery and his commitment to his other team members and those he swore to serve.

On the inside, Wainwright and the rest of the SEALs were giants.

"That must have been challenging," I said, putting it mildly.

"The first team fanned out, covering our route back to the beach. When they were in place I got the signal from the lieutenant to go forward. We went in through the front doors. I was still on point. The doors were glass. They had been smashed. There was blood on the pavement and inside, spattered across the foyer. There was an elevator but I ignored it. The civilians had tried that route and the power was down. The stairwell was through a door at the back of the building. Everything was dark. Inside there was no light from the fires. I had NVG's but we weren't sure they would help against the dreads, so I'd left them on the patrol boat.

"I had a small flashlight we take on ops. I put my foot on the bottom stair, and then suddenly the night exploded into screams and shouts of insane rage."

"Undead, right?"

"In the stairwell. The first floor landing. They had heard me, or maybe sensed me – I'm not sure. Two dreads came swarming down the stairs. They were just dark screaming shapes. I could smell the blood and the stink of them. It was like they had been dug up from a coffin. They were filthy, covered in streaks of gore. One of them had an eyeball flapping against its cheek."

"What did you do?"

"I fired," Mike Wainwright said. "I had no choice but to compromise our situation and go loud. It was either that or become infected. There was no room to work with a knife, even if I had been prepared."

"The zombies went down?"

"Both of them," Wainwright said matter-of-factly. "Double-oh buckshot are pellets each the size of a bullet that spread out up to a killing range of around three hundred feet. In the confined area of the stairwell, the sound was like artillery fire," Wainwright gestured with his hands. "The blast tore the first dread's head off its shoulders, and the rifleman right behind me fired his M16 and took the other one down with a clean head shot."

"Then what happened?"

"We lost the need for stealth," Wainwright explained wryly. "We knew there would be other dreads in the building. We clambered over the corpses and went up the stairs at a run. It was like being back on the BUD/S training ground."

I sat back for a moment and went back through my notes. Mike Wainwright got up and disappeared down the passageway for a few minutes. He came back with a couple of cans of soda. He threw one to me.

I dropped it on the floor.

Wainwright looked at me like I wasn't made of the right stuff.

"Did you meet more zombies as you went up the stairwell?"

Wainwright nodded. He sipped at the soda and then set the can down on the floor. "There was no longer a need for a point man. It was all guns. I went up the stairs shoulder to shoulder with another team member. When we reached the third floor landing a fire door exploded inwards and four dreads came bursting through the opening at us. We opened fire. Two of the dreads were thrown back against the wall. Their guts were shredded. The hail of fire had literally torn them apart. We took out the other two and then capped each of them with a single shot to the head – just to be sure."

"And then you pushed on to the sixth floor?"

He shook his head. "More of the dreads came down the passageway. The firefight had sparked them up. There might have been as many as thirty of them. We could see them spilling out of open apartment doors. Two of the guys in the team had Heckler and Koch MP5 'room broom' submachine guns. They covered the fire door entrance and opened up on the massing dreads. We knew there were too many to take down all at once. We left the two men there to hold back the horde and secure our exit from the building."

"You called it a room broom, right?"

He nodded. I wanted to be sure of my facts.

"It's a compact weapon that's ideal for urban situations. It fires a 9mm Parabellum round," the SEAL explained. "It's only accurate to about a hundred feet, but it has hitting power. We had confidence the two guys would be able to defend the doorway until we came back with the civilians."

I tilted my head to the side thoughtfully. Mike, how long did this operation take? Are we talking about hours?"

"No," he said. "Once we breached the building's entrance, the time until we evacuated with the civilians was less than eight minutes."

"Were the civilians waiting for you?"

He nodded. "They were ready, inside the unit, standing on either side of the door as we kicked it in."

"Can you tell me their condition?"

"They were frightened," Wainwright said. "They had been holed up in that unit for over a week. The food and water had run out. There were eight women and four men, including the VIP. They were haggard and exhausted. Some of the women and a couple of the guys were sobbing. They had heard the gunfire. They knew we were on our way up to them."

"Did the evacuation go smoothly?" I asked. "What was the procedure?"

Wainwright shook his head. "The fucking VIP started bitching the moment we came through the door. The fucker demanded to be the first one taken out. Demanded the team form some kind of a human shield around him to get him to safety."

I was shocked. "What about the others – the rest of the people he had been in the unit with?"

"He didn't give a shit," Wainwright sneered. "The pompous prick thought the rescue effort was all for him."

I sat back. "I don't imagine your lieutenant would have been impressed."

"None of us were," Wainwright admitted. "The guy ended taking a tumble down a flight of stairs as we were fleeing the building." He shrugged his shoulders eloquently, and through a wintery grin he said, "Sometimes accidents can happen, y'know."

Fucking politicians. "What happened next?"

"The whole building was filling with noise," Wainwright's expression became tense. "We could hear pounding footsteps along the corridors on the floors above and below us. The lieutenant posted me and another guy to the end of the hallway and the rest of the team led the civilians back down towards the third floor."

"Did the zombies appear?"

He nodded. "They came down the corridor. The guy next to me opened fire and as he did we started to move back, shooting and then falling back to cover each other – standard urban tactics. But the dreads were relentless. Nothing stopped them. Unless you got them cleanly in the head, they just shrugged off the hits they took. I blew the arm off one – severed it at the shoulder. The dread went down screaming and writhing, then pounced back up onto its feet and came running on. The dread had been a young guy – maybe a college student before he had become infected. There was brown gore splattering across the walls as he ran at me. I fired again and the blast obliterated the thing's head – sprayed the insides of his skull across the passage. The corpse dropped like a bag of concrete."

"So you and your partner got out of the building safely?"

The SEAL nodded. "We rejoined the rest of the team in the stairwell and covered the descent as tail gunners, throwing white phosphorous grenades and everything else we were carrying to keep the dreads off our backs."

I could imagine the screaming chaos of the civilians as the elite soldiers shepherded them down the dark treacherous stairwell, and the din of weapons firing and grenades exploding as the infected ghouls threw themselves at the guns. I could imagine the terror on the people's faces and the snarling hideous cries of the zombies that clawed at them. "Did everyone escape?"

"We got all of the civilians out of the building," Wainwright nodded gravely, "but we lost two good men saving them. The two team members who held the third floor landing stayed at their position until we had cleared the stairs and were assembled on the ground floor foyer. We could hear them firing their M16's. The guys had a dozen thirty round magazines between them, stowed in their load-carrying web gear. Suddenly the firing stopped."

"Did you go back for them?"

Wainwright shook his head. "Coms went dead. We knew they had been overrun. The lieutenant told us to bug out and we went out onto the lawn. The eight man squad covering the building assembled around us."

Something puzzled me. "How did you get everyone aboard the two Zodiacs?" I asked.

"We didn't," Wainwright explained. "We had to change plans. The Zodiacs were our exfiltration route if we had been able to stay covert. Once everything went loud, there was no time for subtlety."

"So…?"

"The RTO jumped on the satcom radio and called in three slicks we had circling offshore," Wainwright began to explain, then saw my pained, confused expression. He sighed with frustration. "RTO is the term for the radio guy, and 'slicks' are transport choppers," he doubled back wearily on his story for my benefit. "We called them up and they swooped in and landed on the beach."

"And that's how you got the civilians and the VIP to safety."

"After a three minute running firefight," Wainwright added somberly. He took a long drink of his soda and then crushed the can in his fist. "We cleared the apartment complexes and four of the team secured the top of the steps. As the helicopters came in, the noise attracted the undead. They came swarming out of the burning buildings all along the shoreline. Some of them were on fire, some of them were moving on the stumps of shattered limbs. There would have been over a hundred, massing together in the courtyard of the closest apartment block and streaming down on us. We opened fire with everything we had, not trying for kills, but merely to hold them off until the civilians and the rest of the platoon could embark.

"The dread bodies were stacking up all around us. We fell back, until we had cleared the steps and were standing on the beach. The dreads came at us, pouring down the steps and launching themselves off the edge of the pier platform onto the sand. That's when we knew we were in trouble," Wainwright's tone suddenly became somber. "We could no longer contain them. We lost the choke point of the steps and they were running past us towards the last remaining helicopter.

"There was four of the team still waiting for us. The civilians and the first squad had been flown off the beach in the first two choppers. The guys opened up fire from the cargo door in the hull of the third bird and we ran back through the bodies and the bullets and made it to the helicopter."

I sat back, flexed my cramping fingers and set the notebook down on my thigh. I looked across at Wainwright and he stared back at me. During the entire retelling of Mission Warwax, the SEAL's facial expression had hardly changed, the tone of his voice had rarely altered. Perhaps it was because the incident had taken place over a year earlier – the memories and emotions were no longer fresh.

Or perhaps it was his training – the way he dealt with the dangers that were inherent in his hazardous line of work. He was a man in control.

I reached across the cramped little ship's cabin and we shook hands. "Thanks for the interview," I said. I meant it. Wainwright nodded, and then a wicked gleam lit in his eyes.

"Just tell it right," he warned me. "If I find out you fucked the story up, or embellished the facts to make the event more dramatic... *I'll come looking for you.*" He smiled, an enigmatic grin that tugged at one corner of his mouth.

I felt a sudden chill of shock wash through me.

I had no doubt the man meant it.

THE SHORES OF LAKE OCONEE, CENTRAL GEORGIA: 33.350°N 83.157°W

The thudding monotony of the roaring Black Hawk helicopter's rotors was a deafening drumbeat. Around me – ignoring me – sat four stone-faced soldiers, their features streaked with camouflage paint, their eyes roaming the terrain that swept by beneath us in a blur.

I heard the sudden crackle of voices through the headset. It was the pilot.

"Two minutes," he said.

The soldiers became restless. They moved in their seats and re-checked their weapons. I felt the helicopter begin to descend, and when I glanced out through the small cabin window I saw a shimmering blue expanse of water, surrounded by a thick green canopy of forest.

The helicopter crawled across the sky and then turned in a slow circle, still descending. We touched the ground smoothly, landing in a field of long green grass that rolled gradually down to the lapping edges of Lake Oconee.

I was in hostile territory.

Six months ago this ground was swarming with zombies. Now we were in what the military termed the 'dead zone' a tract of land that stretched between the border of Florida and the original Danvers Defense Line.

During the second phase of the zombie war, this land had been won back by American ground forces. New forts had been built and new trenches had been dug closer to the Florida state line... but although the area had been cleared of zombies and secured, it wasn't entirely safe.

The helicopter crew chief tugged on the door release handle and the four soldiers spilled out of the chopper at a run, taking up firing positions in a perimeter beyond the slowing blades of the chopper.

I got out of my seat and shuffled towards the open door. The crew chief planted his hand in the middle of my chest and pushed me back down. "Wait here, dickwad," the man warned me contemptuously. "The area isn't secure yet."

I waited. I had been aware of the resentment the soldiers had felt towards me –it had radiated from them in the hostile look in their eyes, the sneers and their laughs as we had flown south. It seemed the helicopter crew felt the same way.

I guess I could understand.

These were fighting men who had been on the front line of the apocalypse. They had fought a hard, dirty war, seen the horrors and the gruesome gore of battles... and now they were playing nursemaid to a civilian journalist.

They hated me.

I sat and stared out through the doorway. The grass was swaying to the downdraft of the big rotor blades, and there was a ripple on the water, scuffing the surface to dark blue. On the far side of the lake I could see a solid wall of densely packed trees that reached all the way down to the water's edge.

The whine of the turbines slowed. The rotors stopped. The crew chief stared out through the opposite window for a few seconds and then visibly relaxed. He glanced at his wristwatch.

"Okay," he said. "The site is secure. You have thirty minutes for your interview, and then we're out of here. Understood."

I nodded. I got to my feet again and stood on the lip of the cargo hold, then turned back to the crew chief. It was eerily silent now. I could hear the distant cry of birds in the trees. I snatched off the headset. "What if the people I'm waiting to meet don't turn up?"

The crew chief stared at me. "Tough shit," he said in a matter-of-fact tone.

I jumped down from the helicopter.

The sun was warm on my back. I walked down to the water's edge and stared across the lake. There was a gentle breeze rustling through the treetops. The air smelled fresh. Somehow that surprised me. I guess I had expected to see rotting corpses, bleached white bones, and circling vultures high overhead – the legacy of a war against the undead hordes that had been crushed and then driven back. But there was none of that. Not here, at least.

I heard another trilling bird cry, and then a few seconds later a man appeared from within the bulrushes that fringed the shoreline. He trudged slowly from the muddy ground, a bow in his hand and arrows in a quiver strapped across his back. The man was dressed in ragged fatigues. He looked to be about fifty years old. He had a grey straggly beard, stained tobacco yellow around the mouth, and dark eyes. His face was a network of deeply chiseled wrinkles. He was broad shouldered and lean. He came up the muddy bank and stomped his boots in the long grass.

"Culver?"

"Addison?" I stared hard. The man turned his head and looked to his left. He waved his arm and I saw a second figure peel away from the dark shadows of a tree. The man came into the bright sunlight holding some kind of a rifle on his hip. He walked past one of the kneeling soldiers and the two men nodded to each other the way combat veterans do when they recognize one of their own.

The second man was also in his fifties. He walked with a heavy limp. He was tall and thin, the features of his face sallow and gaunt. He held out his hand. It was calloused, with half moons of dirt and grime under the fingernails.

"Noyce," he said. "Phil Noyce."

We shook hands, and then I led the men back to the shade of the helicopter's cargo hold.

"You guys are the legendary 'Silverbacks', right?"

Noyce nodded. He looked weary with the kind of fatigue that comes from endless months of strain. He set his weapon aside.

"We're two of 'em," the man said. "We started as a team of eight – all of us retired veterans. There are five of us left now."

"Where are the others? I would have liked to meet them."

"Busy," Noyce said. "They're on a random run along the I20."

I nodded. I don't know why. I had no idea what the man was talking about, but I nodded anyhow. I reached for my notebook and pen. The other man, Addison, set his bow down and reached into his pockets. He rolled a cigarette and stuffed it into the corner of his bearded mouth.

"Just because the war ain't going on in this part of Georgia anymore, doesn't mean there ain't fighting still to do," Addison said. His face disappeared behind a blue haze of pungent tobacco smoke.

I looked from one man to the other. Beneath the layers of grime, the filthy clothes and the weary exhaustion that was carved into their features, I could still see the dark gleam of life glinting in their eyes. They were hard men who had fought for their country and returned home wounded. Now they were at war once again as a tight band of freedom fighters.

"Are all the Silverbacks retired veterans?" I asked.

Noyce nodded. "I was a Sergeant in the Army," the man said. "I did ten years, and was deployed in Iraq with the 1st Cavalry Division. I came home with a bad leg from shrapnel wounds."

"And the gun?" I asked. "Is that the weapon you've been using in your fight against the zombies?"

Noyce nodded again. He seemed a man of few words. Everything he said was for a reason, and uttered with economy. He picked up the carbine and laid it across his lap. "It's a Bushmaster M4," he said. He also had a KaBar knife in a sheath strapped to his thigh. He was wearing multicam pants and shirt and combat boots, and a chest rig that was stuffed with spare magazines.

I turned and looked towards Addison. "And you use a bow and arrows?"

Addison nodded. "I've also got a Smith & Wesson double action revolver," he started to smile slowly, "if things get messy, but I like the bow most. It's silent and deadly. That's important for the work we've been doing," the smile on Addison's lips became broader. "I'm too old for all the runnin' and jumpin' to evade the bastards when they turn nasty. It's easier just to kill the fuckers and sneak away without them being none the wiser."

I looked down at the weapon. It was a compound bow with small wheels and a series of pulleys. There was some kind of a sight mounted to the shaft of the weapon. It looked more hi-tech than some of the rifles I had seen soldiers carrying.

"Is it effective?" I asked.

Addison took one long last drag on his cigarette and flicked the remains out through the cargo door. "Yeah," he said in an exhalation of smoke. "Too effective."

I frowned. "How could it possibly be too effective?"

Addison reached behind his back and pulled an arrow from his quiver. He showed me the point. "I used to have barbed arrowheads," he explained, "but the bow was burying the arrow so deep into the skull of the undead fuckers, I couldn't retrieve the arrow. Couldn't get it back out through the head. So I had to change to blunt steep tips. Just as effective, but easier to pull out of a dead ghoul's eye or temple." He winked, like he had shared some hard-earned valuable piece of knowledge that would one day be useful to me. I smiled, kind of…

"The Silverbacks are all old buddies," Addison explained. "After we served, we became preppers. We all sensed the world was changing and that it was just a matter of time before it went to hell. So we prepared. We packed bug-out bags, we drilled with weapons at the range. We thought about escape routes and kept our survival skills. We didn't expect the apocalypse to come through some towel-head fucking plot, but when it arrived on our doorstep, we were ready," the man said proudly. "That's what keeps us alive – the preparation and the skills we spent years honing."

Prepping was a term I had heard a lot in the preceding twelve months. America had a rich gun culture, but remarkably few people skilled in the robust arts of survival. Millions had died on the streets of Florida because they were unprepared. I imagined the nation would never be so unsuspecting again. Already the government was talking about post-apocalyptic preparedness for citizens, much of the template being drawn from the Israeli experience.

On the inbound flight I had made a list of questions I'd wanted to ask, but now I was face to face with these men, our exchange became more of a conversation than a formal interview. I was genuinely fascinated by these retired soldiers, and their decision to stay 'in country' rather than flee north when the zombie infestation had first swept up from the south.

I wanted to know why.

Addison answered. He seemed the more affable of the two men. His voice was chirpy with an inherent kind of enthusiasm that came out in his tone and attitude.

"What? Run away from the biggest fight the world has ever seen?" he shook his head with incredulity. "Why would we run from that?" he asked me. "We're capable, trained and motivated. This is our land, and Georgia is our state." He paused for a moment like a steam train gathering momentum for the next hilly ascent. "If we had evacuated behind the Danvers line, right now we'd be holed up somewhere in rocking chairs, regretting the fact that we'd run away from a fight." He shook his head. "No, sir. That ain't us. And it's why we still haven't called it quits. It's why we're still running random routes – because the fight ain't over and we intend on seeing it through until the end."

I frowned. "What is a random route?" I asked. "It's the second time I've heard that phrase mentioned."

Noyce leaned forward and shuffled his boots. "It's one of the tactics we've used to fight the zombies," he explained. His voice was steady and calm. It was the voice of an airline pilot – the kind of voice you could put your trust in to get you home safely. "We have a truck with a flat bed on back, and we drive random routes looking for undead. They're drawn to the noise. We run up and down the local roads with the horn blaring, and the undead come rushing from wherever the fuck they are hiding and chase the truck."

"Chase it to where?"

"A dead end street, or a cul de sac," Addison cut across the conversation. "We've got about a dozen places marked out and we lead them to the one we have picked for the ambush."

It sounded like risky work for the driver. Noyce went on smoothly, as though Addison had never spoken.

"We hide in the houses at the end of the street and the truck leads the zombies towards us. When we have them gathered together, the driver high-tails it through a fence and then we open fire from every direction – with everything we have."

I was stunned. "And it worked?"

"Every time," Noyce said dryly. "In the early days – when the infected were running rampage across the south, we would draw thirty or forty at a time. We'd lead them to the ambush place and cut them down. Now, since the Army has driven the ghouls back into Florida, we're lucky to lure a few of the bastards a week. But it's still effective."

I wrote everything down as quickly as I could. Some of my notes were just hasty scratches. I'd have to interpret the mess some other time.

"And the three Silverbacks that were killed?" I lowered my voice to a respectful tone. "Can you tell me how they lost their lives?"

"Bravely," Noyce said.

Silence.

Addison and Noyce exchanged glances, and then Addison sighed. "One of the boys was Phil's brother, Tom," he explained. "Tommy was with a couple of the other guys working on the truck at a safe house we used to stay at. We were trying to fit a 50 cal machine gun onto the flat bed.

The guys got trapped by a swarm of the undead fuckers and by the time the rest of us shot our way out of the house to get to them, all three of the team had been killed."

"I see," I said somberly. "I'm sorry. Can you tell me their names? I'd like to mention them in the article."

"Bob White, Tom Noyce and Scott Horsburgh."

"Did the men have families?"

"You mean wives and kids?" Addison asked. "Sure. We all have. They went north at the start of the outbreak."

"You must miss them."

Noyce shrugged his shoulder. "Sure," he said. "But it's worth the sacrifice. That's what combat is about – you sacrifice the comforts and security of daily life in order to protect the freedom of others. It's patriotism."

I saw the crew chief over Addison's shoulder. He held up his wrist and tapped at his watch. Then he held up both hands. I had ten minutes left with these men, and an hour of questions I wanted to ask.

"The ambush tactic," I asked. "Is that the only method you used to fight the undead?"

Addison shook his head. He tugged at the straggles of his beard for a moment. "The bow," he said, "is the perfect stealth weapon. The zombies have acute hearing – everyone knows that – so you can't take them on in a firefight and hope to get away every time. The problem is that the sound of gunfire just brings more of the fuckers. But the bow – well that was the perfect 'minuteman' weapon. I could lay in wait until one of the ghouls staggered past and take him out without revealing my position. It was like sniper fire. They never knew what hit 'em."

"And so you would just lay in wait in a field… or in the bulrushes like you did when the helicopter landed?"

"No," Addison shook his head. "It had to be an urban situation to be worthwhile. The undead congregated in the towns, so we would go in at night and find a high building with a good escape route. Then we'd wait until daylight and pick them off as they staggered down the streets until I ran out of arrows. The guys with the guns protected the escape route."

I thought back over Addison's comments. I found it ironic that the perfect stealth weapon for fighting undead ghouls was a bow and arrow – one of the most primitive weapons man had ever created.

Warfare, it seemed, had come a full circle.

There was a sudden commotion of movement behind the two veteran soldiers and I saw the crew chief again. He began unloading stores and supplies, carrying them from the chopper and stacking them in the long grass beyond the droop of the big rotor blades. He made several trips.

Noyce reached into the pocket of his multicam pants and retrieved several envelopes. He handed them to the crew chief. Then the two old soldiers got to their feet, nodded at me, and slipped out through the cargo door, back into the afternoon's warm sunshine. I watched them go.

"What's next for the Silverbacks?" I called out suddenly. I could see the four soldiers falling back from their outpost positions, and then heard the helicopter's turbines slowly begin to whine. "Now the war has been won, and the undead are contained in Florida, why haven't you pulled out – disbanded?"

Noyce took the question. He stopped walking away. He turned slowly around to face me. His voice was rasping. "The price of freedom is eternal vigilance," he said, quoting Thomas Jefferson. "The war may have been won, but the only way we're going to be sure the infected don't break from their barriers is to keep a close watch. That's what the Silverbacks intend on doing."

HOLLY SPRINGS, MISSISSIPPI:

"It might look quiet now," Lieutenant Colonel Chris Bond said to me as we stood at the deserted intersection, "but for a few hours on that Sunday afternoon last year, these streets were a glimpse of hell itself."

We had arrived in the little town of Holly Springs in a Humvee – one of the very same vehicles that had brought Chris Bond and troops from A Company, 2nd Battalion 75th Infantry Ranger Regiment face-to-face with the zombie holocaust.

I got out of the vehicle. There was a soldier manning the 50-caliber machine gun, his body tensed through the vehicle roof hatch, and the weapon traversing warily. Four other Rangers spilled out of the vehicle with their weapons ready. They took up positions at each point of the intersection.

Bond looked relaxed, betraying the heightened tension on the faces of the men who protected us. We walked to the corner of Fant Avenue and North Walthall Street, and stared up at the edifice that was the front of the Holly Springs high school. A wedge of cool shadow spilled across the side street. There were houses across the road, their lawns overgrown, trash strewn in the gutters. A bundle of old newspapers drifted on the breeze like a tumbleweed.

The old homes were pockmarked with bullet holes. Windows had been shattered, and several of the houses had burned to the ground, their roofs collapsed around the charred remains. There was an overturned tricycle in the middle of the street and dark brown stains like oil spills on the blacktop. Propped against the front of the school building were the bleached white bones of several broken bodies.

133

The town was eerily quiet, long ago abandoned. The breeze through the trees was like a moan, and the only sound seemed to be the singing of silence in my ears and the irregular beat of blood against my temples.

"Everyone was trapped inside the gymnasium and auditorium," Lieutenant Colonel Bond said, pointing. "There were twenty one school kids and three teachers. They had barricaded the doors as the first of the undead had swept through the town. They were lucky to be alive."

I walked towards the school building. Bond didn't move. "I wouldn't go any further if I were you," the soldier said, his voice remarkably calm and level. "Just in case…"

I turned and looked at the man. His hair was shaved in the standard Ranger buzzcut, but somehow that just seemed to emphasize the chiseled angles of his features. He had a square jaw and a thin slice for a mouth. The line of his nose was ridged with a bump, and his eyes were deep set beneath the jutting slope of his brow. He had the face of experience – the face of a man who had seen the horrors of war and reconciled his conscience to the necessity of it.

I nodded, and retreated the few steps. Bond glanced over his shoulder, and without a word two of the Rangers came forward at a sprint to cover the doors of the school building. I heard the rumble of the Humvee's big engine, and saw it creeping closer to us like a hen protecting her chicks.

"Can you tell me more about that afternoon," I asked. "I'd like to know more about the operation, and how you eventually were able to rescue the trapped civilians."

The corner of Bond's mouth tugged up into a flicker of a smile.

"Mission Exorus was a joint operation," he said carefully. "It was a combination of Delta operatives and my Rangers from A Company. The whole rescue attempt hinged on whether the Delta boys could gain access to the building where the refugees were hiding.

"And they did, obviously."

"Obviously," Bond said dryly. "But not easily."

Lieutenant Colonel Bond explained that eight Delta operatives had been transported to Holly Springs aboard helicopters flown by the elite 160th SOAR. "They roped down to the roof of the building at zero two-hundred hours on the Sunday morning, and were engaged in a bloody firefight to gain entry," Bond explained. "By that time the undead had surrounded the gymnasium and were hurling themselves at the doors. The people inside were unarmed. They had barricaded the entrance."

"How did the Delta teams get in?" I asked.

"Through the roof," Bond said. 'They opened fire on the zombies to clear the press of ghouls away from the doorway while one of the team cut down through the roof with gear the choppers had flown in with them."

"Were the Delta teams necessary to the defense of the gymnasium?" I asked.

"Absolutely," Bond said. "The people were panicking. They had no way to defend themselves. Once the Delta team was able to breach the roof and gain entry to the gymnasium, the mission went from being speculative to possible."

"They were that critical?"

"Sure," Bond said. "In fact if the Delta team's part in the operation had been a washout, I doubt any of those people would be alive today, because I don't think command would have released a column of Humvees to save them. It would have been too risky."

I frowned. "You need to explain," I apologized. "I'm not following you."

Bond's features remained impassive. "Of course you're not," he noted. "That's because you're not military."

We walked a little further down the street until we could see the corner of the gymnasium. It was an imposing dark brick structure with high white columns and long narrow windows. There was a power pole and a fire hydrant out front of the building. Bond strode a little closer and then stopped abruptly.

"You see we had clear access to the front entrance – and plenty of space to draw the column of vehicles up to evacuate the civilians," he swept his arm around, gesturing as he spoke. I noticed several of the building's windows were shattered and there were dark stains of blood on the steps. "But we knew the people inside were panicked. There was no guarantee we could gain access to the building without creating an opportunity for the undead. Once those gymnasium doors were opened, we had no way to control the zombies, or to get control of the people hiding inside. The Delta boys made the rescue possible. They were on hand to defend the opening, and they were able to organize and prepare the civilians."

I got it. I nodded my head.

"But there were delays with the column, right?"

Bond shrugged his broad shoulders. "We brought twelve Humvees from Fort F-004 near the western edge of the Danvers Line, but the roads were choked with abandoned vehicles."

"You must have expected that, right?" I questioned. "Didn't you have satellite images and those kind of things to study when you were planning the route?"

Bond looked like he was a moment away from punching me on the nose. "Yeah, we expected it," his voice had an angry edge. "So we planned on going cross country – which we did. We estimated a ninety minute race to the gymnasium, and we set out at first light on the Sunday morning."

I waited. Bond knew I had more questions.

"One of the vehicles broke down about half way to Holly Springs," he said, like the matter caused him acute personal embarrassment. "I decided we couldn't abandon the vehicle – I needed every Humvee for the evacuation. We radioed back to command and they told Delta there would be a delay."

"What time did you reach Holly Springs?"

"Twelve noon." He spoke like that was all he was prepared to say.

We walked back until we were closer to the Humvee. Lieutenant Colonel Bond turned in a slow circle, his eyes everywhere at once, remembering the fateful events of that warm afternoon. He sighed. Along with the triumph of the operation had come moments of utter tragedy.

"Can you tell me what happened from the moment the convoy of vehicles entered the town?"

Bond nodded, and then his face seemed to change – his features somehow collapsing to make his expression haggard. His eyes went dark, then dulled, and when he spoke at last, his voice had the hollow echo of haunted memories.

"I saw the town through binoculars – that was the first impression I had," he said flatly. "The column was racing along the open ground, and everything aboard the Humvees was jolting and bouncing. I saw the undead swarming through the streets in howling packs. They were moving awkwardly – a kind of shuffling unsteady gait. I tried to guess their numbers but it was impossible – the zombies were sweeping through the town in a snarling surge.

"I dropped the binoculars to my chest, because by then I didn't need them," the veteran soldier shook his head. "The sounds of the chaos carried clearly. I could hear the high piercing screams and the terror in the voices of the people being hunted. It was a world gone mad – something I had never seen the likes of before."

"Were you in the town by then?"

He shook his head. "We were on the outskirts. The undead were clawing people to shreds. It was mindless murder – a relentless insanity of horror."

Bond's voice trailed off for long moments, as if the vision he was replaying in his mind had paused. He sighed again, and turned his face to mine.

In that instant I saw the man behind the soldier.

"There was a young boy," he muttered softly. "He was cowering on the back seat of an old silver sedan. The tires had blown out. It was an old Buick. I could see the white stricken blob of the kid's face, and then a swarm of undead attacked the vehicle. They wrenched the door open and I heard the boy scream. The sound… the sound was like a steam kettle boiling. The zombies threw him to the ground and fell on him. The screaming stopped."

"What did you do?"

Bond shrugged, but this time the gesture seemed almost weary. "We were in column," he explained. "I told the driver to mount the curb, and then radioed for the rest of the vehicles to proceed to the gymnasium. Our Humvee went crashing up over the pavement and ploughed into the zombies, while my sergeant in the turret began opening fire with the fifty."

"You broke discipline?"

Bond stared at me. He nodded.

"When the column arrived out front of the gymnasium, every undead ghoul for miles was swarming around the building. There must have been a thousand of them. They were dripping blood and howling. The lead couple of Humvee's were surrounded by the mob. They began banging on the sides of the vehicles. They smashed their fists against the windows and then swarmed over the roofs. I saw one of the Humvee's begin to rock."

"What happened next?"

"We tried to give covering fire with the fifties mounted on top of the rear vehicles in the column, but the zombies were relentless. The machine guns tore them to pieces, but they just kept coming back, more and more of them every time. There was blood and guts and gore splattered over the vehicles and we still couldn't cut a clear path through to the gymnasium."

I could imagine the scene in my mind. Standing right were it happened a year or so earlier, I could visualize the long line of drab green vehicles parked nose to tail in front of the gymnasium doors, and I could picture the horror of a thousand or more ghouls flinging themselves at the guns and the men bunkered down inside the steel boxes.

"What did you do?" I asked quietly.

"I took my Humvee back to the head of the column, and ordered the rest of the convoy to follow me," Bond said. "We drove around the block again, mowing down the undead, crushing them beneath the tires as they threw themselves at us. We went fast. I could hear the bodies rolling off the top of the vehicle, saw them fall to the road and get crushed by the next Humvee in the line. The road became slick with blood."

"And then you came back to the same place – you came back to the front doors?"

"About eight minutes later," Bond said, his voice still remote and shallow, devoid of emotion or timbre. "Except this time we came back with the 50 cal's firing," he said, "tearing into the undead before they could swarm around the vehicles."

"Did it make a difference?"

"It bought us time and space," Bond explained. "We went up onto the grass and parked the convoy so that the first few vehicles were past the door and the last few were short of the door. That meant the middle Humvees were adjacent. It was like a line of old battleships," he said, "firing machineguns broadside at the undead."

"And that allowed your men in the middle vehicles to gain entry into the gymnasium?"

Bond nodded. "We had warned the Delta boys. They had pulled down the barricade."

I paused for a moment, and so did Bond, both of us sensing that the crisis point of the operation had been reached.

"What happened next?" I prodded gently.

"My Rangers aboard the Humvees got out and formed a defensive perimeter around the gymnasium doors," Bond explained. "I had about fifty men, plus every one of the Humvee machine guns firing. We used the vehicles like a steel barricade. Suddenly the doors of the building burst open and a screaming group of school kids and teachers came bursting out into the sunshine. We flung them into the Humvees as quick as we could. They were crying, sobbing, shaking. Their faces were masks of pure terror."

"They all made it out?"

"Most of them…" Bond said the words like a dreadful warning.

"What happened?"

"The zombies were enraged. I don't know if it was the movement, the sound of the gunfire, or the screams of the civilians," he shook his head. "I still can't work that out. All I know is they flung themselves at the line. It was like they were suddenly incensed. They hurled themselves onto the guns and my Rangers were overwhelmed. The Delta boys had most of the refugees in the back of the Humvees, but it didn't happen quickly enough. A couple of the undead got through the line. They clawed at one of the teachers. I never saw her face, never knew her name. I just saw a zombie crouched on her chest, tearing at the woman's nose with its teeth while she thrashed and kicked her legs in a pool of her own blood. I shot the zombie in the back of the head, and then I shot what was left of the woman before she turned."

I looked away for a moment. A nasty wind was swirling through the street, bowing the trees before it and filling the air with grit and swirling debris. I shielded my eyes. When I glanced back at the Lieutenant Colonel had his head cocked to one side, as if he had heard something.

I got anxious.

"Everything all right?" I asked. I spun round and checked. The four Rangers who were our bodyguards were still in position, and the Humvee was still where it had been parked, the young soldier still vigilant behind the heavy machine gun.

"Yeah," Bond said. "Everything is all right," he reassured me. "I just thought I heard something... peculiar."

I felt my heart stop. Something choked in my chest. "Are we safe here?"

Bond nodded slowly, and then his eyes cleared and his focus came back. He carried on replaying the events of that Sunday afternoon as though he hadn't paused.

"The mission turned into a shit storm," the words seemed to explode from his mouth. "The undead were right against us. The line we had set up was starting to collapse. They got amongst my boys. I pushed myself into the breach and fired point-blank into the snarling face of a zombie. The bullet struck the ghoul in the mouth, snapping off teeth and tearing a hole up through the back of its head. I watched the body fall. Everything had become a scene of milling murder and chaos," Bond said. "There were just too many of them, and they were impossible to stop. We fired until we were running out of ammunition and they still kept coming."

"When did you evacuate?"

Bond nodded, sensing that I was drawing him further along in his retelling of that tragic day's events. He didn't seem to object.

"I stepped over the body of one of my Rangers," he said. "The boy's head had been severed, gnawed clean from its neck. Behind him I heard another man retch. Most of my men were pale-faced and horrified. They were spattered with gore and the blood of the ghouls they had killed. I grabbed one of the men and ordered him into the nearest Humvee.

"We had lost about half-a-dozen good soldiers – heroes all," Bond muttered, "and still the zombies kept coming. They swarmed over the bodies piled around the vehicles. I watched them come like a wave, saw the blood spatter from their howling mouths, the gnashing teeth and the insane shrilling screams of their fury.

"By then all the civilians were aboard the Humvees. Two of the Delta operators had fallen. The rest of them formed up with my command behind the vehicles in the middle of the line that had the refugees inside them."

"And then…?"

"And then we waited," Bond said with a bleak growl. "The zombies were spread across the grass, flailing their arms, clawing for us. They fell back, and then surged again. When they were just about to launch themselves at us, I told the men to open fire. We kept firing until the ammunition ran out and then boarded the Humvees as the zombies finally came crashing through the perimeter."

"You just made it out."

"Only just," Bond agreed gravely. "From that moment on we were utterly defensive. "We couldn't open fire with the fifties because the undead were all over the vehicles. We just had to batten down the hatch and hold on until we could drive our way back out of hell."

"What was that like?" I had to ask. "Did you feel the mission was accomplished at that point?"

"No," Bond shook his head. "I didn't feel that we had completed our mission until we had outrun the ghouls, and that was when we were twenty miles out of town, heading back towards the fort."

It was a harrowing story – a moment in American military history that had been a triumph, but that had hung for so long on the perilous precipice of disaster.

Bond turned and strode back to the Humvee, and the four waiting Rangers at their posts folded in behind us. We clambered back inside the vehicle and the big engine roared. We were moving, and I, for one, felt a little safer.

"Can you tell me what you discovered about the undead?" I asked. "I would like to know the lessons you felt were learned on that day, and whether any of your experiences in Holly Springs were later transferred to the 'Operation Conquest' offensive?"

The Humvee turned a corner, and then another, while Lieutenant Colonel Bond of the 75th Infantry Ranger Regiment gazed across the gloomy cramped confines of the vehicle at me, his body swaying casually to the bumping ride over the uneven ground.

"I learned the measure of heroism," he said softly. "That was the first lesson I got from that afternoon in Holly Springs. The Rangers of A Company that came to war with me on that day were the bravest men I have ever had the honor to serve with. They stood toe-to-toe with the most vicious, ravenous enemy in the annals of history, and they didn't blink – didn't flinch. They sacrificed their lives to save innocent civilians. They spilled their blood for freedom," Bond said, and I thought I heard the barest quaver of raw emotion in his voice.

"And I realized this enemy couldn't be fought in conventional ways with conventional weapons," he explained, as though the thoughts were forming in his mind even as he was uttering the words. "I learned that the immense advantage of our technology was no guarantee of success. Because when it all comes down to it, the only way to fight the undead horde is face-to-face, with a weapon." He splayed his hands. They were hard and calloused – the hands of a boxer maybe.

"We won the war against the zombies because we were prepared to get bloody and muddy," Bond said. "In the end, the zombies were mean and ruthless, but the American soldier was just a little bit meaner."

BURGAW, NORTH CAROLINA:

"I remember this place alright," Captain Danville Spinks said. "Not in a fond way, either."

As the captain and commander of B Company, 1st Battalion, 120th Infantry of the North Carolina National Guard, Spinks and his men formed part of the Danvers Defensive Line, standing in trenches behind thick coils of barbed wire for more than three months at the outbreak of the zombie apocalypse.

B Company, based at Whiteville, were drawn back behind the defensive line and posted along the I40 just beyond the picturesque little town's outer limits.

The National Guard troops stood shoulder to shoulder with elements of the 82nd Airborne as well as other National Guard units that had been called up with the announcement of martial law during the dark early days of the plague.

"We were posted right along this section of the line," Spinks explained. He made a sweeping gesture with his arm.

We were standing beyond Burgaw's town limits in rolling lush countryside. I could see a patchwork quilt of ploughed fields spreading away to the south, and the ugly brown scar of the wide trench like a ragged tear. There were concrete steps leading into the ground. Spinks went down them like a man on his way to the gallows.

He stood in the bottom of the trench and looked about him, and I could see the changing emotions play across his features as memories came flooding back. I followed him down the steps and stood silently while the man paced back and forth, reaching out to touch at a blade of grass, and stomping his boots on the earth that had been packed down hard as concrete.

"When we were relieved from the line," Spinks began speaking slowly, his voice somehow detached and distant, "I started reading books from the Great War, back in 1914. I read about life in the trenches a century ago... and it horrified me to realize that in a hundred years, nothing about this kind of warfare had changed. The lice, the filth, the mud, the rats... it was the same nightmare all over again."

I said nothing. Captain Spinks walked over to the firing step. It was like a wooden bench that stretched for a hundred feet. Beyond it was another, and another... The firing step had been built to allow the troops to elevate themselves above the height of the eight foot deep trench, and to fire their weapons through the barbed wire at the swarming hordes of undead. The raw wood was grey with mud, coated by the feet of a thousand soldiers who had stood to their post during the months of terror and panic.

"Ninety eight days," Spinks muttered, and I was sure he was not talking directly to me. He shook his head. "We stood in this trench and endured ninety eight days of hell — the hell of boredom and excruciating fear."

The nearest Fort was F-039, about eight miles to the north. That fortification, like the entire original Danvers line, had now been abandoned to growing grass and spider webs.

And to the memories of the men who served.

Spinks stared silently out through the rusted coils of wire for a long time, gazing southward, his shoulders somehow slumped, seeming older than his thirty-four years. I sat on one of the concrete steps and waited patiently. The morning was overcast, and the sky charged with the kind of electrical hum that precedes a thunder storm. Heavy black clouds hung low over the ground so that the far distance seemed smudged along the horizon.

Finally Spinks stepped down from the ledge and thrust his hands deep into the pockets of his camouflage fatigues. He stared down at me, his lips pressed into a thin line across his face.

He had a broad face, with a wide forehead and bright intelligent eyes. His hair was black, but beginning to grey at the temples. He blinked his eyes as if his vision was coming back into focus.

"What was it like?" I asked. It was a deliberately open-ended question, as vague as I could make it. I had a feeling that trying to pin down the captain to specific questions would turn the interview into something stilted. I wanted the reality — any aspect of it the man was willing to share with me.

"What was it like to stand in the line, you mean?"

"That will do for starters," I encouraged him.

Spinks inhaled a deep breath. Somewhere nearby, I heard the first rumble of thunder. It rolled across the clouds like the boom of distant artillery fire and then faded away into ominous silence.

"The hardest part was the not knowing," the National Guard Captain explained. "We were always on edge – standing at the firing platform and expecting any moment for the horizon to fill with swarms of zombies. The strain of it frayed a lot of men's nerves."

I frowned. "Was it like that from the very start?"

"No," Spinks shook his head. "The first few days – even the first week were all panic and confusion – sorting out the lines of communication, the rotation of the troops, the supply lines. It was a mad-house of frantic activity."

"But not fear?"

"No – not then," Spinks said candidly. "We knew how far the defensive line was away from the spread of the infected. Every day we would get updates from the satellites and the helicopters and Humvee patrols. We knew the zombies were still down south."

"Was there a point where that altered?" I asked because I was curious. "Did something happen with the lines of communication? How did you and your men go from being aware of proximity of the zombies, to the point where you were standing at your post expecting them to appear at any moment?"

Again, Spinks shook his head. It was an emphatic gesture. "No. The lines of communication were as good as our technology allowed," he said. "We were never left in the dark by command. There was always an update or a briefing."

"So…?"

Spinks shrugged. "So the media…" he said, and his voice trailed away as if he was embarrassed by the confession. He kicked at a lump of clay in the ground and then looked back at me. "The boys were spending all their spare time listening to radio and television coverage – rumors and wild speculation flew along the line like a spreading brushfire."

"So in the absence of a reason to be alert and anticipating action –"

"– We got ourselves all worked up," he admitted ruefully. "It reached the point where we put more faith in the inflammatory sensational media coverage than we did with our own command network. The television stations were filled with terrifying reports – helicopter footage of running hordes of undead. It fucked with our heads."

I said nothing for a few moments. Spinks walked around in an aimless circle, head bowed, boots scuffing the dirt.

"And so you and your men were in a constant state of... what? How would you characterize the state of mind of your men during those three months?"

"Fear," Spinks said. "We were in a permanent state of fear. Fear of the unknown. Fear of imminent attack. Fear of being overrun by the hordes of undead. Fear of dying..."

It was clear to me that the strain of defending this line of trenches had taken a terrible emotional toll on the captain. He glanced at me, and his eyes were skittish and nervous, as though maybe he expected my derision.

"It sounds like an utter nightmare," I said sympathetically. I knew how dangerous a man's rampant imagination could be. I'd talked myself into dark moments of despair readily enough. I didn't know an honest man who hadn't at some stage of his life.

"If there had been activity – something to focus on and apply ourselves to, well maybe it would have been different," he speculated, then shrugged his shoulders. "But there wasn't. There was just the monotony of standing at your post – staring out through the barbed wire, and waiting."

I got up from where I sat and walked across to the firing platform. I stood on the timber ledge and stared across the rolling fields, trying to imagine how it must have felt. The barbed wire entanglements were rusted. The wiring posts, spread along the line at random intervals, were leaning at weary angles. The thirty foot wide snare of wire did not obstruct the view down the gentle slope towards a dense grove of trees.

Another boom of thunder reverberated through the storm clouds.

I looked back over my shoulder. "What was it like when it rained?"

Spinks huffed. "A fucking nightmare," he said.

I stepped back down onto the floor of the wide trench. Further along the line I could see wooden beams fashioned into ragged retaining walls.

"The ground gave way when the rain got too heavy, or it rained persistently," Spinks said. We started to meander along the trench, walking northwards. We came to an upright post and he leaned against it. "This was just one place," he explained. "There were plenty of others along this part of the line." He shook the upright. It didn't move. "The engineers came along and built retaining walls to stop the front of the trench collapsing in," he said. "Or if we couldn't wait, we would use sandbags. It was pretty crude."

"And the mud?"

"It got into everything. We would be standing knee deep in the stuff, and there would be torrents of water running through the trench, following the natural contours and undulations of the land. Let me tell you, when it rained, you wanted to be standing post at a high point in the line, not a low point."

I looked. Where the men of the 1st Battalion had been stationed was a shallow saddle between two gentle rising slopes. Spinks must have guessed what I was thinking.

"Yeah," he said gruffly. "We drew a low point in the trench."

We kept walking. "Did it rain often?"

"Often enough to be permanently wet and cold and muddy," he said. "The mud got into our food, in our boots, in our hair and in our weapons. There was nothing you could do but accept it. Everyone suffered in some way or another."

"Was that the worst part of trench life – dealing with the mud when you were standing at the firing line?"

Spinks shook his head. "No. The worst part was trying to sleep in the rain," he said. "It couldn't be done. The mud was inches deep, like a quagmire, sucking at your boots every step you took. No man could lie down. We had to sleep standing up."

"What if you weren't on duty?" I asked. "I mean if you were not posted to the line that day?"

"Off rotation?"

"Yeah."

Spinks shrugged. "It was a little better," he admitted. We walked to the rear wall of the trench and climbed more concrete steps back out of the hole. "Behind the line were thousands of tents – temporary camps for headquarters and supplies," he explained. He made a broad sweeping gesture that seemed to encompass as far as the eye could see. "And the Army took over the town."

"Took over Burgaw?"

He nodded. "We made use of the town's infrastructure and the road network for transporting supplies. Burgaw became a hub for command to co-ordinate troops. It also became a USAMRIID hospital. They were all along the line."

"So if you weren't standing at your post, conditions were a little more comfortable?"

"Sure," Spinks admitted.

I had seen historical photos showing the soldiers of World War 1 enduring the grind of trench life. There were differences here, but perhaps they were only cosmetic. The

Danvers trench was twenty feet wide. The trenches in the First World War had been narrow warrens that had become homes for the men who inhabited them. I got the feeling the nature of the enemy had been the difference in the way this trench had been used by the men who served. There had been no need to fear artillery fire, so the trench could be wide. And there had been no need to fear air attack or naval bombardments, so the support system could be brought close to the trench and left in the open and undefended. There was no need for concealment or fear of a counter-strike from a zombie horde.

"Do you remember the rotation system?"

Spinks looked at me. His eyes had lost some of their sparkle. They seemed glazed over. "I'll never forget," he admitted. He stood silently for long moments, overcome by a melancholy of more bitter memories. "The first sixty days were the worst," he said softly at last. "Because panic ruled everything. We were vulnerable — there just weren't enough men in the line, so we stood in the trench for nine days, and then had one day behind the lines. The infrastructure was limited; the supply routes were still being established. After the first two months it got easier. Fresh troops were pouring into the defenses, and the Army was beginning to mass our forces in preparation for 'Operation Conquest'. We stood in the trench for a week, then were relieved for three day breaks."

"The men knew about the second phase of the zombie war?" For some reason I was surprised by that.

"Sure," Spinks shrugged. "Along with the rumors about the zombie horde sweeping north that were fuelled by the media, we also heard rumors about a counter-offensive."

"How did the men feel about that?"

"We were excited," he said. "The build up of troops behind the lines was impossible to miss. The Army was bringing in artillery and tanks. We knew they weren't for defense. We knew there had to be an attack coming sooner or later."

"And your men were excited?"

Danville Spinks stared at me hard and I could see some emotion pass behind his eyes. He frowned.

"Don't misunderstand the motivation of the men who served along this line," he said with sudden passion. "We weren't all elite 82nd Airborne. There were plenty of National Guard units just like my men and me. And while the time in this trench was soul destroying, it never altered our commitment to protect this country from the zombies. We never lost our bravery or our dedication. We never wavered. What we did in this trench was endure – because America needed us to."

"Did you ever see combat during the months in the trench? Did the zombies ever test the line this far east?"

Spinks shook his head with something like regret. "No," he sighed. "But I wished we had seen action. It would have made the sacrifice worthwhile in a tangible way." He lapsed back into silence and we started walking away from the trench, towards Burgaw. The ground here had been flattened and turned to earth when the Army had mobilized. Now it was overgrown with long grass and weeds and flowers.

Spinks gave me a sideways glance. "We heard about the Battle of Four Seasons at Hendersonville," he said. "Some of my buddies were there. They saw action. When it happened, everyone was keyed up, expecting the zombie surge to come our way, but it never did," he lamented.

There was a Humvee and a driver waiting for us under the leafy canopy a gnarled tree. Spinks pulled open his door, and then paused to take one long last look at the trench line. "Ninety eight days," he muttered softly once again, and shook his head, "and nothing to show for our service apart from the knowledge that we did our duty. No medals, no recognition, no act of valor... just mud in our boots and a gut full of fear."

It started to rain.

HENDERSONVILLE, NORTH CAROLINA: THE BATTLE OF FOUR SEASONS

The 'bone yard', the man called it.

The Bone Yard.

I shook my head slowly – it was the most horrific sight I had ever seen. I walked through the long grass, and the undulating field was a riot of beautiful yellow flowers... littered by the bleached white bones of over one hundred thousand skeletons.

I turned around, numbed. "My God," I breathed. "I had no idea." Some of the bones were still shrouded in tattered rags of cloth. They had been picked clean by the scavengers and burned bright white by the North Carolina sun. In places the bodies had fallen in great heaps, and closer to the rusted entanglement of barbed wire, the bones were scattered so thickly that no grass had grown, no ground could be seen. It was a floor of fragmented skulls.

"You wanted to know what the Battle of Four Seasons was like," Colonel Clayton Paris of the 82nd Airborne said. His voice was deep and made harsh. "This was the reality of it."

He came to join me, leaving his aides by the bulky shape of the Black Hawk. He walked with his hands clasped behind his back, his shoulders straight, but his head bowed. He moved like he was stepping through a cemetery.

"One day," the Colonel stared hard into my eyes, "I hope this battlefield will be treated with the same awed reverence as Gettysburg. It deserves it... but I doubt it will happen."

"Why?" I asked. My voice was hushed. It didn't need to be — the battle had been fought almost a year ago. And I hadn't meant for my voice to be so restrained. It was perhaps, merely a reflection of the desolate, eerie surroundings.

The Colonel shook his head. He had a worn face, the granite features of his younger self abraded away by the ravages of life and the horrors he had seen. His eyes were deep and dark like fathomless pools, and the silver pelt of his moustache drooped into the corners of his mouth when he smiled.

He wasn't smiling now.

"There will be no monuments from this war, no statues and no medals conferred," his deep voice rumbled. "There will be no parades to remember our heroes or fallen comrades — because it wasn't that kind of war. It wasn't the romantic notion recorded in the history books. There were no bright uniforms and no glorious moments to be turned into song. This was a dirty war. A harsh, terrible war. A war I wish I could forget."

When the zombie hordes had swept north and crashed against the Danvers Defense Line, Colonel Paris had been commanding the Battalion of the 82nd Airborne who had repelled the initial attack. It had happened right here — right where we were standing, early one morning as the sun had begun to rise.

Just fifty feet away, behind the coiled wire, was the length of trench where the Colonel's men had faced down over one hundred thousand of the undead in a battle that had raged throughout the entire day, and well into the evening. I shook my head slowly.

One hundred thousand zombies — a Superbowl crowd, swarming from out of the distant fringe of dense trees and hurling themselves up the gentle rise of ground, and onto the waiting guns.

It was simply too overwhelming – too vast for me to possibly visualize.

"They came from out of those woods," the Colonel said, pointing to the south. "We knew they were coming – we'd been preparing for twenty four hours. We had satellites, and helicopters thick in the sky, tracking their approach. We knew the storm was coming, we just didn't know the precise point of impact."

I followed the direction the Colonel was pointing. About three miles away I could see a dense barrier of forest. The ground ahead of the trees was strangely undulated, like grass covered sand dunes, before leveling out as it rose gradually to where we stood.

"How did you survive?" I asked. "How could so few men hold off over one hundred thousand undead? It just doesn't seem possible."

The Colonel said nothing for a moment, but there was a flickering shift in his eyes. "It wasn't just my men," he said. "The defense of Hendersonville was the culmination of a lot of careful thought and planning. It was the first time those plans had been put into practice. Thankfully, they worked. If they hadn't… well, you can guess the rest."

"So what were these tactics? How were they different from the standard military tactics you might have employed on any other battlefield?"

Colonel Paris rummaged into his pocket and found a cigar. He jammed it into the corner of his mouth and lit it. He inhaled deeply and the sweet aroma of the expensive tobacco carried on the breeze, enveloping me in a soft scented cloud for a moment.

"The tactics we drew up to deal with the zombies were totally different to the way we would normally go about combat," the man said. "They had to be, because the nature of the enemy was so unlike any other we had gone to war against."

"In what ways?"

"In every way," Paris gruffed. "But the two most important factors that determined the way we fought them were the issues of morale, and motivation," he said.

"Morale and motivation?" I felt I should write this down. I flipped open my notebook and started scribbling.

"You see the zombies don't suffer from issues that affect their morale, son," he said between puffs of hazy smoke. "You can't demoralize them – you can't beat them into submission. You can't encircle them and call on them to surrender. They're mindless. They keep on coming *because* of their motivation."

"Which is?"

"To kill," he said. "To kill no matter what. They're driven by sound. It makes them crazy. It incenses them. They have no regard for self-preservation. The mindlessness of them makes them a brutal enemy."

I wrote frantically. "Okay," I said. "So how did these factors affect your tactics?"

"We had to go back to the drawing board," Colonel Paris explained. "We had to remember our history if we were to safeguard our future. Eventually, we found the answers in the lessons of the First World War, and the Zulu warriors of Africa."

What?

"Sorry," I muttered. "I don't think I heard that last part clearly. Did you say your tactics came from the Zulus of Africa?"

Paris looked kind of pleased by the dumbfounded expression I wore. He nodded. "It was where we took our inspiration from," he clarified... without being any clearer.

I waited. Colonel Paris seemed in no particular hurry. He nudged a shattered pelvis bone, buried in the grass, with the toe of his boot.

"On the other side of that wire I had close to a thousand of the best men in the Army," he said. "Every one of them a veteran, every one of them proud to be in the 82nd," he explained. "And further along the trench in both directions we had Battalions of the 14th Infantry Regiment – the Golden Dragons. Together, the five miles of this line were defended by some of the very best soldiers ever to go to war. They were steady and experienced."

"Against one hundred thousand?"

"Behind the trench, on the high ground, we had a battalion of Abrams tanks, and in fields beyond those trees way back yonder, we had massed artillery batteries of Paladins."

"What are they?" I asked, and then added quickly, "and what good were they? I didn't imagine artillery would make an impact on a horde of zombies. Surely the artillery wasn't effective?"

"Paladins are 155mm self-propelled howitzers," The Colonel said crisply, as though I was interrupting the flow of his retelling. "They're like a tank and an artillery piece combined," he gave me the vague dumbed-down description. "And they were effective."

I shrugged and moved on. I decided I would come back to the artillery issue later.

"So clearly, advance warning gave you a fighting chance."

"Absolutely," the Colonel agreed. "Having that kind of intelligence – knowing where the enemy was massing and having some idea when they would smash against the line gave us time to organize. It gave us the opportunity to pull together the armor and artillery to support the front line troops. Without that notice, there was no way we could have activated the plan to defend Hendersonville."

I nodded, made a note to find out more about Paladin self-propelled artillery pieces, and then looked up into the Colonel's face.

"So what was this plan – and how did the Zulu's inspire you?"

Colonel Paris suddenly became more animated, drawing shapes in the air with his fingers as he spoke around the stub of his cigar. "The Zulu warriors are famous for a tactic called the 'Buffalo Horns'," he said. "It's a variation of a classic flanking manoeuver where the Zulus move forward into battle with the strongest, fittest men forming the 'chest' of the buffalo. That's the part that absorbs the ferocity of the attack. Then, when the enemy is engaged, the 'horns' of the buffalo sweep forward on either side and attack the enemy from both flanks."

I nodded. And then flinched suddenly. "Jesus! You didn't have your men storm out of the trench and through the barbed wire to outflank the zombies, did you?"

"Of course not, you damned fool!" the Colonel's voice suddenly boomed in the silence of that tragic, monstrous graveyard. "We employed what we called the 'static buffalo' – a tactic that played on the predictability of the zombie behavior."

I waited with my mouth shut. The Colonel drew deeply on his cigar and then waved it at my face. "I wanted the zombies to attack here," he said. "Right here where my men were waiting. So we opened fire – drew them towards the sound – lured them onto the defensive line at a place we were prepared for them. That was the first step."

"And it worked?"

The Colonel nodded. "They responded to the sound of machine gun fire. It was like a huge flock of birds, suddenly wheeling in the air and all flying towards the one point. That was when the artillery opened fire."

"The Paladins."

"Yeah," Colonel Paris said, his voice gruff. "The artillery started shelling the area two miles south of here – just pounding away in a pattern. By then they were firing right amongst the zombies. It didn't deter them. They kept raging towards the trench."

"Were your men still firing?"

"Sporadically," he said. "There was no point. The ghouls were well out of effective range, but I had to keep some fire up to keep 'em interested enough to hit the wire where we wanted them."

I ran my eyes quickly back over my notes. "Can you tell me more about the artillery?" I asked. "Conventional thinking would say that it would be ineffective against the undead swarms because of the slim chance of getting fragments to actually penetrate the brain. Was that the reality?"

The Colonel dropped what was left of his cigar in the grass and ground it down with the heel of his boot.

"That was not the case," he said. "The artillery wasn't meant to wipe out the zombies. Yeah, they took some of the bastards out, because the effective blast zone of each shell fired was about fifty yards. We scored some kills, but we did a hell of a lot of damage to them, slowing them down. That's what the artillery was for – it was a backup to the barbed wire."

I tried to look like I understood. I don't think it worked. "Um…"

The Colonel sighed. "We were dealing with over one hundred thousand undead, maybe a hell of a lot more, and they were all enraged and charging up the slope towards the barbed wire. There was too many of them – we knew that. The artillery fire slowed them down. They fell in their thousands – arms and legs torn off – some decapitated, but thousands of them *incapacitated*," The Colonel emphasized the word. "It meant that when they hit the line they weren't all stormin' and a hollerin'. Some of them were dragging themselves towards the trench. Others were thrown down and didn't get up again."

"Okay," I said with a little more conviction. "And the artillery worked with the barbed wire? Is that right?"

"Yes!" Colonel Paris exclaimed. "No one in their right mind expected the zombies to hit the barbed wire and then suddenly turn back in surprise! They flung themselves at the entanglements, and became entangled. *It slowed them down*," the man said again, talking to me like maybe I had some kind of a learning disability. "We couldn't hold the line against so many zombies unless we could find ways to halt or delay their attack and make them easier for the troops in the trench to pick off. We wanted to stagger the onslaught – and, by God, that's exactly what the artillery and barbed wire did."

"And so then what?" I prompted. "How did the attack develop?"

"Quickly anyhow," the Colonel admitted. "That's what combat is like. It's the endless days of boredom and anticipation, followed by a sporadic burst of gut-churning action and panic. When the zombies came within range, every man in my Battalion opened fire."

"And the tanks? You mentioned there were tanks on the reverse side of the defensive trench."

"They opened fire too," the Colonel said. "That was the reason for the trench being so deep. Eight foot is higher than any man. So we built firing steps. The battalion was lined up on the steps, with just their heads and shoulders visible, and the tank-mounted heavy machine guns were able to fire over the troops and into the zombies."

"The firepower..." I confessed, "... it must have been awesome."

The Colonel actually smiled – a grim little twitch one corner of his mouth. "It was unlike anything I had ever experienced before," he admitted. "Normally firefights are sporadic affairs – one guy shoots and then the other guy shoots back – that sort of thing. But this was a full Battalion of the 82nd Airborne opening fire with everything we had, supported by Paladin artillery and the machine gun mounts on a line of Abrams tanks. It was a sound to shake hell itself."

I glanced over my shoulder and saw bones spread across the ground amongst the barbed wire defense. "Some of them got caught in the wire," I said and pointed.

"A lot reached the entanglement," the Colonel said, "but none reached the trench. Once they were ensnared in the wire, we picked them off quickly. Some of them fell and others tried to clamber over the bodies. We picked them off too. And some of them literally hurled themselves into the wire. They died where they fell."

"So it worked?"

"Yeah," the Colonel said.

"But still... one hundred thousand zombies... how did the line hold against the tremendous weight of numbers?"

The Colonel tapped the side of his nose and smiled slyly. "That was when the static buffalo tactic came into play," he said. I got the sense he was enjoying himself now. Not enjoying the horror of the battle, but the elegance of the plan he was revealing. There was a sense of grim satisfaction in his voice.

"We held the line against the horde for as long as we could, but simple math made it impossible to sustain. There were just too many of the enemy pressing at the one point. When I felt we were about to be overwhelmed – everyone in the 82nd stopped firing."

"They did what?"

"They stopped firing," the Colonel said like he was relishing my surprise. "And then they stepped back down off the firing step, below the eye line of the trench. Suddenly the undead couldn't see anyone. All they could see were the hulls of the Abrams tanks, covering the wire."

"And then?"

"And then the Battalions on either side of my men opened fire. From the left and right of our position the 14th started shooting."

"What happened?"

"The zombies pressing against the line were drawn to the new sound – they couldn't help themselves. They're like moths to a bright light if sound catches their attention. They began to spread away on either side onto the 'static horns' of the buffalo."

"So it was kind of like a spillway for a dam," I said, nodding with admiration despite myself. "When a dam is about to overflow, they let out excess water to decrease the pressure. You did the same kind of thing."

The Colonel wrinkled his nose and then sniffed. "I prefer the buffalo analogy," he said stoically.

"And so the 14th Infantry began drawing the undead onto their guns, right?"

Colonel Paris nodded. "We had more tanks covering their men from the reverse slope – not firing their main weapon, but merely adding the fire from their machine guns. As the undead were repelled, the Paladins opened up again, catching those who had been disabled and finishing them off."

"Was there ever a point during the battle where you thought the plan would fail, or when everything suddenly went wrong?"

"No," the Colonel said, and I believed him. "We had a twenty foot wide trench with all the ammunition we could stockpile, and the ability to bring more men from further along the defensive line in to support the troops if necessary. It was a cohesive plan tailored to the specific enemy we faced – and it worked flawlessly."

"Did many zombies get entangled in the wire?"

"Thousands," The Colonel said. "But very few made it beyond the first ten feet of the entanglement before they were head-shot. We left them sagging in the wire until the battle was over, and then burned the bodies with flamethrowers."

"How long did the battle last?"

"All day," Colonel Paris said. He folded his arms across his chest. "The Paladins stopped firing just on sunset, and by then the field was littered with the dead. More dead than I've ever seen. More dead than in the great Napoleonic battles. The fields were red with zombie blood and slippery with their gore. It was a charnel house."

"I can only imagine…" I said softly, my voice muted.

The Colonel sighed. "The field of glory is never a pretty sight," he said, like he was maybe quoting some long-forgotten General from the pages of history.

The man became somber for just a moment, and then seemed to shake the mood off like a heavy coat. "We fired flares throughout the night and kept the men standing at their posts until sunrise," The Colonel said. "The Paladins began firing again in the middle of the night and continued firing throughout the next day."

"Why?"

"To make sure every one of the undead sons-of-bitches was dead once and for all," the Colonel growled with sudden passion. "There were thousands of them, mutilated in the grass. We left it to the artillery to finish them off. By then they weren't moving much. The artillery pounded them into dust."

I stared again at the stark white bones that were thick on the ground. "I'd like to talk to one of your men, if that's all right. I'd like to hear what the battle was like for one of the men in the trenches as the zombie horde crashed along the line."

The Colonel snapped a speculative glance at me, and then slowly nodded his head. "Sure," he said...

"It was a target rich environment," Specialist Marcel Rodriguez said to me without relish – without any hint of pleasure. "They were thick on the ground, pressing against the barbed wire. From that range, we couldn't miss."

Rodriguez, one of the 82nd Airborne's designated marksmen was posted in the middle of the line when the zombie horde spilled out across the rolling fields that fateful dawn. He remembered the battle clearly; the sights and sounds of that action still a harrowing torment to him, as it was for many of the men who stood in the trenches throughout the Battle of Four Seasons.

Rodriguez was armed with an M14, equipped with a Sage stock and with a mounted Leupold scope.

"We started firing when the dreads were five hundred yards away, and we didn't stop firing for near eight hours," the soldier explained. "We were pissing while we stood and shot. There just wasn't an option. No one could be spared, so we just urinated against the wall of the trench and got on with the business at hand."

Rodriguez was one of the men who formed the 'chest' of Colonel Clayton Paris's static buffalo defense. He said the undead horde that came towards Hendersonville that morning was nothing like he had expected.

"We had seen the media stuff," he said. "You couldn't avoid it, but even so the reality when they came through the trees was a lot more intense than anything the television had shown."

"What do you mean by 'intense'?" I asked. Rodriguez was a young man, not yet twenty-five, with jet-black hair and one single eyebrow that seemed to reach right across his brow. He had flashing white teeth and Latino features.

"The sound of them," he shook his head like it still echoed inside his mind, "was terrifying. It wasn't a cohesive kind of battle cry – it wasn't like a chorus of voices all calling out the same words. It was more animalistic. More raw than that. It was a wild insane sound. It was chilling."

"How were the men around you at that point?" I asked. "The rest of the guys you must have hung out with in your unit?"

Rodriguez shrugged. "We were all pretty scared," he admitted. "Nothing wrong with that. Everyone gets scared before going into action. The guys around me were nervous. We just looked at each other with this kind of *what the fuck* expression in our eyes."

"And then you started firing, right?"

He nodded. "At five hundred yards," he said again. "There was artillery coming in from behind our position, falling amongst the dreads once they cleared the trees. The rest of the guys sat tight, but as an SDM, it was up to guys like me to start picking off the nearest dreads before they got too close."

"So you're a sniper, right?"

"*Like* a sniper," Rodriguez said, "but we're not snipers – our training isn't that specialized. Our role is to lay down accurate fire for our fire team at a range up to around eight hundred yards. Snipers work differently."

I made a note of that.

"So tell me your recollections of the battle," I encouraged the young soldier.

He was a shy, quiet man. He felt uncomfortable being questioned. He flicked a glance sideways and saw the Colonel standing with his staff well out of earshot. Rodriguez and I were sitting in the shade of the Black Hawk. The Colonel had wandered away down the slope, walking the battlefield while a small cluster of neatly uniformed subordinate officers shadowed his every step.

"The dreads were like a nightmare," Rodriguez confided. "Their faces…" he shook his head. "They were covered in blood. Some of them had arms and legs missing. Some of them were horribly burned, and others had chest wounds. It didn't matter. They threw themselves at the barbed wire like savage dogs."

"And you and the rest of your Battalion held them off."

"Yeah," Rodriguez said softly, like he still didn't believe it himself.

"Was it hard to concentrate?" I asked the impulsive question, trying to get the man to open up to me. "With all that noise, the sound of a battle raging and so many zombies trying to get through the wire to tear you to pieces – how did you keep your focus?"

"Training," came the automatic answer. "After the first few rounds, and after the initial shock and fear of seeing so many dreads swarming towards us, we just fell back on our training, like robots," he said.

"And that helped you concentrate?"

"No. That helped us get through the action and do our job," he said. He paused for a moment to pluck one of the bright yellow flowers from the ground. He held it up, close to his face and studied it carefully, then glanced at me furtively. "I only shot men," he whispered.

"Sorry?" I frowned and leaned closer. "I missed that."

Rodriguez lowered his voice to a confidential whisper. "That day – I only shot and killed men."

"Male zombies?"

166

"Yeah."

"Why?" I was intrigued.

Rodriguez shrugged his shoulders again. "I don't know," he said softly. "I just couldn't... y'know...?"

"You couldn't fire at the women and children?"

"Yeah," he said and lowered his head.

"Even though they were zombies too?"

Rodriguez pressed his lips into a thin pale line and looked away. "The kiddies were gruesome," he said. "Just young ones, no more than six or eight years old. They were covered in blood too, snarling just as ferociously as the rest of them, but I just couldn't bring myself to line one up in the sights and squeeze the trigger."

"And the women also?"

He nodded. "I know they were dreads," he said. "And I know they would have torn my throat out if they got the chance... but they were women once, and that kinda shook me."

I nodded. It was an aspect of the conflict I had not thought about before. Perhaps it made the whole apocalypse even more harrowing for those who had served.

"So you only fired at male zombies?"

Rodriguez nodded. "I did my duty," he added quickly. "It's not like I avoided my mission, or put any of the other guys around me at risk. I just made a choice about my targets."

PART 2: 'OPERATION CONQUEST'
The Interviews...

UNDEAD RESPONSE COMMAND POST, KNOXVILLE, TENNESSEE:

There could be no mistaking this man. Even if you didn't recognize his face, you could tell in an instant he was Army. It was in the way he walked, the precision of his mannerisms – and it was in the force of his presence.

"Operation Conquest was about gaining the ascendance over the zombie horde," SAFCUR II looked up from a detailed map he was studying and said to me. "The victory we sought to achieve over the undead was a combination of military superiority, and a concerted effort to raise the hopes and faith of the rest of the nation."

General Zachary G. Winchester was a West Point graduate and a career soldier who had led American troops on battlefields throughout the Middle East. The President, replacing 'Tug' Horsham after the Battle of Four Seasons, had appointed him SAFCUR.

"As I understand it, that was always the plan," General Winchester said curtly. "When the struggle against the undead transitioned from a posture of containment into one where conquest became the priority, it was decided in Washington that a new skill set was required to lead our military. Horsham did a remarkable job. The man is an American hero for the way he pulled so many different organizations together and got them working as one for the defense of the country." The General paused for a dramatic beat, and then said, "My skills were different."

"In what ways?" I asked. We were in a basement – an empty cavernous room below the city of Knoxville. There was no carpet, no bright paint on the walls, and no decorator pieces of furniture. It was just an empty space with a cement floor, a long table, a dozen chairs and a million maps. Every spare inch of available space was covered by empty coffee cups and overflowing ashtrays.

I had to remind myself that aggressive hostilities against the zombies had ended a couple of months ago when the barrier across Florida had been completed. And yet this dark musty space still felt very much alive with the hum of activity and the intangible sense of tension that seemed to permeate the walls.

"When I interviewed General Horsham, he said the change of SAFCUR for 'Operation Conquest' was like a football coach switching from defensive to offensive teams. Would you agree with that analogy?"

Winchester laughed and ran a hand through his neat thatch of short sandy brown hair. "Yeah," he said. "That sounds like a good way of putting it." He dropped into a big leather chair and propped his feet up on the table, crossing his ankles. His shoes were black and polished like a mirror. Someone walked past us, obscurely hugging the edge of the room. Winchester snapped out a hand and caught the person on the arm. "Coffee," he snapped, then looked at me. I nodded. "Two. Black and strong. Pronto."

It could have been a Major, or a private. It could have been a civilian contractor. Winchester never bothered to look. He barked the order and expected it to be obeyed.

"So the Battle of Four Seasons marked the end of the containment phase. Why?"

"It didn't mark the end of containment," Winchester made the point. "It marked the beginning of a transition towards the conquest phase of the war." He was like that, I discovered. He was precise in his words, clear in his explanations. He was the sort of man who left no doubt about his exact meaning, and his exact requirements of those around him.

"The Battle of Four Seasons was an indicator that the tactics we had developed were working. That conflict gave us confidence that we could repeat the same procedures at any point along the line and achieve the same result. It was a moment – just a moment – of satisfaction. It gave us a chance to pause because it signaled the end of the terror. We had drawn a line in the ground and we had been able to defend that line. We used that as a kind of launch pad into altering our stance – going from being on the back foot, to planning our first aggressive counter strike."

"You mentioned the American people before," I said, seizing on a thought. I had to flip back through my notes to find what I was looking for. "You said *'Operation Conquest' was about gaining superiority and restoring hope and faith.*"

General Winchester nodded sagely. "That's correct," he said. "With the success of 'Operation Containment' we gave the people of America hope. Up until that point there was rioting in the streets. People were filled with panic. There were food shortages, fuel shortages, and the roads north as far as Canada were choked with cars. People were fleeing for their lives. Even martial law was unable to suppress the terror. But once the nation realized we had managed to stem the surge of undead, they began to settle. They began to adjust, take a breath. That was why the next phase was critical. We needed victories over the undead, and we needed the world to know about it. That's what gave America faith."

I nodded, while I wrote everything down. "So how did you go about gaining these victories?" I asked. "If I remember, there was quite a lull between the Battle of Four Seasons and the victory you won at Rock Hill."

170

"Correct again," General Winchester said. He was about to say more, when a young uniformed soldier came into the room carrying two Styrofoam cups of coffee. He set them on the edge of the big table and backed out of the room. "There was a pause," the General went on again. "Because we had to learn how to beat the zombie fuckers. We needed to reinvent how we took the war to a unique enemy. That took time, and experimentation."

"Can you tell me more about that – the tactics you developed?"

"No," Winchester said, without any temper. "Because I'd be taking credit for the work of others. I can tell you this though," he swung his legs off the desk and leaned forward suddenly, thrusting out his jaw and fixing me with his gaze. "The first thing I did when I got this job was have a long talk to an old buddy of mine, Colonel Chip Biggins. He's the CO at the 278th Armored Cavalry Regiment, headquartered right here in Knoxville. The 278th is one of only two armored cavalry regiments in the US Army. It was Chip and his men who developed the techniques we used when we came up against the undead at Rock Hill."

I made a note of the name and the unit, and then reached into my bag for a fresh notebook. There was more I wanted to ask SAFCUR II.

"Is it wrong to claim that 'Operation Conquest' was more of a public relations exercise than an actual military success?"

"Fuck yes!" Winchester exploded. His face darkened with blood and his eyes glinted like the points of bayonets. He slammed the palm of his hand down hard on the tabletop. "Where the hell did you get that impression from?" he raged.

I met his stare with an expressionless face. "Well I got the impression from you," I said openly. "You just told me that a lot of emphasis went on reassuring the public, and that victories over the zombie hordes were vital to restoring the faith of the American people."

There was one other person in the room. It was a lieutenant. He was pouring over a filing cabinet of maps in the far corner, trying to locate something that had eluded him ever since I had arrived. General Winchester turned his eyes from me and focused his attention on the officer. "Out," he snapped.

The lieutenant looked up, startled. He saw the General's expression and all the color drained from the young man's face. He left the mess of maps strewn across the bunker floor and beat a hasty retreat, closing the door very quietly behind him.

We were alone.

General Winchester stood up. He was imposingly tall, like an avalanche of attitude. He came and stood closer, then leaned in to press his face next to mine.

"Listen to me, numb-nuts," he seethed. His jaw was clenched, his teeth gritted together. The words seemed to hiss from his snarling mouth. "Operation Conquest was a vital part in the overall plan to save America from extinction." As if he wasn't exerting enough influence, he prodded me in the chest with a gnarled finger. "Young men risked their lives to develop the tactics that were ultimately employed to drive the zombies back to Florida. They were young men *under my command!* Don't you dare publish anything that diminishes their contribution to the effort to free this country. Don't you fucking dare!"

We had a ten second staring competition. I could see all kinds of emotion boiling behind Winchester's eyes.

"I'm just trying to discover the truth," I said calmly.

The General's eyes narrowed to slits. His face seemed to fill with wrinkles that spread out from the corners of his mouth, and across his brow. "And I'm telling it to you!" he snapped.

He pushed himself away from me and stalked a circuit of the long table, hitching up his pants and muttering to himself. When he came back to where his empty chair waited, he slammed it against the edge of the table like he wished it had been my head instead.

"Operation Conquest was a phase in the war against the undead where we developed specific tactics, and learned to co-ordinate all aspects of our capabilities in a concerted effort," he said in a moment of brilliant double-speak. "Write that in your fucking book."

I nodded. "I will," I said, and recorded everything the General had just said. Then I looked up at him. I think it bothered the man that I was unruffled. He was used to quaking obedience from everyone who surrounded him. "Now, can you tell me what that bullshit means in real words?"

Winchester blinked. Something flashed across his face, and then he blinked again.

He started to chuckle.

"Wise ass," he muttered without hostility. He rubbed his chin and slumped back down into the big chair with a resigned sigh, as if all the bluster had gone from him.

He spun around and stared at a map-covered wall for a moment, then turned all the way round to face me again.

"Look, the simple truth is that we were standing in a deep pile of shit," the General said. "We had stopped the zombies, but we had no idea how to drive them back. We thought armor was the answer but we had to re-learn how to use it, and at the same time we had to develop a way to make use of the artillery we had. That's it. That's what 'Operation Conquest' really was. It was the training and development phase of the war."

I didn't write that down. To me it was an off-the-record kind of confession.

"I remember seeing some news footage of the tanks rolling across the countryside of South Carolina in tight formations, like bulldozers, with the rest of the armor sweeping in lines behind them," I said to the General. "Can you tell me what would have happened if the plans you and your officers developed using armor hadn't worked?"

Winchester was watching me as I spoke like he could barely wait for me to finish before he replied. But he didn't. He didn't say anything for over a minute. I sat in the strained silence and waited.

"The tank and armor tactics we developed were part of the overall operation," he began, measuring every word like it was important. "But the plan also included the use of artillery and aircraft. That's the first thing. You'll obviously get the detail from Chip Biggins. As for the rest of your question… no comment."

That surprised me. I sat back in the chair.

"You won't tell me what other optional plans you were developing in case the armor assault wasn't successful?"

"No."

"Why?" I persisted. And then had a thought that sent a chill down my spine. "Was there any other plan?"

"Yes."

"What were they?"

"No comment."

I sighed. I set down my pen, carefully folded the cover of my notebook closed and laid it down on the edge of the table. I leaned forward, and rested my elbows on my knees. "You were going to use nukes, weren't you?" My voice was level and subdued, but filled with a sense of foreboding. "The Army was actually considering the option of using tactical nuclear weapons against the zombies."

Winchester's face started to break. There was a twitch at the corner of one eye. The rigid façade of his features began to dissolve into something more human, more emotional.

He looked down at one of the maps spread across the table and then slowly lifted his eyes to mine. "Yes," he said. "But that's not for publication."

Something dreadful and cold slithered in the pit of my guts. I nodded my head in slow agreement. "How close did America come to the use of nuclear weapons?"

"Close," Winchester said. "The decision went all the way to the top."

"The President?"

Winchester inclined his head.

"Is it still an option?" I had to ask. "I mean is the military still considering employing nukes against the undead now that they are barricaded in Florida?"

"Everything is still an option," Winchester said diplomatically. "Every weapon at the nation's disposal is constantly being considered and assessed for its viability against the zombies." He was back to the political double-speak of just a few minutes earlier. I knew I needed to get past the recited lines if I was ever going to learn the real truth.

I doubled back. Sometimes it's the best way to gain momentum forward again. "When the option was presented to the President," I began, "Who actually recommended the use of nuclear weapons?"

"I did," Winchester admitted.

I wasn't completely surprised. I doubted the recommendation would have been treated seriously if it had come from some pencil-pushing politician in the relative safety of his Washington office. This man was the Supreme Armed Forces Commander. He would have been listened to.

"But I didn't make it a recommendation," Winchester hastened to add. "I presented the option to the President with several other alternatives."

"Can you tell me what those other alternatives were?"

The General got out of his chair again. He was restless, uncomfortable. He stalked around the room. He was so tall, and the ceiling of the headquarters so low, that he almost looked stooped as he paced.

"Experimental weapons," he said vaguely. "Lasers and the like."

"What else?"

"Evacuation."

"From where... to where?"

The General shrugged his shoulders and then looked down at his shoes. "From the lower forty-eight," he said. "Maybe to Alaska, or Canada."

I recoiled, stunned. "You mean surrendering the entire nation to the plague was an option?"

"It was," Winchester said. "If we hadn't been able to drive the zombies back."

I frowned. "But you had them contained in the southern states. Why would evacuation then be necessary? Wouldn't the worst-case scenario be that the status quo was maintained and that we conceded the loss of the southern states?"

Winchester shook his head. He didn't agree. "The Danvers Defensive line held against the undead, and after the Battle of Four Seasons, we knew we could hold our position. But we didn't believe we could contain the infection indefinitely," SAFCUR II said heavily. "We didn't have a buffer. If the virus had somehow been carried into the trenches, it would have burned across the rest of the country."

Okay, I got that. I could see that it would be possible for the virus to somehow break out beyond the thin trench line of defenses. It only took one infected ghoul...

"But now?" I brought the interview back on course. "We have the buffer zone – the dead zone as everyone calls it. There are hundreds of miles of arid abandoned land between the original Danvers Defense Line and the containment line across the Florida peninsula. Mississippi, Alabama, Georgia, South Carolina – they're all dead zone. Surely that's an extensive buffer."

"It is," Winchester agreed. "But the only real assurance we will ever have that the zombie virus has been beaten, is if every one of the infected is destroyed."

"So nuking Florida is still on the list of options."

A ghastly transformation had overcome the General in just a few quiet minutes. He looked somehow older now, aged and wearied. It was in the hunch of his shoulders and the dull sheen of his eyes. And it was in the dry empty sound of his voice.

"Yes. Using nuclear weapons against the undead in Florida is still an option," the words rasped in his throat. "If it ever comes to it."

FORT F-037 NEAR SPARTA, TENNESSEE
35°55′56″N 85°28′11″W

First Sergeant Larry McMaster, 3rd Battalion 3rd Marines rolled up his sleeves and then kicked at the weeds that had grown along the length of the chain link fence, as though their presence here personally offended him.

"Relics now," McMaster growled. I wasn't sure what he was referring to – the weeds, or the fort itself.

"You mean the fort?"

"Yeah," McMaster scowled. We were standing inside the perimeter of fort F-037, just south of the little town of Sparta. The fortification had long ago been abandoned after the military had pushed the undead swarms back towards the south and built new fortifications that measured the stages of the offensive. Now, these very first forts that had defined the Danvers Defense Line were rusting ugly skeletons, abandoned to time and the ghosts who haunted them.

And there were plenty of ghosts.

Fort F-037 had been attacked by the zombie hordes just a few days after the undead had tested the trench defensive system at Hendersonville. It was McMaster's men – the troops of 3rd Battalion – who had fought off the undulating tide of dead in a battle that had raged for several hours.

"There was no surprise," McMaster explained. "Reconnaissance satellites and choppers gave us plenty of warning – but there was still an element of shock," the man admitted candidly. It was hard for me to imagine a Marine like the First Sergeant being shocked at anything. He was the classic cutout of a hard-nosed warrior. He had muscled forearms, thick as posts, and a huge barrel chest that stretched the fabric of his fatigues. His face was like granite – the features too hard to ever be called handsome. His eyes were black, hooded under the overhanging ridge of his brow, and his mouth was a wide thin slash beneath the beak of his nose. His demeanor bristled with confidence and a sense of disdain for anything or anyone who failed to measure up to his expectations. He would be a hard task-master, I imagined. Not a man who would tolerate fools or incompetence.

He was the kind of tough no-nonsense veteran you wanted at your shoulder in a fight.

"And so the reconnaissance warnings you were receiving – did that mean you had all your men ready as the undead advanced?"

McMaster looked at me bemused. "Advanced?" he wrenched the word from his throat and made it sound like a curse. "Son, they didn't fucking advance. They fucking charged at the fence – hurled themselves at the wire barrier like insane berserkers. There was nothing methodical about it. There was nothing remotely civilized. Calling it an advance portrays the moment they came surging towards us as though it was part of a tactical military conflict. It fucking wasn't."

I flinched. The bark of the man was like a physical thing. He brooded silently for a few long moments, then rested one boot on an old jerry can and clasped his hands behind his back in the pose of some long lost military commander from the past. He stared out through the wire, narrowing his eyes as the memories came back to him of that afternoon the fort had come under attack.

"We knew to expect the fuckers," McMaster's voice had become subdued. "But we didn't know *what* to expect. Does that make sense?"

I nodded. He nodded back. "I had my men drawn up twenty feet behind the fence line, with India and Kilo companies in the front rank, and Lima company in close reserve."

I frowned. "That must have been awkward," I said. "I don't imagine that you would have practiced those kind of straight-line formations too often in previous conflicts, surely."

McMaster grunted. "You're right," he said wryly. "It was totally fucking foreign to everything I had experienced and encountered on the field of conflict," he said. "My men had never formed up like that – ever. We were all about our spacing, ragged formations, one man covering his buddy as we moved forward. Now we were suddenly kneeling in a line like it was the Battle of Waterloo, or a battle from the Civil War."

"Is that really how it felt?"

McMaster nodded. "Yeah," he said. "It was a major mental issue that we needed to overcome. The fact was that we were in no danger of incoming fire. We were under no direct threat. We couldn't take hits. We could position ourselves out in the open like the men were on the firing range." He shook his head like his world of warfare had been forever turned upside down and he was still not adjusted.

"That must have made it easier."

"You would think so," McMaster confessed. "But it didn't."

"Why?"

He shook his head again. "The enemy was so fierce. So utterly mindless in the way they assaulted the fence. They threw themselves onto the barbed wire. They clawed at the chain wire beyond it. They smashed themselves without any regard for their own safety against the locked gates across the road. They were furious, and that carried with it its own intimidation," he admitted.

I was intrigued. I had imagined a tough veteran unit like the 3rd Marines would have relished the freedom of the combat – being able to reign down overwhelming firepower on a primitive enemy. McMaster's admissions had startled me.

"How did that affect your men?"

"Initially, we were ragged," he said.

"Ragged?"

"Undisciplined," McMaster barked, as if he was resentful at having to explain himself. "The men were awed by the ferocity of the assault. Our first rounds were all over the place."

"Did you have men in the observation towers?"

"Heavy machine guns," McMaster grunted, "and the base itself was fully mobilized. We had a column of Humvee's drawn up behind the rifle companies, pouring machine gun fire at the zombies through the wire, firing over the heads of the men."

"The sound of the battle – "

"Was deafening," the First Sergeant finished the sentence I started. "It was a constant barrage of violent noise – the rip of automatic fire drowning out the howls of the enemy."

"Was it difficult to command in such a situation?"

McMaster stood straight and went walking off along the edge of the wire fence. There were skulls and shattered fragments of white bone on the opposite side of the fence, half-buried in the swirling dust and dirt. He looked away into the distance, following the line of the road until it dropped down beyond the horizon between the saddle of a far-off hill. He didn't move, He just stood there, staring out into the afternoon, and eventually I followed him.

The road was potholed and torn ragged along the edges. The shoulder of the blacktop was gravel, giving way eventually to long grass that was turning slowly brown with the change of season. McMaster rested his hands on the wire, fingers through the narrow links like a prison inmate dreaming of escape.

"I was wondering if it was difficult to command in a situation like that," I repeated the question, then felt myself flinch, anticipating some kind of barked retort. McMaster turned his eyes to mine slowly. "It was impossible to command," he said. "It was impossible even to be heard. The men fired long bursts at the undead, and over that was the endless rattle of the machine guns on the vehicles and in the towers. It became a cluster-fuck."

"But effective, right? I mean you beat them back. There was one report I read afterwards that claimed as many as thirty-five thousand zombies had been killed."

McMaster shrugged his broad shoulders. "I don't write the media reports," he grumbled, like he was indirectly contradicting the numbers the government had claimed.

I sighed. I sensed there was something bugging the veteran First Sergeant. "You seem disappointed." I threw the comment out there.

"I am," McMaster said gruffly. "I am disappointed."

"Why?"

He shrugged again and then let his fingers slip from the wire. He folded his arms across his chest and the muscles in his forearms coiled and rippled like pythons.

"Because it was so fucking disorganized," he said. "It was such a heavy firefight, but without the discipline expected and required of US Marines. There was no order, there was no concentration of fire in any tactical way — everyone just blazed away until the ammunition ran out."

"And you had expected something else?"

"I had demanded fucking discipline!" McMaster roared suddenly, and the bull sound of his voice seemed to echo around the abandoned compound. "I studied the battles of the past — the massed ranks of muskets facing a massed enemy, and the limitations of their weapons had made them disciplined."

"Can you explain what you mean?"

McMaster scowled. "Isn't it obvious?"

"Not to me," I admitted. "But I'm a journalist, not a soldier."

He stomped his boots in the dirt. Little devils of dust swirled around his legs. "The musket needed to be reloaded. That took time. Therefore each shot had to be controlled and weighted to achieve the maximum effect. Men listened to the barked orders — everything was regimented. The firefight here at the fort was nothing like that. We should have been fucking surgical!" McMaster hissed. "Instead we were like a panicked rabble."

I could see how the veteran disciplinarian would take the reaction of his men as a personal offense. He was like that.

He was a proud warrior with a distinguished past. He had dedicated his entire adult life to the Marines.

But the conflict against the undead was something no one had experienced prior to the outbreak. It had demanded fresh tactics, and new levels of *olde worlde* discipline.

At least that's what McMaster seemed to think.

"How close did the zombies get to the fort?" I enquired with all the polite tact I could muster.

"Close," McMaster admitted. "They were at the gate, throwing themselves against it. The barbed wire kept them off the fence, so they swarmed at the gate."

"But it held."

"Yeah," the First Sergeant said grimly. "It held." He walked over to the gate and held the old padlock in his hand. The chain was thick, the lock massive. A red dust of rust came away and dusted his palm. "When they started to pile up right here, I brought Lima Company forward and diverted the other two companies to fire at the flanks. Lima Company formed up across the road."

"And drove the undead back?"

"Yeah," McMaster said. "The bodies piled up. They were climbing over the corpses trying to get over the gate. There must have been a thousand of the fuckers torn apart, like a barricade of limbs and gruesome bodies... and the others were scrambling over them."

"Was there a point where you worried that the gate might collapse, or that they might breach the fort?"

"Twice," McMaster said. "When they first crashed against the gate I thought the whole structure might collapse. But it didn't. We fired into a solid wall of 'em and ripped them to pieces. The firefight was intense. The road was awash with blood and gore."

"But they kept coming."

"Yes, they did," the Marine nodded his head. "They were climbing over the other undead like they were scrambling up a man-made mountain. The captain brought up some of the Humvees and we hit them with heavy machine guns to hose them off the wire. It was like riot police firing water cannon – except each time they fell, more would climb over them. They were utterly relentless."

"How did you eventually stop them?"

The veteran Marine shook his head, like maybe he was still wondering that himself. "Once we had contact, we sent for reinforcements," McMaster explained. "We knew a battalion – even of Marines – was not going to be able to hold them off forever. We had good lines of supply out through the back entrance of the camp. We brought up more Humvees and heavy machine guns from further along the trench system to the west."

"So it was weight of numbers?"

"No. It was weight of firepower," he said. "That's all it was. That was all that saved us – the defensive system of the fort, and the ability to bring an overwhelming amount of fire to bear."

"What lessons do you think were learned from the battle around the fort?" I asked the Marine. "Did the conflict create any revision of tactics for future encounters of this scale?"

Larry McMaster kicked at the dirt for a few seconds. There was a tuft of weed growing like a vine up through the wire. He severed it with the tip of his boot, and then turned his back to the distant horizon and swept his gaze across the compound, maybe seeing yet again the position of his men from 3rd Battalion as they had been drawn up to fend off the assault.

"We had to change the way we communicated," McMaster thought carefully before he answered me. "There is no doubt that overwhelming firepower won the day, and that was something we expected and planned for. But what we hadn't anticipated were the troubles we encountered in keeping the fire directed at tactical points that demanded attention." He paused again like he was playing the words back over in his mind to be sure they made sense. "So we began to develop a series of hand signals," he explained. "Because in the intensity of the moment, communication lines were overwhelmed by the sheer volume of the firefight. Simple hand signals became the best way to reach the troops and direct their fire."

"Like in the battles of old?"

"Yeah," McMaster conceded. "Just like the battle of old. Except in those days, captains and generals carried swords and they swept them down to order the troops to open fire, and used the weapon to rally their men."

"Anything else?"

"Drills," McMaster said. "We drilled in the line formations until the men were comfortable and adjusted to the din of battle, and trained to watch for command signals. It was parade ground stuff – things we hadn't reviewed since basic training. Since this battle it has become the approved way to manoeuver troops into a defensive position and to form them up for combat."

I tried on a wry smile. McMaster looked like he might punch me on the nose. He found nothing at all about this moment in America's military history amusing. "History repeats itself," I offered. "The lessons of the past re-learned."

"Yeah," McMaster grunted. He still looked like he wanted to punch me – maybe just for the satisfaction it would give him.

"Coming back to the battle at the fort," I changed the subject to distract him from any brewing violent intent. "Did the zombie attack just peter out, or were they driven off?"

"They were slaughtered," McMaster said grudgingly. "But it still wasn't over. They didn't just retreat to lick their injuries. They didn't flee the field carrying their wounded under a cover of smoke or anything remotely familiar. They just died. And those that weren't killed in the initial battle, were finished off throughout the night. In the morning, we burned the remains. Now, all that's left is this rusted old fort, and thousands of shattered broken bones, burning in the dirt and dust."

KNOXVILLE, TENNESSEE:
278TH ARMORED CAVALRY REGIMENT HEADQUARTERS:

While I sat and waited for the Colonel to arrive, all I could do was focus on the hat that sat on the polished surface of the desk.

It wasn't an ordinary hat – it was a military headpiece as famous as the bicorn worn by Napoleon, or the feathered war bonnets worn by red Indians.

It was a Cavalry Stetson.

The acorn band was a black and gold weave, just below gold crossed sabers. The winged eagle above the sabers, designating a 'full' Colonel, was silver. Like I said it wasn't just a hat: it was an iconic image of the Cavalry, and America's military heritage.

Colonel Chip Biggins' office was large and utilitarian. Behind the desk was the American flag, and a view of barracks buildings through a large window. The rest of the office was uncluttered. Everything was in its place, and there was nothing that did not belong, or serve a purpose.

When the Colonel came into the room, he glanced at me quickly and then went around behind his desk. He had a fistful of papers in his hand. He set them down, and then stared at them for a moment as though their presence somehow bothered him. He scowled, and then moved the papers into a drawer. Finally I had his attention.

I leaned across the wide space of the desk and we shook hands. "Colonel. It's nice to meet you."

Chip Biggins' expression was stern. He reminded me of one of those old portrait photographs of a grim man staring out at the world with a fearsome expression darkening his features. His eyes were hard and wary. He had light brown wavy hair that was beginning to turn grey, and a fleshy face. The sun had browned his skin so that his eyebrows looked almost invisible. He stared at me for a long second and then said, "Pleasure."

That was it.

I sat back in my seat. I had my notebook in my lap and a page of prepared questions. Colonel Chip Biggins glared at me like he was almost daring me to open my mouth.

He was an intimidating man – a big barrel-chested body and huge forearms. He swayed in the leather chair like it was a rocker.

"Colonel, I wanted to ask you some questions about your unit – the 278th Armored Cavalry Regiment. SAFCUR II – General Winchester – told me in a recent interview that you and your men were instrumental in developing tank tactics against the zombies during 'Operation Conquest'."

Colonel Biggins nodded. "We did our job," he said obliquely, and then lapsed once more into silence.

I have the utmost respect for our fighting men and women, but they're difficult subjects to interview. Men like Biggins are guarded when dealing with the media – partially because of mistrust, and partially because of matters of operational security. I had thought by mentioning SAFCUR II's name, Biggins would be a little more willing to talk.

Apparently not.

"Can you tell me about the tactics you developed? How were they different from the normal tank tactics that would be employed against conventional armies?"

The Colonel stopped swinging back in the big padded seat. He leaned forward and clasped his hands together on the desk, forearms resting on the polished surface like he was about to deliver a lecture... or a sermon.

"Let's start at the start," he said. His voice was deep and gruff. "Even though the 278th is referred to as an Armored Cavalry Regiment, its make up is actually an Armored Brigade Combat Team."

"Is there a difference?"

The Colonel nodded. "There is," he said. "The ABCT structure we operate under now uses a few less vehicles, but it gives us more flexibility and the ability to deploy more efficiently. The ABCT is a modular unit. The change in structure is to enhance our ability to be deployed to overseas theaters of action quickly."

I nodded and wrote everything down. The Colonel paused and waited. When I looked up again, he was staring at me impatiently.

"Don't you take shorthand?"

I shook my head. "And normally when I do these kind of interviews people prefer me not to record the conversation. That's why I have to write everything down and then decipher my notes when I get back to a hotel.

"Inefficient," Biggins said. "You got a phone?"

I nodded.

The Colonel grunted. "Then record the conversation. I'd rather take a chance on you catching something off the record than you writing everything I say down wrong."

I dived into my pocket for my cell phone, and threw the notepad down, glad to be rid of it. I set the phone down on the edge of the desk and started recording. The Colonel looked grimly satisfied. His eyes flicked to the office door, as though he was reassuring himself it was closed and we were completely alone.

It was… and we were.

"Chariots," the Colonel said.

I blinked. "I beg your pardon?"

"You asked about the tank tactics my unit developed to fight the zombie horde. I'm giving you the answer. Chariots."

I did a double take. "Can you tell me more?"

Biggins got up from his chair and paced around the room. Every step was measured and precise. It was like he was marching on a parade ground. He circled the office twice, and stopped beside the American flag. I turned a little in my seat until I was facing him, and then slid the phone closer across the desk.

"You've probably heard this before," Biggins explained, "but the fact is that we were forced to rethink all of our tactics when we went up against the zombies. Normal tactics no longer applied, because the circumstance was different, and because our enemy was vastly different from those we had beaten before."

"So you turned to history?"

"Of course," Biggins conceded. "Every commander knows the history of warfare – the tactics of the great strategists that shaped the world we live in. In every aspect of this conflict, it was the lessons learned from the past that allowed us to fight an enemy from our future. The tank tactics we employed were no different."

"But chariots?"

Biggins looked bleak. "Why not," he shrugged. "When I was first approached by SAFCUR II, and told about 'Operation Conquest' my team and I went back through time, looking for comparative scenarios that were similar to what we were facing. Tanks first appeared on the battlefield during World War I, and they had some military success. But their biggest success was the shock value."

I was listening, but not understanding. The Colonel's explanation seemed a contradiction.

"But what use was shock value when you're fighting an enemy like the zombies? They couldn't be shocked. Not in the same way. You couldn't affect their morale, right?"

"Of course," the Colonel snapped. Maybe my interruptions were affecting his train of thought. I decided it was better to sit quietly and shut my mouth. I sat back and stared up at the man.

"That's why we kept going back through time. Finally we explored the great ancient battles – and that was where we found the real key to success."

He paused for a moment, like maybe he was waiting for me to nod my head or mutter some sound of sudden understanding. But I had learned my lesson. I kept quiet. The Colonel went on.

"The tanks employed in the First Great War were against an enemy that was entrenched. The other problem with focusing on the First War for our ultimate strategy was that the early tanks in theater were few and far between. So we went back to the first ancient battles where chariots were employed. In ancient times, chariots were used against tightly packed infantry formations. But they were used in a *specific way*."

I couldn't help myself. "Which was?"

"In dense formations," Colonel Biggins declared like it was significant. "The first chariots were formed up wheel-to-wheel and unleashed on the unsuspecting infantry. They ripped through the ranks and shattered the enemy formations. They weren't about delivering a platform that killed thousands of soldiers, they were impact weapons that broke apart columns and left them exposed for the infantry that followed the chariots into the breach."

"And that was the inspiration for the tank tactics you employed – the tactics that won the Battle at Rock Hill?"

"It was," Biggins said. There was an air of grim satisfaction in his voice. He stepped away from the flag and dropped down into the big leather chair.

'Zombies are the most lethal enemy America has ever faced," the Colonel said emphatically. "You can't demoralize them – but you can *immobilize* them. Do that, and they become target practice. A running zombie is a hideous, terrifying threat, and a critical danger to everyone. A crawling, broken zombie is a sitting duck. We needed to develop ways to rob them of their speed and their ability to move."

"You crushed them?"

"Absolutely," the Colonel said. He stopped for a moment, and bit his lip. The silence in the office stretched out. Finally he lowered his voice to a confidential level. "We FUBARed them," he hissed.

I knew the expression, but I wondered whether the Colonel could be tempted to say the words, knowing they were being recorded.

I frowned. "I… I don't understand…"

"Fucked Up Beyond All Recognition," Biggins said, wrapping his tongue around the words with a kind of relish. "That's what we aimed to achieve and, by God, that's exactly what we did."

There was another long pause. I did and said nothing to fill the awkward silence. I was content to listen to the Colonel explain the tank tactics in his own time. He gave me a look that suggested he didn't much like me.

"We practiced new tank formations," the Colonel explained. "We rehearsed driving across open fields with our tank elements close together in long impact lines. It took some time, because the concept was totally foreign to every man who has ever driven a tank, but eventually we got it. Eventually we were able to take the field in long solid lines of armor that swept down on the zombies and took advantage of their greatest weakness."

I sat up. "They have a weakness?"

"Of course," Biggins said, then leaned across the desk and dropped his voice to a whisper again. "They're mindless, and they're insatiable. They can't help themselves but attack sound and movement."

"So what happened?"

Biggins pointed a big gnarled finger at me. "First, you need to understand that the tank tactics we used would never have succeeded without the support from artillery," he cautioned me. "The massed bombardment we used was like nothing ever witnessed in the history of warfare before – every piece of equipment the Army had available was drawn up and opened fire in a barrage to reduce the enemy's effectiveness. That had to happen before the tanks could roll."

I had heard mention of artillery fire being effective against the undead before. Now this Colonel of an Armored Cavalry Regiment was reinforcing the claim. "What use was the artillery?" I asked. "Why was it so essential?"

"Casualties," Biggins said simply. "The whole plan depended on being able to wear away at the enemy's efficiency and effectiveness. The artillery fire killed tens of thousands of zombies. The barrage of air burst shelling ravaged the undead. And those who weren't destroyed were severely disabled. Only when we had saturated the area around Rock Hill did I set the tanks rolling."

"You destroyed the towns?"

"Every one of them," Biggins was unapologetic. "We flattened every structure that lay before us. We leveled the ground – had to. The zombies infest urban areas. They congregate in numbers around the towns. I wanted a flat-earth policy. There could be nowhere for them to hide, and no obstacles in the way that would disrupt the formations of armor. It was vital."

I rubbed at my forehead, trying to imagine the awesome power of a vast artillery bombardment, and the impact it would have on buildings and roads. "How long did your artillery fire on the area around Rock Hill?"

"Twenty four hours – solid," the Colonel said. "Through the night, the sky was lit like the world was on fire, and the sound shook the earth under my feet."

"And then you sent in the tanks the following day?"

"A few hours after sunrise," he said.

"Can you tell me more about that, please? I'd like to know what tanks you used, how many... what the result was... everything actually."

Biggins leaned forward and rested his elbows on the edge of the desk. He laced his fingers together. He stared at me.

"An Armored Brigade Combat Team like the 278th consists of about ninety M1 Abrams Main Battle Tanks, as well as ninety M3 Bradley Fighting Vehicles and more than one hundred M113 Armored Personnel Carriers. That's a lot of steel, son," Biggins explained. "And once it's rolling, it is an unstoppable force. The Abrams weighs around sixty-seven tons. The Bradleys weigh about twenty-five. Hell, even the M113's weigh more than twelve tons. It's a massive amount of weight when it's rolling. You run someone over with an Abrams, and they're going to have a bad day, you know what I mean?"

I nodded my head. "So you used the vehicles like a battering ram?"

Biggins looked disappointed. He shook his head. "When you say it like that, you miss the importance of the tactic," he scowled. "You miss the value of what we did, and why it worked."

"Okay, sorry," I said. "Then tell me what I'm missing."

"You're missing the combination of elements that worked together at Rock Hill to win the conflict," the Colonel insisted. He got back out of his chair and leaned across the table like it was a wargames sand box used to explain tactics to new officers. Suddenly he became more animated, gesturing with his hands as he explained the battle.

"Our artillery pounded the area around Rock Hill for a full day while we were drawing up the Regiment, and then we rolled out through Fort F-042 which was just south of Statesville on the I77. We had a lake on our right flank, and the AFV's were spread out in a long line with the Abrams and Bradleys in front, and the M113's two miles behind with troops in each vehicle." The Colonel found a couple of rulers in his desk drawer and laid them out end-to-end on his desk to simulate the line of Abrams and Bradleys.

"The fort was our Forward Operating Base and we had an LD two miles to the south. By the time we crossed that Line of Departure we were in formation and the battle really began."

"What happened once the zombies were engaged?"

"It was like mowing the lawn," he said suddenly. I looked up at his face. It was such a surprising analogy that I frowned. "What do you mean?"

He shrugged his shoulders. "When we swept south towards Rock Hill, the undead were scattered and in disarray. The bombardment had been brutal. The ground was torn up and there were undead bodies thick in the grass. We mowed right over the top of them, just like when you mow your front lawn."

I tried to imagine the similarity. I couldn't.

"An Abrams will do close to fifty miles an hour. Imagine that," Biggins said. "Imagine a sixty seven ton steel monster coming at you at close to fifty miles an hour. And then imagine having nowhere to run, because there is another one right beside the first one, and another Abrams right beside it. We swept the ground clean of undead and buried them in the dirt. The machine guns on every vehicle tore them to pieces, the tanks rolled right over them, and then the infantry in the M113's, who were finishing off the remains after we had done with them, killed anything that still writhed in the dirt. Nothing could stand in our path."

I nodded, but something didn't seem quite right to me. I wasn't sure what it was. "But there must have still been tens of thousands of undead between your tanks and Rock Hill," I said. "That's a lot of bodies, and a lot of obstacles. You couldn't have killed them all, surely."

Biggins made a face that looked close to a snarl. "They're tanks, not cars or trucks. They're not wheeled vehicles, son. They're tracked vehicles that can't be stopped. They move faster than the undead can run, and a pile of zombie bodies thirty feet high is not an obstacle. The tanks just run right over them."

"And then the troops in the Armored Personnel Carriers got out of their vehicles and killed the remains?"

Biggins nodded. "We had the men in hazmat gear. The 113's were a couple of miles behind. Anything that moved got sprayed with machine gun fire, and then the troops disembarked the vehicles and head-shot anything that hadn't been crushed."

"Were the main guns on the Abrams firing? Can't they fire some kind of canister shell?"

Biggins nodded, then shook his head just as abruptly. "We removed all the main ammunition from the Abrams and the Bradleys before they went into combat. Every available space inside those vehicles was used for machine gun ammunition."

I sat back, staring at the two rulers on the desk. "But what about beyond the reach of the rulers... the tanks? At the end of the line... there are still going to be thousands of undead. Weren't the men in the troop carriers in danger?"

The Colonel conceded the point with a curt nod of his head. "There was some risk," he admitted, and then went back to his bizarre lawn-mowing comparison. "When you run your lawn mover over a swathe of grass, you never cut every blade down. That was why we had the M113's to finish off zombies that somehow survived the assault. And yes – when you mow your lawn, you can only deal with the grass that the mower is wide enough to reach. But we had Apache's in the sky, covering the left flank."

I was starting to understand. "And so what was the purpose of the battle?"

Biggins regarded me carefully for a moment. "It wasn't to win," he admitted. "That wasn't the point. What we wanted to do was to test the tactic – examine the impact of a combined assault using heavy armor and artillery... and the cover of helicopters. The Battle of Rock Hill was the testing ground. We knew we didn't have enough armor to cut a deep path into South Carolina, but we needed to know whether the tactics were sound. Once we had established their validity, we could muster more armor and attack through several forts at once."

"With the ultimate goal of killing the zombies?"

"No," Biggins shook his head. "That was never possible. Our goal was to win back land. The final mission stage was called 'Operation Compress', not operation 'Kill', for a reason. We conceded that it would be impossible to wipe out the undead infestation by military conflict alone. Ultimately, this was all about an effort to drive the undead back to Florida and then quarantine the state."

"Did you lose any men during the battle? Surely it couldn't have gone exactly to script."

Biggins made a face like he was trying to decide whether he wanted to answer the question. On the surface, his explanation had sounded flawless — as though everything during the battle had proceeded with text-book efficiency. I wasn't an expert on the military, but I knew enough to realize that rarely happened. The fog of war, the unexpected... the things that could not be anticipated were often the cause of causalities and disasters.

Biggins pointed at my cell phone and frowned. I turned the record feature off.

"You sure that thing is switched off?"

"Yes."

Biggins grunted, then leaned forward, becoming an intimidating presence. "I'll give you a version for your article, and I'll give you the facts. The facts have to be off the record. Deal?"

I was intrigued, but at the same time I was conflicted. Journalism was about seeking the truth. I wasn't sure I could be comfortable with the compromise. But on the other hand I wanted to know the story... at any price.

"Okay," I said grudgingly.

Biggins seemed to relax. The tension went from his shoulders, but his expression transformed into something dark and disturbed. I could see a troubled look shift behind his hard eyes.

"Officially, the Battle of Rock Hill was a stunning military success," the Colonel declared. "Casualties were minimal. We lost less than a dozen men, and those were as a result of an accidental collision between two of the M113's that were taking part in the mopping up operation behind the battle tanks. One of those vehicles overturned, and the crew and soldiers aboard were all killed." He paused for a moment, and then said, "You can write that down for your article."

I did. I jotted a few quick notes and then laid the notebook and my pen back down on the desk. "And what about unofficially?"

Colonel Biggins rubbed his forehead and for a moment his eyes were hidden behind his hand. "We lost seventy four men, killed by the zombies," he said. "In turn, each of those infected men were terminated once they began to turn."

I stared. Gaped. The Colonel scraped his hand down his face like he was trying to change his features by rubbing them into different shapes. Suddenly he looked haggard.

"Seventy four men killed?"

The Colonel nodded. He closed his eyes for a moment and when they blinked open again they were dark and vacant. "Two of the Abrams broke down during the operation," he shrugged. "Mechanical difficulties. The vehicles were recovered after the battlefield had been cleared, but at the time, the men in those vehicles panicked. The tanks were overrun by undead. The crews radioed for help but didn't stay in their vehicles. They tried to make a run for it. By that time the line had moved on. The tanks were isolated. The M113's were closing, but couldn't get there fast enough. The crews were attacked by zombies and all killed. When the M113's arrived on the scene, they were confronted with their own comrades, turned into zombies."

The Colonel lapsed into a long silence, and I sensed there would be nothing gained by a barrage of questions. I glanced out through the window behind the desk. Men in ACU's – Army Combat Uniforms – were marching purposefully across the parade ground. Overhead, the sky was filling with dark storm clouds.

"It turned into a cluster-fuck," Colonel Biggins said bluntly. "The men in the M113's hesitated. They should have opened fire with the machine guns. They didn't. We lost five troop carriers and all the crew and soldiers aboard those vehicles. Ultimately, Command radioed for air support and three of the Apache's were called away from the left flank of the attack to terminate the infestation."

"Command? Who?" I asked. "Who gave the actual order to have those soldiers killed?"

"Me."

"Oh," I said then fell silent. "That... that must have been a difficult order to give, Colonel."

The man didn't say anything for a long time. He didn't need to. I could see the agony in his face, the torture of the memory. He sighed at last – a deep shuddering breath of air like he was deflating. "When I gave the command to go into battle I knew the risks and the dangers I was placing those boys in," Colonel Biggins said. "It's something that no leader ever becomes comfortable with. Tragedy is the close companion of triumph," he said philosophically. "It's rare that you can have one without a little of the other."

I nodded. "Is that how all commanders learn to reconcile combat casualties?" I asked.

Biggins smiled but the expression was as bleak and bitter as winter. "That's how we're supposed to do it," he said, then shook his head gravely. "But it doesn't work, son. The pain of losing good men never goes away."

THE BATTLE OF ROCK HILL
ROCK HILL, SOUTH CAROLINA

"It would have been nice if the machine guns on an Abrams were mounted in the hull, but that kind of weaponry hasn't really been popular for years," Captain Rory Walsh said to me. "You're probably thinking about Tiger tanks and Sherman's from back in World War II." He slapped his hand against the warm steel hull of the tank we were standing beside, and I had the sense that it was a gesture of affection – the way a man might pat a faithful dog. "The main machine gun on an Abrams is mounted on the turret," the captain said, and pointed. "So the Army built cages – these god-awful contraptions that were kind of like a small shark cage. We were supposed to fit them atop the tanks so we could fire the weapon from the turret hatch as the zombies came into range."

"Supposed to?"

Walsh shrugged. "They were fitted," he conceded. "Every Abrams and every Bradley in the 278th had one. It was done as part of the Army's new tactics they were employing to fight the dreads. But they didn't work," he admitted. "In theory they were fine – a steel cage so the machine gun could be operated without the danger of zombies climbing aboard the tank and attacking the gunner. But in reality, they were hopeless. Some geek in an office came up with the idea, I guess. That's the way these things usually work. Once they were fitted, we couldn't effectively traverse the turret."

"So a lot of the machine guns weren't firing during the battle of Rock Hill? Is that what you are telling me?"

The tank captain shook his head. "No," he said, "I'm telling you that a lot of the guys removed the damned cage before we went into battle. We fired from the turret and then dropped down into the tank and closed the hatch when the dreads were right beneath our tracks. It was the only way we could operate effectively."

Rory Walsh had the calm demeanor of a man that looked hard to shake. His gaze was steady, his eyes the color of a deep blue ocean. He had the slow unhurried speech and accent of someone from out west, maybe Wyoming. He had a close cut crop of sandy hair and the hint of a moustache I doubted would ever amount to much.

"The turret cage was supposed to give us a sense of security – the freedom to fire the 50 cal and the 7.62, even if there were zombies somehow climbing aboard the vehicle. But they built it without enough room to traverse the weapon. Basically all we could do was fire at what was directly in our path."

"So you didn't feel secure inside that cage once the undead came close?"

"No, sir," Walsh said. "I felt like bait."

"Bait?"

He nodded his head. "The sight of us drove them crazy. I know a lot of the other guys felt the same. I wasn't the only one to abandon the weapon and shut the hatch when we started rolling over the undead."

"Did many zombies manage to climb aboard?"

Walsh shook his head. "Hardly any, it turned out. We had removed everything from the vehicles that might have given them something to grab hold of, and we were traveling at up to forty miles an hour when we hit the open fields around Rock Hill. Even on rough terrain we had trained to keep our speed above twenty clicks."

I wrote down everything the tank commander told me and then we walked together in a slow circuit of the tank. The Abrams was a mighty monster – a steel goliath. The tracks were thick with chunks of dirt that had been torn from the ground and the rear of the vehicle was black with exhaust smoke, grimy over the paintwork of camouflage.

"Your C.O, Colonel Biggins, explained the long-line tactic, like ancient chariots. What was it like on the ground inside one of the vehicles? Was it as smooth an operation as I was led to believe?"

Walsh looked suddenly pained, as though overcome with a sudden conflict of loyalties. "Yes and no," he said vaguely. "As the commander of one of the Abrams, I can't tell you how many hours we spent drilling for the attack – too many to remember. It was day after day of precision manoeuvers, trying to keep each tank in line, trying to maintain steady speed and position in undulating terrain. I would be lying to ya if I said it went perfectly, because it didn't."

"What went wrong?"

"Communication was a bitch," the young man admitted. "Coordinating all those heavy vehicles and getting them to work as one cohesive battering ram was impossible. At one end of the line the ground was smooth, and at the other end of the line we were rolling up ten and fifteen degree inclines. One end of the line had to always be slowed to accommodate the terrain being encountered at the other end of the line. The plan was to hit the dreads at something like forty miles an hour. It never happened. As we came up towards the ridge when we first saw them, we probably weren't doing more than twenty-five."

"And afterwards?"

"The fog of war," Walsh said vaguely. "The sky was filled with smoke. The sun was blood red. I kept contact with the tanks on either side of me. That was all I could do. We were smashing through the undead like they weren't there, and they just kept coming and coming. Once we broke through the first wave, I got back up behind the machine gun and fired at the bodies we had crushed. We couldn't have done that with those shark cages. It would have been impossible."

I frowned thoughtfully. "How could you actually see where you were going?' I asked naively. "There would have been smoke and thousands of zombies crawling all over the place. How did you maintain formation?"

"It was good luck as much as good management," Walsh admitted. "The driver sees through three periscopes called vision blocks. He's also got an integrated display that gives him navigational data, speed… that kind of thing. The driver did a fine job."

"And the rest of the crew?"

"We were all in the turret basket," Walsh said. I had my loader and gunner taking turns on the machine gun once the battle started, because so much of my time was spent in contact with command, trying to co-ordinate each tank. I tell ya, it would have been easier on one of those old chariots. At least they could clearly see what they were doing and where they were going."

We started on another circuit of the Abrams. Walsh glanced at me sideways suddenly. "Do you want to climb aboard and see for yourself what it was like?"

I shook my head. As big as the Abrams was, I was claustrophobic. Sitting inside the tank would have been like sitting inside a steel coffin. "I'll take your word for it," I tried to smile and failed.

Walsh shrugged his shoulders like he was a little surprised, but not so surprised that he was going to insist. "When the battle was over and we came back to the FOB, we finally had a chance to see the way the conflict had played out on monitors during the de-briefing," the young tank commander explained. "Observer helicopters had been in the air, ya see. One of them carried journalists but the rest were following the battle, recording the conflict for analysis. Between those birds, Command was hovering above us, trying to co-ordinate the attack. When we came back and played through the tape, it was like a football team on Monday morning going over the weekend game."

I thanked Captain Walsh for his time. I realized I needed a different perspective of this epic battle that had begun to turn the tide against the zombies. I wanted a broad overview – a sense of how vast the conflict had been.

I needed to speak to a journalist.

Another perspective from the Battle of Rock Hill

Tracy Camberwell lined me up in the viewfinder and snapped off three quick shots before I could react.

"I'm supposed to be interviewing you," I reminded her casually.

Camberwell smiled and flicked an errant strand of long black hair away from her face. She set down her camera and crossed her legs. "Occupational hazard," she said.

We were sitting by the side of a road, just outside the town limits of what remained of Rock Hill. The scene was one of devastation; torn mangled iron, crumbled rubble that had once been buildings. The road had been heaved up and broken by relentless artillery fire. Everything was grey and dusty and destroyed.

Camberwell was a seasoned journalist – a war correspondent who had filed reports from Syria, Iraq, Afghanistan and the troubled African continent. She worked with a camera and a laptop, filing freelance news releases for several of the world's major media outlets. But like many correspondents, she had returned to America when the zombie infection had spread like wildfire through the southern states, reporting as one of a handful of journalists who had been embedded with the US Army throughout the epic zombie war.

"I got this for you," I said. "To thank you for this interview." I reached into my bag and held up a bottle of shampoo. Tracy's eyes grew wide with astonishment. She reached out for the plastic bottle and I handed it to her. She snapped the lid open and inhaled. "It smells like apples," she said with a wistful smile. "Thank you!"

I nodded. The shampoo had cost me a small bottle of scotch, traded to a dubious character lurking in a dark Nashville alley.

Camberwell was wearing a man's shirt and pair of dusty denim jeans. She rolled up the sleeves of the shirt until her forearms were bare. Her hands were those of a woman who had worked for a living. She wore no rings, no nail polish.

She uncrossed her legs and then held a hand up to her face to shield her eyes from the low angle of the afternoon sun.

"We flew directly over this place," Camberwell said after a long moment of silence, the tone of her voice haunting and reminiscent. "At the time it was teeming with zombies. They were swarming towards the sound of the oncoming tanks. It was quite incredible – a seething mass of bodies moving like a wave."

Her voice tailed away as a gust of wind scattered debris and dirt into the air. All around us was the flat grey rubble of a wasteland. The wind moaned through the broken buildings like it does through the shifting dunes of a desert.

"You were in one of the observation Black Hawks, right?"

She nodded, and then turned her face to fix me with her gaze. "Yes," she said softly. "There were four of us – all print media journalists, naturally."

"Naturally," I nodded my head. The Army had refused all television media requests to film or broadcast any footage of the apocalypse. No media aircraft were permitted to cross the no-fly zone beyond the 36th parallel. The only journalists offered the opportunity to cover the military response to the zombie outbreak were newspaper journalists, and even their photographs were censored before publication was permitted. The government's control over what the American public had witnessed of the outbreak had been rigid and strict.

"What was it like?" I asked.

Interviewing another journalist isn't as easy a task as it might seem. To the casual observer, another journalist would appear to be the perfect interview subject – after all they know the kind of comments that work for media and they know the value of accurate description. But it often doesn't work that way. Sometimes journalists can be the hardest interviews of all, because they tend to filter the spontaneous honesty of their comments like they're writing the copy in their heads before committing to the words.

Camberwell shrugged her shoulders, and then flicked me a wry smile. We were old friends. We had worked on a major newspaper together several years earlier.

"C'mon, Tracy," I said. "Make it easy on me."

She laughed, and the sound was one of unaffected delight – like the tinkle of a delicate crystal bell. It seemed out of place in such a desolate place of devastation. She nodded her head.

"The whole town had been flattened by the artillery fire before we got in the air," she said. "So when we flew over, it already looked pretty much like it does now."

I nodded. "What did you see from the Black Hawk?"

"Tanks," Tracy Camberwell said. "Hundreds of them rolling down from the north," she flung her hand at the distance, indicating the direction the 278th's armor had appeared from on the day the battle had been fought. "I think that whole ridge had once been forested... but you would never know it now. As we flew over, all we could see from the air was grey rubble and brown earth."

"Like... what? Give me a word picture."

"Like the images I've seen in the history books," she said softly. "Like the fields of Europe during the Great War." She shivered involuntarily and hugged her arms around her shoulders. "John, it was like flying over an alien world. And the tanks – these huge great steel monsters racing across the ground in one long line..." she went quiet and began to slowly shake her head. "... It was unreal."

I raised an eyebrow and regarded Tracy carefully. She was a seasoned journalist who had reported the cruel savagery of war for over two decades. Now she was in her mid-forties. I had a high regard for her work, and for her as a person. Most journalists became bitter and cynical after a time, but not this lady. She had an integrity about her I envied and admired. But I found it hard to believe that a woman of her quality and experience couldn't come up with a better word than 'unreal' to describe the events leading up to the epic battle of Rock Hill.

I stayed quiet for a few moments, just watching her face – studying the distance in her gaze that gave her expression a kind of dazed cast. I had no doubt she was replaying those images in her mind. And I waited.

"I've never seen so many tanks on a battlefield," Camberwell said slowly. "And never in such a formation. It was a long line, like they were charging on horses towards the undead. I could see the licks of flame from the machine guns. The Black Hawk pilot flew along the line as the tanks rumbled across the ground, and it was the most awesome, terrifying sight I had ever seen. It was incomprehensible just how much power the Army was unleashing. It was a steel battering ram, travelling at high speed. It couldn't be stopped."

I nodded. "I think that was the plan," I said gently.

Tracy Camberwell looked up into my face and her eyes snapped back into focus. She took a deep breath and her shoulders heaved. "Yes, well they were right," she said. "The zombies came towards the sound in their thousands."

"Did you actually see the zombies? Did you see what happened when the tanks rolled over them?"

Camberwell nodded her head. "There were thousands of them down to the south, maybe a couple of miles from where we are sitting," she said and scribed directions in the air with her hand. "They were like ants – like the ones you see in the Amazon rainforests. They swarmed towards the sound of the tanks in one solid heaving mass of rage. We were circling overhead, maybe three or four hundred feet above the town. The tanks came through the devastation of these buildings and the actual contact took place just past that fold in the ground up ahead, there."

I was fascinated. I got to my feet. Camberwell stood as well.

"Do you feel like a walk?" I asked. "I'd like to take a closer look."

Camberwell dusted dirt off the bottoms of her jeans and we stepped through the debris of broken buildings, following the crumbled path of a road that had been torn up by tank tracks and massed artillery. When we reached the wreckage of the last building we stopped and I swept my eyes across the barren landscape.

I had the sense that once this had been a lush green field, spattered with stands of trees. But now the ground was heaved into unnatural undulations that were the result of shell bursts and the churn of over one hundred armored vehicles. The ground was bare earth, with errant tufts of green grass and gay splashes of color where weeds had begun to flower.

"Can you tell me what you saw?" I asked Tracy Camberwell again.

She put one hand on her hip and shifted her weight. The breeze was picking up. It flattened her shirt against her chest and tugged at the tendrils of her hair. She clawed it into a ponytail and tied it with a rubber band that had been around her wrist.

"The entire skyline was filled with bodies – undead zombies that just poured over the distant rise in a solid press," she said.

"And the tanks?"

"They came right through here," Camberwell explained, "Right where we are standing, spread out in a long line that reached all the way to our left as far as that distant ridge."

"And you were in a Black Hawk directly overhead when this happened?"

She nodded. "There were other helicopters flying over that ridge on our left I told you about," she said. "The

Army had a dozen Apache helicopters thick in the sky. I think they were to stop the zombies from spilling around the end of the line and getting to the troops that were following in the carriers."

I nodded. I knew that already. I said nothing.

"As the tanks came through this field they accelerated. We could see this huge wall of dust and dirt kicked into the air like a smoke screen as they roared towards the ridge. The sky turned brown and the haze of smoke from the artillery and the exhausts of the engines thickened the air."

"But you saw what happened – even through the dirt and the smoke?"

Camberwell nodded. "I saw," she said. "And I took photos."

I nodded. "Tell me what was in those photos, Tracy. Tell me what happened when the tanks raced towards the ridge where the zombies were."

"It was a massacre," her voice became an eerie whisper. "The tanks rolled right through the zombies like they weren't there. Thousands of them – literally thousands of them were crushed under the tracks of the tanks."

"And the zombies? What did they do once they tanks hit them?"

Camberwell shrugged her shoulders. "Some tried to clamber aboard the Abrams, and a few succeeded. I think the Army must have had some kind of a rule that insisted no tank stop for any reason, because they kept moving. As the zombies climbed onto the tanks they were thrown off. Most of them didn't get that far. Most of them were cut down by all the machine guns, and then crushed under the tracks."

"How did the zombies look as they reached the tanks?"

Camberwell frowned and glanced at me like it was the dumbest question she had ever been asked.

"What do you mean?" she tilted her head curiously.

"I wanted to know whether the massed artillery had an impact," I explained. "If the zombies that swarmed towards the tanks were all running like berserkers, then clearly the artillery wasn't effective."

She understood. She frowned thoughtfully. "We couldn't see that clearly," she said hastily, but I do think the artillery worked. The zombies didn't hit the tanks in one long line. It was more fractured than that. It was like a comet."

"A what?"

"A comet."

I scratched the side of my nose and frowned. "What the hell does that mean?"

Camberwell sighed. "It was like this big explosion of rage against the tanks, but there was a long tail of undead behind the first wave. They were slower, struggling. I think that's what the artillery did – it slowed a lot of them down."

This was all making sense, and matching with other accounts of the battle I had heard. I nodded, and took Tracy by the elbow, guiding her down a gentle slope of ground to where I had spotted a shard of white bone, buried in the earth.

I crouched down and scraped around the edges of the bone with the tip of my pen like an archaeologist who had discovered some rare fossil. The bone was just a fragment – no larger than a box of matches.

"They're all like that, I would guess," Camberwell said. "Fractured. Shattered. Crushed." She was standing close beside me. I looked up into the sun so that her figure was silhouetted and the expression on her face masked by shadow. But the tone of her voice carried a sudden trace of melancholy. I got to my feet. My knees cracked.

"Are you okay? I asked.

Camberwell nodded. Her lips were pressed into a thin pale line. "Tens of thousands of zombies were slaughtered during the Battle of Rock Hill," she said, measuring her words. "The ones that weren't killed by the artillery barrage, were killed by the machine guns as the tanks raced towards them. The ones that weren't killed by the machine guns were crushed under the monstrous weight of the tanks as they rolled over the top of them. Anything that survived was killed by the men in the personnel carriers that followed a few miles behind the tanks... and anything that survived all that was gunned down by the Apache helicopters."

I nodded. "And that's a good thing," I said. "It proved the Army's tactics worked. Rock Hill was a great victory for the Army. It was the first conflict during the war where we took the fight to the zombies and crushed them."

Camberwell nodded. "Yeah," she said without any enthusiasm. "And on the surface, you're right. The zombies were massacred and we won an important victory."

"But..."

"But we forgot they were once *people*," Camberwell said. She wrung her hands together. "During the war, the enemy was zombies, but they were also victims. They were victims before they became zombies – before they became the enemy. We lost our humanity, John. We saw them as a dangerous threat, and they were. But before all that – before they became infected zombies, *they were our brothers and sisters, our mothers, fathers, sons and daughters*. Somewhere along the line we forgot that. We forgot to remember that once, these undead were our fellow Americans."

I stared at Camberwell, and saw the glitter of unshed tears welling in her eyes. It was that aspect of humanity she had become famous for as a journalist. She saw what others didn't. She remembered what the rest of us forgot.

"You're right," I conceded softly. "They were Americans, Tracy. They went to ball games, celebrated Christmas and Thanksgiving. They worked at jobs and loved their kids." I looked back down at the shard of white bone and saw it in a new, somber light. "But when you're fighting for survival…"

"I know," she nodded. She rested her hand lightly on my forearm and I fell silent. "I just want people to remember, that's all," she said. "That's why I'm still writing. That's the passion that keeps me working as a journalist. I want readers to know that every victory we celebrated against the zombie hordes was also a terrible tragedy for the American people, and a terrible, terrible conflict for our fighting men and women."

Another perspective from the Battle of Rock Hill

"I'm not flying at the moment," Buddy Nichols said as he stared down at his hands. They were shaking – a gentle but persistent tremor that couldn't quite be controlled. "I haven't even been near an Apache helicopter again since…"

I nodded and gnawed sympathetically at my lip. I felt the man's pain, his anguish and the deep emotional scars that the Battle of Rock Hill had seared into this young pilot's consciousness.

They were wounds that might never heal.

"You were piloting one of the Apaches choppers that Command pulled away from the left flank of the battle when the M113's were overrun, right?"

Nichols nodded his head. "That's right," he said in a voice that was soft as a whisper.

Every journalist has his or her own moral and ethical compass. We each decide how to handle an interview, and whether an interview should even be conducted. I've seen some TV reporters thrust microphones into the faces of grieving parents who are distraught at the death of a loved one, and that kind of aggressive, careless reporting makes me cringe.

We were sitting under the canvas roof of a makeshift Army Hospital tent behind the lines. Buddy Nichols was perched on the edge of a narrow cot, hunched over with his head bowed and his elbows resting on his knees, staring down at his hands that wouldn't stop shaking.

I set down my notepad.

"We don't need to do this interview," I made the decision. "I don't want you to re-live those moments if it's too traumatic for you."

Buddy's head shot up sharply and he stared hard into my eyes. There was a tortured, beseeching expression on his face, twisting his mouth into a grimace. "I want to…" he said and then broke off the sentence. "I *need* to…"

We spent a long moment staring at each other before I nodded my head slowly. I left my notepad on the ground. "I'm not going to ask you any questions, Buddy," I said softly, "but if you feel you need to talk about what happened that day at Rock Hill, I'm keen to hear your story – whatever parts of it you feel like you want to share."

His head jerked. He swallowed hard, and then his eyes lost their intensity and his gaze became distant. He turned his face a little, like he was staring at some invisible television screen just past my left shoulder. He wrung his hands and clenched his fists so that his knuckles turned white.

"We were covering the left flank of the battlefield," he said slowly. There was a hollow kind of echo in his voice so that the words seemed to come from far, far away. "We were working low, and firing at the zombies that threatened to sweep around the edge of the tank line. Then Command called us up with an urgent order. The line had been broken and several of the M113's were under attack."

Buddy Nichols rubbed his brow the way a man does when his head is pounding. There were beads of perspiration on his top lip like he was in the grips of a fever. An orderly in a crisp clean uniform leaned over Buddy's shoulder. He was carrying a small white plastic cup and a handful of tablets. The orderly smiled in the benign perfunctory manner of someone with too many other patients waiting for attention. Nichols accepted the cup and set it down beside him on the cot.

"At first we didn't understand – we didn't realize the crews of those carriers had been infected," Nichols said. "We thought it was a breach in the line between a couple of the Abrams. We turned west and flew back along the advancing line of tanks. The zombies were like ants – swarming ants thick on the ground. We could see the heavy tanks crushing them and the trails of blood and gore like… like snail trails across the grass and dirt. In the distance, to the south, we could see the troops in the M113's mopping up. There was a cluster of the vehicles parked at crazy angles, and a tight knot of the undead around the troops. The undead were in uniform. That was when we realized the crews were being overwhelmed – infected."

"And you opened fire?"

Nichols shook his head. "No," he said. "Not immediately. We radioed back to command, told them what was happening to the crews of those M113's."

"And then…?"

"Command repeated the order to execute the attack."

Buddy chewed his lip. He started clenching and releasing his hands. I could see unshed tears welling up in his reddened bloodshot eyes. "I gave the order to my co-pilot gunner. I told him to open fire."

I said nothing. Nichols wrenched his mouth into a twist of pain and began to sob softly. A tear ran down the man's cheek and he cuffed it away with the sleeve of his uniform.

"Once wasn't enough," the Apache pilot muttered. "If it had been, then... then maybe it would have been all right. But the zombies... the guys that had been in the M113's kept getting up," his voice pitched higher with the stab of his anguish. "We had to sweep over them again, and again. We fired until there was nothing left of them — nothing but mush and gore and blood." His voice trailed off into tortured silence. He gave a long shuddering breath and his shoulders heaved as if the burden of some great weight had been lifted from him.

I reached out and shook his hand. I thanked him for his service to our country. Buddy Nichols stared at me like he was seeing right through me — seeing something else entirely.

"They were our men," he croaked, his voice strangled by his despair. "One minute they were American soldiers... and the next..."

OUTSIDE OF ROCK HILL CITY LIMITS, SOUTH CAROLINA

As I sat and watched the man picking through the ruins of his life, I wondered if this was how it felt for the survivors of Hurricane Katrina. I wondered if it might be the same overwhelming flood of emotions that swept over those who had lost their home in a forest fire, or any other terrible natural disaster.

It was a wrenching experience.

The house that had kept him and his family safe was gone now, destroyed in the battle and the relentless bombardment of artillery that had turned the surrounding farmland to cratered dirt. But even though many months had passed since the day he had been rescued by the Army, this moment was still filled with powerful emotion for him.

He knelt over a small jewelry box and lifted the lid like he was peeling open a tender wound. I heard the soft tinkle of broken music, and the man's shoulders began to shake as he sobbed.

Karl Penrose stood slowly and clutched the tiny box tight within his hand. He turned towards me and shook his head in a silent gesture of despair. He took a couple of halting steps and then stopped again, sifting through the empty recesses of his memory.

The compound walls that surrounded the man's home had been reduced to rubble. The wrought iron gate was a twisted mangle, and the land had become overgrown by weeds. Of the house itself, nothing remained but for the blackened burned beams that had supported the roof. Clay tiles lay like shattered pieces of glass amongst fragments of crockery – chipped cups and broken plates. Penrose's steps through the wreckage were like the reverent footfalls of a man respectfully making his way through a cemetery. He came to where I stood at last, and let out a long anguished sigh that had been choked in the back of his throat.

"There's nothing else," he said. His voice was hollow. He held the jewelry box up to show me. It was a small wooden shape, covered in dust. The corners had been chipped, the timber battered. "My daughter's…" the words drifted away and he fell silent.

I glanced down at the old photograph I held in my hand – the photo he had given me when we had first arrived. The image showed a home like a Hollywood mansion: leafy green trees behind a high solid fence that surrounded the entire property.

He was a tall man, stooped at the shoulders as though the weight of those months surrounded by the zombie horde had crushed him. He had a long straggly beard, and was dressed in flowing robes and sandals. He looked like some ancient biblical figure who had wandered lost in the desert. His face was deeply lined, the skin burned to the color of old leather. His hair was white and hung lank to his shoulders. He scraped it away from his face with the back of his hand and lifted his eyes to mine. They were empty.

"How long did you hold out here?" I asked. My voice was soft, as though to talk too loud would break the heavy spell that seemed cast over this wasteland.

"We didn't flee when we heard about the outbreak," Karl Penrose answered. His voice was unusually high-pitched so that it seemed wrong for his body. "Everyone else we knew packed up their cars and ran north," he said. "Those first few days were a madness of panic. There was looting and riots. At night I could hear the gunfire and the screech of tires. Civilization seemed to collapse. Friends turned on friends. Neighbors abandoned each other to fend for themselves. It was Armageddon. It was a horror ripped straight from the pages of an apocalypse."

"But you didn't flee? You and your family stayed here, on your property."

Penrose nodded. "My daddy always told me it was best to be prepared," he said softly. "I learned that as a small boy, and I never forgot it." He set the little jewelry box down on the ground and sat beside me on a mound of grey rubble. "For a long time people used to look at me like I was crazy," he confessed suddenly. "They'd watch me walking down the street, or see me in a store and laugh behind my back." He shrugged, like he was shrugging off all that ridicule. "It never bothered me," he said. "It bothered the wife and my children, of course. They felt like pariahs. This area was pretty close-knit. Everyone knew everyone else. It wasn't much fun being regarded as the local 'crazy old fool'."

"I can imagine," I said kindly. "But you had the last laugh, didn't you?"

He looked at me like it was a poor choice of words. And, on reflection, it was.

"People laughed at me. I never laughed at them," he made the point. "Folks used to call me Noah. They would torment my children, and called the compound here an 'Ark'. The kids were social outcasts. Everyone stayed away from us. It was hard on the children and my wife. It really was."

I noticed I had asked the man two fairly specific questions, and he hadn't answered either one directly. I tried again.

"Why did you decide to stay here? Why didn't you leave and head north where your safety was assured?"

Penrose smiled thinly. "I didn't believe our safety would be assured by heading north," he countered. "There was nothing to guarantee we would have a place to stay, and nothing to assure me that we would be able to make headway in the jams of panicked traffic. And there was no guarantee that food and water and electricity would be available." He shook his head. "To me the danger was in fleeing. The only way I could assure my family's safety was to stay right here."

"Because you were prepared?"

"Yes," he said. "I've been preparing for disaster for years. At first it was because I had children. I started stockpiling drinking water and canned food. Then I looked around me one day and saw what was happening in the world around us. Terrorism, militants, food shortages... horror on every page of the newspapers and on every TV station. I knew it could only end one way."

"What did you do?"

"I got serious about survival," he said. "I felt it was every person's duty to ensure the safety of their loved ones in the event of a disaster. I started researching. I learned about survival techniques, and we created a vegetable garden in

218

the back yard of the compound. We learned to become self-sufficient. Then I began gathering weapons – even taught the children how to fire bows and cross-bows. We got ready for the inevitable."

I had to ask the question. "What if you had been wrong? What if you had devoted so much of your life to preparing for a disaster that never came? Wouldn't you have felt cheated?"

Karl Penrose looked hard into my eyes for long seconds. He narrowed his gaze. "I would have been thrilled," he said. "It would have delighted me if this day had never come."

"So you didn't see this zombie apocalypse as some kind of vindication?"

"No," he said flatly. "I prepared for a disaster event just like the way people take out insurance. Health insurance, life insurance… I took out my kind of insurance. I don't regret the investment of time and energy, and I wished it had never come to this."

We sat in silence for a few moments. I set my notebook down and we just listened to the singing of the insects. The day was warm – the kind of warm that makes the mornings inviting, and the afternoons oppressive. Karl Penrose scuffed his sandals in the dirt, as though he might uncover some small precious fragment of his old life just below the surface. He didn't.

"When the zombies came, how did you react? Can you tell me what happened when you first saw them?"

"We had spotlights along the top of the walls overlooking the ground beyond," he said. "And we had more spotlights around the house to light the entire compound, all powered from a generator. We knew they were coming," he said.

"How?"

"By the panic, and then by the screaming." He stood up, stretched his back, and then sat back down again. "At first we could hear the blood-curdling screams. They were coming from that a ways," he pointed towards an area of destroyed rubble that might have once been a suburban street. "Then there was gunfire. Not just the occasional shot. This was a panicked fusillade. I got Milly and the kids inside and went around the compound making sure the gate was bolted and chained."

"What happened next?"

Karl Penrose became distraught. His eyes clouded over. "Vicki Creighton suddenly appeared at the gate."

"Vicki Creighton?"

"One of our neighbors," Karl explained. "The lady who lived a couple of doors down the road from us. She suddenly appeared in the night, bashing against the gate and screaming for help."

"What did you do?"

"I... I watched her," Karl said softly.

"You didn't let her in?"

He shook his head. "I couldn't," he said. "There wasn't time. The undead were swarming over the streets. I could see them moving in the night. They were howling and hunting in packs. They were tearing at people. Literally tearing at them. The screams were the most horrible sounds I have ever heard in my life."

"And Vicki Creighton?"

"She was covered in blood. I didn't know if she'd already been bitten. She was bleeding from the nose, and there was blood dripping down her face from a cut she must have had on her head. There was blood all over her dress and running down her legs. She shook the gate and she was crying and screaming for help. I couldn't take the chance..."

"You let her get killed?"

"I protected my family."

"What happened to her?"

Penrose shook his head. "I don't know," he admitted. "I walked slowly back towards the house. I could hear Vicki screaming at me – pleading for me to help her. Then she cried out – louder and more piercing."

"And then?"

Penrose looked down at his sandals. "Then she was gone. She had been taken by the undead. All that was left was a pool of blood at the gate."

"What happened next?"

Penrose seemed to lift a little, like he was relieved to change the subject. "I took Milly and the kids up onto the roof," he said. "We had a two-story house, and I had a rooftop porch built, like an observation platform. It was overgrown with vines because we had incorporated it as a trellis for our vegetables. We stood on the porch and watched the unfolding horror."

"Could you see much?"

"Enough," Penrose said. "The power was still on in some parts of the suburb, but by then there were dozens of houses on fire. Cars too. Everything seemed to be burning. The zombies were shadows against the flames, and the sound of the terrified screaming measured their progress. They swept around the compound and spilled across the road, heading north."

"Did you open fire?"

"No," Penrose said. "It was pointless. What help could I have been? A few shots in the darkness at running zombies wouldn't help anyone. I decided to save the ammunition. I figured I needed every round to protect my family."

"But you said the zombies swept past the compound."

He nodded. "They did – the first night."

"So they came back?"

He nodded again. His expression became darker. He shook his head. "I don't know if they could sense us, or if they could maybe hear us... I just don't know. But by the

221

following morning, the compound was surrounded by zombies."

"That must have been terrifying."

He looked at me as if it was something he had never considered before. He frowned a little and stroked his fingers through the strands of his beard. "It was, actually," he said at last. "I stayed up through the night. I kept guard at the gate. I could see them moving in the shadows, but the spotlights on the walls only reached fifty feet beyond the compound. I didn't know what was in the night. I didn't know until sunrise came. That was when I realized we were surrounded by hundreds of them."

"What did you do?"

Karl Penrose shrugged. "I stayed calm," he said. "I knew we were safe behind the walls, and we had plenty of food and water – everything we needed to last for months. We had power, fuel stored. It was all there. It was just a matter of waiting them out."

"As simple as that?" I found it hard to believe that anyone could remain calm when hundreds of undead zombies were howling for your blood, separated by just an iron gate and a wall. "You didn't go all Rambo, or something?"

"Shooting them all, you mean?"

I nodded. That's exactly what I meant.

Penrose shook his head. "There was no point," he said. The man had an inner tranquility about him that seemed utterly unshakable. "I didn't have enough ammunition to kill them all, and I was pretty sure opening fire on them would just attract more by the sound of gunfire."

"So you just sat tight – went about your normal daily life?"

He smiled, but there was no humor in the gesture. The expression slipped off the side of his mouth. "Daily life?" his voice became hollow and wistful. "I don't think any of us will ever experience normal daily life again."

"So what did you do?" I persisted. The man's evasiveness to direct questions was becoming a little annoying. With a shave and a suit, he would have made a fine politician.

"We endured," he said, like the words were a family motto. "We waited until the authorities got control of the outbreak and came back to free us."

"You waited several months."

"Yes."

"And then you nearly got killed when the tanks rolled through."

"No."

"No?"

"No," he said again. "We were rescued by helicopters a few days before the battle. The sky was filled with Black Hawks for forty-eight hours. They must have been sweeping the area looking for any survivors before the artillery barrage and the tank assault. They saw the sign we had painted on the roof. They lifted us to safety."

I nodded. Karl Penrose seemed completely unshakable. "What about your family?" I lobbed the question like a grenade. "How did the months in the compound affect your wife and two children?"

Karl Penrose could have thrown himself over the grenade and smothered the impact. I would never have known the truth. But he didn't. He looked at me with a sudden flood of compassion in his eyes, like I had at last, probed a deep wound.

"My wife – she hates me," he admitted. "She's gone to Canada to live with her mother, and she has taken the children with her."

I was shocked and bewildered by the sudden admission. "I don't understand."

Penrose shrugged his bony shoulders and stared fixedly down into the dirt. "When the helicopters came," he said slowly, like it was a struggle to form every word," I… I tried to wave them off. I didn't want them to rescue us."

What the hell?

"What do you mean — *exactly?*" I asked with a dawning sense of horror. "Why would you do that?"

Penrose didn't look at me. His eyes moved evasively. They focused on the small jewelry box between his feet. "I thought we were safer in the compound than we would be in the outside world," he tried to explain himself to the dirt. "We had everything we needed here. We were self-sufficient. We had water and food, and the garden would have provided for us. We had a stockpile of fuel for the generator. It was safe and secure. It was an oasis away from the horror of the unfolding world."

"So you refused to leave?"

He nodded at the jewelry box. "I refused to let the helicopter crew take any of us. I clung to my kids, and they had to draw their weapons on me."

"You mean you… what? You held the kids like hostages?"

He nodded.

"And what happened?"

"One of the helicopter crew hit me and pinned me to the ground. Then they dragged me into the helicopter."

I sat back and stared at the blue sky, stunned. Penrose sighed heavily and then turned his face until he was gazing at a pile of rubble that had once been a part of the compound wall. "I just thought we would be safer if we stayed here…" he said softly to the pile of bricks and crumbled mortar.

I guess he got tired of talking to the dirt.

FORT DETRICK, MARYLAND:
USAMRIID HEADQUARTERS

Sergeant Major Julio Moranes arrived for the interview perspiring, and out of breath.

He was a slight man, lean rather than muscled. He was wearing sweat-stained fatigues and an olive drab t-shirt. He had a towel draped around the back of his neck. He shook my hand and then used the towel to mop across his brow.

The sound of the man's steps echoed through the big empty arena of the gymnasium, loud on the timber floor. He dropped wearily down onto a weight bench, caught a glimpse of himself in one of the wall mirrors, and then smiled ruefully.

"Sorry," he said. "I've been for a five mile run."

I made a face. "Too much exercise can kill you," I quipped.

He looked back at me. "So can no exercise at all."

Touché.

I had found a plastic chair against a wall to sit on while I had waited. I reached into my bag for a notebook.

"You and the rest of your USAMRIID team were the first ones to discover the bodies at Fort Mill," I said.

The Sergeant Major nodded. The United States Army Medical Research Institute of Infectious Diseases troops had been the first men on the ground after the Battle of Rock Hill. "That's correct," Moranes said. "We were air-lifted into the area around Charlotte about a week after the battle."

"For what reason?"

"Intelligence and information," the Sergeant Major said. "The Army wanted a close monitor on the effects of the infection in an urban area. We figured it was part of the larger plan."

I frowned. "So this wasn't part of the re-occupation of the dead zone then, was it?"

"No. It was not," Moranes said. "We were flown into the area by Black Hawks. They dropped teams of us along route I77. My men and I were lifted to Fort Mill."

"How did you feel about that?"

The Sergeant Major seemed to think carefully before he answered. "We knew we were being placed in harm's way," he admitted frankly. "The Battle had been fought just a week earlier. We had been told the undead had been slaughtered and driven back towards Columbia…"

"But…?"

He shrugged. "We didn't believe that *every* dread had been taken out," he confessed.

"So you thought it was possible that zombies were still active in Charlotte and the surrounding towns?"

"Yes."

"That must have been a difficult assignment," I tried to prompt the man to open up a little. "You must have been scared."

"Sure," Sergeant Major Moranes said. "We were in full-faceplate biohazard outfits, and communication between each member of the team was through two-way radio. Hell, the air packs we wore weighed forty pounds. Just moving around was an effort."

"All that biohazard gear…" I began curiously. "That was to protect against a zombie attack?"

Moranes shrugged. "It was to protect against every possible risk of infection," he said instead. "We didn't know what we would be walking into."

I nodded, and then asked the sixty-four thousand dollar question. "What *did* you walk into?"

Moranes buried his face in the towel for a moment. His forearms were glistening with sweat. The air in the room was stuffy. It smelled of liniment. When he looked up and lifted his eyes to mine, his expression was bleak.

"We walked into hell," he said softly. His eyes had a haunted hypnotic stare, the pupils like little pinpricks. He was looking directly at me, but visualizing somewhere else entirely.

"Tell me," I said softly.

Moranes sighed. "The Black Hawks were circling in the sky, the crew chiefs at their miniguns looking for signs of zombies," he said, "while we were on the ground, sifting through the rubble."

"In Charlotte?"

He nodded. "There were teams in Charlotte. Most of the city had been utterly destroyed before the battle. Fort Mill was the same. The artillery and the Air Force had laid waste to just about every building. When we jumped out of the helicopter it was like stepping into some third-world war zone," he muttered.

"Did you have other soldiers on the ground with you?"

Moranes nodded. "We landed with a Marine escort," he said. "They shadowed us while we worked, and while the choppers kept top cover."

"What were you looking for?" I asked. "What was the point of sending USAMRIID troops into areas like Fort Mill?"

"We were looking to measure the effectiveness of the artillery bombardment and the air bombing," the Sergeant Major explained. "It was an intelligence gathering mission. We had biohazard bags and we went through the rubble collecting samples."

"Samples?"

He nodded. "Pieces of zombie," he said.

"That must have been..." my voice tailed off because I couldn't think of any conceivable word that would be suitable.

"Gruesome," Moranes said. "It was gruesome. We had multi-layer gloves. They were so thick we could barely grip anything, and we were foraging through the debris collecting limbs and heads – lots of heads. We bagged them all up and left them in a pile at an intersection for when the Black Hawks came back down to retrieve us."

"And is that how you found the bodies – the civilians at Fort Mill?"

The Sergeant Major nodded. "Eventually," he said. "We worked in teams, picking over the site. We didn't comb through every building because we were sampling. One of the other men and myself found the dead in a basement."

"Tell me about that moment," I insisted in a gentle voice. "Describe to me what you saw."

The Sergeant Major's tone began gruff, like he was forcing the words from his throat. "The house had been blown apart by the bombing," he said softly. "There wasn't really anything left except piles of brick, covered in grey dust. The building must have taken a direct hit – there was rubble strewn across the lawn and pieces of the roof in a nearby tree. It was like the whole street had been torn to pieces by a twister."

"And the people?"

He nodded. "The basement," he said. "When we started picking through the debris we moved a pile of broken rubble. It was covering a small square door built into the floor, like a trap door. The door was broken and hanging off its hinges, so we were just staring down into a broken black hole. There were smears of blood on the wood."

"And the people were down there?"

"There was a ladder. I climbed down."

Moranes fell silent. I waited. He wrung his hands and then wiped them on his fatigues as though the sensation of what he had touched that day was still on his fingertips. "They were all dead, he said finally. Every one of them."

"Were they killed by the bombing?" I prodded.

The soldier shook his head. "They had suffocated," he said, as if it was the most remarkable and bitterly ironic moment he had ever witnessed. "There had been an air vent to the basement concealed in the back yard amongst the plants of a garden. It had been blocked off by falling debris from the shelling. The people had tried to claw their way out through the trap door, but they couldn't shift the rubble. The basement had become their tomb."

It was so cruel. The people in that dark hole had survived for months while the zombie plague had raged above them. Then they had been killed by the very same bombardment that would have liberated and saved them.

"How many?" I asked.

"A man, a woman and six children," Moranes said. "They were all laying in bunks, as though they had been sleeping."

"And you're sure they died of suffocation?"

The man nodded. "The basement was an enormous underground kind of bunker. The people must have been preppers. They had canned foods, plenty of fresh water..."

"Just no luck," I said.

Moranes nodded like I had uttered some deep and meaningful universal truth. "That's right," he said with an empty voice. "Just no luck."

I left it at that. I closed my notebook and stuffed it back into my bag. Moranes seemed surprised that the interview had ended so abruptly. He looked up into my face, and there was a twist of puzzlement across his mouth. "Is that all you wanted to know about – that family in Fort Mill?"

I shrugged. "Is there anything else that happened on that day you wanted to talk about?"

Moranes looked blank. "I... I just thought you wanted to interview me about the heads – the zombie heads," he said.

I frowned, and there was a sudden tingle of something up my spine. Maybe it was a journalistic instinct. Maybe it was just a sense of premonition. I sat back down again and lied.

"Of course," I said. "I'm sorry. I was so drawn in by the tragic story of that poor family, I completely forgot. The zombie heads. That must have been a defining moment in the war against the undead, right?"

I hoped so.

I was going out on a limb, feigning knowledge. Sergeant Major Moranes knew something, and he clearly thought that I knew the same information.

I didn't.

"Yeah, I guess it was," he admitted. "When we were out there in the field, gathering the remains, we all thought it was purely for analysis of the skulls. You know – trying to determine the effect of our artillery by the impact wounds and evidence of fragmentation."

"Of course."

"It was only later that it occurred to us all that we were actually gathering the first samples of undead for scientific analysis," he said. "The Battle of Rock Hill was the first time the Army went into the field and collected extensive specimens that could be analyzed by the USAMRIID scientists."

I furrowed my brow. "Didn't the Army have other undead corpses that they were studying – trying to trace the cause of the infection and work on antidotes before then?"

"No," Moranes shook his head.

"But what about the Battle of Four Seasons? That was months before Rock Hill. There was a hundred thousand of the undead spread across the ground. Surely other

USAMRIID teams went through the remains and gathered samples for analysis."

"No," Moranes said again.

"Why?"

"The infection was still spreading – it hadn't reached saturation point," the Sergeant Major explained. "The zombies were still killing survivors, infecting them during those first weeks and months of the outbreak. Our scientists had to wait until there were no more people left; to be sure the virus wasn't a mutation. We needed a pure strain of the infection before we could determine its origins. That's why we were on the ground that day along the I77."

It had indeed been a pivotal moment – a turning point in the history of America. Without the gruesome work done by men like Julio Moranes, the western world would never have ultimately traced the virus back to Iran's insidious act of terror.

BOSTON, MASSACHUSETTS:

It was one of those little streets that looked like it had been photographed for a travel brochure. Golden leaves fell from the trees and drifted into the gutters, and as I climbed the steps and tapped lightly on the door I could hear the strains of classical music from within.

A young man answered the door. He had a narrow serious face and a pallid complexion, as if he hadn't been out in the sunshine for months.

"Culver?"

"Yes."

The room he led me into was a jumble of books and files – an organized chaos that had taken an adult lifetime to accumulate. Somewhere under the mess, I was sure there was furniture. Two of the walls were lost to full-length bookcases, and a ladder on rollers that allowed access to the shelves near the ceiling. The room smelled of dust, and yesterday's cat food. There was a window set into the wall opposite, and beneath the misted panes of glass sat Professor Igor Vavilov.

Vavilov was a stick figure − a thin fragile looking man with stooped shoulders in a dark grey suit that was rumpled and too large for his slight frame. He had a face full of wrinkles and more hair sprouting from his ears and nostrils than on his head. He looked as though he was a hundred years old, his skin like the musty parchment of the ancient books that surrounded him.

In the wedge of light that spilled in through the window was a stainless steel flask of steaming coffee, several slices of buttered toast, and a plate of eggs and sausage all balanced on a silver tray.

Vavilov looked up at me as I was led into the room. He had a mouth full of food. He pointed to a chair I hadn't noticed with a fork.

"You want coffee?" Vavilov asked me around a chunk of sausage. He had a thick eastern European accent.

"Sure," I said.

He poured from the flask and handed me a chipped enamel mug with a picture of Mickey Mouse on it. Then he sat back in his chair and clasped his hands across his emaciated stomach contentedly.

I sipped at the coffee. It was thick and sweet, not a flavor I had tasted before. Maybe he imported the stuff.

"So," he said as I set the cup down and pushed it a couple of inches away from me, "Russian coffee is not to your liking, eh?"

I made an apologetic face. "I think it's an acquired taste," I replied politely.

Vavilov chuckled – a wheezing sound that rasped from bad lungs. "But you won't drink any more to acquire the appreciation necessary, right?"

I nodded. "I think it would take more than one cup."

He made that same asthmatic sound again, then pursed his lips. His eyes were bright and cunning within the deep folds of his withered skin. I could imagine him leaning over a chessboard, his skeletal claws moving pieces with the deftness of a master. Not a man to be underestimated.

Vavilov flicked a glance at the young man who had escorted me into the room, and then gave a dismissive wave of his hand. "That will be all for now, Dimitri," the old professor said. "I think Mr. Culver wants to talk to me in private, yes?"

I nodded. "Yes," I said.

The young man disappeared like he was part of a conjurer's magic act. I didn't even see him go.

The room was silent. I could hear the tired old bookshelves creak and groan under the weight of all they carried. Tiny motes of dust drifted in the air. Vavilov dropped his chin onto his chest in a contemplative gesture and then raised his eyebrows in mild surprise. He had an egg stain on his tie. He brushed at it with the tip of a finger and then sighed.

"What do you want?" he asked at last. He spoke very slowly. Perhaps it was because his accent was so thick. Every word was carefully measured on his lips before uttered.

"I wanted to talk to you about your work on the zombie virus," I said. "I'm fascinated to learn more about your involvement in the analysis of the outbreak, and the information you passed on to the CIA."

Vavilov nodded his head sagely. He had known exactly why I was here. I had explained it all several times to his assistants before being granted the interview.

"Da," he said. Somewhere in the house the classical music ended abruptly. He seemed reluctant, or perhaps he was in no hurry. "Do you know who Napoleon Bonaparte was?" Vavilov asked me suddenly.

"Of course," I said.

He nodded again, and heaved himself upright in the chair with the kind of grunts and groans that suggested this required a major effort. "Bonaparte blazed a trail of death and destruction through Europe for almost twenty years," Vavilov said. His eyes went to a bookshelf for no apparent reason, then darted back to mine. "Countless people died on battlefields and in the streets. No country seemed untouched by the little Corsican's deathly touch."

I didn't say anything. I just sat and listened to what I assumed was an old man's ramble. Vavilov paused dramatically. "They called him the first Antichrist," the professor said. "And they called Adolf Hitler the second Antichrist."

"Yes," I said patiently at last. "I know."

Vavilov nodded his head. "When I learned of this virus, the horrible infection that had come to America, I was suspicious," he admitted. He closed his eyes. The corner of his mouth twitched and one of his eyebrows seemed to take on a life of its own. Then the old man fixed me with an intense gaze. "I thought that the man behind this act of terror must surely go down in history as the third Antichrist," he said.

I leaned forward. "So you knew, right from the outset of this zombie infection, that it was a man-made strain? You knew this was not the same kind of epidemic as Ebola, or any of the other contagious infections that have swept the world?"

Vavilov started to shake his head in denial, and then stopped. "I had my suspicions," he said softly.

"Why?"

Vavilov tapped at his temple with the tip of his finger, then lapsed into secretive silence.

"You worked at the Institute of Ultra Pure Biochemical Preparations in Leningrad with Professor Vladimir Pasechnik back in the 1980's didn't you?"

Vavilov nodded. He said nothing, but his eyes narrowed shrewdly. I heard a little catch of his breath.

"And you were Pasechnik's right-hand man."

Professor Vavilov shook his head. "No," he said. "There you are wrong, Mr. journalist. "I was the *KGB's* man in the facility." He laughed then, a loud, high-pitched guffaw. The humor was lost on me. "Pasechnik was a fool," Vavilov said contemptuously. "A brilliant man – but a fool."

"Why?"

"He thought the research at the Institute was to benefit mankind. He thought we were working on antidotes to biological substances that would be used to fight their outbreak."

"What kind of substances?"

"The plague."

"But you weren't?"

"No," Vavilov said, like the answer should have been obvious. "The facility was used to develop biological weapons. Our research was being used to create a means to modify cruise missiles so that they could deliver payloads of plague-like infections to our enemies."

"You mean the USA?"

He laughed again, but this time with less conviction. "My friend, in those days Mother Russia had *many* enemies."

I sat back thoughtfully. This man had worked closely with the CIA in hunting down the origins of the zombie infection, and tracing it back to Iran. There was something I was missing.

"What aroused your suspicions," I tried. "There must have been something that first raised a warning."

Vavilov nodded his head. "The CIA and some of your USAMRIID scientists came to visit me," he said. "But by then I had already begun to wonder. Once I saw the data they had gathered from the infected bodies… it was apparent to me that the original strain of infection was a *created* of evil."

"A creation?"

"Creation," he corrected himself. "It was not of this world. It was created in a laboratory."

I got my notebook out. "Can you tell me more?" I asked. Outside the sky was darkening. I could see storm clouds building on the horizon through the window behind Vavilov's back. The room suddenly became gloomy, like a light had been turned off. The hushed sound of the big rambling house turned eerie.

"When I was at the Institute – long, long before the Berlin Wall came down and I defected to the West – several of the scientists were tasked by the government to create a new strain of infection – something that mankind could in no way prepare for. We gave the project a special name and the work produced several promising pathogens that we called the F1 *smyert*."

"Smyertch?" I tried the word. It sounded awkward on my tongue.

"Death," Vavilov said. "We called them the F1 deaths."

"What did F1 stand for?"

He shrugged his shoulders. "Formula," he said – but I got the sense that he was lying, or embellishing the real meaning. I didn't pursue the matter.

"Did Vladimir Pasechnik know of this work? Did he head up the research?"

"No," Vavilov spat with sudden contempt. "The man was a romantic!" He waved his hands in the air like a conductor before an orchestra. "He had no idea for many months what we were working on, and by then, the plague mutations we were creating were already in the advanced stages of development."

Despite myself I reached out and took another sip of the coffee. It tasted just as bad as the first mouthful. I stared into the mug for a moment, wondering if I could see grains of dirt.

"What happened to the F1 pathogens?" I asked quietly.

For a very long time, professor Vavilov said nothing. He seemed distracted by the storm that was gathering outside. He kept his eyes fixed on mine, but his senses were attuned to the rising sound of the wind and the changing temperature.

"They were abandoned," he said guardedly.

"Abandoned? Just like that?"

"Yes."

I didn't believe him, and he knew it.

"You had several promising strains of plague-like pathogens under development... and the government ordered you to stop the research, right at the height of the Cold War?"

I might as well have said, *"Are you kidding me?"*

Vavilov shifted uncomfortably in his chair. He crossed his legs, and then reached a long arm for a crumpled packet of cigarettes. He lit one and became fascinated by the feather of smoke that crawled towards the ceiling.

"They were stolen," he said at last.

"Stolen? By who?"

"You mean by whom."

"Whatever," I snapped brusquely. The man was stalling. I had the feeling he had told me more than intended, and now he was looking for a way to wriggle out of the mess he had begun to unravel.

"Who stole the pathogens?"

"His name was Glavinoski," Vavilov said. "He was a drunk and a notorious womanizer. He was one of the scientists at the facility who was working on the F1 project."

"Did you know this man?"

"Da."

"Why was he employed if he was a drunk?"

Vavilov shrugged. "The facility employed over four hundred scientists and support staff, Mr. American journalist," the old professor's tone became belligerent and grating. "Glavinoski might have been a drunkard, but in Russia that is not such a big thing. He was also a genius."

I could guess the rest. "You told the CIA about this man and your suspicions after you analyzed the data they brought to you a few months ago, and they since traced him to Iran, didn't they?"

"Da," Vavilov said. He drew on the cigarette and tried to hide himself behind a thick swirling screen of smoke.

"Tell me more about Glavinoski," I said. "If you are right, he will go down in history as the third Antichrist. What was he like?"

"I *was* right," Vavilov said petulantly, as though I was questioning his intelligence. "The CIA had the evidence they needed before they launched the revenge attack on Iran."

I nodded. "Okay, then tell me about this man."

Vavilov shrugged his shoulders eloquently. "I have told you," he insisted. "He was a drunk and a womanizer."

"And a thief."

"Da, and that too."

"What was he like to work with back at the Institute?"

Vavilov chewed his lip for a moment. He took one last deep draw on the end of the cigarette and then stubbed it out in an ashtray that he found behind a pile of books. "He was young then," he said. "And a firebrand. Do you know that word?"

I nodded. Vavilov looked satisfied. "He would come to the facility with red eyes and smelling of alcohol and women's cheap perfume. He liked the ladies. And he liked the prestige of being one of the mother country's elite scientists. He had a big ego," Vavilov gestured with his hands, drawing a large circle in the air. "He thought he was the brightest of the bright."

"And was he?"

"Yes," Vavilov said in a moment of pure candid honesty. "He was a ruthless fucking genius."

PART 3: 'OPERATION COMPRESS'
The Interviews...

FORT BENNING, GEORGIA:
FORWARD BASE – NATIONAL UNDEAD CONTAINMENT COMMAND

I felt like I was suffocating – like all the air was being sucked out of the room by the man's restless energy and overwhelming presence.

SAFCUR III stalked impatiently across the width of his office and then came back behind his desk again. I could sense his brooding resentment of me, but I didn't believe it was personal. I hadn't been in the room long enough to piss the man off yet. Rather, instinct told me that it was the imposition of his time he really resented. He had more important things to do than answer a journalist's questions.

General George Tash thrust his jaw out at me and there was a curl of distain at the corner of his mouth. He balanced on the balls of his feet like he wanted to leap across the desk and choke the life out of me.

He was a tall, spare man with a wavy crop of black hair just starting to sprinkle grey. He had a thin nose and fleshy jowls that made his face look long, and gave him the countenance of an undertaker. He glared at me.

I flipped open the cover of my notebook. "Thanks for your time, General Tash," I began politely. "As the current active SAFCUR responsible for the containment of the zombie outbreak, when did you take over from SAFCUR II?"

"I took over from Zac Winchester about a month after the Battle of Rock Hill."

'Were you surprised by your appointment, especially given the success of that engagement?"

"No."

"Why?"

"Because I was part of General Winchester's team that planned that attack, and he has been an important part of my team in planning the assault across the southern states to win them back."

I frowned. I had no idea the succession of leadership against the zombies had been so overlapping – so cooperative. I had thought each appointment had been quite separate.

"So there was never the possibility that SAFCUR II would maintain his overall command once the decision was made to invade the southern states and push the undead back into Florida?"

"No. It was a matter of horses for courses," General Tash said. "My experience, and my knowledge of the area we were moving into were critical." The General folded his arms across his chest and narrowed his eyes warily. "If you're fishing for some kind of conflict or friction, you can forget about it," he snapped suddenly. "Commanding our armed forces against the zombies was not some kind of pissing competition, son. It was an unprecedented display of cooperation between every aspect of America's military from the top, all the way down to the men on the ground that risked their lives. Understand?" He barked the last word like an order hissed on a parade ground.

I got the message. I let the matter rest and changed tack. "Can you tell me about the offensive, then?" I was working hard to keep my tone neutral. The General's personality was as prickly as a barbed wire fence. I wondered if he had grandchildren. If he did, I was pretty sure he would be the grumpy grandfather...

"Was there a key attack during the operation you think is deserving of mention?"

General Tash shook his head. He still had his arms folded. "No, because the offensive wasn't made up of a series of battles. Instead, it was all one rolling push right across the line."

I arched my eyebrows in surprise. "The *entire* Danvers Defense Line?"

"That's correct," the General said. His voice had lost its edge like maybe his mood was slowly thawing. "We put over thirteen hundred tanks into the field – everything that was made of steel and ran on tracks we could mobilize went through the fortifications along the line at the same time. An hour later over a thousand troop carriers and engineering vehicles came behind them, using the same tactic that had been employed at Rock Hill. Above the advance were Black Hawk and Apache helicopters…"

"And before the attack? Did you use artillery?"

"Yes," the General said. "What we lacked in field artillery we made up for in Air Force and Naval bombardments."

I took a deep breath. "You turned the states of Mississippi, Alabama, Georgia and South Carolina into a wasteland."

The General glared at me. "Not my problem."

"You devastated thousands of hectares of forest."

"Not my problem."

"You destroyed every town, city and community across the entire south of America."

"*Not my problem!*" The General was simmering with growing resentment. His eyes became black. "My only task was to win," Tash's tone was like acid. "And to do so with the least amount of risk to the men under my command. That's what I did, so don't give me that fucking tree-hugger bleeding heart shit about the goddamned environment, son!

I don't give a fuck about trees, or buildings. I care about my men. Their lives were in my hands." He stabbed his finger at me like he wished it were a weapon. "That was where my responsibility began and ended."

I sat back. The room seemed filled with electrical static the way the air crackles before a thunderstorm. I had pushed the General's buttons deliberately because I wanted to see what kind of a man had led our troops into the most epic military assault in America's history.

I didn't like him.

But I respected him.

He was a cold bastard – a confrontational man with an imposing presence and a fierce temper. But I accepted too, that he wasn't given the burden of SAFCUR III because he was a media darling. He got the mission because he was capable of doing the job. I decided I had seen enough. I backed off, softening the tone of my voice and letting the tension melt from my body.

"General, can you talk me through the assault? I'd like to try to understand how you were able to orchestrate such a massive drive into zombie territory, and how your units were able to defeat literally millions of zombies."

George Tash let out a long breath, but his eyes still smoldered. He remained standing. He went to the window of his office and stood staring out through the glass for several seconds, his hands clasped tightly behind his back.

"Every fort along the Danvers Defense Line was an FOB for our troops," he said, talking with his back to me, his shoulders stiff and his voice remote. "At zero hour, when the assault began, the tanks poured into enemy territory and formed up into line at their designated LD."

"You mean one long line that stretched all the way from the coast across to the Arkansas border?"

Tash turned around. "No, of course not," he said harshly. "That wasn't possible, and even if it was it would be fundamentally bone-headed. The terrain prohibited anything so simplistic."

I scribbled notes. My cheeks were burning. The man's lack of tact was pissing me off.

"The tanks formed into lines, each one up to a hundred vehicles wide, in exactly the same way they had at Rock Hill," he went on to explain."

"But the zombies… weren't you worried that too many would escape through the gaps between tank formations? Was that a consideration?"

"Of course," Tash growled. "But after more than seven days of non-stop artillery bombardment and air attacks, with the skies thick with helicopters, the risk was minimal. Most of the undead that were marauding near the Defensive line were obliterated or made redundant by the barrage and the choppers."

"Redundant?"

"Incapacitated. No longer a viable threat. Dismembered…"

"What about as the tanks rolled further south?"

The General turned around at last and I could see the altered set of his face. His expression had softened, the darkness had gone from his eyes. He wasn't smiling, but he was no longer snarling either.

"You don't seem to have a clear picture of exactly what we were facing," Tash said bluntly. He dropped into the chair behind his desk and rested his bunched fists on the table like two hammers. "First, the largest mass of zombies we encountered during the early days of the assault was estimated at just a few thousand. And second, those undead we did fight had largely been rendered useless by the artillery and air support."

"Just a few thousand? I thought there would be millions…"

"There was," Tash said. "There still are. But they're not all swarming over Alabama and Georgia," he said like the notion was utterly ridiculous, and naïve. "The majority of the undead are still in Florida – never left. They never spread far enough north to be a threat. The only undead we ever had to fight were the ones who came out of Florida, or were infected in the states from Mississippi across to South Carolina. We didn't have to kill them all. We only had to destroy the ones we encountered."

I made a note of the General's comments and then underlined the words. It was critical, and a point that many people had probably never considered.

Me included…

"So as the assault struck deeper south, did the numbers of zombies increase?"

"Considerably," SAFCUR III nodded his head. He swung his chair around until I was staring at him in profile, as if he was sitting for a portrait painting. "The first seven days of the assault were the most challenging because we were operating across a broad front, but as compensation, the undead numbers were less and the artillery and air attacks had been concentrated over many days. But as we moved further south, we were gradually able to compress the line. The offset to this was that the number of zombies we were fighting increased as we neared the border, and we were also unable to be as thorough with our rolling artillery barrage and air assaults. We had to keep the assault moving – that was a critical element."

"Why?" I honestly didn't understand. "Surely you couldn't run tanks as big as the Abrams and even the Bradleys twenty-four hours a day. You would run out of fuel, and there would be mechanical problems, even if there were no zombies to contend with."

General Tash straightened and swung the chair round to face me once more. "That is correct," he said. "But I never said we ran the tanks continuously. I said the assault was continuous." He got up from the chair and started pacing again. The restless energy that had lain dormant suddenly came back and he sparked back into perpetual movement. "We used the tanks in carefully planned stages," the General explained, "with units moving forward and then halting once each new objective was reached. They were then overlapped and replaced by another wave of vehicles while the first tanks were repaired and refueled, and the crews rested. It was at those points that new outpost fortifications were constructed."

"You built more forts? Where? Across Georgia and Alabama?"

"And South Carolina and Mississippi," General Tash added. He cracked his knuckles and then flexed his fingers like a strangler about to do murder. "The outposts were not forts," he explained. "We didn't have the time. Behind the troop carriers were Army engineer units. As a strategic point was seized – such as a hill or a vital intersection – the tanks were posted, the troops in the M113's formed a perimeter... and the engineers built small fenced installations that would house troops and vehicles if the assault faltered or failed. We needed outposts – safe places for the men if our line was breached, or if the weather set in and delayed the attack."

How big were these outposts?"

The General shrugged. "It depended on the environment," he admitted, "and it depended on what was available to the men on the ground. Often materials were flown to the location by helicopters. If there was an abandoned airfield nearby, then we would airlift heavy equipment."

"Were these outposts ever required?" I leaned forward suddenly. "I mean, was there ever an instance...?"

246

"No... not a situation where the attack was ever in danger of faltering or failing. However there were two occasions where individual elements were forced to make use of the defenses until they could be rescued by Black Hawks."

"What instances?"

The General made a face like he was deciding whether he should share the details. He took a long time. Finally he sighed. "We lost several men who were operating out of M113's," he said at last. "They were mopping up in an area south of where Athens, Georgia once stood. Our satellite images of the artillery bombardment had shown the city devastated, but you can never obliterate an entire city – you can never really flatten it and remove all threats. The men were head-shooting zombies that had been crippled by the artillery and the rolling wave of armor. One of them got bitten..."

"And he turned?"

The General nodded his head. "He was working with a team in the rubble. He attacked several of the other men nearby, and we had multiple losses."

Multiple losses... the clinical term sounded like the kind of antiseptic expression a man used when he didn't want to admit the reality.

"You mean several soldiers turned into zombies and then attacked others that were working in nearby vehicles?"

"Yes."

I frowned, and picked my next words carefully. "How many men were infected with the zombie virus, sir?"

General Tash pressed his lips into a thin stubborn line. "I'm not at liberty to reveal the number of casualties."

I sat back in the chair and shook my head. I had a feeling the interview was about to turn hostile once more. I shrugged my shoulders. "Well if you won't tell me, should I make up the number? Should I say *over a thousand* men were

247

killed when an infected zombie attacked a group of brave soldiers who were mopping up behind the advance? Should I say it was more than *two thousand...?*"

Tash glared at me and I glared right back. "It wasn't anything like those numbers," he snapped. "And to print that kind of bullshit is inflammatory and irresponsible."

I shrugged my shoulders again, this time in an off-handed way, but said nothing. Tash narrowed his eyes. "Sixty-two," he said grudgingly. "They were Marines who had been called in to work with the troops assigned to the M113's.

"Sixty-two?"

"That's right. By the time the men were able to react and retreat to the protection of the vehicles, they were being over-run. The surviving Marines opened fire from the cover of the troop carriers and were eventually able to reach one of the outposts that the engineers had built the day before just a few miles to the east. Black Hawks later extracted the men. One of the rescued Marines died later in a field hospital from gun shot wounds."

"A zombie shot him?"

Tash shook his head. "He was wounded in the battle – the fog of war..." the General's voice lowered. He clenched his hands together. "It can happen..."

I set down my notebook and rubbed my forehead. Tash and I lapsed into a respectful, but uncomfortable silence for a few minutes. I was thinking about the Marines who had become infected – their bravery and the tragic circumstances that had overwhelmed them. I was thinking about their families, and the men who were their comrades being suddenly forced to open fire on guys they knew to save their own lives.

I looked up. "What was the other incident?" I asked.

Tash looked deliberately bewildered for just an instant. Perhaps he was hoping I would forget to ask. He went back to the office window. Outside, the sun was beginning to set. "We lost a small number of men from the Arkansas National Guard... and quite a few engineers."

"How?" I didn't ask about the number of casualties. I wanted to know the circumstances of the incident first, in case the General tried to stonewall me for details again.

"They were men from the 1st Battalion 153rd Infantry Regiment based in Malvern. They were mopping up undead on the west flank of the front in Mississippi," SAFCUR III said in a careful measured tone. "They were a team of soldiers in an M113. One of the men went down injured – bleeding. No one apparently saw what happened. The soldiers evacuated the man to a fortification that was being built along the I55 about fifty miles north of Jackson."

"Had the wounded soldier been infected with the zombie virus?" I asked with a slow dawning sense of horror.

Tash nodded his head. "The M113 reached the fortification just as the man was turning. He infected everyone within the defense."

"Everyone?"

Tash's expression was grave. "Several more men from the 1st Battalion and almost one hundred engineers that were completing the fortification."

"My God..." I breathed softly. "How did... how did you contain the outbreak?"

"Once we realized the installation was overcome with infected, we destroyed the fortification and everything – everything within the compound – using helicopters and artillery."

I let the General wander around the office. He thrust his hands deep into his pockets and prowled across the carpet with his head bowed and the burden of those soldiers' deaths heavy on his shoulders.

"Now the zombie hordes have been pushed back into Florida and the final containment line has been built, do you feel the worst of the crisis is over? Can America begin to rebuild?"

Tash's head snapped up. "No!" he said fiercely. "The work still isn't finished. One day we need to take Florida back – we need to terminate every zombie and every trace of the infection. Until then, we can't relax, we can't rest and we must not lose our focus."

"Is the Army still on alert?"

"Of course," the General gave me another one of his withering glares. "We have troops all along the abbreviated Florida border in trenches and behind barbed wire, and we have armor and infantry here at Fort Benning and more at Fort Stewart. We remain on high alert. We remain ready to finish the job we started."

"Fort Stewart?" I flicked back through my memories. I hadn't heard the base mentioned before.

"It's the largest military installation east of the Mississippi," the General explained. "It's outside of Hinesville, Georgia. A few years ago it was the staging area for American troops en route to serve during Operation Iraqi Freedom."

"And you have more men and tanks there?"

"Plenty," Tash declared, "with more arriving every week. Fort Stewart is close to the Florida line. It gives us the ability for rapid response and deployment if the containment line is ever broken. It was one of the last pieces of ground we recovered when we drove the undead back."

"So you didn't flatten the military installations the way you devastated every town and city? You didn't bomb the buildings in case the bases were concealing zombies?"

Tash shook his head. "No, we didn't," he said. "We deliberately preserved Fort Benning, Fort Stewart and several other key installations because we knew they would be needed in the aftermath of the apocalypse. We needed the runways, the facilities and the equipment that had been abandoned as the troops were forced to withdraw to avoid the spread of the infection."

"Then how did you get them back?" I asked. "How did you recover Fort Benning, for example?"

"The hard way," Tash said. "The fucking hard way."

"Meaning?"

The General finally stopped pacing the floor and came to lean over his desk, palms planted on the edge of the wooden tabletop. He pushed his face closer to mine – so close that I could see discolored spots of sun-blemished skin on his cheeks and across the bridge of his nose. "I sent in the Rangers," he said. "It was the home base for a lot of those boys before the apocalypse. They knew the lay of the land. They did the job."

"The Rangers re-took the base?"

"Yes," he said. "They were on the ground, fighting for every yard, face-to-face with the enemy and supported by armor and helicopters."

"That must have been one hell of a fight," I breathed. I was fascinated. Throughout the zombie apocalypse, the Army's leaders had gone to great lengths to place our fighting men and women behind barbed wire and in trenches, or within tanks, troop carriers and forts. This was the first time I had heard macabre news of soldiers confronting the zombie-infected hordes in direct action.

"Can you tell me about the battle?"

"No," the General said, and then seemed to relent only a moment later. "All I can tell you is that the operation was conducted over a twenty-hour period and in that time several thousand of the enemy were destroyed. The base was re-taken by the Rangers supported by Abrams tanks which swept the area beyond the Fort."

It wasn't the kind of answer I wanted, but I suspected it was the best I was going to get. Besides, I was tired of dueling with this man. He was exhausting to be around. His energy was combustible.

"So the Rangers confronted the zombies and fought a kind of urban street-fight to secure the base's buildings, while the tanks protected and crushed the undead around the perimeter?"

Tash shrugged. "You can describe it that way if you want."

"Was that what happened?"

Tash said nothing. He stared at me defiantly. "I've told you all I can about the operation to re-take Fort Benning," he said again. "The operation to re-take Fort Stewart employed similar – equally successful – tactics."

"But you won't tell me exactly what those tactics were?"

"Correct."

"Then will you tell me how many soldiers died in the battle to win back the two Forts?"

"Casualties were less than we anticipated, but more than we had hoped for."

I sat straight in the chair and arched my back. I could feel the burn of being hunched over spread across my stiff shoulders. I tilted my head from side to side to loosen the muscles in my neck.

"General," I said calmly, "have you ever considered a career in politics?"

He knew I was being sarcastic. He narrowed his eyes.

"Have you ever served, son?"

"No, sir. I haven't."

Tash's mouth curled into an ironic sneer. "Then you have no fucking idea what it is like to go into combat. You have no fucking idea what it is to lay your life on the line for your country."

"No," I admitted. "I can only imagine the bravery and selflessness that would require," I said sincerely.

He shook his head. "No!" he roared suddenly. "You *can't* imagine. You can't possibly imagine what it is like to be so filled with fear but still do your duty. And you can't possibly imagine what it is like to aim your weapon and fire at someone with an intent to kill them." He pushed himself away from the desk. There was a bubble of spittle in the corner of his mouth. He wiped it away with the back of his hand.

For many minutes the General stood silently in the corner of the office, simmering. I could see the tension in the way he held himself, the clench of his fists and the rigid line of his back and shoulders. Finally, he turned around to face me.

"Every man and woman who served America during this conflict was a hero," General George Tash said in a low rumbling voice. "They deserve to be honored. Their exploits and their efforts deserve to be celebrated and appreciated. I've given you everything you need in order to fulfill that obligation. Now go and fucking do it!"

FORT STEWART, GEORGIA:
EASTERN COMMAND BASE – NATIONAL UNDEAD CONTAINMENT COMMAND

"Colonel, am I right in saying that your role during 'Operation Compress' was to serve as second-in-command to General George Tash?"

Jeremiah Richelson nodded his head. "I was in command of the eastern flank during the push into zombie-held territory," he carefully qualified his answer. "I oversaw our tank and troop-carrier movements through South Carolina and into the eastern parts of Georgia."

"What was that like?"

Richelson narrowed his eyes. "What was what like? Serving under the General, or overseeing the movement of almost five hundred armored fighting vehicles across a front that was over a hundred and fifty miles wide?"

"Both," I said. "But tell me about your time working with the General first."

The Colonel was a dour looking man. He was taller than average with a wiry physique. He had the foppish habit of glancing at his own reflection in the windows of a nearby Humvee every time he thought I wasn't looking. Maybe it was a vanity thing, or maybe he merely wanted to ensure he presented himself in the correct military manner at all times.

"Have you spoken to the General personally?" he asked.

I nodded. "He granted me an interview."

The Colonel's expression became cynical. "Then you can probably imagine what it was like."

I could. Personally I would have thrown myself out of a helicopter. Tash had been the most demanding of all my interviews. It didn't surprise me to know that SAFCUR III's confrontational, abrasive attitude was something the men who served underneath him were also very aware of.

"With respect, sir – that's not really an answer."

Colonel Richelson conceded the point with a jerked nod of his head. He stopped suddenly and clasped his hands behind his back, straightened his stance a little and fixed me with his gaze. We had been walking around Fort Stewart in the late afternoon sun. The base was a buzz of activity, the air filled with the purposeful kind of noise that comes from men in preparation for war.

"When you work with the finest men in the military, you need to be prepared to lift your performance to meet the exemplary standards they set and expect," The Colonel said in a monotone voice. "It has been my experience that serving under General Tash was the defining highlight of my own personal career. The man is the best we have, and he made me better for the honor of working as his second-in-command."

His gaze flickered, to be sure I wrote everything he said down word-for-word. I did.

He relaxed a little then. I saw it in the eased set of his shoulders and the softening of his features. He gave me a speculative glance. "Do you drink, Mr. Culver?"

I nodded my head and smiled self-deprecatingly. "Colonel, I'm a journalist. We all drink. My therapist told me once that drinking alcohol was my sub conscious way of washing my mouth out."

Colonel Richelson hesitated, processing my comment as though he analyzed everything said with great care. Finally he smiled.

"Clever," he muttered. He turned on his heel without another word and I followed him across a vast concrete parade ground and into one of the base office blocks.

Colonel Richelson's office didn't come with an ornate antique desk, shelves of leather bound books or even deep comfortable chairs. The office had the feel of being temporary because it was. When the base had been re-taken from the zombies there had been no time for luxuries. The desk was standard military issue and so were the chairs. The carpet was threadbare, worn down in patches and deeply rutted where other, better furniture pieces had once sat.

The Colonel tossed his cap onto the desk, and brushed his fingers carefully through his hair. He went to the filing cabinet in the corner of the room and pulled open the top drawer. From within he produced a bottle of scotch and two small glasses. He set them on the desk and raised his eyebrows in a question.

I nodded.

The Colonel splashed scotch into both glasses and carefully screwed the cap back onto the bottle. He dropped down into his chair with a sigh and reached for his glass.

"To victory," he said.

I picked up the other glass. "To victory."

We drank in silence. The scotch was good. Behind the Colonel's shoulders I could see the sky slowly darkening through a window as sunset approached. Long shadows stretched across the ground and clouds went scudding across the sky, pushed along by a strengthening breeze.

Finally I set the glass down on the edge of the desk and looked more carefully around the room. There was a vast map of old America on the side wall. It had been there for some time. There were brown water stains through the paper.

"Colonel, can you explain to me in more detail how 'Operation Compress' actually worked? General Tash sketched a broad outline, but it was a wide-ranging interview," I deliberately understated my time with SAFCUR III.

Richelson set down his own glass and I noticed he had barely sipped at the alcohol. He sat up straight behind his desk and clasped his hands together in a studious pose.

"When the first wave of tanks came out through the defensive forts we formed them up into line, just as they had been at the battle of Rock Hill," he said. "When they began the push south, I was in a Black Hawk controlling the advance."

"And were there any problems?"

"There are always problems in battle," the Colonel said seriously. "Good leadership requires a commander to deal with those issues."

"So... what were the problems, and how did you resolve them?"

The Colonel looked thoughtful for a moment. He was an organized man. He had an organized mind. I felt like all the information he shared was sorted and processed. Nothing came out of his mouth that was unfiltered or thoughtless. I had a hard time believing he would be capable of spontaneous decisions during something as harrowing as a major tank battle – but clearly he was. General George Tash was no fool. He had selected this man as his second-in-command for good reason.

"Coordinating the tanks with the rolling barrage of protective artillery fire was the first obstacle," Richelson said. "The artillery was firing at map co-ordinates in a carefully scheduled plan that was designed to keep the shelling five miles ahead of the tank line. As the tanks moved forward, so would the bombardment move. That didn't always happen with the precision required."

I arched an eyebrow.

"What problems did that cause?"

The Colonel shook his head. "It didn't, but it could have – if we hadn't stayed vigilant. We needed to keep open lines of communication with the various elements of artillery we were working with, and we had to adjust the speed of the tanks. There were a couple of times when the armor was moving through flat open ground where they got too close to the barrage. We had to slow them down."

"Couldn't they have just stopped?"

"No. We were in zombie territory. The first rule of our tactics was that we must be constantly on the move at a pace that is faster than the undead."

I nodded. I should have remembered that. Maybe I needed another drink...

"Were there many undead? What casualties did the rolling column inflict?"

Colonel Richelson probably knew down to the last zombie. He was the kind of perfectionist who would probably have had other helicopters in the air counting the bodies as they fell beneath the heavy tracks of the Abrams and Bradleys.

"We estimate enemy casualties at between fifteen and twenty thousand over the first few days," he said. "That was only from the troops and tanks under my command on the eastern flank of the offensive. Those numbers became even higher as we pushed closer to the Florida border."

"How much higher?"

The Colonel shrugged. "Another thirty thousand," he said with concealed pride.

I was impressed. I didn't ask about our own casualties. Instead I asked about the lessons the Army had learned between the time of the Rock Hill engagement and the massive armored push into the southern states.

Richelson considered the question, naturally.

"We didn't modify the concepts we had already developed," he said at last. "The only variation was the need throughout this massive assault to keep the tanks constantly on the move. In finding the solution to the problem, we also inadvertently were able to significantly reduce the number of casualties the Army on the ground incurred."

More careful technical speak. I was becoming accustomed to the sanitized, antiseptic answers to my questions from the men who had commanded our soldiers. At another time and in another place I might have been satisfied with the vagueness of the answer. But not this time.

"What does that mean, exactly?" I asked. "Can you explain in terms my readers will actually understand?"

If he was offended, the Colonel didn't show it. His expression remained the same. He swung around in his chair and glanced out through the window. I saw him sweep his hand through his hair, then turn back to me.

"We advanced in long lines of closely connected tanks, and two miles behind the advance was another long line of M113 personnel carriers. We had Apache helicopters in the sky, covering the flanks of each line... all that, I suspect you have already been told."

I nodded.

"But during the offensive, the need to constantly press at the enemy demanded a second wave of tanks be moving behind the advance in order to take up the assault when the first line of vehicles needed to refuel, and required maintenance. Now the Abrams is one of the most reliable Main Battle Tanks the world has ever seen. It proved itself in the deserts of the Middle East. It's reliable and trustworthy, so we didn't factor on long maintenance delays. We did factor in the need to rest the men and refuel."

"And so you had a follow up column of more tanks?"

"Yes. They trailed the line of personnel carriers. When the first line of tanks reached the objective of its advance, the rear column of tanks moved forward and spread out to continue pressing the zombies. The first vehicles were refueled."

"And this saved lives?"

"Yes. Undoubtedly."

"How?"

"Because at the Battle of Rock Hill the troops in the M113's were the last line of our attack. They were required to head-shoot any of the undead that were not eliminated by the tanks. With the rolling assault that pushed south, we had the column of tanks in the rear that meant we could deploy them in instances where the men in the M113's were unable to deal with the vast numbers of maimed zombies requiring extermination."

I was writing all this down, but even as I did so, my mind was racing ahead to the next questions I wanted to ask. The Colonel's explanation of the way the attack had been coordinated had made me more curious.

"What about at night?" I asked. "Did the attack roll on in darkness as well?"

"No," Richelson said. "It was deemed too dangerous."

"Too dangerous?" I frowned. "In comparison to waiting in the darkness for the zombies to attack?"

Richelson pressed his lips together. "The times when the vehicles were being refueled and repaired were always the moments fraught with the most hazard. It was always possible that stray surviving undead might break through our perimeter. Fortunately the covering Apache's were thorough."

"And during the night, when the advance was forced to halt. How did you handle that situation?"

"We dropped a constant curtain of artillery fire across the front," the Colonel explained and then revealed an incredulous fact with a stab of his finger. "During the offensive south, we fired more shells than the Army has fired collectively in every other military conflict during the Twentieth Century. That includes Vietnam, Korea and the Middle East engagements."

"And this curtain, as you called it – that kept the undead at arms length?" I asked.

"That, and the false insertions by the Black Hawks."

I blinked. I hadn't heard anything about false insertions. I flipped over to a new blank page. "What are false insertions?"

Colonel Richelson reached a long arm for his glass of scotch and took another prim sip. "From sunset until sunrise each day of the assault, we operated sticks of Black Hawk helicopters in zombie occupied territory, working in areas ahead of the tanks," he explained. "The Black Hawks would fly very low level operations to draw the attention of the enemy. Because the zombies are attracted to sound, we were able to set the helicopters down and then take off again quickly in a series of manoeuvers that were designed to lead the zombies away from the tanks, and to concentrate them into areas where the armor would advance the following morning."

I grunted my grudging respect. It was a clever tactic.

"And this helped distract the undead while the men involved in the assault were being rested?" I prodded.

Richelson nodded. "It certainly did," he confirmed. "And it also served to maximize the enemy losses. Drawing them into clusters made the work of the armor as it advanced the following day even more devastating."

MARIETTA, GEORGIA:

It was just a desolate nightmare landscape of grey rubble, black charred timbers and the burned out wreckage of cars. For miles in every direction the land was flat – made that way by the relentless artillery bombardment, which had preceded the Army's rolling assault through the heartland of the south.

There was nothing to indicate that where I stood was once the thriving city of Marietta.

"We found the bodies over here," the soldier pointed. He stepped away from the Humvee and went towards a broken pile of wreckage that had once been a large building. In the eerie silence I could hear the vehicle's big engine popping and ticking as it cooled.

I followed the soldier over the broken ground. Steel girders had been twisted by artillery fire. The smell of smoke still seemed to hang in the air, even after so many months.

A rat scurried over my boot and disappeared into a crevice of rubble.

"When we found them, they were laying beside their weapons," the soldier intoned, his voice hushed and respectful. "We figure they were from the Georgia State Defense Force. We found thirty-one bodies."

I paused in mid stride. "Georgia State Defense Force? I didn't know such a unit even existed."

The soldier nodded his head. He was a grim-faced, serious young man who still looked too young to shave. "Yes, sir," he said earnestly. "The State Defense Force is comprised of men and women who make up an unpaid, volunteer component of the US Defense Forces." The soldier paused for a moment. "My father was part of the State Defense Force in Mississippi. A lot of retired veterans join."

I was fascinated, but also curious. "And what makes you think that the bodies you recovered from this site were members of the Georgia State Defense Force?"

The soldier shrugged. "This was the Clay National Guard Center," he said simply. "It was the unit's Headquarters. When the Georgia National Guard was mobilized to fight the zombies, the State Defense Force was tasked with securing the buildings and equipment while they were fighting at the front. It's one of their primary missions."

I looked around again. I could see a bombed and cratered airstrip in the near distance. It was overgrown with weeds and littered with debris.

The soldier followed the direction of my gaze. He nodded again. "This site used to be a Naval Air Station," he explained, "and the underground bunker we discovered is about another half-mile in that direction."

We walked.

"As best we could figure it, there were twenty six men and five women inside the bunker," the young soldier explained as we stumbled across the rough ground. "Each of the bodies was evacuated and returned to relatives for burial wherever possible."

I was struggling to keep pace. I stopped for a moment and took a second look around, more to catch my breath than for any other reason because there was nothing to see. "How long ago did you discover the bodies?" I asked.

The soldier made a thoughtful face. "We found them a few weeks after the armor rolled through this part of the state," he explained. "One of the mopping up crews in an M113 was checking the area for dreads. They reported the bunker."

"Did they go down inside?"

"Yes, sir."

"What did they find – apart from the bodies, I mean?"

The soldier shrugged his shoulders. "A letter."

I felt my heart skip a beat. "A letter? Written by one of the men?"

"Yes, sir."

I paused for a moment. "What did it say?"

The soldier reached into his pocket. "Here," he said. "The Colonel told me you would want it. You can read for yourself."

The soldier handed me a folded piece of paper within a small clear plastic evidence bag. I realized my hands were trembling.

"Who wrote it?" I asked in a whisper.

The soldier shook his head. "It's unsigned, sir."

I opened the bag and carefully unfolded a single page of paper that was wrinkled and stained with spatters of dry blood and the grime of dirty fingers. I held the letter in my hands like it was a priceless relic and sank down onto my haunches to slowly read:

We're surrounded by the undead. There is only enough ammunition for another day, then no more. We're fighting at night now, heading up to the surface after it gets dark to take the war to the enemy. Each shot brings more of the undead down on us. Last night they almost found us.

No food left, but we still have water. Jerry thinks the zombies will move on, but they haven't yet. Most of us want to make a last stand here and save a bullet for ourselves at the end. There's no way we'll go easy. There's no way we will let them get us – we won't be turned against our own troops and families. We'll die with our boots on. All we have left to fight for is each other. There's no escape. It's too late for that.

I miss my wife and kids. I pray to God they got away in time. This will be hard on my little girl.

We're all going to die here…

I handed the letter to the young soldier. He slid it back into the evidence bag and tucked it carefully into one of his pockets.

I turned away…

And smudged a tear from my cheek.

'SEPIA' RESTAURANT: WASHINGTON D.C.

The Secretary of State eased his shirt sleeves far enough to reveal the diamond-studded cufflinks, and glanced at the face of his gold wristwatch. "I'm on the clock," Vincent McNab said. "So don't fuck around with formalities, okay?"

I nodded. This man had a reputation for being a hardline tough guy. His straight-talking approach to diplomacy had won him no friends internationally since the zombie apocalypse, but within America he and the

President were seen as exactly the kind of team the nation needed as it had faced its most perilous crisis.

Personally, I liked him.

It was rare to find a politician who didn't care for politics – and Vince McNab was one of those guys. He had no political ambition – just a desire to do his job to the best of his ability. He didn't have one eye on his re-election prospects, or an eye on the Oval Office. He didn't care for Washington, he cared about America. He was a man on a mission, and that mission had nothing to do with his own popularity, or a looming November election.

A waiter brought drinks. McNab bared his teeth in a fierce grimace that was probably his idea of a warm friendly smile.

"Are you gentlemen ready to order?" The waiter had menus tucked under his arm.

McNab ran his eyes quickly down the list. "I'll have the usual," McNab snapped. "And he will have the same."

The young man retrieved the menus and scurried away. McNab stared at me across the restaurant table and set his hands down on the starched white tablecloth like a gunslinger ready to reach for his pistols. "So?"

I sipped at my drink to buy a few moments of time. The man was like a whirlwind, and I didn't want to get swept up in his bluster. This interview was important to me. I needed to get it right.

"What did you order for me?" I asked.

"Tuna salad sandwich," McNab said. "It's all I've got time for. And I don't think it's right that the nation's leaders are swilling alcohol and feasting on three course meals while the rest of the country is still struggling to survive. Do you?"

"I see your point," I agreed carefully, "but why bring me to a restaurant at all? Couldn't we have done this interview in your office?"

"No," McNab said. He glanced past me, his eyes moving in his head. The restaurant was all but deserted. We were sitting in a dark corner, with the drapes drawn across the windows to block out the afternoon sunshine. There was only one other occupied table – a couple of dark suited men wearing sunglasses and sipping at bottles of water. The men were both young, with short neat haircuts. Secret Service, I guessed.

"I didn't want this conversation to take place anywhere near the State Department."

I didn't pursue the matter. I shrugged my shoulders and took another sip of my drink. The Secretary of State picked up his glass and swallowed his bourbon like it was medicine.

McNab was a tall man with curly grey hair and the kind of soft pouches of skin under his eyes that made you think he was sleepy. He had a beaked nose, and deeply etched lines across his brow that formed a V between his eyes. His gaze was dark and hawk-like, his restless presence disconcerting.

"So?" he said again impatiently.

I took a deep breath. "You know I want to quote you, right? You know this interview will be on the record?"

McNab swatted the words away like they were flies with a flick of his hand. "I know that," he growled.

I shrugged. I pulled my cell phone out and laid it on the tabletop. It was recording.

"During the height of the zombie apocalypse, America was vulnerable internationally," I began. "Would you agree with that?"

McNab nodded his head. He sucked at his teeth for a moment, glanced down at the cell phone, and then he literally launched himself into a tirade.

"You don't know the half of it," the Secretary of State hissed. "Nor do the American people. But they should. They should know that the fucking Chinese and the fucking

Russians have seized on America's vulnerability and taken the opportunity to place the world right back on the brink of global conflict."

I sat back, stunned. "Are you serious?"

McNab gripped the edge of the table. "Do I look like I have a sense of humor?"

He didn't. McNab looked like the kind of man who never laughed. He was intense, bristling with energy and passion.

"Can you explain what you mean in more detail? They're fairly inflammatory claims. I don't imagine the Chinese or Russian governments would be pleased to hear your accusations."

"Fuck 'em!" McNab said like he meant it. He leaned across the table and fixed me with his hard eyes. "What I'm telling you now is exactly the same thing I have already told the Russians and the Chinese to their faces, and in exactly the same kind of language."

I raised an eyebrow in surprise. "I don't imagine the Chinese took the criticism terribly well."

"Fuck 'em," McNab said again. "The days of delicate diplomacy are long gone. We're in a different world now. For years America was the world's policeman – we intervened in global conflicts and we exerted military and economic influence to maintain the peace. But this zombie outbreak changed all that. We were forced to become isolationist – we were forced to pull out of Europe and the Middle East to protect America from infestation."

"And you claim the Chinese and the Russians took advantage of that, right?"

"They did," McNab said flatly. "America is on the brink of financial ruin. Our economy has collapsed. Wall Street, our industries... everything broke down when the apocalypse spread through Florida. People left their jobs to protect their families. Others tried to flee north to Canada.

We had martial law introduced. Everything ground to a halt, and then collapsed from under our feet. The Chinese… the fucking Chinese… what did they do? Did they offer to help? Did they extend any aid to America? Of course not. They called in their fucking debts! They sent a delegation to Washington insisting that we repay all loans immediately," McNab's face was twisted with his rage and loathing.

"And naturally we couldn't," I prompted gently.

"Of course not!" McNab was seething. "We were on the brink of Armageddon."

"So you think the Chinese demand to repay the loans was what… a ploy?"

McNab nodded. He waved his hand at the waiter for another drink. "When we met the delegation, they had a compromise," the Secretary of State smiled bitterly. "They would forgive all loans – wipe the slate clean. All we had to do was turn our back while they invaded Taiwan."

"They used the loans as leverage?"

"They blackmailed us," McNab said. "And there was nothing we could do. We couldn't defend Taiwan because we had every piece of American military hardware fighting to defend America. So they bought tacit permission to invade Taiwan, knowing we couldn't do a damned thing to stop them."

My mind leaped ahead to a frightening thought. "Are we still vulnerable, Mr. McNab? Is America at risk of a Chinese, or maybe a Russian invasion?"

"No," the Secretary of State said emphatically. "The bastards wouldn't be game." His drink arrived. He moved the glass away to the side of the table. "The Chinese aren't interested. Their focus is on Asia. Now they have Taiwan, and the North Koreans are massing on the border to South Korea. They're backed by the Chinese – but they're keeping their expansion plans firmly in the Asia region. The

Russians… well they've swept through the Ukraine and they've also taken Poland. They have troops on the border to Germany, but that's as far as they'll go until next spring. They wouldn't dare try to invade America."

I raised my eyebrows at that. "Really? Given America's current position?"

"*Because* of America's current position," McNab corrected me to make his point. I didn't understand.

"I don't understand," I said.

The Secretary of State glanced down at his watch and then stared back into my eyes. "When the apocalypse swept through the southern states of America, civilization *as the American people know it* collapsed. We have power supply problems, blackouts and brownouts. We have food shortages, no exports, no economy. We have no social media, limited cell phone capabilities. We have drinking water problems and in some states we have riots in the streets. We still have martial law."

I nodded, but I didn't see the man's point. If anything it seemed like he was making the case *for* the very real prospect that America could be invaded by Russia.

"The point is that America has changed," McNab went on. "Americans have changed. We used to be the wealthiest, most envied nation in the world. We used to be financially the strongest nation in the world. Not any more. Now we have become a nation of gun-carrying survivalists. We've become like Sparta."

"Sparta? You mean ancient Sparta?"

McNab nodded. "The Greeks and Romans were the affluent cultures in the ancient world. They had art and civilization. They had philosophy and literature. The Spartans were warriors. They were no-frills fuckers who terrified the ancient world because their focus was solely on their own survival. That's who we have become. We got king-hit by the zombie outbreak, and when a man gets hit he tucks his chin onto his chest and regains his balance. That's what America is doing. Then the guy gets back up off the floor and he fights back," McNab enthused, and there was a rising tone of passion and fire in his voice. "That's what we're going to do when the time is right, only it won't be the old America, it will be the new America swinging punches – a tougher, leaner nation filled with people who haven't been made lazy and apathetic by everything they have been blessed with. It will be an America filled with warriors who know how to survive, and know what it's like to fight for their life."

I was about to ask another question when. the waiter arrived with our sandwiches. He was a nervous young man. He set our food down on the table and fussed over how the plates were arranged. The Secretary of State gnawed on his lip like he was stifling his temper. When the waiter had disappeared, McNab took the top off his sandwich and examined the filling.

"NATO has collapsed," McNab said as he prodded a piece of tomato with the tip of his finger. He pushed the slice to the side of his plate and replaced the bread. "The fucking French – the chicken-shit bastards have pulled out of the organization, and maybe Belgium will do the same. They don't have the balls to stand up to Russia without us propping them up."

"And what does that mean, do you think?"

"I know what it fucking means!" the Secretary of State's voice rose and took on an edge of frustration and temper. "It means the fucking French are a useless pack of cowards who haven't won a fucking fight since the time of Napoleon. Now they're trying to hide from Russia because they don't have the guts to stand and fight. They left NATO, and that means they've abandoned their European partners."

"Which means…?" I kept prompting gently. I felt like a kid poking an angry snake with a stick.

"It means we now have Germany and Britain left on their own to man the Fulda Gap against Russian armor. We can't help them, and no one else from NATO is coming to their aid. The fucking French have seen to that."

"You blame the French?"

"Yes," McNab said. "If they had held firm, NATO would have held together. Now Europe is in danger of becoming a total fucking shambles. War seems imminent. Once Russia has got the Ukraine bedded down and smashed Poland, Germany could be next."

"And we're powerless to stop them."

"Exactly. We can't be the international cop while the police station is burning to the ground. We've got to sort out the crisis here at home before we can begin to project our influence internationally again."

I picked up my sandwich in my fist and took a bite. McNab looked at me like I was something repulsive he found on the sole of his shoe. He stabbed his fork into one corner of his own sandwich and cut off a piece with his knife. He held the fork up as if to show me how the sandwich should be eaten.

Who eats a tuna salad sandwich with a knife and fork?

I dropped my sandwich back onto the plate and reached for my own fork. McNab looked grimly satisfied.

"With respect, sir," I said, "but America has certainly contributed to global instability. I mean, what we did to Iran… and the implications of that action across the entire Middle East…"

"That is horse-shit!" McNab growled. He dropped his knife and fork and shifted his weight in his chair like he was itching to reach across the table and grab me by the throat. "What we did to Iran was exact revenge for the most heinous crime ever committed against America and mankind," he said. "We got payback, and those fuckers deserved every bomb, and every bullet."

We glared at each other across the table. I nudged my cell phone a little closer to the Secretary of State with my forearm. "Yes, but as a result of that action, the Middle East is now embroiled in war." I held up my hand and counted off each point on my fingers. "Israel has been locked in conflict with the Palestinians for the last four months. Iran's government has been destroyed, and now half a dozen different terrorist insurgent groups are laying claim to various parts of the country. Syria is in the grip of civil war. Egypt's government has been toppled…" I rested my hand on the table, "and all these dominos have fallen since we attacked Iran to avenge the zombie outbreak. Surely we must accept some responsibility."

"Horse-shit," McNab said again. "Iran got everything it deserved. What happens there now isn't our responsibility. Our duty is to America, and to protect the American people, by any means… *any means* deemed suitable by the President. We might not be able to protect the rest of the world at the moment, but we can damned sure protect ourselves, and the message to Iran and anyone else who wants to take a punch at America was sent loud and clear – fuck with us, and we'll fuck you over."

I sat back in my chair and drummed my fingers on the edge of the table. McNab took a bite of his sandwich and then stabbed the fork in my direction. "What else do you want to ask?"

"What about the United Nations?"

"What about it?"

"Well… why didn't we go to the United Nations over what Iran did? Wouldn't that be the normal way to deal with the kind of international act of terrorism they perpetrated? Sanctions could have been called for. Iran could have been pariahed by the rest of the world."

"Sanctions? Fucking sanctions?" McNab spat the words at me. I was playing Devil's Advocate. Personally I was delighted we had bombed the Iranians back to the Stone Age, but in the interests of journalism I wanted to put the question to the Secretary of State.

"Sanctions don't work," McNab said. "Never did and never will. You're talking about trying to slowly strangle the life out of an Islamic nation that has vowed an eternal struggle against the West." He jabbed a finger at me and his eyes took on a peculiar gleam of passion. "That's the point here. Sanctions would have been a slap on the wrist. We wanted to punch them in the nose, and then kick them in the balls. That's why we bombed the fuckers."

"And the United Nations? Was there ever a thought within the Government to gather collective support for the attack?"

"No."

"Why? We did that in the Middle East before."

"Because we didn't *need* anyone's support, and we sure as hell didn't *need* anyone's approval. You fuck with us, we fuck you over," he used the phrase for a second time.

I could understand why this man had become so popular across the country, despite – or perhaps because – of his confrontational, abrasive nature. He was a throwback to the glory days of America when men like John Wayne were film stars.

"Do you realize how close we came to total collapse?" he asked me around a mouthful of food. "Do you have any understanding of just how perilous our situation was when the terror of the apocalypse first broke out in Florida?"

I shrugged my shoulders. It wasn't really a question I could answer. I frowned down at my food for a moment. "How close?"

McNab pressed his fingers together like he was taking a pinch of air. "This close," he said, giving the words and the gesture heavy emphasis. "We were on the very fucking verge of falling apart."

"Until?"

"Until our President closed the border to Canada and Mexico and stopped everyone fleeing the country. When he went on television and gave his, *'United we Stand'* speech, everything began to turn around."

I leaned forward and pushed what was left of my tuna salad sandwich aside. "Closing the borders caused riots," I said, remembering those frantic first weeks of utter panic that gripped the nation. "It was anarchy, and troops had to be posted. Troops that could have been used protecting the defensive line the Army had created against the spread of the zombies."

McNab nodded. It was the first time he had actually conceded a point. "You're right," he said. "For the first few weeks everything hung in the balance. That's why the President made his address. And that's when everything began to settle."

"Could you explain that to me?"

"You mean the why and the wherefore?"

"Yes."

McNab rubbed his chin. I caught another glance of the expensive cufflinks. They were out of character for the man, as was the suit and tie. He struck me as someone more comfortable in work clothes than dressed like an over-priced lawyer.

"Closing the borders made a statement. It said, loud and clear to the American people, *'this is where we are, and we're making a stand. If we go down, we do it together. If we get out of this mess it's because we stand together'.*"

I couldn't help myself. I smiled. The Secretary of State had just quoted from the President's famous speech almost word-for-word.

"And you think that made a difference?"

"I know it did," McNab said earnestly. "I saw it in the way people responded, the way they reacted. They went from fighting to keep their family alive to fighting to keep America alive. People began to band together. We stopped being individuals and became united again. Men volunteered for duty. They stepped up, knowing that protecting America was the best way to protect their own families. We saw people begin to give and share again. We saw Americans at their finest. That's what the President did when he gave that address. He reminded everyone of who they were, and he got us fighting for each other again."

I picked up my glass and stared down into the contents like I was a fortune teller trying to divine some clairvoyant glimpse of the future. I looked up at last. McNab was staring at me.

"Will we ever recover?" I asked.

McNab nodded his head. "We will," he sounded certain. "It's going to take a lot of time. We've got to get the nation back on its feet and we've got to rid Florida of the infected, but we will recover," the Secretary of State declared. "But we won't be the same. We can't be – not after all we have endured and the damage that has been done. When we come out of this, and when we're ready to be part of the world again, we'll be a different America… but better and stronger because of it. You mark my words."

THE ATLANTIC OCEAN:
SOMEWHERE OFF THE COAST OF FLORIDA

The sky was a sullen endless vista of clouds the color of old bruises as the ship steamed north. I was standing on the port side, the wind blowing into my face. As the warship's bow cleaved through the rolling swell, a fine mist of sea spray fell like rain. It was uncomfortable – not the ideal place for an interview, and yet the sailor standing beside me didn't even seem to notice.

He was aged in his mid thirties – a man with a mop of black hair and one of those wicked smiles that flashed mischief every time he talked. His eyes were dark, his facial features animated. He had the stub of a cigar jammed into the corner of his mouth and there was a sense of world-weariness about him – as if he were an old soul in a young man's body. He took a deep breath, like the smell of the salty air was invigorating.

Gunners Mate 1st Class, D.K Murphy swept his gaze towards where the distant Florida coastline lay, somewhere beyond the grey heaving horizon.

We were aboard *USS Mahan* DDG-72, an Arleigh Burke class destroyer. The *Mahan* was one of the Navy's guided missile destroyers that had been built around the formidable Aegis Combat System. The ship was a multi-role vessel, bristling with weaponry that included over ninety missiles.

"What was it like to be part of the Navy's fleet during the apocalypse?" I asked the sailor. When we had first met he had insisted I call him 'Murph'. The man frowned, as though he was rummaging around in his mind for the right words.

"We were part of the Navy's bombardment once the dreads had been pushed back into Florida," he explained. "At that stage the zombies were being crushed by the army, but there was still no defensive line along the Florida border. That was why the Atlantic Fleet was called in – we shelled the north of Florida while the army engineers threw up the final defensive trenches."

I nodded. The ship nosed her bow into another wave and a wash of seawater came slopping along the deck.

"Do you remember what other ships were involved in that bombardment, Murph?"

He smiled easily. "Hell," he rubbed his chin, "I think the whole damned fleet must have been out there. It seemed like you could have walked the entire coast of Florida from one bow to the next stern. We were just one long grey line steaming up and down the coast, raining hate, hell and discontent in its wake."

"And what was your role in the conflict?" I asked. "I was told you were part of a gun crew. Is that right?"

Murph nodded his head. He snatched the stub of the cigar from the corner of his mouth. "I was Mount 51 gun captain of the MK45, 5in 54."

I stared at Murph and he must have seen the utter bewilderment in my eyes. It was as if he had suddenly begun speaking in a foreign language.

"What does that mean?"

He smiled, and the expression twisted and contorted the rest of his facial features. "It means I was in charge of making sure the gun went 'boom' when it was supposed to, and kept on going 'boom' until it wasn't."

I turned and glanced over my shoulder, staring back along the superstructure of the ship. "Was it that gun?" I asked, pointing like a wide-eyed child at the forward weapon, closest to the bow.

Murph nodded. "The weapon itself is above deck, and the control and ready loader room sits just below it. It was Johnson and me on the control panel, and down in the deep mag Smitty was in charge of our ammo handler crew."

"Deep mag?"

Murph nodded. I think it was then that he finally realized I knew nothing at all about ships or their weapons because from that point on in the interview he went to great pains to explain everything in more detail.

"The deep mag is the ammo load point for the weapon. It's three decks down," he said.

I made the kind of facial expression that showed I was impressed. I had no idea so many men and so much complex design went into the firing of a naval gun.

I clung for the ship's rail. The sea was becoming more agitated. The swells were rising. I heard the distant sound of rumbling thunder and the wind became biting cold. I looked longingly back towards the shelter and warmth of the ship's superstructure again and then sighed wistfully.

"What exactly was your task during the bombardment of the Florida border?" I asked. My teeth were starting to chatter.

Murph wedged the end of his cigar back into the corner of his mouth before he answered. Remarkably it made no difference to the way he spoke.

"We were tasked with drawing away and destroying as many of the undead from where the engineers were building the fortification lines as we possibly could," Murph said. "The Marines and Army artillery units were doing the same sort of thing from behind the lines." He paused and shrugged his shoulders. "We were in a much better position to accomplish the task. Every round we fired not only killed dreads, but also drew them towards the sea and away from that line."

"How did you draw them away?" I asked.

Murph smiled. "Nifty tricks," he said, and winked at me. I waited.

"We started our first barrage at 0300hours, well before sunrise. We did it on purpose, you see. We began firing starshell illumination rounds." He gestured with his hands to help me understand. "They're kind of like a giant flare. They make a shit load of noise and explode in bright colors. Like a firework," he decided the word was more descriptive than 'flare'.

"We were trying to lure the dreads – so we were firing all kinds of shit we knew would attract their attention."

I help up my hand. "Can we go somewhere else?" I asked impulsively. My lips were turning blue and I was sure I was losing feeling in my feet. Murph looked at me quizzically.

"You cold?"

"No," I muttered the lie. "I just need to write this all down. I don't want to miss anything," I shrugged apologetically.

Murph stared at me for another long moment and then nodded his head reluctantly. He pulled the cigar from between his lips and glanced at it with regret. He tossed the stub over the rail with an expression on his face like he was burying a close friend at sea.

He led me along the deck and through a door. We walked through narrow passageways lined with steel pipes. The air smelled faintly of stale sweat and engine grease. Murph led me to the mess deck and we sat on opposite sides of a small table. I found my notebook.

"You were saying?" I looked past the blank page. Murph leaned back in his chair with his hands behind his head.

"We lobbed the flares as far inland as we could reach – that was about thirteen miles, and we set 'em to go off high up, so the dreads would be sure to see and hear them from even further away. That went on until sunrise. Every hour or so, we'd drop some Willy Pete a little closer to the coast.

"Willy Pete?"

"Phosphorous rounds," Murph explained. "They burn bright and long. We kept dragging the zombies towards the shore. Every time we fired we were shortening the range."

"To lure them towards the coast, right?"

Murph nodded. "Just like a carrot on a stick."

"And you said you kept these flares and phosphorous rounds firing until sunrise?"

Murph nodded. "By dawn all the dreads close enough to hear or see the initial cannon fire were piling up on the beach. That was when the frigates opened fire on the fuckers," he said with sudden relish. "There were special boat units and SEALs just off shore – a little past the breakers. They were in fast boats. They were spotting groups of undead and then calling in fire missions."

I wrote all this down as quickly as I could while Murph watched me with a curious kind of fascination. I glanced up and he was still watching me.

I blinked. "Is something wrong?" I asked.

Murph shook his head. "Just wondering how you do it," he said.

"What?"

"Your job. Being a journalist. Is it hard?"

"It can be," I admitted. "But not as hard as serving your country like you have done."

Murph smiled again. The darkness seemed to drift away from his expression. I had the sense that the Navy was not just a job for this man. It was his life.

I steered the conversation back to things that mattered. My work was not one of them.

"What happened at sunrise, Murph? Did the artillery barrage continue?"

The man shook his head. "Come daybreak the carrier started launching unmanned recon drones. They flew inland at high altitude, but flew back low as possible. You see we were doing everything we could to keep the dreads moving towards us, and away from the engineers digging the trenches. Every time the drones spotted a big enough group within our range we'd shower the area with high explosive – high frag rounds. The shells were armed with mechanical time fuses so they would go off in the air and rain shrapnel." Murph's gaze became distant for a moment. He shifted his weight on the chair trying to make himself more comfortable. "Every once in a while the drones would catch sight of a big group way inland and one of the cruisers in the flotilla would send a missile down range."

I flipped over to a new page and then stopped suddenly, my pen poised, as a question came to me. It was spontaneous. It just spilled from my mouth in a moment of curiosity.

"Were you scared?"

Murph looked at me like he didn't understand. He shrugged his shoulders. "No…" he said slowly, his voice kind of guarded.

I shook my head as though I wanted to erase the question and replace it with a better one. "I mean were you scared about your own role in the bombardment? There must have been some pressure on you when it came to firing and being effective, right?"

Murph straightened suddenly, and in that moment his demeanor seemed to change. He had been a laid-back and casual since we had begun talking, but now there was a flicker of some deep and significant passion in his eyes. He stared at me.

"This was the Navy's time," he began, his eyes fixed and unwavering. "We hadn't performed a major bombardment since the Vietnam War. It has always been the missile men or the flyboys for as long as I can remember." He clenched his fist. "This was the hour of the gun."

"So you were under pressure?"

"Of course!" Murph's voice rose. "Just before we came on our station in the gun line, the Captain and the Gunnery Officer stopped in '51 to make sure we were ready. As the Old Man was stepping out through the water tight door, he suddenly thrust his head back in and glared at me."

I leaned forward a little, watching Murph's eyes. "What did he say?" I asked, intrigued.

Murph smiled wryly. "The Old Man said, 'gunner, if we come off our first trip up the gun line with anything other than deck hands in our deep mag, I'm going to be very disappointed in you'. Then he dogged down the hatch and we opened fire."

"Was the Old Man disappointed afterwards?"

Murph's smile broadened just a little. "No fear!" he said. "We sent everything we had down range that trip!"

I couldn't help myself. I smiled. Murph's enthusiasm and passion for the Navy was almost a tangible thing. He had such a complex personality – talking to him was like experiencing four seasons in a single day. He could drift from moody to sullen, to affable and expressive in a matter of seconds.

"How long did the bombardment last?" I asked.

He glanced up at the low ceiling as though searching his memory, and then his eyes came back to mine. "We fired half that first day, and then came off the line to onload more ammo at sea while another ship took our place. Then we stood down to rest for six hours before coming back on station to start the attack all over again. It was a long week," Murph admitted, "but I wouldn't have been anywhere else."

I went back through my notes. Some of the writing was smudged, the paper I had written on tattered and grimy. But within these pages was a compelling piece of America's fight against the zombie hordes. I thanked Murph. He got up from the table. On the way back through the maze of narrow steel passageways I had a final question.

"Did it ever bother you, Murph? Firing on the zombies, I mean."

He stopped suddenly and folded his arms across his chest. He shook his head.

"For fifteen years my home has been a sea bag and a hull number. But my parents retired ten years ago to Ocala, in Florida. I never heard from them after the apocalypse started, and I'll probably never know what happened to them," his tone lowered and his voice became softer. "They might have been in those hordes of undead we fired on," he admitted. "I tell myself sometimes at night that they were. Then, at least I can believe they are now at peace."

QUINCY, FLORIDA:
WEST OF THE FINAL FLORIDA CONTAINMENT LINE

"You were one of the Army Engineers that worked to create the fortifications of the final Danvers Defense Line, right?"

Sergeant Wally Bunton nodded his head. "That's right," he said around a mouthful of gum. "I was in one of the Engineering units assigned to closing off the western side of the Florida border."

"The new abbreviated border, right?"

"Right," Bunton said. "The Army drew a line from Panacea, to Tallahassee up to a little town called Havana. That way we liberated the Panhandle from the infection."

I looked around me. We were sitting in the shade of an Army truck in the rubble and ruins of Quincy. Like every other town south of the original Danvers Defense Line, this little corner of Florida had been laid to waste by endless artillery bombardment. Naval ships stationed in the Gulf had done some of the damage. The Air Force had done the rest.

"What was it like?" I asked the generic question. "It must have been risky as all hell."

Wally Bunton nodded his head. "I worked on the original Danvers Defense Line, digging the trenches east of Jackson in Tennessee. That was a cake-walk," he said with a tone like fond reminiscence. "Back then we had time, we had equipment, we had structure. It wasn't like that digging these trenches let me tell you. Down here, it was like trying to take a shit behind a tree in a crowded park full of people."

The pen paused on the page of my notebook and I looked up suddenly. Sergeant Bunton wasn't smiling. He was grim-faced.

"What did you say?"

He cleared his throat and spat the gum out. He repeated the analogy again and watched my face as I arched my eyebrows. "What I mean by that is to say it was an endless butt-pucker," the man tried to explain. "We were digging furiously, excavators, heavy trucks… every piece of equipment we could beg, borrow or steal to get the trench line dug and the barbed wire laid… and at every moment we were expecting to see fucking zombies fill the skyline. We were trying to work quiet – trying not to make any noise. Like I said, it was like trying to take a shit…"

I nodded. I got it.

"Did you see any zombies? Was there ever a point when you and your men came under attack?"

Bunton shook his head. "We had the Louisiana National Guard protecting us. They had units all along the western Florida flank while we were getting the fortifications ready. They were posted a few miles inside the zombie zone… poor bastards."

I frowned. "Why do you say that? Were they attacked?"

"I say it because it was the most nerve wracking duty a guy could draw," he looked at me like maybe I was a visitor from another planet. "They were *inside* the zombie zone covering our ass while we threw up the fortifications."

"So they did get attacked?"

Bunton shrugged. "Man, there was contact all along the line from St. Marys on the coast to Monticello. It couldn't be helped. We were working right on the edge of the infection zone."

"Deaths?"

Again, Sergeant Bunton shrugged. He rummaged around in his pocket for another stick of gum. He was a broad-shouldered brawny man with tattoos along his muscled forearms and his hair buzzed close to his skull. His uniform was covered in dust and dirt as a testament to his work. Even now, when the defensive line was established, the Army Engineer Corps were still at work maintaining and improving the hastily prepared trenches and earthworks.

"There were no deaths amongst my men," he said. "And none that I heard about from the National Guard guys protecting us. But further east... well you hear all kinds of rumors," he said and eyed me speculatively, as though inviting me to probe for details.

I did. It was my job. "What rumors did you hear?"

Bunton got to his feet and stretched. The sun was hot. He mopped his brow. Even in the shade the heat was sweltering. My shirt stuck to my back and I could feel beads of sweat popping up across my brow.

Bunton glanced over his shoulder. Two soldiers were repairing another truck. I could hear the clank of tools and the soft curses of their frustration. He jerked his head. "Let's take a walk," he said.

We couldn't see the western trench line from here — it was a few miles further to the east. Around us were heavy vehicles and some tanks. In the distance I could see the trail of dust kicked up by trucks carrying troops.

When we were away from the vehicles, standing in a pile of grey rubble, Bunton stopped and squinted up at the sun. "I heard that a whole Company of National Guard boys from Kentucky got overwhelmed by zombies further to the east," he said. "But the Army has kept it quiet."

I frowned. "Where further east?" I asked.

Bunton glanced at me. "Around Jasper," he said.

"Are you sure?"

Bunton looked away warily for a moment, as though he had suddenly heard a sound carried on the air. When he turned back to me his eyes were narrowed. "That's what I heard," he said. "At first the rumor was that the blanket of artillery fire we were laying down close to the border had taken out the Company. But a day later I heard that it wasn't artillery fire at all. The zombies had attacked the line and run into the National Guard. What I heard was that thousands of the undead came out of the night and overran the perimeter. They got to the trenches and were held up by the barbed wire just long enough for reserves to be called up."

I didn't write any of this down, but I paid careful attention. "Who told you this?" I asked.

Bunton shook his head and gave me a *'do you think I am that dumb'* kind of look. "Check it out," he said.

"How?" I asked. "I can't check it out if you won't give me your source?"

Sergeant Bunton clamped his lips tightly shut and shrugged his shoulders one final time. "Then I guess it will remain a rumor," he muttered. "And a mystery."

CIA HEADQUARTERS:
LANGLEY, VIRGINIA

The Director of the Central Intelligence Agency sat hunched over his desk, hands clasped together and eyes closed like he was in the attitude of prayer.

Calvin Maitland was a short, solid city-bred man who looked like an accountant. His hair was cut short and swept across his forehead to disguise a receding hairline, and his skin was darkly tanned. As I spoke the man's face changed, his features animated as he followed every word of the question. He frowned deeply, and then a moment later he smiled.

"Good question," he said as his eyes came slowly open and he fixed me with his gaze. "And I'm glad you asked it."

"Do you have an answer?"

Maitland's smile clung precariously to his mouth as he started to speak. "Gathering intelligence is a complex proposition at the best of times. The United States has a highly sophisticated network of satellites as well as human resources and other more oblique resources. That's how we piece together what is happening in the world, and where threats might come from."

I wrote everything down, and then looked up. The man was still smiling – a relaxed expression, like he was toying with me and doing it easily.

"Thank you," I said politely. "Now would you answer the question I asked?"

The smile faded. "I just did."

I shook my head. "No, sir, you didn't," I kept my tone respectful but firm. "I asked you specifically what lead the CIA to draw the conclusion that Iran was behind the zombie apocalypse. I asked you for the actual evidence you gathered to support your claim that the Iranian government perpetrated this act of international terrorism."

The Director leaned back in his chair and set his hands on the armrest. He crossed his legs and narrowed his eyes. "I think the answer I gave you will be suitable for your interview," he muttered the words carefully.

I shook my head again. "Sir, your answer sounded like something you would dish up at a press conference, but this isn't one of those. I was told you would be fully co-operative."

Maitland said nothing. I tried again.

"I happen to think the work the CIA did to follow the trail of terrorism back to Iran was quite brilliant. I'd like the opportunity to portray that to my readers. You sandbagging me this way is just going to come off as arrogance. I don't want arrogance. I want reality. You're giving me filtered fiction."

The Director's eyes flicked down to a single piece of paper on his desk. It could have been a Presidential directive, or it could have been a shopping list. He scanned it, his eyes moving in his motionless head, and then he looked up at me again and gave the kind of heavy sigh that sounded like a child blowing out birthday candles.

"HUMINT and OSINT were critical to following the trail back to the Iranians," Director Maitland revealed at last. "Everyone thinks the majority of espionage work these days is done through satellites. They are important, but they don't tell you anything more than what is in a picture. They can't tell you the 'why'… and that's often critical when an organization like this one is analyzing data."

Better. I wrote furiously. Maitland was talking quickly, as though he was keen to be done with the explanation and it took all my concentration just to keep up. When he paused for a breath my hand was aching.

"We also were fortunate that some of the men and women involved in this investigation were 'blue skyers'," Maitland said.

I looked up from the notebook. "Blue skyers?"

The CIA Director nodded. He steepled his fingers together as if he was trying a different kind of prayer position. "Yes," he said. "Men and women who go above and beyond the normal means of investigation – they're people that don't follow a trail. Instead they see a situation and ask *'what if'*. Those folks were the ones within the team that made the biggest breakthrough."

I was intrigued. Fascinated. I had come to this interview at Langley with little expectation. Now my journalistic instincts were screaming. This was a thread of conversation I knew I needed to unravel. I also knew instinctively that I needed to be patient.

"What exactly is HUMINT and OSINT?" I asked.

"HUMINT is short for human intelligence – it's the information that might be gathered from traditional spy sources."

I cut in quickly. "You mean spies on the ground in Iran?"

The Director inclined his head. He rested his hands palm-down on the desktop. Clearly he had given up praying I would go away quietly. "That's right," he said.

"And OSINT?"

"That is an abbreviation for Open Source Intelligence," Director Maitland explained. "It's something that the average man in the street might not think about much, but over the past twenty years it has become a valuable form of intelligence gathering... without the James Bond glamor." He smiled then, amused by his own comment.

I shifted my weight in the chair, arched my back as I sat up straight. "Can you explain the kind of OSINT you are referring to?"

Maitland glanced past my shoulder. I knew behind me was his office door and a wall lined with books. He hesitated for a moment and then brought his eyes back to mine.

"You have to understand that I am reluctant to divulge every source of intelligence our Agency uses..."

"I do understand," I said. "And if Iran was still functioning with a government and an Army, I would understand it even more. But since that's no longer the case..."

Maitland's expression became pinched with a flicker of annoyance. He shifted his gaze back down to that single piece of paper on his desk. His eyes were moving like he wanted to look anywhere except directly at me… so I stared at him.

He capitulated with one final sigh. "Open Source intelligence is the gathering of material that is readily available to everyone," the CIA Director began to explain. "In the old days it might be things like newspaper clippings, footage of foreign events broadcast on television… you understand?"

I nodded.

"In the last twenty years that has grown to include the kind of information that is transmitted through cell phone communications, and social media."

"Facebook?"

The Director nodded. "It includes all forms of social media," he confirmed.

"And Facebook gave you clues about Iran's involvement in the zombie terrorism attack?" If I sounded incredulous, I was. I felt certain the Director was still playing his games.

"Yes," Maitland said with conviction. "Facebook actually provided some of the early clues that ultimately led us to confirm that the zombie outbreak was an Iranian terrorism plot."

I wrote all this down, but I wasn't sure why. I had the feeling that at any moment, the CIA Director was going to break out into a bullroar of laughter, amused by my gullibility.

"Sir, are you serious?"

"Yes."

I raised a questioning eyebrow and sat back in disbelieving silence. Maitland's expression never altered. His features were set and rigid, almost as though this conversation was painful for him.

"I need more details," I said.

Maitland nodded his head. "The Open Source Center is based in Reston, Virginia," Maitland began. "Ironically it is the least understood intelligence discipline. That's probably because the information gathered there doesn't need to be stolen. The Center employs a large number of staff, and some of those staff operate social media accounts. Not all of those accounts are genuine. Do you understand where I am leading?"

I shook my head. I didn't. "You're talking about people at the Open Source Center operating fake accounts on social media?"

"I am," Maitland said. "And not all of those fake accounts are created with American profiles. Understand?"

I shook my head again. The CIA Director was trying to lead me somewhere and I didn't know where. I was getting frustrated.

"Can you just tell me where this is going, sir," I asked. "I'm really not good at quizzes or puzzles."

Maitland looked disappointed. Perhaps it had been his last attempt to answer my questions without actually having to directly say the words. He shook his head like a disappointed father when his son drops a high ball.

"We had people based at the Open Source Center and they operated social media accounts in the names of Middle East citizens," he said softly. "They created profiles as Iranian students, or young adults and they interacted over social media networks with genuine Iranian citizens."

"Like friends?"

"Online friends," Maitland said. "They would log onto the accounts at times that corresponded with mornings and evenings in the Middle East, and they would assume their fictitious identities to engage in conversation with students, doctors... the youth of Iran."

I was baffled and confused. "Just like that?"

"No," Maitland shook his head. "Some of the accounts we operated have been established for several years. It wasn't something that we just did overnight, and it's not something that we operated only in Iran. We had fictional social media accounts created for various people right across the Middle East."

"Had?"

"Have… had… Draw your own conclusions, Mr. Culver."

I had stopped writing. Maitland and I spent a few seconds eyeballing each other, like we were locked in a staring competition.

"I didn't know the youth of Iran even had internet," I said warily.

Maitland smiled bleakly. "They do," he said. "In fact the leadership of Iran itself is not immune to the power of Facebook and other social media sites. Some of them have used those sites to post messages and information."

"But the country had internet filtering, surely."

"Yes," Maitland said. "They had draconian measures in place because they feared online social networking's potential to challenge the narrative the regime was articulating. The 'Twitter Revolution' that threatened Moldova a few years ago and that swept the Egyptian government from power would have given the Iranian's plenty to worry about. So they had draconian internet filtering. That wasn't enough to stop the Iranian youth. One third of the nation's youth were interconnected and politicized by virtual social networks."

"So you are saying that the Iranian youth were actively disobeying or circumventing the social media bans imposed by the government?"

"Of course they were," Maitland said bluntly. "In fact, according to Iran's Ministry of Sciences, almost sixty percent of Iranian university students use Viber and

WeChat, and almost the same amount admit to using Facebook. Iranian university students are just like students all around the world, Mr. Culver. They're social – it's just harder for them, so much of the social media activity was underground."

"And your staff at the Open Source Center tapped into the social media network of information?"

"Yes."

"What did you discover?"

"Nothing – directly," Maitland admitted. "But in the weeks leading up to the outbreak of the zombie infection in Florida, there were photos and commentaries coming out of Iran's social media about long lines of people around Tehran. Now normally that's nothing too extraordinary. But the lines of people being photographed were all young men. Normally if the government was vaccinating the population for a strain of desert flu, then the lines would be mixed groups of men and women, and mixed ages in different parts of the city. But these groups were all young men, and the lines were not out front of hospitals or medical facilities – they were outside military barracks."

I nodded my head in slow understanding. "And that was your first clue?"

"It was, but we didn't realize it at the time," Maitland confessed. "It was just something interesting that made it into a report and was then forgotten. The speculation in Iran from the people we were connected to through social media was vague, and certainly not alarmed. They didn't know what the government was doing, and neither did the men in the lines. They received an injection – that was all they knew. They weren't told what it was for."

"And the human intelligence?"

The CIA Director didn't flinch – didn't resist. He adjusted the knot of his tie and fell back into the soft padding of his chair.

"Not ours," he admitted. "The fact is that we have never been able to place a source high enough into the Iranian regime to be of any use."

I shrugged my shoulders. "So where did the information come from?"

"The Mossad and the British."

"Mossad – the Israeli secret intelligence?"

Maitland nodded. "They had a source in the Iranian government – a contact they only referred to as 'Pegasus'."

"A politician?"

Maitland made a face like he had bitten into something sour. "Most probably," he agreed. "All we know is they had been running him since 2010. Apparently they caught him in a honey-pot operation during some European delegation visit. Quite frankly, that's all we know about the guy."

"Honey-pot? What is that?"

"It's a standard method of trapping a source and blackmailing them," Maitland said frankly. "This guy got caught with his dick inside the wrong under-aged girl. The Israelis set him up and he rolled over."

I nodded. "And he told the Israelis about the zombie virus?"

Maitland shook his head. "If he did, Mossad didn't tell us," Maitland said softly. "They told us that the Iranian government was immunizing its Army – injecting them with some kind of antidote."

"The antidote to the zombie virus, right."

"That's the conclusion we made – eventually. Once it was too late. At the time, it dovetailed in with what we were hearing on social media, but the reports were separate. No one put the two pieces of information together until later."

"And the British? You mentioned their involvement somehow."

Maitland nodded. "They intercepted two phone calls, one from France and one from Tehran, both made by a

Russian scientist to a former comrade and fellow scientist. Apparently the two men had worked together in Russia. The man who received the call had defected to Britain."

"And the caller? Who was that?"

"A scientist by the name of Glavinoski."

I sat back in my chair again, and recalled my conversation with Professor Igor Vavilov. "So then you went to Boston and spoke to one of the other men this Glavinoski worked with – a man the CIA had brought into America after the end of the Cold War."

"Vavilov," Maitland confirmed.

It was all making sense. I could see the trail: the Russian scientist who had been employed by the Iranians to develop the zombie virus, telephoning an old associate who he had worked with at the Institute of Ultra Pure Biochemical Preparations in Leningrad. "Were those phone calls you intercepted between the two Russian scientists specifically about the development of the zombie plague?"

"Yes," Maitland said, "although when we played through the tapes the British sent us, everything was naturally abstract. Again, on its own, the information was interesting, but not specific. We only put everything together when our blue-skyers started asking questions."

I leaned forward in the chair again. I was perspiring. The heating in the room was turned up high, and the air was stuffy. Maitland seemed strangely unaffected. I felt a trickle of sweat run down my back.

"Tell me more about these blue-skyers you keep referring to. I don't understand their role, or how they operate."

Finally Calvin Maitland seemed to relax. A trace of a smile touched his lips, and it was an expression of grim satisfaction. I sensed that here, at last, was something he was willing and eager to share.

"Generally intelligence gathering is a join-the-dots kind of process," he explained. "Sometimes you can come across a piece of information and use it to take preventative counter-measures. At other times, the intelligence gathered simply confirms a current belief. Occasionally… too rarely… you can use that intelligence you have to create a case. That's what we did. We created a case against Iran by assembling all the fragments of information."

I was disappointed. The whole explanation was too abstract for me to grasp, let alone for me to describe to readers. I set down my pen and notepad.

"Can you explain that in a way I can understand?" I asked. "Can you put it into a relevant context that relates to the zombie infection?"

Maitland was still smiling smugly. He sat forward and the springs of his expensive executive chair creaked.

"Back when Ronald Reagan was President, America and Russia were locked in the grips of the cold war. It was the 1980's and all the data coming across the CIA's desk suggested that Russia's economy was growing – almost booming. But one or two of our guys didn't believe it, so they sat down and asked themselves 'what if'. What if Russia was actually on the brink of economic collapse – despite everything we were being told. What sort of conditions would we expect to see? What indicators would there be to support the idea? Then they went looking. That was the key. They asked a question and then went looking for evidence. They didn't wait for the evidence to come to them and they didn't accept anything at face value. They went looking for truth."

"And found?"

"And they found that Russia was teetering on the brink of imploding," the CIA Director explained. "They drew up a list of the economic and social indicators they expected to see and then put the word out to agencies around the world.

Within weeks the data started coming back, all of it supporting their speculation. Reagan used that information to end the Cold War. He essentially dared the Russians to compete in an arms race they couldn't afford. Ultimately, they had to concede. The Cold War ended."

"And your guys did the same thing?"

"Essentially, they did," Maitland confirmed. He got out of his chair suddenly, leaped to his feet and paced across the room. He thrust his hands deep into his pockets and when he reached the door, he stood perfectly still with his head bowed, like he was concentrating all of his will on a problem. I swiveled in my chair to follow the man. He looked up at me at last.

"For months after the initial outbreak of the zombie infection we all assumed it was some terrible disaster, but a natural disaster. Something that just happened," he shrugged his shoulders. "But one of the guys here at Langley wasn't so sure. He started to ask questions, and one of the questions was 'what if'. What if this was some kind of monumental monstrous terrorist attack, the likes of which mankind had never known? What would we see if that was the case?"

"And he started digging, right?"

Maitland nodded. "He started assembling those fragments of information I mentioned earlier. We started looking in the Middle East, and when we put the fragments of information together it became clear that Iran might have been involved. Then we went to the satellite data, and other social data that suddenly became relevant.

"Social data?"

Maitland nodded. "The Iranian government – the key members of the regime – had not been seen in public for months. No national broadcasts. No sightings at all. No military exercises. The entire Army had been basically confined to barracks. Their defense systems had been on alert, but there was no imminent threat."

"And the satellites?"

Maitland peered hard at me. "In 2014 the US government launched a satellite from Vandenberg Air Force Base named NROL-25," he said quietly. "It's operated by the National Reconnaissance Office, and it is fitted with technology known as 'synthetic aperture radar'... which means it can see through cloud, it can see in daylight and dark... and it can identify underground structures, such as military bunkers."

I raised both eyebrows in stunned surprise. "Really? We have satellites that can do that?"

Maitland nodded and then went on. "The NROL-25 was tasked to fly over Iran. We found the secret bunkers beneath Tehran. Then we went back through the records of previous satellite images and saw the sudden flurries of activity around the diplomatic quarter of Tehran where the bunker is concealed. They were stocking up."

"Stocking up with supplies?"

"And people. Key people. They were all underground. That's why we hadn't seen or heard anything from their government. Every crucial person in the regime was underground – hiding... or waiting."

"You took your findings to the President?"

"Of course," Maitland came back to his desk. "When we were sure of the facts, I took everything to the President and laid it out for him. The two intercepted phone conversations between the Russian scientists were the smoking gun. Now that we looked at them and were able to give them context, everything fell into place. I assure you, there was no doubt." The CIA Director paused for a moment. "Mr. Culver, even though I haven't told you everything about our investigation, I've told you more than enough for your interview. Safe to say that when I detailed our conclusions to the President directly, he too was convinced. It was no coincidence that seven days after we pushed the zombie hordes back into Florida and cordoned off the state, we declared war on Iran and bombed them back into the sands of history."

I sat back in my chair, frowning. For long moments the room was silent. I was groping for something buried deep within my subconscious – some critical question that remained just out of reach. I furrowed my brow. I could see the CIA Director watching me like I was a fascinating science experiment. Finally, I had it. My eyes went wide.

"Sir, when all this information was assembled, and you were sure the Iranians were behind the plot, why didn't we just fly into Iran one night and snatch a dozen soldiers? Couldn't we have manufactured our own antidote? Couldn't thousands – perhaps millions of lives – have been saved if we had been able to lay our hands on the formula?"

Maitland grunted. He folded his arms across his chest. "We did," he said.

"Did what?"

"We did exactly what you suggested, Mr. Culver. The SEALs flew into Iran and we captured eight Iranian soldiers. Three of them were Revolutionary Guard."

"What happened to them?"

Maitland shrugged his shoulders in a gesture to suggest that he knew damned well, but he wasn't about to tell me. "Officially those men disappeared."

I took a deep breath and jerked my head in understanding. I wasn't about to detour down the perilous path of discussing detainees and the ethics of the government's actions. "Well before they disappeared, did you manage to discover anything about the antidote? Are we making this stuff in a lab or something?"

"There is no antidote," Maitland said flatly.

"What? But the Iranian soldiers… the long lines outside the barracks. Your intelligence information…"

"There is no antidote," the Director said again. His tone was bleak and unwavering. "Whatever those soldiers were injected with, it was either a temporary preventative to the infection that wore off and left the bloodstream within just a few days, or it was a placebo. We found nothing – no cure, and no traces of anything in their systems that might offer protection against the infection. There is no cure, Mr. Culver. None."

AIR FORCE ONE:
ANDREWS AIR FORCE BASE, MARYLAND

I watched the President give his speech down on the concrete tarmac from a swing-up TV screen that was mounted to my seat at the rear of the iconic VC-25B.

In the years before the apocalypse, the televised Presidential departure address was rarely broadcast by news media. But now – when the nation's fate hung precariously in the balance – the people needed to see their leader as often as possible.

The President stood before the microphone with Air Force One looming in the background. He smiled. He spoke about a future where America would rise from the ashes of the zombie horror into a new era of prosperity and strength. Then he took his wife by the elbow and guided her to the stairs because Air Force One had never had a jetway. A sergeant saluted. At the door of the aircraft the President and the First Lady turned and waved.

I felt a sudden jangle of nerves.

I got up from my seat and walked towards the front of the aircraft. The President's Director of Communications was waiting for me. She flicked me a harried, anxious smile.

Her name was Connie Collins. She had worked in the media before joining the President's team. She had a clipboard clasped tightly to her chest. She ran her eyes down a page of names and details, then glanced sideways at me.

"The President's accommodations are in the nose of the plane," Connie said. "He wants you to meet him there for the interview. I'll lead you through to his office."

I followed the woman forward through the lower deck of the modified Boeing 747 airliner. The upper deck was cordoned off. It was packed full of military-style electronics gear and a team of communications specialists. Connie led me to a wooden door near the front of the plane and knocked.

"Come in," the man's voice was a boom of bass even through the wall. Connie smiled at me and arched an eyebrow. "I'll be back to collect you in exactly twenty minutes. Be ready. We depart in half an hour. If you're not finished by then, you will be flying all the way to Europe with us." She gave me a pout of pink lipstick and then silently mouthed the words, "Good luck."

I took a nerve-settling breath and pushed open the door to meet the President of the United States of America.

Joseph Mace was sixty-three years old; a hulking solid framed man with intelligent, searching eyes set in a web of fine wrinkles. His hair was grey and wavy, tidy without being styled, and his smile seemed genuine. As I entered the office he rose from behind his desk and shook my hand. He was wearing a shirt and tie. His coat was draped over the backrest of the chair and he had the sleeves of his shirt rolled up.

"John, nice to meet you."

The President just called me 'John'.

"Mr. President," I smiled nervously. My palms were sweaty. "Sir, thank you for granting this interview."

The office was functional – nothing elaborate, nor extravagant. It seemed a reflection of the way this man ran the country, and perhaps of the man himself. We sat down. I slid the strap of my bag off my shoulder and set it down on the carpeted floor. The President sat back, relaxed. He crossed his legs, propped his elbow on the armrest of his chair, and then rested his chin in the cup of his hand like he was giving me his full attention. "Welcome to Air Force One," Joseph Mace said. "Do you want anything to drink before we start? Coffee perhaps?"

I shook my head. "No thank you sir. I've been told I'm on the clock and I don't want to take up any more of your time than I need to."

The President started to smile. "Did Connie read you the riot act?"

I nodded. "She's efficient," I conceded, "and a little bit scary."

Mace chuckled. It was an unaffected, genuine sound. "She needs to be, I'm afraid, otherwise I wouldn't get any work done."

I sat back. I felt a little of the anxiety seep away from my body. President Joseph Mace was going out of his way to make me feel comfortable. He struck me then as the kind of man who could easily be your next-door neighbor – the kind of guy who might drink a beer on Sunday afternoons while watching a ball game. For all his stature and power, somehow he had retained his humility and humanity… and his willingness to connect with the people who had elected him to represent them.

I reached into my bag for my notebook, and flipped back the cover to a new blank page. The President didn't change his relaxed posture. He didn't stiffen, and he didn't suddenly become wary or guarded. It felt like a friendly chat rather than an interview with one of the most powerful men in the world.

I glanced at President Mace. He inclined his head. "Go for it," he invited me. I could feel my throat tightening. Suddenly my mouth felt dry and stuffed with cotton wool. I took another deep breath, and then blurted out the first big question.

"Do you have any regrets about ordering the attack against Iran?"

"No," the President said. He fixed me with his eyes as a way of letting me see the truth of his words. "The Iranian government was behind the zombie terror attack against America. Of that there can be no doubt. They created the virus and they unleashed it on our unsuspecting citizens. They purposely set about inflicting the most damage to our country they could. They wanted America destroyed. It was only the fast, heroic actions of our military that prevented the entire nation being over-run." He sat up suddenly in his chair, drawing himself upright, his shoulders squared, the etched lines of his face changing his expression so that his features became grave and his bearing Presidential. "The fuckers deserved everything we threw at them," he said bluntly. The words seemed to boom around the room, bouncing off the walls like an echo. I blinked. President Mace went on ominously.

"There was a time not so long ago when America turned the other cheek. We became too tolerant. We didn't do enough to enforce peace around the world — we didn't attend to the tasks that we, as a nation, were obliged to, given our great wealth and strength," Joseph Mace said, suddenly launching into a speech filled with passion. "That lack of attention cost us credibility and respect. Respect," he said again for emphasis like it was a cornerstone word and a foundation for all he believed. "Well all that has changed now," the President declared. "It's not about politics. It's not about whether the President is a Democrat or a Republican. The days of party politics in America have disappeared because we can't afford the luxury of divided opinions and hesitation. From these days forward we need to rebuild the nation, and we need everyone pulling the same weight and fighting for the same causes."

"An end to politics?" I quipped. "That doesn't seem likely, surely?"

"It's already happening," President Mace declared. He shifted in his seat again and then his eyes bored into mine. "Right now we don't have time for politics, so I am inviting the opposition to nominate a suitable candidate to fill the role of Vice President. It is my plan to see America through this crisis through joint government, with representatives of both sides of the political spectrum making the decisions for the nation as we go forward."

I wrote everything the President said dutifully. I wasn't sure about the ideology or the legality of a joint government proposal… but the concept was one the people of the nation would probably encourage. But the fact was that Americans were too concerned with the day-to-day survival of their families to care what the politicians in Washington were doing. The nation was in economic tatters. Food and fuel shortages dominated daily existence. Since the FAA had grounded all flights during the early days of the outbreak, people had become isolated and almost tribal within their small communities. We were all Americans, but the things that had bound us together had been abandoned for those things we needed merely to survive.

I wondered if this President's term would be defined by the zombie outbreak, or by his ability to somehow steer the country through the crisis. Would he be the last President?

"No," President Mace declared with complete conviction. "The zombie outbreak crippled us, it hasn't killed us. Right now the infection is contained within the abbreviated borders of Florida. That has come from over twelve months of military conflict, and it hasn't been for nothing. There is every reason to believe that one day, Florida will once again be American soil. We're through the worst of this apocalyptic crisis. We'll go forward from here."

I realized then that it didn't matter what I believed about the President's bi-partisan political plans, or even whether I believed that Florida might once again become a populated state of America.

He believed it.

And he had the power to affect the changes.

"Sir, was there ever thought given to considering a limited nuclear option against the Iranians? I mean… our government's stated policy concerning a response to the use of weapons of mass destruction against the United States has always been a retaliation of equal severity."

The President nodded as though he was conceding the point, but his gaze remained level and unwavering. "I thought about it," he admitted. "I thought long and hard about the use of tactical nuclear weapons. We certainly would have been justified in taking that course of action. In the end, those around me persuaded me that an equally effective option was to use conventional weapons and a more 'surgical' approach to eliminating Iran's capabilities to function at every level of government as well as economically." The President's eyes never left mine. He wanted to make his message clear. "The people of Iran were not involved in the terrorist attack. This was State sponsored terrorism, and our target was specifically those who were behind the evil plot, and those capable of prohibiting our revenge. The only reason I did not proceed with a limited nuclear option was the social collateral damage. Millions of innocent people would have been killed."

I looked up from my notebook. "So the fear of a Russian or Chinese response to a nuclear strike was not something you factored into the decision not to nuke Tehran?"

"No," President Mace said, almost dismissing the question with a growl. "We would have stared them down and taken them on if they so much as made a sound of protest. We didn't start this terrible, tragic episode in the world's history, Mr. Culver, but we still have all the resources we need and the determination to finish it, no matter who comes at us. We will be the last one standing. I think our Soviet and Chinese friends have a new respect for our position and attitude."

"Where do you see America right now?" I asked. "I mean our station in the world?"

President Mace tilted his head thoughtfully as he considered the question. His lips were pressed tightly together and I could see tiny etched lines form around his mouth as he concentrated.

"We're alone," he said bluntly after a few more seconds of silence. "Essentially we have been cast adrift on the seas of uncertainty by the global community. They want to know if we're going to sink or swim before they tie their boat to us again." He spoke matter-of-factly, but I sensed an undercurrent of bitterness. "The only measurable support we have had is from the British and the Australians – allies that have stood with us since the Second World War. But what can they do?" he shrugged. "Australia's support is an open provocation to the Chinese who have just invaded Taiwan and have troops on the border with South Korea. The British have always stood shoulder to shoulder with us, but in doing so they risk the wrath of Russia if they move deeper into Europe. Everyone else has abandoned us, or fallen mute."

"Are we vulnerable, sir?"

"In what way?" the President became wary. The question was vague and he was too experienced merely to answer without first seeking clarification.

"Vulnerable to attack from the Russians or the Chinese?"

President Mace shook his head. "No," he said. "We still have a fearsome nuclear arsenal and a military that has the advantage of intense combat experience. Neither the Russians or the Chinese would dare to directly attack us."

"Are you certain? Both the Russians and Chinese have been very aggressive since the zombie outbreak has restricted our influence globally."

The President nodded. "That's true," he conceded. "But Moscow and Beijing still believe we're going to fall. They still believe the zombie infection will break out across the containment line, so they don't *need* to attack us. They're waiting for us to implode..." his voice lowered and then tailed off into a moment of silence before he fixed me with his eyes. "They're wrong, Mr. Culver. I'm right," The President of America declared. "We're going to come through this, and when we do, we're going to be meaner and tougher and stronger than before. That's what I believe."

He made me believe it too.

EPILOGUE:
Operation 'Fire Cauldron'.
America's Revenge...

WHITE HOUSE SITUATION ROOM:

As a room it was…. underwhelming.

I set my notebook down on the tabletop and pulled out a chair. The uniformed man standing in the doorway glared at me.

"Do you know what this room is?" he asked. He had a voice that sounded like his throat had been sandpapered, or coarsened by years of heavy smoking.

I nodded. "The Situation Room."

The officer shook his head. He was Brigadier General Bartholomew 'Bart' Cowlishaw, the Assistant Commanding General of the Joint Special Operations Command. "There are several conference rooms," he corrected me. "This is the small one. It's also the room where one of our former Presidents and his national security team watched live feeds during 'Operation Neptune Spear' back in 2011 when operators from SEAL team 6 killed bin Laden."

I raised my eyebrows, overcome with a new sense of reverent respect. "I saw that photo," I admitted. "The one with the President and the rest of his staff watching a monitor."

The Brigadier General nodded. He was immaculately uniformed, and smelled faintly of after-shave. "That's the same monitor," he said, nodding at a dark screen mounted to the wall at the end of the room where we were standing. "And this is the very same room our current President and his team watched live feed of Operation 'Fire Cauldron' when our soldiers went into Iran and destroyed their leadership in reprisal for the zombie terror attack."

I was impressed. Genuinely. This small cramped room had been the center of two defining moments of America's recent history. "Are you sure?"

"Yes," the Brigadier General said. "I was here."

He fiddled with something in his hand and the dark screen of the monitor came to life with a crackle like static. Cowlishaw gestured. "Sit down," he said gruffly. "You're about to see what the President and everyone else in this room watched."

I dropped into a chair. I reached down for my carry bag, and then remembered it was in a plastic tray beside a metal detector on the other side of the door. I cleared my throat awkwardly.

"Do you have a pen?"

The Brigadier General looked at me like I had committed some treasonable offense. "Excuse me?" he asked without it sounding anything like a question.

"A pen," I said apologetically. "Mine is in my bag…" I flicked a glance beyond the doorway. Cowlishaw made a face like he had just inhaled smelling salts. He sighed. He had a pen in his shirt pocket. He slid it across the table to me the way a bartender in a western movie slides a beer along a countertop to a thirsty cowboy. The sound was jarring in the oppressive silence. I clamped my hand over the pen and smiled weakly. "Thanks."

I turned my attention to the monitor. The screen was filled with hissing swirls of static. "This footage was captured by drones that followed our strike teams into Iran," Cowlishaw explained. "Some of what you will see is the attack against the bunker in Tehran where the Iranian leadership were ensconced. Other footage will show you our attacks against the oil fields and Iranian military installations. I suggest you make notes. The edited film will run for six minutes. If you have any questions… tough."

I turned my head in time to see the Brigadier General leave the room. I heard the door lock behind him and then a series of bright flared flashes of light in the corner of my eye tore my attention back to the unfolding drama on the large screen.

I sat transfixed. In eerie black and white images I saw the blast of several explosions, each one a brilliant flare of white against the grainy grey silhouettes of buildings and vast structures. I saw the ghostly grey shapes of helicopters, silent on the screen as they hovered, and dark running men spilled from their bellies. I saw figures fall, saw soldiers running. I saw death and gruesome, clinical destruction, devoid of sound, but somehow all the more compelling and shocking because of the silence.

Finally the screen went black. I heard the door behind me open just a few seconds later. Brigadier General Cowlishaw's face was set and grim. He had a sheath of dog-eared folders in one hand.

"That…" I shook my head. I was a journalist but I was at a loss for words. "…what I just saw… was brutal."

Cowlishaw nodded. "Operation Fire Cauldron was not an action planned just to sever the head from the monster," he said coldly. "We decapitated the head, then the arms, and the legs. We dismembered the beast so that it will never, ever rise to threaten America again. Iran – as the world knew it just over a year ago – is gone for good."

I nodded. I glanced down at the notes I had written. "I'd like to interview some of the men who participated…"

"No," Cowlishaw said bluntly. "That's not going to happen. Everyone you want to speak to is on operational duty in various parts of the world. They are unavailable."

I frowned. "You don't know yet who I wanted to speak to."

"It doesn't matter," the Brigadier General said like there would be no discussion. "It's non-negotiable."

I took a deep breath. I wondered if Cowlishaw knew I had already interviewed the President. I opened my mouth. Cowlishaw narrowed his eyes like he was daring me to protest.

"This is all you will get," he said after a few tense moments of prickly silence. He slid the folders he was holding across the desk to me. "There are reports from the bombers, the special forces teams, 160th SOAR pilots and the Navy. Read them. Write your own account. You have four hours."

"I beg your pardon?" I came out of my chair. "I don't understand."

Cowlishaw shrugged. "It's simple," he said. "You have four hours in this room with those reports. Write an account of the operation."

I shook my head. "But it will be fiction," I protested.

Cowlishaw narrowed his eyes. "It will be fiction based on fact," he corrected me. "It's either that, or you have no story."

OPERATION 'FIRE CAULDRON': ACROSS IRAN

They came out of the night without warning – three B-2 Spirit bombers, their two-man crews weary from the twelve hour flight from Whiteman Air Force Base in Missouri.

The pilots were grim-faced. This was a 'no-mercy' mission.

This was a war of revenge and retribution.

The target for the B-2's was the Iranian underground bunker that satellites and intelligence had revealed beneath the Embassy district of Tehran.

They were armed with 30,000-lb GBU-57 Massive Ordnance Penetrators, 20-foot long GPS guided bomb capable of penetrating over one hundred feet of concrete before exploding. The pilots dropped the Bunker Busters in sequence – placing the second bombs from each aircraft into the hole created by the first to ensure double penetration depth.

One bomb would have been enough. With six of the massive bombs raining down on the underground command bunker, the devastation was assured to be catastrophic.

The ground erupted as though the surrounding city had been torn apart by an earthquake. From the cameras in the circling unmanned drones, incandescent white flashes blotted out the relayed infrared footage to the White House Situation Room. When the flashes died away, the air above the capital was filled with roiling billows of thick smoke and a debris cloud of dust.

Just a few minutes after the bunker had been hit, the silhouettes of four Black Hawk helicopters appeared in the bottom right corner of the screen. They seemed to glow ghostly green on the monitor. The helicopters hovered above the rubble and then dark running figures spilled from the bellies of the beasts as operators from SEAL Team 6 roped down to the ground. The men moved quickly, wraith-like apparitions.

As the survivors of the massive Bunker Busters clambered bleeding and torn from the wreckage, the SEALs opened fire.

This was a 'no-mercy, take-no-prisoners' mission.

The B-2 Spirit bombers turned for the long flight back home. As they left Iranian air space their flight path took them past sixteen inbound B-52 bombers, on their way to oil refinery sites within the vast Iranian deserts. Further to the south, more B-2 Spirit bombers were flying in tandem teams towards Iran's five main nuclear facilities.

Apart from the men of SEAL Team 6, there would be no boots on the ground. This wasn't a war of conquest – it was a war of decimation.

The strike force of ten B-2 bombers out of Diego Garcia broke into pairs and turned onto final course settings for their targets. Armed with more of the massive Bunker Busters, two of the bat-winged stealth bombers attacked the heavy water plant near the eastern town of Arak. Another duo of B-2's dropped their payload of bombs on the Bushehr nuclear power station. Even before those guided bombs were released, two more of the US bombers were targeting the Gachin uranium mine in the south. Twin teams of B-2's also destroyed the Isfahan uranium conversion plant, and the Natanz uranium enrichment plant. Within the space of less than an hour, Iran's nuclear program had been sent back to the dark ages.

The B-52's picked up their escort of F-18's and flew on to their targets. The Fighters had been launched from the flight deck of a 5th Fleet carrier stationed in the Gulf. The giant bombers of the American Air Force flew missions throughout the dark night, destroying missile base targets at Bakhtaran, Abu Musa Island, Bandar Abbas and Imam Ali.

Iran's extensive surface-to-air missile assets were obsolete against the incoming attacks. Most were easily rendered useless by the American electronic warfare and defense suppression weapon systems. The American fighters and bombers had freedom of the skies as they pounded the Iranian defense installations. F-15 fighters from Al Dhafra in the United Arab Emirates flew missions around the clock, while the Iranian Air Force was left floundering. It had been critical to the Americans to swarm the skies and seize air superiority with fighters because several of Iran's air bases were located within minutes of key targets.

But the Iranian Air Force was no match for the advanced US fighter jets. The best the Iranians could put into the air was a small number of Su-24's and MiG-29's, but with avionics that were less advanced than the Russian versions. It was a critical weakness that the Iranians were unable to overcome. Their inability to respond to the US air strikes meant most of the country's fighters were destroyed in their hangars.

A hail of Tomahawk missiles rained down on key military and political locations within Tehran, fired from US Destroyers patrolling the gulf. Air raid sirens wailed like mournful laments and citizens scurried into shelters, or clung to their loved ones and cowered in the dark corners of their homes as the missiles continued to fall and the destruction seemed without end.

As dawn came the following morning, the sun rose behind a pall of black smoke hanging across the Middle East, drifting like a black haze.

Beneath the smoke, Iran lay in ruins. The entire nation's religious and political leadership had been destroyed in the bunker below Tehran. The nation's nuclear facilities resembled the craters of a lunar landscape, and – while elements of the Iranian military still remained – the Air Force and key Army installations had been decimated.

The B-52's returned just after sunrise. They flew unchallenged beneath the protective shelter of their fighter escorts, and bombed the Iranian naval base of Bandar-e Abbas, as well as commercial shipping harbors along the Iranian coastline.

In less than twelve hours, Iran and everything the nation had grown to be, had ceased to function.

The evening after the attack on Iran, the President of the United States, Joseph Mace, broadcast an address to the

American nation. It was televised from his desk at the Oval Office, and repeated through the Emergency Alert System.

My fellow Americans. The events that unfolded over the past many months almost tore our great country apart and brought us to our knees. The zombie apocalypse that swept across the southern states of our great land killed millions of people and attempted to destroy our way of life, our trust for one another, and our faith in God.

It tested our military as no other conflict in the history of this nation has done. It turned our fighting men and women against those who had once been our brothers, sisters, sons and daughters.

The zombie apocalypse was not just an attack on our people but also an attack on our freedom – that right which we cherish most dearly.

For many months during the terrifying spread of the contagion we lived under the assumption this diabolical disaster that had befallen us was just that – a natural disaster. During these trying times, we struggled to survive; we struggled to adapt and to carry on in the face of fear, the face of doubt, and deprivation.

Today I am happy to announce we have won our battle. We rose above the threat that challenged us. We showed the true grit for which we, as Americans, are admired and respected by all the free nations of the world. We did not surrender. We did not go meekly into the darkness. We stood up. We fought back.

And, we won.

I can now reveal to you we have discovered new evidence proving this event was more diabolical than we could ever have imagined.

This was not a virus Fate brought to our shores. This was not an accident, or a natural epidemic.

It was, instead, the most brutal insidious act of State sponsored terrorism the world has ever witnessed.

The tireless work of our collective intelligence organizations has proven beyond all doubt this zombie outbreak was, in truth, a plot perpetrated by the government of Iran against America and her people. It was a callous, criminal act unmatched in the history of mankind for its evil, and malicious disregard for the sanctity of life.

We were targeted not because we were a military threat, but because we stand as a beacon of freedom and fairness throughout the world. Today that light still shines because, despite the challenges we faced, we endured and survived.

Last night I issued orders for a retaliatory strike against Iran, targeting several key installations in Tehran along with several other major military and industrial complexes. Those missions were successfully accomplished and, as a result, Iran is no more.

We have suffered. We have struggled. We have endured, and we have survived.

Iran has been destroyed.

Iran has been torn apart at every level of its government. Its economy and military forces have been broken.

We have ensured Iran, as a nation, will never rise again as a threat.

Dark times have descended upon our world. The unprovoked terrorist attack upon us had dire global consequence. People now live in fear, and we are embroiled in a new age of international uncertainty.

But through it all, America has endured. We have stood against the enemies of freedom before, and we will continue to do so. To those who might threaten us in the future we give this warning. We will no longer act with an extended hand of conciliation, but with the clenched fist of our total force and the unfaltering conviction of our will.

We will preserve and protect our fundamental right to defend ourselves.

We now begin a new age – a new time in the history of this planet, and we embark on this uncertain path no longer as the world's greatest power, but as the world's most dangerous enemy to those who would seek to benefit from our adversity.

To the people who may threaten us in the future, remember our forefathers once warned, "Don't tread on me."

Heed that warning.

America will bite back.

Today we have proven it and tonight we stand committed to doing so in the future, should it ever again be necessary.

We remain the land of the free because we are the home of the brave.

Thank you. Goodnight, and God bless America.

AFTERWORD:

When I decided to write this account of the zombie apocalypse, it was my intention to record interviews that showcased America's *military* response to the virus, and the way the men and women of our armed forces went to war to defend our nation.

That was my intention.

And, I fear, I have failed.

I didn't plan to write a record of this tragedy that detailed the human side of the conflict. I wanted this account to be removed from the emotional civilian reports that have made up so many other books about the zombie war.

But it's just not possible.

As I read back through these interviews now, I realize the humanity of our soldiers pervades every page. I read it in their words, their fears, their determination and resolve. Indeed it is the humanity of the men and women who fought the war that rings like the clear chime of a bell calling to us all...

To remember their valor.

Their sacrifice.

Their patriotism.

—   John Culver
        Washington D.C.
        New America.

Acknowledgements:

I would like to thank the following people for their contributions to the writing of this book. I am forever in their debt for their willingness and enthusiasm.
Nick Ryan.

- **Larry Bond:** Larry is a bestselling techno-thriller author and worked closely with Tom Clancy on some of his most famous novels. When I first had the idea for this book, Larry was very gracious and helpful with thoughts and suggestions.

- **Galen, 'The Arkenstone':** Galen is one of the foremost experts on Iran, its politics, culture and its military. He was an enormous help with the early sequences of this book.

- **Samuel C. Garcia:** Sam is a former US Army Black Hawk helicopter pilot and an all-around nice guy. He helped me with the combat sequences in *'Dead Rage'* and generously backed up for this book, giving several of the interviews a much needed touch of authenticity.

- **Tommy Towery:** Tommy is a retired U.S. Air Force Major and a man amongst men. He has been an enormous help throughout the writing of this book, contributing ideas, and information as well as sharing his experience and knowledge to make the sequences in the book as realistic as possible. Tommy was instrumental in writing the B-52 bomber interview as well as many other parts of the book.

- **Dale Simpson:** Dale is a US Special Forces Operator. He helped a great deal with the writing of *'Dead Rage'* and re-enlisted to help with the interviews for this book. His specialized knowledge was vital to the book's authenticity.

- **Bill Seery:** Bill was a phenomenal help in writing this book. A former US Navy man, Bill championed the cause for Naval involvement through this novel, and then went out of his way to help me research and create the necessary sequences. Bill's input to the authenticity of the finished novel was invaluable.

- **Randy Harris:** Randy is a retired Cavalry Major with more than 43 years experience in the US Army and Army National Guard. Randy is a fine man, and was instrumental in developing the sequences involving the armored battles that take place in the book.

- **Ty Harris:** Ty is a cool guy I met online. He owns a comic book store. We were chatting on social media and I suddenly had the idea to include him and his family as refugees who had survived the apocalypse. He agreed… and that makes him very cool indeed.

- **Dave Moon:** Retired USAF Major, David Moon, was a great help sorting through the Air Force interviews within this book. He also opened doors for me to reach out other contacts within the Armed Forces.

- **Ron Page:** Ron is a former US Marine who served two tours in Iraq before joining the police force. He is currently a SWAT Team operator. His help fact-checking the manuscript to ensure accuracy was invaluable to the finished authenticity of the novel.

- **Rusty 'Waldo' Walden:** Rusty is a retired USAF Colonel who flew F-16 fighter jets. He was a tremendous help checking through the fighter patrol sequences.

Other titles by Nicholas Ryan available through Amazon:
*Ground Zero: A Zombie Apocalypse
*Die Trying: A Zombie Apocalypse
*Dead Rage: A Zombie Apocalypse

All titles are stand-alone novels. They can be read in any order.

Made in the USA
Middletown, DE
05 May 2015